Well here I am again!

Sorry about the last wait, but I in the original story of this book, I wrote a subject that was not permissible. Another lesson taken on board and more work!

I never dreamed when starting to write my first book, 'The Mistletoe Run' when I was only 75. That I would get it into print, which was last year 2017. Also I thought I was only writing that one novel!

Unfortunately I have now reached 78! and this is my second book Happiness Never Lasts. I hope dear reader you enjoy reading it as much as I enjoyed writing it and rewriting it?.

Although it has not been without stress, because the new Laptop I purchased 31st May 2017, purposely for my novels, had a manufacturers fault. It could only happen to me!! I thought I had lost this novel and the third which is 'Love Will Find A Way'. Fortunately I found early draft copies of both on our computer, not sure how they were still there? But it was still like starting again, but I have got there.

Because I am a first time writer, 'Literary Agents' do not want to know you, until you are known! I keep asking, if no one gives you a break, then you how do you get known known!?!

So I have to do what an agent would normally get done. I cannot believe what a load of rubbish my computer types for me! I am pleased there is a delete key!

Lets face it when I started work at 15, when typing, if you needed 4 copies, you put in three sheets of carbon paper, therefore you had to get it right - no delete key, in those days!

Happiness

Never

Lasts

by

Margaret Loxley

Acknowledgments

First, I could not have written any books without the
support of my husband Phil,
Who never knows when he will get his next meal!
At first he was very supportive and made it known that
he was proud of my achievements.
He may now be having some regrets,
because I have now the completed the third
and well into a fourth!
So now it's "Oh no not another one!"
I know he is only joking!
Thank you my darling, for all your help,
support and encouragement
especially when I have been feeling down.

Also without the patience of my
daughter-in-law,
Alison Streets.
I would be nowhere whatsoever, without her!
She's had to deal with my many emails and
telephone calls, answering my endless questions,
Through her know how, experience, imagination and
artistry, especially for the covers of
The Mistletoe Run and Happiness Never Lasts
My sincere thanks and love.
I know how hard it is for her with her debilitating illness.

Chapter one

Great Aunt Celeste was born in 1932, she is a distant relation on my fathers side of the family, she has no immediate family left. She has lived with us for as long as I can remember.

My father is the youngest of three sons, Ernest the eldest was born in 1944 he is married to Emily but they do not have any children. Next was Thomas born in 1946, he was married to May, they have one daughter Amy but they are divorced.

My father was born in 1948 Lawrence Cartwright, he always looks fit and toned he exercises regularly and I love him dearly. He married Rosalind in September 1971, she was born in 1950. They always slept in separate bedrooms which until I was older, thought was the norm.

The three brothers inherited the family business, which is seven luxury five star country hotels, which at one time before they were turned into hotels belonged to the landed gentry. Their Office is based in Nottingham.

I am Natasha, (Nat) I was born June 1977, I have blue eyes and fair hair like my father. I have two older brothers Charles, (Chas) who was born August 1974 and Matthew, (Mat) born February 1972. Both are like mother, dark almost black hair, beautiful brown eyes and very pale olive skin. Both went to boarding school and subsequently to University, so I only see them during the holidays. I went to the local private school.

We live in a seven bedroom house in West Bridgford, South of Nottingham. My uncles also live in West Bridgford, nearby.

Aunt Celeste does all the cooking, she also looks after us children, like a biological mother would normally do, she looked after me from being born, mother did not want me! Because I was taught by Aunt Celeste I was very advanced for my years and I loved her dearly.

When I started school I could read, write and do maths, the same as an eight year old. I was also a very good cook.

Mummy what does she do? Well we never see her until she has had her breakfast in bed every day, then she will not make an appearance, until her hair and make-up is in place. She is slim, beautiful, but does nothing in the house, everyone dances to her tune, she is good at organising other people and looking busy, she this has down to a fine art. She goes out every evening and never gets home before 1 or 2am!

I am now sixteen, it is July 1993, I have just finished school, my father says I only looked presentable when I went to school in my uniform and my long hair in plaits, the rest of the time, my hair is loose, really tousled. I wear old jeans and baggy jumpers or shirts, I am a tomboy because I only knew my brothers. I do not have any friends, mummy demanded I come straight home from school, I am never allowed anywhere at the weekends and school holidays, despite my father objecting frequently, but mummy says she gives the instructions not him. Which as she never wanted me it seemed odd?

The only concession was when I was seven my father bought me a pony so mummy reluctantly had relented and let me go on Saturday mornings for four hours to groom and ride him, I was allowed to go more frequently during school holidays, again that was because my father had insisted she let me go.

We never had a family holiday because she never came with us, I think we had a fairly happy childhood, I love my brothers very much, they are drop dead gorgeous, they have both have had a lot of time for me when they were home.

There was one sad time however, when we lost Peter, I was then eleven. He had suddenly appeared in September 1983, after mother had been away for six weeks, he was not like any of us, he was very pale with a shock of ginger curly hair and big green eyes, but she adored him and so did I.

Of course Aunt Celeste had to do all the normal things a mother would normally do. When she was busy and it was not a school day, I used to mind him, I used to play with him, it was like having a living doll and he would laugh as soon as he saw me.

Mummy had given me strict instructions I was never to go to her room, so I did not.

Six months after Peter had appeared, my father came and said I had to go to her room, I followed him upstairs, he opened the door, I walked in, the door closed behind me, when I turned my father was not there. Now bearing in mind I will be seven in June, I had never spoken to her. I always had my meals in the kitchen, even when my brothers were home, they ate in the dining room I was always excluded. I was not sure what to do so I said "Mummy," I got no further.

"I am not your mother, you were found on the doorstep, my husband took you in, they let you think you belonged to them, you do not they just gave you our name, you may call me Mrs Cartwright! Do you understand?" she snapped I was close to tears my lips trembled.

"I do not understand what do you mean I am not yours?" I sobbed.

"Exactly that you are not one of the family, if you are going to stand and cry like a baby I will give you something to cry about. Now shut up you horrible child, you have work to do. You were took in, and as you are a girl, you have to start to repay me for looking after you!" Well that stopped the tears, she looked after me? I have never even spoken to her, so perhaps she is right, I am not a true Cartwright, I will have to ask Aunt Celeste or daddy they will tell me. As if she had read my mind she said "I do not, I repeat, I do not want you to go pestering anyone in this house asking if what I have told you is true, it would not be fair when they have been so good to you, and I will find out then I will punish you severely, so what's it to be?"

"I understand Mrs Cartwright," I stuttered.

"Right now come over here and look at my darling son Peter, isn't he beautiful?"

As soon as he saw me he laughed, and held his chubby arms out to me. I was not sure what to do, so I looked at the woman I thought was my mother.

"He has obviously seen you around, so he knows you," she explained.

"No, I have always played with him, when Aunt Celeste was busy," I said.

"Did I ask you to speak. You are out of order, you do not speak until I allow you. However, seeing as he does like you, it will make life easier, because I want him in your bedroom with you. I could not put him in a room of his own, I would worry. So you will move his cot in with you, and every night he will be with you, I need my rest and he disturbs me too much, I cannot function and do all my work, if I do not have my sleep."

Do all her work, I have never seen her do anything? What do other mothers do then? I thought. But I don't mind having him with me.

"After you have had your tea and done any homework, you can mind him for Aunt Celeste. Then put him to bed. During school holidays you can help Aunt Celeste with him, so she can do her duties."

It was like having a living doll. I was happy doing it, I used to get bored in the school holidays especially, with having no friends, so I loved looking after him and I know he loved me. Sometimes at night when he grizzled I put him in bed with me, he was no trouble, he went to sleep with my arms round him. In fact he got as he was more in with me than in his cot.

Then during the school holidays, that is when I used to see Mat and Chas she started taking me and Peter on holiday with her, although I never saw her until mid morning, then she would disappear until Peter and I had an early meal and she would come to our room for an hour before his bed time and make a big fuss of him kissing and saying how much she loved him. We never went to her room, which was always on another floor a long way away.

I desperately missed Chas and Mat, apart from when the holidays were more than one week long, that was the only time I saw them. Daddy and Aunt Celeste often said I should not spend so much time with Peter, but I always said I was happy doing it, and did not want it any other way. Good job I had no choice!

When Peter was five, I started taking him to see my pony, he was very good and sat and watched me for weeks, eventually he talked me into to letting him ride, but I said we had to get him a riding hat and everything he would need first, which daddy got for us.

One Saturday in December 1988 I woke up with a temperature, a sore throat and cold, Great Aunt Celeste told me I was to stay in bed and she went to tell Mrs C I was ill, and she had better get up and take her own son riding. Apparently she was fuming because she was meeting someone and had now to alter her arrangements. Peter was insistent she take him so she had no choice. I do not think she had seen 9.30am for years!

Unfortunately they had not been there long when a man in a car arrived at the stables, and according to the staff she ran to greet him and was in his arms kissing.

The staff were unaware she had sat Peter on the pony without his hat and harness, nearby a car had back fired, the pony must have reared and Peter fell off and hit his head on the concrete and died.

That was when my nightmares started. It was terrible for us all but I felt so guilty because I should have been there, I really missed him, added to which even though I was not there, Mrs C maintained it was all my fault her darling Peter had died, she was totally blameless and she believed it. It did not matter how many times the others told me it was not my fault, she would shout at me that it was all my fault and that I was an ugly, ungrateful little bastard! To top it all she got rid of my pony without telling me or Daddy I did not find out until I went a few weeks after Peters death and the staff told me. My nightmares were getting worse.

From then on I rarely saw her and when I did, she would totally blank me. She gave instructions I had to continue to eat my meals in the kitchen. I never knew what happened behind closed doors, so I do not know why my father let her get away with it.

She continued going away and taking me with her, I was always on my own, I never went to her room. The first time we went after Peter had died, I was shown to a room at the top of the hotel where the staff slept. I assumed the normal rooms were all full, until I went down to the restaurant for my evening meal and was told the dining room is for guests only. All maids and servants had to eat with the hotel staff!

That is when I realised how vindictive she could be. I did not tell anyone, I just accepted her vindictiveness of which she was an expert. Although I did not mind too much because I was left on my own all the time, so it was a holiday for me. We never went to any of the Cartwright's hotels!

Last Christmas 1993, was lovely Mrs C disappeared just before school and university finished for the holidays and was gone for three whole weeks so I had my brothers, Daddy and Aunt Celeste all to myself. We had a brilliant time, during this time Mat and Chas started asking questions about their mother and Peter, so I told them everything, they were absolutely astounded the way she had been treating me and to say I was not really one of the family, they were outraged.

A few days later daddy asked me to go into his study, when I went in not only was daddy there, but Mat and Chas. They were looking equally as puzzled as I was.

Then daddy said, "I was hoping this would never happen, my wife promised me she would not say anything, however, as is her norm she cannot keep her word, she delights in making trouble, as long as it does not affect her."

None of us spoke, we looked at on another wondering what was coming.

"My darling Nat, I love you with all my heart, but the truth is, you are not my biological daughter, I have always thought of you as my own sweetie! I could not love you any more if I was, I am so sorry." he had tears streaming down his face.

Suddenly my world was in bits, she was right, no wonder she did not like me. I just sat there sobbing. At first I think my brothers, no they are not, are they? were in shock, then they both started talking together.

Daddy pulled me over to him and sat me on his knee, wrapping me in his strong arms. "Nothing changes my darling, as far as I am concerned you are mine and always will be," he held me tight and was kissing me.

"What do I called you now," I said through my sobs?

"Darling I am still daddy and always will be."

"But I thought I took after you, with my fair hair and blue eyes?"

"Pure coincidence sweetie, but it did make it conceivable. Please sweetie nothing changes, I could not love you any more."

Chas and Mat agreed, they still think of me as their sister and loved me to bits.

Last November she'd booked for us to fly up to Scotland for ten days at Easter, I mentioned it to Daddy he said to go as she left me alone, he would make sure that two en suite hotel rooms were booked, and that I was not a maid and ate in the restaurant, so I decided to go.

I am pleased I did because I made friends with the owners daughter Helen, the first friend I had ever had, and we went for walks, she took me to her room where we played music, went shopping and just had a good time although she did work in the hotel so time was limited.

One day she said "Are you the witches alibi?" I had told her all what was what. Also I had started calling her that, obviously not to her face.

"I am sorry what do you mean?" I asked.

"Well there is a man Henry Russell, apparently a divorced millionaire registered in room 20, but he never uses that room, he has a bottle of our best champagne delivered to Suite 3 at 9.10 every night, I discovered that is the witches suite?"

"I have no idea? but I cannot see her having sex with anyone, she does not sleep with my daddy! Has he got ginger hair?"

"Yes he does, do you know him, I hope you don't mind me being nosey?" she said.

"No I am glad you are, that has really got me thinking she perhaps is using me for an alibi, although at home nearly every night she goes out, not with my father. She did have Peter with ginger hair who was clearly not Daddy's, thank you Helen," then she went to start work.

Early that evening I decided to ring home and speak to Mat and told him what I had discovered, at first he wasn't sure to believe me, but said to keep quiet, we will discuss things when he comes home in July. Because he was to go back to Uni before we were due home. I sat wondering how I could get into her room, or at least her attention. I had an idea, I stood on the top of the dressing table, my plan was to try and sprain my ankle, so I jumped and before I landed I turned my foot and bingo one sprained ankle. I hope I have not broken it, it made me cry, it soon began to swell up I was in considerable pain.

After a while I struggled up and hopped and limped and went in search of Suite 3, I knew where it was as soon as I rounded the corner, because of the a DO NOT DISTURB sign. I tapped on the door nothing, so I knocked very loudly and shouted, "I need you," and shouted again, suddenly the door opened a fraction, she well I think it was her hair all tangled, very flushed and red, puffy lips holding a wrap to her naked body, it did not cover much. She hissed "Get back to your room now, I will come as soon as I can."

I tried to push the door open. "Can I come in, look I have sprained my ankle." The glare was something out of a horror film, she could win an Oscar I thought.

"You get back to your room now, you are going to regret you ever knocked on my door." It was little more than a whisper but I heard her loud and clear.

I managed to get back to my room, my ankle was really swollen, I could have been dead for all she cared, I should have known. She eventually arrived over an hour later, she marched in, got hold of me and started shaking me, I thought my teeth would drop out, then she started hitting me across my face and I screamed.

"You can stop that right now. Do not ever come to my room again," and slapped my face again really hard "Next time it will be a cane not my hand."

"But I've sprained my ankle look." I cried.

"It is no excuse, you should have picked up the telephone and told reception, what do you expect me to do you are so stupid, you bastard. You know how fragile I am and I need my rest," she stressed.

Well she gets my title right! "Does a bottle of Champagne every night help you rest then?" it came out before I thought what I was saying. Her face was a picture the shock was palpable. Her mouth opened but nothing came out, so I carried on "This is the last time you drag me away for your dirty affairs, you look down your nose at everyone, yet you are no better than a cheap prostitute. You are selfish, everything has to be done for you. Does my darling Daddy know what piece of work he is married to?" It all came rushing out, before I thought about it.

"You do not say anything to your father, you do not understand these things, I will try to make it right with you Natalie," she tried to make it sound soft and nice.

"Who the hell is Natalie, for your information I am Natasha. I do not want you to try and make anything right. You even let my Peter die, that's how good a mother you are. I am glad you are not my mother, I would hate to think I had anything of yours," I spat with real venom.

She raised her hand at that, but she was a bit too slow, I caught it in mine and gave her a good hard slap with my other, she wilted on to the bed, the look of shock was brilliant.

Then she said "I could teach you how to dress and use make-up."

"Did you forget something else you could teach me?" she looked up at me questioningly, I carried on "You should be very good at teaching me how to lay on my back and open my legs wide, for any man who wanted to fuck me," she shot up, her hands ready to smash into my face, she was furious. I moved as fast as I could, even though my ankle hurt, somehow she tripped and fell face down.

"You will regret that for the rest of your life, I will make your life a misery, I will not use my hand, it will be a cane my girl and I will enjoy every minute of using it on your bare skin."

I picked up the telephone and asked for Suite 3, she looked astonished, a very well spoken man answered the phone "Could you please come and collect this apology of a woman from room 110?"

"How do you know," I stopped her there.

"I am not stupid," after about ten minutes there was a knock on the door, I opened it and there he stood quite magnificent, he clearly was a lot younger than her, his dark ginger hair needs combing, but I guess he must have come in a hurry.

"Come in and take her with you she is not welcome, I will be flying home tomorrow, so please leave my ticket and some money at reception. Do not worry I will not say anything to my darling daddy, I love him too much to pile on the hurt," Henry looked shocked, I added "I am so sorry to have troubled you Mr Russell, I really do not know what you see in this human, although I have heard tell she is good in bed! Good night."

Then I think I went into shock, I started trembling uncontrollably, crying, I am not as grown up as I thought.

I rang home to see if Mat was in, and he answered, I told him everything that had happened, between sobbing and snuffling. Very calmly he said "I know there is a flight up at 1am, I will catch that and bring you home, you cannot travel on your own, I know where you are staying, do not contact her at all, get packed. See you very soon."

I packed what I did not need and lay on the bed, I must have fell asleep the next thing, there is a tap on the door and there stood my Mat, I threw myself at him and we hugged, he stroked my hair, he kissed me on the forehead and his lips just gently and swiftly passed over my lips, something he has been doing for a while now.

"Come on get ready, I will order some food for us," at last my big bossy brother.

I limped into the bathroom, dressed in my new suit, I had bought with the aid of my friend Helen, along with delicate underwear, blouse and high heels. Instead of putting my hair in the usual pony tail, I brushed it hard and it fell in nice natural waves and curled up at the ends. Also for the first time in public I put make up on, which she encouraged me to buy. Although I was not hungry, when I opened the door and smelt the bacon sandwiches he had ordered, I could not resist eating. As I emerged from the bathroom Mat looked up and did a double take.

"Christ where's my little Nat? you really have changed." That was it we sat and ate our sandwiches, then he said "Let me look at your ankle it is very swollen," and he removed my shoe, he felt all round it "Thank goodness, it is not broken, shall I bandage it, to give you some support?"

"No thank you because I will not be able to get my shoe on, can I lean on you, you're a big strong lad," I said laughing.

"Okay, but the taxi will be here in a minute," it arrived soon after, we drove to the airport, sat in silence waiting for the flight to be called. When I looked towards him he was looking at me a bit strange.

I said "What?"

"You, you have changed, you have grown up and got a lovely figure, that you have been hiding under all those big baggy things you wear. I think I will be having to keep my eye on you! I will be home for good in July, ready to start work full time in September for the Cartwright empire, so I will be able to get to know my not so little sis better." Then the flight was called.

We arrived home a long time after my father had left for work, he was to be away for several days, as all the brothers were regularly, travelling round all the hotels, so he did not know I had returned early, so no need for excuses. Mat had to leave more or less straight away for Uni and I was in tears.

"Come on Nat it won't be for long, I will be back before you know it, be a good girl and when she returns keep out of her way," he hugged me and kissed me on the forehead, his lips again brushed mine again. He looked me in the eye and said "Nat you are going to drive men crazy."

When the trollop, that was Mat said we should call her, returned five days later I was at school. When our paths did cross a few days later, I said "I would like a word with you," I said.

"Shall we go into Mr Cartwright's study then?" I followed her in. "What can I do for you," she asked. I shook my head in disbelieve, she really should be on the stage she is such a good actress.

"I know Peter was his, it was obvious when I saw him."

"Your father accepted Peter, you know we do not sleep together."

"Well you do not have to share a bed with a man to become pregnant, for all I know daddy could have been fucking you on this desk," I felt so wild that she could not see she was wrong in any of this.

"I will not have that language from you, I was going to say it isn't lady like, but that is one thing you will never be," she spat.

"That could be because you are certainly not a lady in fact a prostitute is to good a word for you. If Henry meant so much to

14

you why did you not divorce daddy and marry him?"

"I am not having this conversation with you of all people. You think that was an idle threat I made, I promise you it was not, I am going to make your life a misery," and she was gone.

Before I knew it, it was the end of term 20th July and the end of school for me.

When Chas arrived home I ran to his out stretched arms, he picked me up and swung me round like both he and Mat had always done. I went and helped him unpack and sort his dirty washing, he took off his shirt as I lay on his bed "Wow look at you, your muscles what have you been doing then?" I said looking in amazement.

"It's been hard work going to the Gym, sis, but it has been worth it, you should see some of the girls I have been dating." They have both, still carried on calling me sis.

"You are growing up, you have got really tall but still in all these baggy clothes. Come on get gone I want to take a shower."

"It's okay I will lay here and watch," I giggled. He did no more he jumped on the bed and started tickling me, I screamed for him to stop.

"Nat what happened to my little sis? You have suddenly developed in a place I should not have my hands, I think you should go my pet, my thoughts are certainly not of a sis," he seemed subdued.

"Chas I am still the same, does that mean we will not be having any fun any more?" I said as I slid off his bed.

"Please darling go," I got up and left his room very dejected and suddenly feeling lonely.

I went downstairs and met daddy in the hall, he led me into his study. "We are having a dinner party a week on Saturday because Mat will be home then. You, my sweetie, will be joining us, and the whole family will be here, plus Celeste's friend Olive, as will our friends Andrew, Pamela, George and Sheila. We will be dressing for dinner. He passed me a credit card and a form to sign. I want you to purchase everything you need for a family dinner, from a cocktail dress to footwear and jewellery, there is no limit spend what you must, I am going to prove to her how wrong she is, about my lovely daughter,"

"So I do not need any money?" I asked.

"No spend whatever you need to, I want you to look a million dollars my darling, not sure about your hair, but do not have it cut and please no pony tail," he said laughing "Remember her beauty is only skin deep, she is very cruel, demanding and selfish so please my sweet do not cross her," he was very serious.

"But it is too late," I muttered

"What did you say, too late?"

"Because of everything, she has told me she is going to make my life a misery, I am not sure but she says she has got a cane for the future."

"She is very cruel, well you know that, with what she promised to keep a secret. She no feelings, and certainly no conscience."

"Why did you put up with her?" tears were streaming.

"It was anything for a quite life, not any more, I promise you my darling she is going to regret what she has done to you," he was fuming.

"I won't let you down, I promise," we kissed and hugged.

I went shopping, bought everything, I went to Griffin and Spalding, to their beauty counter, they taught me how to use make-up.

I went to a jewellers and saw a pair of Diamond earrings set in Platinum, they were expensive, so I thought I had better ring daddy on his mobile.

"Hello my darling, is everything alright?" he asked.

"I have seen some earrings but they are a bit pricey."

"How much" he asked

"They are £1,050.00, but a big, drop and very beautiful."

"Do they look good and expensive?" he asked.

"Yes very much so and definitely classy."

"Get them sweetie, bye darling," he said and was gone.

Mat arrived home, I helped him empty his car and clutter up his room "Thank you my darling, come here I have not had my hug yet," he scooped me up in his arms. He put me down and kissed my forehead and brushed his lips across mine, "You are really beautiful Nat, are you all ready for Saturday?" he asked.

"Yes, however, I really need to talk to you sometime," I hesitated.

"Now is a good time, come on darling spill what's on your mind?" he quizzed. I told him about the trollop and what I had told daddy after, I could not stop the tears.

"Nat I cannot bear to see you like this. If she says or does anything, you fetch me but I am not letting you out of my sight, I wonder what Pa has in mind?" he was holding me close, I felt safe there, as always.

That evening after dinner Mat said "I want a word lets go to your room," so I followed him wondering. We went to my room "Nat your room is lovely and tidy. Pa and I have been talking, we plan on Saturday you do not come down, until I fetch you, when they're all here Pa will say aloud 'I had better come for you' On cue I will take you to the lounge where, and tar-la the big entrance?"

"I will keep my fingers crossed something is bound to go wrong" I said cautiously.

Saturday 8th August arrived, poor Aunt Celeste was rushing round, no sign of the trollop, so I stayed and helped. We were sitting down at 7pm, the drinks were to be in the lounge at 6.30pm. Whilst I was busy I was alright but as soon as I got to my room I was nervous, I felt sick.

Normally I could be showered and ready in 15 minutes but I knew this would take longer! It took a while but I got there, I put on the knee length scarlet figure hugging dress, which showed my cleavage, the bra made my boobs look bigger, I had silver high heeled sandals, finger and toe nails and lipstick all matched my dress. I was pleased with the make up, and false eye lashes. The only jewellery was the diamond earrings. My hair I brushed, it shone and I left it loose, it slightly curled at the bottom, I tucked the sides behind my ears to show off the diamonds hanging from my ears.

Now the nerves really took over I was trembling, I felt sick, I'm not going down, I had just made my decision, when there was a tap at the door and Mat walked in, I could see him in the reflection of the window, I was stood at.

"I am looking for my baby sister, do you know where she is," I turned slowly round, his mouth wide open.

"Do I look that bad? It does not matter because I am not going down, you will have to say I am not well," I was visibly shaking head to toe.

"My darling, you look absolutely you incredible. You've done something that should not happen to me. My darling, you have to come down I want to see the trollops face."

"I can't Mat," I was close to tears.

"Darling please don't cry you will spoil that beautiful face, hold on" he crossed to my phone. "Hi Pa, Nat is in melt down, she says she cannot come down, please bring a big glass of something." Shortly after there is a tap at the door and in walked daddy.

He looked amazed "My baby you are so beautiful, I hardly knew you, you look out of this world, darling sip this sherry, it will make you feel better, I want this big entry, I am right aren't I Mat?"

"Yes Pa you are so right, the trollop has serious competition. Right my gorgeous sis, let me take you down and show the trollop how wrong she can be or I will carry you, what's it to be?"

"I'll walk," we made our way down stairs it was very noisy, like there were a lot of people instead of a dozen or so. They are all talking at once, when we heard a clap of a hands, it was the trollop.

"Lawrence we will go in to dinner, your daughter can eat in the kitchen."

Mat opened the door a bit further and said "That will not be necessary she will be dining with us," he stepped to one side, took my hand grinning from ear to ear.

The whole room was turned as one, I kept my eyes on Daddy, Mat put his arm round my waist, as though I was his possession, there was an audible gasp around the room, I looked towards her, she stood with her mouth wide open, not believing what she saw, then everyone started talking at once, they were all buzzing round me telling me how beautiful I was.

Mat whispered in my ear "The trollop is going to burst, she went from near white with the shock, to green with envy now she is bright red and it certainly does nothing for her," we both laughed.

Daddy whispered in the other ear "My darling I am so proud of you, you have made my nightmare of a life worth it, just to see this, how jealous the trollop is of you, also she is not the center of attention and compared to you she looks positively haggard and old."

Mat whispered again "It's all this shagging around it is destroying her," thank goodness Daddy could not hear, but then he would probably agree, he has joined in quite happily calling her the trollop.

Chas approached "Bloody hell Nat, I thought Mat had brought one of his girl friends, you look fantastic, what I want to know is what's going on, with you three? it's like a secret society," he stated.

"I will tell you later bro," Mat said.

We all drifted in to dinner, Daddy sat at the head of the table with Mat next to him then me, and then Chas next to me, when "No, no you are sitting all wrong Mat and Chas one each side of me now!" she was about to say something else but Daddy cut in;

"We are alright as we are down this end thank you very much Mrs C," she physically flinched, sat down going red, very red indeed. She hardly touched the first two courses, but drank plenty of wine. As they were filling up the glasses, I picked mine up to Daddy, he started to pour the dessert wine into my glass when;

"She is not old enough to drink she can have water," but it was said with such venom everyone turned to look at her, daddy very calmly said;

"I hardly think one glass of dessert wine will make any difference, but thank you for pointing it out. However, you should think twice before you open your mouth, you were drinking at fourteen by all accounts, you were frequently incapable of knowing what you were doing, or who was doing what to you. They used to wait in line for their turn, what was it you charged?"

She was beetroot red, everyone was looking at her for her denial, which did not come. "I think you should practice what you preach, this household has had enough of you, you should start acting like the lady you keep telling us you are, and not the dirty slut, you actually are," the gasps were very loud.

Mat was holding my hand and I was gripping it tight. Chas was holding my other hand. Daddy then added "Also do your shagging elsewhere not under my roof."

Suddenly she got up and came round the table to where I sat, and said in my ear "My room now," and left, Mat had heard and told Pa what she said the three of us stood up as one, he said to Chas;

"Take our guests into the lounge for coffee or something stronger in my absence please."

We left together daddy whispered "Go in, leave the door ajar I want to hear what she says, also I want be able to get in quickly."

Mat said "WE want to get in quickly."

I entered her room. "Yes you little bitch, you have been blabbing to your darling daddy, I told you I was going to make your life a misery, it starts now, I also told you I would be using this," she raised her hand and began swishing a cane through the air "I want to know who you have been fucking to get money for that outfit?"

"I am not sure, I think his name is Henry dark ginger hair?" I thought she was going to have a heart attack. I was trembling head to foot.

"Thanks to you, you lost me Henry after all those years, I knew I was good and I pleased him, I even had Peter for him, but thanks to you he said he did not want to see me again. Now he's fucking you, you little low life. I should have left years ago and took my boys with me. I am going to give you your first of many to come thrashings, get that dress off this is going to be straight on bare flesh, you will not be able to sit down for a week," how could she think I would have sex with anybody, let alone her old boy friend.

Daddy came in, walked passed me, Mat came and took my hand and put his other arm round me, "You are not laying a finger on my beautiful daughter, not now, not ever. You are one very depraved, sick, trollop, I don't know what I saw in you, especially as you had both my brothers before me, why did you decide you wanted to marry me, although I should say trap me?"

"You were the best of the three in bed, you had Great Aunt Celeste, so I would be the lady of the house. I decided any contraceptive was to go you got me pregnant, I knew you would marry me. I told you not to take that thing in, bringing up someone's bastard, you are pathetic. I started going out and met Henry and let him get me pregnant, he said I was beautiful pregnant. I realised life was much better going out at night meeting people and going to clubs, the men all wanted me because I was beautiful," she showed no guilt or anything, I could not believe it.

"You mean because you cannot keep your fucking legs closed, you do not know how to make love, you just fuck, you disgust me, but not any more I want you gone, out of this house. I will get you some cases and bags, once you are out all the locks will be replaced. I want to just put the record straight, I bought all my daughters clothes and I will continue to do so, she makes you look old and fucked up, you are a has been. I will buy her everything she needs, and the same for my sons. You promised you would not say anything, to anyone about my beautiful daughter, however, you cannot keep your word. I cannot believe you thought my daughter would do anything with your old boyfriend. Monday I will start divorce proceedings, I doubt the open court will award you much in view of everything. You can always carry on opening your legs, but hurry up, at the side of my beautiful daughter you are positively old, haggard and definitely a has been. Start packing now!"

He moved quickly towards her and grabbed the cane before she realised what he was doing, she was seething, she still held on to it with one hand and raised her other, to rain blows down on his head, he was too quick the cane snapped in two with such force, her hand shot up and the cane hit her in the face, there was an ugly gash from her forehead down the side of her nose and lower cheek, it was bleeding badly, she shrieked, "What have you done, my beautiful face, I will take you to court for this I'll sue you for millions," she was shrieking like a fish wife.

"I do not think you'll get far, you forget there are two witnesses that father was only trying to remove it, so you did not beat my beautiful sis, so it would be a waste of your money, you will not get anywhere with it," Mat stated.

"My own son turning against his loving, caring Mother, I have done everything for you, took care of you from a baby and you repay me like this! And she is not your fucking sister, stop calling her that." she yelled through tears.

"Well I have heard many lies in my time, you have always done as little as possible with any of your children. We had wonderful times without you, you are the one who missed out. Start packing you lying bitch," Daddy was furious, I have never seen him cross with anyone. He threw the piece of cane to her, took hold of me and said "Come on Mat, help me find some old cases and old bags, for the bag!"

I waited with them while they dug out the oldest cases and bags they could find, they dumped them outside her door, daddy said "Don't be too long packing, I want you out by 10am tomorrow, you will not be allowed anywhere in the house, apart from your room, the stairs and the front door. I will ring a friend with a large van, it will be here tomorrow at 10am, all the locks will be changed! Come on kids we have some serious celebrating to do," and he literally ran downstairs.

"I cannot believe all that has just happened I feel like it was a dream," I said as I looked at Mat.

"No Nat neither can I, I really feel for Pa he is too nice for his own good," he said simply.

The following day, daddy stood guard to make sure she did not go to the kitchen, he said "You have sponged off me long enough go and buy your own breakfast."

He did not lift a finger to help her, we had strict instructions to stay out of the way. The man with the van arrived just before 10am and was loaded and gone before 10.20 with her in the passenger seat, because whilst the man was finishing off, she went to drive her car round, but daddy followed her and snatched the keys from her hand.

"I think you will find that was purchased with my money," she had the grace not to argue. Hence the reason why she was travelling in the van, for her it was a big humiliation.

Chapter two

We were having dinner the Tuesday after, daddy put some brochures on the table "I will be away for two weeks from next Monday, so I thought you three could go away together, I have some details here of a beautiful island in the Mediterranean, there is a main building with restaurants, bars, dance floor every amenity but you sleep in little thatched chalets. I thought I would treat you to ten days together, travelling Friday the 13th, I have provisionally booked a 3 bedroom chalet, what do you say kids?"

I said "That would be brilliant I have not been away with my brothers since I was little."

Mat said "Sounds good to me."

Chas said "I can't, I have already booked to go away for three weeks, with my friends, so I am sorry I can't, although it sounds wonderful and I think we would have a marvellous time, sorry Pa."

"Well do you two still want to go? I can phone and see if they can change the chalet for two bedrooms and a lounge?"

"Yes," Mat said with no hesitation.

"Good I'll do it now. I know you will look after her, it's time she had some fun. I got up and plonked myself on his knee and kissed him all over his face, and hugged him tight.

"Daddy I love you so much."

"In the meantime Mat, will you go with her to do some shopping, she has a debit card, I thought you could help her?"

"I think you had better see what Mat says, he may not want to be seen with his little sister in town," I said, forgetting I am not his sister!

"Fine by me I hadn't anything organised anyway, so my darling I am all yours," he said giving me the sexiest smile.

Daddy managed to change the chalet.

I could hardly sleep Thursday night I was so excited. We were up bright and early to go to the Airport, we would be flying first class to Sardinia, it would take about two and a half hours, so would arrive there approximately 14.00 hrs. Then we would go from there to the little island by helicopter possibly thirty minutes to arrive at the hotel.

When we arrived at East Midlands we checked in, then shown to the V.I.P lounge and the steward asked if either Mr or

Mrs Cartwright, (at which point Mat nudged me, as I opened my mouth to correct her,) wanted any refreshments, we declined. "Why did you stop me from correcting her," I laughed, as I asked when she left.

"Well you thought it was funny and I thought it sounded nice we can have some fun see who else gets it wrong," he said looking me.

We sat in comfortable silence, we did decide to have a drink and a snack, another steward brought our refreshments she asked "Can I get you anything else Mrs Cartwright or Mr Cartwright?" we told her we were fine, as she closed the door, I burst out laughing, Mat turned to me with his serious face on.

"I do not think that is funny Mrs C," he said smiling "I think we should go with the flow, it could be fun."

"Wow Mat are you serious, you want me to pretend to be your wife?" I asked in amazement.

"I would like that very much, I cannot think of anyone who I would rather have, than you as my wife," there's that sexy smile again, it does something to my insides.

"Okay, I'll go along with that."

"In that case then," he said, and took my face between his hands and kissed me full on the lips, I kissed him back, we were locked together, until the door opened and some more VIP's came in.

"Mat," I whispered "That was a lovely kiss, I have never been kissed before, apart from daddy, does that mean you might kiss me again now I am your wife?"

"Oh yes my darling, you do not realise what you do to me. We are not doing anything wrong, you are not my real sister" he stated. I just sat open mouthed looking at him. "Darling you are catching flies," and put his hand under my chin and closed my mouth.

The steward came to tell us we were boarding, were shown to a first class cabin with luxurious armchairs. "We will be taking off shortly darling fasten your safety belt," he did no more he leaned over me and did it for me. While he was close he gave me a quick kiss on the lips "That's a good girl," I leaned back and closed my eyes trying to take in what Mat said. I know I felt different, all my insides were jumping around. I must have fell asleep because the next thing Mat was saying;

"Nat darling wake up, you are crying and whimpering in

your sleep," I could feel tears on my cheeks.

"I am sorry Mat, I have nightmares, they just will not go away, they started years ago when Peter died, and she kept telling me it was my fault, gradually they got worse, after each terrible episode with her."

"Darling who have you told?" he looked very concerned.

"No one," I replied.

"You have been suffering all these years and never mentioned it to Pa and Aunt Celeste?"

"No what is the point?" I asked.

"You could have had help. Oh my love, what you have been put through all those years," I was in his arms, he was holding me close and kissing my face.

"I will take care of you Nat, you mean the world to me, I will not let anyone hurt you again."

We were soon coming in to land, we had to fasten our safety belts. We were through the airport, onto the helicopter and landing close to the hotel in next to no time.

We signed in, again they said Mr & Mrs, we were shown to a round thatched roof chalet. It was perfect, the front was floor to ceiling windows, which opened right back, giving you an uninterrupted view of palm trees and silver/white sand and turquoise sea.

There was a comfortable lounge in the centre with en suite bedrooms either side. I freshened up and put one of my new sun dresses on, it was very hot outside. As I was walking towards the open windows Mat appeared, he'd changed into shorts and a thin shirt, he looked so handsome "I have just been looking round getting familiar."

We walked back to the main building, and had a snack and drink. We sat reading all the leaflets regarding the hotel and the island.

We went to change for dinner I put on a full length pale lemon rather close fitting dress, with shoe lace straps, with little shiny beads all over, but I was unsure because it was rather low. When I emerged Mat was stood looking out at the view, all the palm trees had little twinkling lights through the branches, it was beautiful.

"Mat I think this is too low, don't you?" He turned round and looked at me.

"My darling you look gorgeous, no it is not too low, god

Nat you are so, so lovely, come here," he held out his hand which I took, he put his arms round me "I want to kiss you but I do not want to smudge your lipstick. I think what you are showing is perfect, it is certainly doing things to me. There is dancing later, can you dance?"

"Yes we were taught the basic ones at school, can you?"

"Yes and I cannot wait to get you into my arms," he kissed my forehead, then brushed my lips. He looked at my hands.

"Take that ring off your right hand," which I did, "Here," he said, placing it on the third finger of my left hand, but turning it to look like a band. "There that's right Mrs C," I stood mouth open wide "Darling you are catching flies again," he laughed, took my hand and we walked to the restaurant, where we had a delicious four course meal, with wine.

We could hear distant music, so we went to the ballroom, it was quiet full as we entered they were just starting a waltz. Mat turned to me and said "Mrs C can I have my first ever dance with you?" before I could answer, I was in his arms and we were Waltzing "You dance well Mrs C."

I laughed "So do you Mr C," we danced on and off for an hour and a half, drinking in between. Mat suddenly said;

"Come on darling, I can hear my bed calling," we strolled back to the chalet with his arm round me.

"Mat I love you, I always feel safe with you, will it be the same after we get back and are not Mr & Mrs any more?" I whispered.

"My darling, I am not going to stop being your husband, I want us to get married for real, I am in love you Nat, I want to fuck you, I have tried to keep my distance, but I keep being drawn to you, when Pa suggested this holiday and Chas could not come, I thought all my prayers had been answered. Nat say something, have I over stepped the mark? and you are catching flies again," he gently closed my mouth. "Nat I know I will be your first."

He picked me up took me into my bedroom. He began kissing me, but this time it was different, as we were locked together, he opened my lips with his tongue and it was in my mouth doing all sorts of things to me, I felt on fire, the throbbing was intense, my insides were in turmoil, my legs were weak. He let me go looking deep into my eyes, that was worse than ever, I felt like fainting I flopped onto the bed, he was quickly undressed, and stood there naked in front of me, I think he had an erection, I have never seen one, so who was I to know?

"You see my Nat what you do to me, not for the first time I might add." He pulled me up, my dress was off, and my underwear before I could blink, he threw the covers back off the bed, picked me up and lay me down, very gently, then lay beside me, kissing me again, then he gently pushed my legs open and his fingers went inside, I know I was moaning and sighing I was in heaven, I do not think I can take any more excitement I think I am going to burst.

"Mat, I feel funny, excited I can't get my breath?" he looked at me.

"My lovely Nat, nothing is wrong with you, when I put my prick into you, the feelings will become more and more intense. I cannot hold out any longer my darling I have to get inside you, I want to feel you round my hungry prick," he was gasping. He removed his fingers and gently pushed himself in.

"Mat, oh Mat that is I don't know it feels out of this world."

"Sweetie just relax do what ever you want, just let yourself go, do whatever you feel, yes that is wonderful," I had started to push myself towards him, I cannot put it into words, all I can say no one tells a virgin that they are really missing out. He kept pushing in and pulling out then began to go a bit faster. I was gasping, sighing, I do not know what the hell I was doing but I was certainly enjoying Mat, was doing to me. He gave a hard push and it hurt, I made some sort of a noise.

"Sorry darling, you have let me take your virginity," he then started going faster than ever. Everything was happening, he was really ramming in and groaning, grunting "Yes oh yes Nat," I thought he was in pain. Then it all stopped.

"Mat are you alright are you hurt?" I asked.

He laughed and stilled, "Nat that was wonderful, I could stay like this for ever. I love you so much, and yes I am more than alright I am ecstatic, no definitely not hurt that was me coming," he said whilst trying to get his breath.

"Thank you Mat, is it always like that?"

Eventually he was able to answer "I am hoping so my darling, but at some stage, you will come as well. Do you want a drink I am gasping," he rang room service for a bottle of their finest champagne and two glasses.

"Come on my treasure let me take you into the shower,"

he picked me up and took me into the shower, he gave me the best shower I have ever had, his fingers worked magic when they got between my legs, I calmly opened my legs wider and stood with my eyes closed enjoying everything he was doing to me. I put my arms round his neck and kissed him on the lips, we just melted together with tongues entwined.

"My darling will you marry me? I cannot let any other man take a fancy to you, you are mine Nat, mine I'll never let you go."

"I do not want anyone else Mat I love you, I have always loved you, (but I love Chas as well?) I love all the things you are doing to me, I could not bear to be without you my darling," so he finished showering me and wrapped me in a big white fluffy towel and carried me to a chair. He dried me very carefully kissing me all over as he went along.

He then went and fetched the champagne and poured us two glasses, he came and took the towel from of me and dried himself quickly and threw it on the bathroom floor, I stood up as he passed me a glass, "Here's to us my lovely Nat," I said the same, "Nat I am surprised you do not seem shy seeing me naked, a lot of girls are until we get better acquainted."

"Well I've seen you naked loads of times, so what's new."

"Ha yes but that was donkeys years ago we were all a lot younger."

"Well to me we are the same, it is just that there is more of you now," I laughed.

"I have seen you so many times in my imagination, I love what I am seeing, you have a gorgeous body and your tits, Christ Nat they are fantastic," he was eating me with his eyes.

"Do you really think I have a good body, I can't see that myself, but then if you are happy, that is all that matters, so you want to keep fucking me Mat? I love you and I am so happy," I said dreamily.

"I love you, I want to make you happy and keep you safe. Enough now you need some rest and sleep my little darling."

I must have fallen asleep straight away, until Mat woke me up, it was dark with the moon shining through the windows.

"Darling you were screaming, I had to wake you I cannot bear it, look you are wet through I will get you a towel," he came back and proceeded to dry me, he even rubbed my hair avidly to try to dry it "Darling we will have to get you to the Doctor when we get back?"

"I do not want to go, they will only send me to a shrink and I will have to go through it all again, please Mat don't make me," I began to cry.

"Darling, no I won't make you do anything you do not want to do, please don't cry, that is the last thing I want my lovely Nat," he soothed. He took me in his arms and lay down, I was soon asleep, however it happened again, so we went through it all again getting me dry.

We had a wonderful time we swam in the turquoise sea, visited the other islands, lay on the beach, or just walked. Every night we danced until the early hours, we made love, we were so happy, the only thing that spoilt it, was my nightmares.

"I don't want this to end, I wish we could stay for ever."

"So do I Mat, so do I."

Soon we were back at East Midlands and home.

We arrived home to an empty house it was so quiet so we took our cases upstairs to our rooms but left our doors open so we could talk to one another. "Bring your washing out, I will do it tomorrow, do you want anything to eat or drink Mat," I shouted as I had almost finished.

"Yes Nat you between two slices of bread," he laughed "No darling perhaps just a cold drink or whatever you fancy, I am dead beat I think we should have an early night, sleeping in our own beds," there was a pause "Nat did you hear me?"

"Yes Mat in our own beds." I couldn't get any further for the tears.

"Correct, why don't you agree," he came, and saw me he said "My sweet I was joking, you don't think you will be sleeping on your own, no, together every night, it is just that we will have to be careful when the others come home, and once term starts Chas will be gone."

We suddenly realised I should have some kind of contraception. We made a private appointment for two days later the Wednesday. Then late Tuesday my monthly started so we breathed a sigh of relief.

We had the rest of August together before we started working for the Cartwright Empire. Father came back and my goodness he did look well he was in very high spirits. Aunt Celeste came back and said she was going to live with her friend Olive now we were all grown up. I cried and cried and told her I would miss her greatly, but she'd said I would have to go and visit she was the mother I never had.

Our first day at work was so very different to school. It transpired that a big Hotel Conglomerate were buying four of our hotels, leaving us with just three. They paid four and three-quarter million, Daddy and Uncle Ernest and Mat, were to have £1,550,00.00 each, Uncle Thomas, wanted out altogether, hence Mat getting his share, also any profits. He did not want his ex wife, having any more money. Any oddment remaining, was to go into the business.

Charles had previously told Daddy, he wanted to have his own company of "Chartered Accountants and Financial Advisor" so he had been given £700,000.00 with another payment in the future.

We were then told Uncle Thomas had inoperable cancer, he had six to ten months maximum.

Once Mat and I were confident in running the company, Daddy and Uncle Ernest wanted to leave the running to us. We said it would not be rocket science with only three hotels.

We thought everything was sorted, then daddy announced he wanted to sell the house, because he was moving in with his lady friend Suzanne, apparently he had been seeing her for three years. They will be living in Wollaton, she is a widow with four children, but they are scattered all round the world, none near Wollaton. Here we were feeling sorry for him, and all the while he was getting his leg over elsewhere.

He planned to give the three of us half a million each to buy a house or apartment or whatever, then he would sell the house. They were going to give Chas another half a million because he was not joining the company.

We knew we were going to move in together, we told daddy, but he did not realise our full implications, he was very happy, he knew Mat would look after me. We told him we were quite happy with his arrangements. We knew if we had any problems at work we could ring him or Uncle Ernest.

We decided to look for an apartment but with space for an office it seemed stupid to have an office elsewhere. It would then close all aspects involving Daddy and Ernest, releasing more money with the sale of that building, which would go to Daddy and Ernest, we told them, they said Mat would receive a third of the sale, that was what it would have been if Uncle Thomas was still in the business.

Early October we had a big shock, dearest Great Aunt Celeste, suddenly died of a heart attack. She had only been with her friend for three weeks, we were all gutted, me especially, she had always been the nearest I had to a mother. It was a very quiet funeral just the family and her friend Olive. We had thought daddy would invite Suzanne but he didn't, so none of us said anything. Aunt Celeste didn't have much Mat, Chas and I received the money she had, we received four thousand eight hundred and forty pound each, but she left me her jewellery and there were some really beautiful old pieces, daddy said they were all real stones, they could be quite valuable, I said I would keep them safe and not part with any, ever.

No one heard anything of the trollop once she left, which was a surprise really, we thought she might have made contact with her son's but no neither had heard a thing.

Daddy decided there was no use to leaving it until the last minute to get rid of some furniture, and decided to get the auctioneers in to assess, what was going in the sale, all we were not using. There were several pieces that I said we would like, he said we could have anything we wanted, as I was to show the Auctioneers round, I was not to include anything I wanted.

The second Sunday in October and the door bell rang, daddy was here fetching the last of his stuff. "I'll get it daddy," I opened the door, there stood a policemen and a man in a suit.

"Is Mr Cartwright at home please?" said the suit.

"Yes please come in," I showed them into the snug "I will fetch him," Mat was just coming downstairs.

"Who is it?" he asked.

"Policemen they want to see daddy, is he still upstairs?"

"No darling I am here," he appeared in his office doorway.

"There are two policemen I put them in the snug," he looked bemused and went into the snug Mat and I automatically followed him, the police looked at us.

Daddy said "This is my daughter and son, is it alright if they stay?"

"At this stage yes, this is just enquiries, if you are sure? Mr Cartwright do you know where your wife is please?"

"No I, I threw her out on Sunday 9th August at 10am sharp!"

"Have you had any contact with her?"

"No she knew better than to try and contact me."

"Has she made any contact with either of your children?" In unison we both said "No."

"I have another son, but I know he has not had any contact either."

"Was that not a bit strange do you think? not to contact her children even if you two had fallen out, especially her daughter?"

"No, she knew better."

"So did she leave a forwarding address?" they asked.

We chorused "No."

"Well sir we have reason to believe your wife has been murdered, a body of a woman was found on some waste ground near the river at Wilford, she had no jewellery or hand bag but in her pocket we found an old business card, we scrutinised it, it was a 'Cartwright 5* Country Hotel card' We made enquiries and your name and address came up, so with what you say sir, we would like you to accompany us the the morgue to identify the body. If it is your wife, we would like you to make a statement at the station whilst you are with us, we will take you in our car."

Daddy grabbed his coat and they left, then we scrambled round and we set off in Mat's car for the police station.

We waited for ages, when he appeared, he did not look very happy, I ran and put my arms round him and kissed him and he held me tight.

"It was her, they asked some very funny questions, they think I killed her, I asked how she had died and they said they could not tell me anything and when I said I was moving, they asked me to stay where I was for a few days, even though I said it was only to Wollaton, they still demanded I stay put. They want photo of her as recent as possible, so that will be a problem."

"Come on Pa we will take you home," Mat said. Daddy was very quiet on the way back and when we got in he went straight to the drinks trolley and poured a large neat whisky and knocked it back in one. "I had better telephone Thomas and Ernest, I had to give the police their details, then I will phone Suzanne she will wonder where I am. It's a good job I have some clothes left here and you haven't got rid of my bed!" he did actually laugh.

"I had better go and make his bed up again Mat," I said.

"I had better come up and check that it looks as if we are not sleeping together. You don't think they really thought he killed her, do you?"

"Mat everything is going pear shaped," I began to cry.

"Come here darling," he wrapped me in his arms "Don't get upset I will take care of you, you know that," so we were back to three.

Monday while we were at work they took Daddy in for questioning again, he came straight to the office to tell us what had happened, he looked very drawn and pale "Apparently the Post Mortem has shown she died sometime between the 22nd and 28th August. They said it was a very frenzied attack. I told them it could not possibly have been me, I was away in Malta from the 16th August to the 7th September, with Suzanne, they telephoned her whilst I was there, she confirmed what I had told them, she gave them the Hotel and various detail's, which they actually checked, I could not believe it. They said when the body is due for release they would let me know, I thanked them and told them, I was not interested, for what she put my daughter through for years, she can rot in hell."

Mat and I looked at each other, I took daddy in my arms and hugged him tight, smothering him in kisses "I love you so much my darling."

"I love you both, but I can never make it up to my Nat for all her suffering, I wish I could turn the clock back, it is tearing me apart, but Suzanne is helping," he said with the hint of a smile.

"Pa you go and get on with your life, Nat and I are very happy together and I am taking over the role of looking after her, so please Pa go and be happy as we are."

A few days later her photograph and a statement appeared in all the daily newspapers and the Nottingham Evening Newspaper and asked if anyone knew of her or had seen her between 10am Sunday 10th August and the 24th August. It was on the T.V news the following day.

We started looking for an apartment, we didn't want a house with a garden. Mat soon found some, they were being built in the Park, which was in Nottingham fairly close to the centre. He took me to see the agent, the two ground floor had been sold. There were the two on the first floor and the large expensive Penthouse which covered the whole area of the building, which included a large space outside which went all the way round, obviously there would be a secure frame work with reinforced safety glass panels, that you could only see out of. The building was already finished, the interiors were on hold to see if anyone, wanted to set the layout as they wanted it.

It was just what we wanted, so the following Saturday we met the Agent there and he took us up, there was a lift to the first floor but only the Penthouse had access to the top via the lift. The floor was not finished because pipe work and electrics, had yet to be installed. We paid £250,000 deposit, off the asking price of £650,000.00, well Mat paid, he said I was not paying for anything. We came away with a copy of the plans, with exact size of everything. We decided on the layout of Lounge, Dining kitchen, Office, Large Master bedroom with en suite and walk-in dressing room. The guest room had a walk-in dressing room, a separate bathroom, with shower, toilet and wash basin off a small hall.

I was so excited I rang Daddy, and told him all what we were doing, he said he was pleased I was happy, I deserved it.

We were told they were pulling out all stops to get it completed, which would be early January.

Daddy phoned frequently, he said he was going away with Suzanne for Christmas, to America, because all her children were to travel there and all meet at her eldest son's big house.

We started packing the office up ready for the move, which we would probably be doing over Christmas. We knew we would not be seeing Chas, he had moved in with his girlfriend, her parents had bought her the flat, so he wasn't coming home.

Daddy said the police had telephoned to say they had, had quite a lot of response, and did he know she came from London and owned a large house there, which she rented out as flats.

"Mat I still cannot understand why she stayed with us if she had money of her own?"

"That's just it my darling, she was greedy," he answered "You know I am already quite wealthy, Grandma who had died, left me a million pounds, because I am the eldest, it has been growing interest, I had a very generous allowance from Pa, he has been paying it into my bank account for years."

Christmas is near, I didn't know what to buy Mat, he seemed to have everything. I suddenly remembered something daddy had said once about Golf, so I rang him on his mobile, he confirmed yes Mat loved golf, but seemed to be to busy at the time, he had let it drop. So I went and purchased, on the salesman's advice the best set of clubs, then I hid them, we had so many empty rooms now, it was easy.

Christmas Day, Mat bought me the most beautiful big diamond solitaire engagement ring, some Chanel No.5 perfume, chocolates and a teddy bear that had the name Matthew embroidered on it, I was in tears he kissed me, saying I could not cry on our first Christmas together. I told him I did not know what to get him, but I had a little something but I had left it the Aunt Celeste's bedroom would he please fetch it. He was ecstatic, I could not have got him anything better. Would I mind if he went playing golf? I said of course not.

Boxing Day we went to the office, to get some sorting out and packing done, we wanted to be ready for the big move.

12th January 1994 we were informed the penthouse was ready, so Mat went to pay the remainder of the purchase price. He came back to the office with the keys and paperwork etc. We had already signed with the utility companies, so he telephoned them to say it was completed and we had taken possession. We went to look at the finished apartment during our lunch break, we key our own number to let ourselves out for the penthouse, we stepped out, Mat opened the door, he picked me up and carried me over the threshold, as he put me down we were locked together kissing, we looked round it was fantastic just as we had imagined.

We had already selected carpets, curtains and blinds, so it was just a matter of letting them have a key to get it all finished. We packed everything we would need, we packed the best of everything, including some original paintings and mirrors, we did not have to purchase any household items, we took everything for eating, cooking, cleaning etc. As carpets were laid we had the beds delivered.

The day arrived for the move, it was a Saturday because of the office, then by Monday the office was in the apartment. We had already taken most of our clothes and unpacked loads of boxes. A removal van came early for daddies furniture, we were having. We were soon there and everything unloaded and put in place before lunch time. We sat in our new dining kitchen and had a cup of coffee and some biscuits, then decided to have a shower, it was a wet room, so there was plenty of room for us both.

I asked him what he wanted for his dinner, to which he said it was all in hand and not to asked any more questions. We sat in our lovely luxurious lounge with the curtains all drawn back and we could see over the roof tops, it was as though we were in heaven, life could not get better than this. At 6.30pm he said we will go and lay the table but do not ask questions, just before seven the bell went and Mat went out of the door and opened the lift doors, I could hear him talking, then heard him thanking whoever.

He came in with a big bouquet of red roses "Just for you my very, very special sister," then he went out, when he returned he had a big hamper which he put on the work top. He began unpacking things, he looked up I was still stood there "My darling you are catching flies again," and he came over to me and kissed me "Now my sexy little thing close your mouth, here let me take your roses and you sit at the table." When I sat down I could not see what he was doing, he was putting things in the oven. He came with a bottle of champagne, which he opened with a flare, he did not loose one drop, he filled our glasses and passed one to me, so I stood opposite him and he looked me in the eyes "To my one true love, here's to us my darling and I promise you, by this time next year you will truly be my wife," we had a drink, well I only had a sip, the tears poured down my cheeks.

"My darling Mat, I love you so much, you are one very special person, I have never been so happy, and you have done all this for me," I had to put my glass down because I was shaking. He put his down and took me in his arms.

"I only want you to be happy, I don't want you ever to look back, we go forward together, please don't cry, I thought you were happy?"

"I am but I am overcome by how romantic you are and so thoughtful, you have changed, because when you were young you were so down to earth, matter of fact, no nonsense, romance wasn't in your vocabulary," we laughed.

"It is you who changed me, I have never bought a girl flowers and as for presents I had to think she was special for me to put myself out and go out and buy something, I love you my darling, that must be why and I have to take care of you, I could not bear it if I thought you were on your own, as you have no friends," he looked at me, "You are so lovely and sexy and you let me fuck to you, you are amazing," and he took me in his arms and kissed me.

After some time he said "Come on sit down I am going to feed you." The three course meal was out of this world, he had ordered dishes he knew were my favorites, all the dishes went in the dishwasher. I did not have to lift a finger he had thought of everything. When I had quizzed him about the food, at school he was friendly with Mick, his father owned a restaurant in Nottingham and he used to meet him and they would have meals. When he went to the bank he bumped into his Mick, he had took over the restaurant from his father, hence he had got everything from there. So that was our first meal in our own home together, one of many to follow.

We put the old office building on the market, it sold very quickly for £1,200,000.00 although it was not a vast building, it was in a prime position in Nottingham and covered three floors, that gave us (well Mat) another £400,000.00!

One day Mat said he had bumped into another old friend Max, he used to play Golf with, and he was going to get him membership at his club, was the okay with me? I had told him it was fine.

He started going out a couple of evenings, with Max for a drink, he was only out for under two hours, and he always made it up to me when he returned home.

Everything was running smoothly, in fact we did not have to spend much time in the office, well correction, Mat didn't, I did everything.

Mat announced we were getting married, 2nd September this year, 1994, in Gretna Green. I have told Pa we want a few days off from the 1st September to 4th September he said that was fine, I omitted to tell him why we wanted time off. He'd told him all he had to do was answer his mobile if any hotel rang and we would explain the situation to our hotels," he stopped and looked doubtful.

"Mat my darling that is fine by me, if you are going to be my husband, I would do anything you know that, besides we do not want anyone here, they might discover the spare room isn't used," he came and gave me a wonderful kiss.

Time flew fast the 31^{st,} August arrived we did all the last minute preparations, I telephoned Daddy and told him there were no problems, and they would be speaking to you if anything cropped up.

We set off late that evening to start on our journey, we stopped at a hotel on the way up. Mat had made all the arrangements. We were married at 2pm, with two witnesses provided by the office.

Everything settled down on our return. Mat started playing Golf a few weeks after he had seen Max in March. They went fairly early on a Saturday but he was home early in the afternoon and during the light nights they used to go Wednesday about 3pm to around 8pm.

One Saturday early in October the bell rang, when I opened it there stood Chas, we hugged and kissed. "Why didn't you let me know you were coming?"

"I wasn't sure I was coming, Nat you look wonderful," he was holding me at arms length looking at me.

"How long are you staying darling?" I asked.

"Well if it is alright, until Wednesday, I have some visits to make down here and some people to see, show me where to put my bag, then you can show me round," he said.

I took him into the spare room "I will make the bed up for you."

"Come on show me the rest, he was impressed it is wonderful Nat, are you happy?"

"Yes of course I am why?" I asked.

"Okay, so you have just taken me round, you have shown me the spare room, there is only one other bedroom? When I took your hand not only were you wearing a diamond ring, but a wedding ring? What's going off Nat, you haven't got married and Mat moved out? because you would have both told me, when we speak regularly," he stood looking at my left hand.

"Chas, Mat and I are married."

"You cannot be, your related? Christ I forgot, we're not!. So when did all this come about, when did he start fucking you Nat," he was shouting at me, he had never ever shouted at me, the water works began "Nat, Nat my darling I am sorry, I should not have shouted at you, come on sit down, I am sorry, please darling, I need to know," so I told him the story from the holiday.

"So I gave you to him on a plate, when I said I could not go. He did not lose any time of getting into your knickers!"

"Chas I know it is a shock but we do love one another, he is so different to how he was when he was younger," I said.

"Well where's he now?" I explained about the Golf clubs and Max.

"I don't mind Chas, I would not have bought them if I did not want him to have friends besides me," I looked at him.

"And where do you go?" when I hesitated "Don't bother,

nowhere you sit at home like a good little sis-wife, and I would like to bet you, you do the work in the office?"

"There isn't that much now there is only three hotels."

"I know my brother better than you will ever know him, and do you know Nat, I have seen his ex girls and the devastation he leaves behind, and you know what makes me so bloody mad," he looked at me "The fact that I had and have deeper feelings for you than Mat will ever have, I backed away because, I did not think it was right, being brought up as brothers and sister. Then left you vulnerable to his manipulations, Nat I love you so much, I have tried everything to get you out of my mind, I have tried staying away, but I am still in love you and I always will be, and I do not mean as a brother. I know I have Heather and live with her, but it is not working, that is why I am here, I am looking to starting my own business now I have finished Uni, I want to get back nearer Nottingham," he looked at me "Nat I am so sorry for shouting at you please forgive my darling," and he put his arms round and pulled me close to him "You feel so soft and smell so sweet, let me just hold you a little longer," when he released me he said "I'll go and put my things away, you are sure it is alright to stay?"

"I would be cross if you went elsewhere," he went into the spare room, I went and put some towels in the shower room.

"We do not dress for dinner." I called to him.

When Mat came back, he was surprised to see Chas and he welcomed him happily as any brother would. I lost no time telling him Chas knew everything, "In that case then I don't have to pretend," he said and took me in his arms, he really went to town with kissing me, I wondered if he was doing it on purpose, did he know how Chas felt about me? When he let me go, Chas was looking out of the window, I felt awful for him.

While I got on with dinner, they sat at the table chatting with a lager, every now and again Mat would ask if I needed any help. Any awkwardness soon went, we started chatting as if we had never been apart. We had a good few days, although I was the one in the office Monday, with all the weekly paperwork from each hotel.

Chas left about 11am and said he would be back later this evening, he would not want dinner, and would be going tomorrow around 7am, and would be late again.

Wednesday, Mat had a pre-arranged appointment with the

bank at 9.30. Chas was not up. I went into the office to work.

He came in to me, "I am glad Mat is not in, I had a call from Heather, she says she wants me out before next Monday, the last thing I want is staying with the two of you. If I could dump my stuff here, I could book into a hotel."

"Chas no you can't, I do not have to ask Mat if you can stay, you are our brother, I do not have to ask permission. Mat might think there was something funny if you went to a hotel, don't you think?"

"I suppose," he said "It's just that he's all over you and I am not sure if he is doing it on purpose? Is he like that normally? Tell me Nat please, honestly?"

"Well no, we were kissing and cuddling at first, however, we usually wait until we go to bed, I think you could be right it is because you are here, did he know how you felt about me?"

"God no Nat, he had no idea, but then I did not know he had, he used to say things about you, that made me wonder how he felt? You know sexual innuendoes. No I am not going to stay, I will sort something else out. I cannot sit and watch him mauling you. I am making a coffee and then I am going Nat, do you want one darling"

We left the office, and went into the kitchen together, he had his coffee. "Do not say anything about what I am doing, if Mat asks you do not know, just say I said see you soon, okay?"

"Chas I am so sorry," and the tears started.

He pulled me to him "So am I, I have to go, I will see you soon, but I will ring first. Nat can I kiss you please just once?" he looked so sad, I lifted my lips to his, he did not hesitate, his lips were on mine, his tongue slipped between my lips, entwined with mine. He was really doing things to me, I didn't want him to stop, he was having a different effect on me to how I felt with Mat. This kiss really got to me, I wanted more, a lot more.

He still held me close and looked deep into my eyes "Nat that was the best kiss ever. I have frequently dreamed about what it would be like, now my darling I know, please take care my love, any problems please let me know immediately," and he was gone leaving me feeling devastated.

Chapter three

The afternoon came and no sign of Mat, so at 2 pm I rang his mobile, it went straight to voice mail, I asked where he was?" Nothing, rang again at 4.30 pm, still nothing. I rang Daddy and asked how he was, and had he seen Mat, he said no. I rang again at 6 pm and 8 pm.

At 9.15 pm he staggered in drunk, I ran to him "Mat darling I have been so worried where have you been, why didn't you phone?"

He looked at me "I do not have to answer to you, just because I went for a few drinks, don't think I have to ask your permission, I have already eaten and I want you in bed now, I feel like giving you a bloody good fucking, that will shut you up, now move bitch," I just stood looking at him, I could not believe what I had just heard "Nat I will not tell you twice," he got hold of my arm and pulled me into the bedroom, "Get undressed" I was frozen to the spot, he grabbed my dress and tore it off , "I want to see what I own," he picked me up threw me on the bed and tore my under wear off and it hurt, really hurt.

"Now lay still, open you're legs wide, while I get undressed," I did as I was told, I was so scared, "That is all mine, I own you all of you," he stood swaying, I am praying he sways and falls over. "Now Mrs C remember a wife's duty is you keep your husband happy and satisfied in bed, otherwise I will go and fuck someone who will let me, you never complain, if I like to rough you up a little, you never, never ever say NO, do you understand?" I just nodded.

He was now undressed and kneeling on the bed in front of me "How's that for a cock Mrs C, you know where this is going don't you?" that was it. I can't say it was making love, he was rough very rough, he hurt me, he put great big love bites on both breasts. Eventually he rolled over and I think he was unconscious, I went to the bathroom had a shower and cried. When I went back in he was still in the same position, I covered him up and slid in on the edge of the bed, I could not sleep, all the while he snored loudly at the side of me.

I got up went to where we keep the drinks and took a big drink of whisky from the bottle, I regretted it straight away, I felt sick, so I ran into the shower room, and was sick until I was just heaving. I crawled into the spare bed where Chas had slept, I could smell his after shave, and began to cry and sob as quietly as I could, but I doubt an earthquake could have woken Mat.

I did eventually fall asleep only to be woken by a night mare, I went to the shower room and dried the sweat from my body, when I looked in the mirror my body had bruises all over, grazes and scratches, from him ripping my clothes off. He had been rough between my legs, I was badly bruised, I looked as if I had been in a road accident. Then I went back to bed but by now in was nearly 4am, I dozed on and off but could not get to sleep.

Then at about 9.15 I heard this thud and Mat thumping around the bedroom I think he's going to the en suite, he was I heard him flush the toilet. Then "Nat, Nat darling where are you?"

I got out of bed, put the bathrobe on which Chas had worn, and went round the bedroom door, he was sitting on the edge of the bed "Christ Nat I feel awful, how did I get home?"

"I have no idea how you got home, or where you had been all day. I do know what you did when you did come home though," I felt like screaming! He looked at me in amazement.

"You sound unhappy Nat, come here let me make it better sweetie," and he held out his hand, so I went towards him.

"I think you have done enough," and opened the bathrobe to show him my battered body, he looked shocked, saying; "Did you have an accident? Where were you? darling had I better get you a doctor, come here my darling," he said.

"Mat you did this, you who had a job to stand, you who ripped my clothes off, you who treated me like a common prostitute, you who forced yourself into me, you who put all these bites on me and you have the audacity to sit there and say did I have an accident, yes I did you!" I was sobbing by now.

"Nat I can't remember anything."

"Where were you? why didn't you answer your phone? I was going out of my mind I was so worried and then when you did appear I wish you hadn't."

"I didn't do that, I couldn't, I love you."

"Christ all bloody mighty Mat, I have just told you, but I am telling you now, you do anything like this again, I will be ringing the police, as much as I love you, I am not going through anything like this again!"

He could not stop apologising, all day he was full of remorse telling me how much he loved me, I never did find out where he had been. "I am telling you this now Mat, you get drunk again, you will not get in here, you will be locked out, it is entirely up to you, you can go elsewhere and fuck a prostitute they don't mind a bit of rough."

He did not go anywhere for over a week, not even golfing, he did begin to get on my nerves telling me how sorry he was, and it would not happen again, but something had changed, I could not put my finger on it.

One night he was in a weird mood and said "I want to feel your mouth on my cock, give me a blow job."

"A what? what do you mean?" I queried.

He pulled his erection out "Sit on the bed and open your mouth," he more or less demanded.

Not thinking, I opened my mouth, and he started put it in my mouth, I moved back in horror "No sorry Mat, I am not doing that, please don't be mad with me," I said. He pushed me roughly back onto the bed and ripped my panties off. "What are you doing?"

"Shut your fucking mouth, or I will put it in," that stopped me. "Open your fucking legs, you little slut," he pushed two or maybe three fingers inside me, and suddenly his mouth was on my clit, he removed his fingers, then his mouth, tongue and lips were doing wondrous things, it felt wonderful, in a short time I was having an orgasm, I had never felt anything like this before. He did not stop he kept doing it until I climaxed again, he still didn't stop but he was getting very rough he was sucking very hard on my clit non stop, but I still climaxed and he carried on until I did again, he suddenly stopped. He grabbed me and pulled me over to him and lay me over his legs (it happened in a second) and began spanking me hard "You dirty, filthy, slag letting me do that, you even came, you have never done that when I fuck you, you would let anyone do what they liked with you, you are worse than the trollop," all the time he was spanking me. He stopped and was groaning and he was coming all over me.

"Get up on your fucking knees, you dirty bitch," he was on his knees behind me. "I am going to fuck you like the cheap bitch you are," he began pushing into my bottom.

I screamed "No Mat, not there, please," I am pleading.

"Shut your fucking mouth, I will not tell you again," and he rammed into me. I screamed, he stopped moving and next thing he is leaning over stuffing the corner of the sheet into my mouth, then I felt blows on my bottom, he was not slapping, he was using his fist. "Go on bitch scream now, then he started the ramming in again, the pain was excruciating, he kept going, he was drawing out and then ramming in hard. I felt so sick, everything was hurting inside and out, the internal pain was excruciating.

"Nat you are my wife, you have to let me do what I want to you, you haven't any choice now we are married, you have to do whatever I tell you and you do not complain, if I do something you do not like, as wife you keep me happy always and you do not say no, ever," He was still ramming me, then it all changed, I realised he was coming again. After a while, I dare not move he said "I thought that would have lasted longer, but you are tight, we will stretch it, if I fuck you there regularly, go and get in the shower you filthy bitch."

I scurried into the shower, I did not know where hurt most and I looked down and there was blood pouring down my legs, I felt faint, I wobbled but grasped the towel rail, to steady myself, I moved out of the shower and tore some toilet paper off and put it to my vagina, nothing I moved it to my back passage and it was pouring out of there. I felt faint again, but went back in the shower and kept the head spraying onto it, in the hope it would stop the blood.

He suddenly appeared in the door way, with a glass it looked like whisky and he gulped it down in one "Come on baby help me shower, hold out your hands," and he squeezed some body wash onto my hands, "I'll do the rest you look after my prick," he was weaving all over the place.

He was suddenly Mat again, drunk, but he was normal. Will you go and fill it for me babe and hurry up," so I put a bathrobe on and grabbed some tissues and wedged them at the top of my legs, so the blood did not get everywhere. When I got to the bottle of whisky it was nearly empty, yet it was full earlier, I got a new one out. and took both bottle and glass back to the bedroom, hoping he would have enough and pass out.

He came out of the bathroom "It's a new bottle can you open it for me?" I asked.

"Course babe, anything you want, I love you so much, do ya want some?" he was really drunk, I took the bottle from him and filled his glass to the top, it was not anything like a small glass, more like a tumbler. He sat on the bed, I thought we would get back to normal, I didn't know where the pain was the worst.

"Mat I do not feel very well, can I go and make a drink and have some tablets," I tried to sound calm, I didn't want to upset him.

"Hang on babe, I have something that will make you feel better," and he started rummaging round in his bedside drawer. "Here," he said and tipped some white powder on to the glass top, "Sniff this up your nose," I looked aghast, he grabbed my arm and the bathrobe opened. He looked closer at me "Nat you've started your period, go and get it sorted you dirty bitch," I am not going to hide it.

"I haven't Mat it's not my period," I said very calmly.

"What is it, there is a lot, I think you ought to get a Doctor, where's it coming from?" he genuinely had no idea.

"My back passage Mat, it's what you have done," he sat and looked as if he did not understand, I will make it clearer. "Mat you have done this forcing yourself into me, like the animal you are," I still sounded calm, but inside I was screaming.

"Nat I would never hurt you, you know that. Now what really happened?" he took a deep drink of his whisky the glass was nearly empty again, he put his hand to his head, "Oh god," and fell face down.

I went and got some panties, I took them in the bathroom, had another shower and find a towel and rip it up to make a big thick pad and put it between my legs, and pull the panties to hold its in place. When I come out I see the duvet in covered in blood, but leave it.

I go and put the kettle on find some pain killers, the sit down and cry. I went into the spare room and went to bed, I hardly slept, I was frightened in case he came in. The bleeding eventually stopped but I could not go to a Doctor, I was to embarrassed.

He did not emerge at all the following day, each time I went in unfortunately he was still breathing. He eventually got up and 10.30 the day after, he was his normal self, but looked like he had an hangover from hell, serves him right, I thought. He did not say much, he just had two large cups of black coffee, then he got ready and said I am going to play golf, I won't be late and left, it was Saturday and he did not come home at his usual time I began to worry, the phone rang about 5 pm it was Mats mobile, a woman voice said "I am ringing for Matthew, he will not be able to get home tonight, don't worry he is alright, see you tomorrow," I did not get a chance to ask anything.

I am so worried I had no one to turn to, there was only Chas. I rang him, I thought it was going through to his mail but he answered "Hi Nat how are you?" I couldn't speak I was crying "Nat what is it?"

"Sorry Chas. where are you?"

"I'm in a hotel why, darling is everything alright you sound upset."

"Can you come, please come, Chas I am frightened."

"I'm on my way it will take about 10 to15 minutes, I am on Mansfield Road," then he was gone. 13 minutes later he was at the door, I opened it and fell into his arms crying.

"Nat come on darling, let me get you sat down and tell me, where is Mat? Could you not have phoned him?" I shook my head. He made me a cup of strong tea and we sat at the table, "Come on darling, spill I can see this is serious?"

So I told him everything from that morning when he'd gone to the bank and every step of the way, when I got to when he got home drunk, look," I said as I unbuttoned my top and showed him part of my breasts. Then I told him about two nights ago and what he did, then I showed him my severely bruised bottom, lower back and the top of my legs.

"Nat did he do that? and the bleeding have you been to a Doctor?" he asked, he already knew the answer.

"Yes he did do that and a lot more, I am not only frightened, but why did he get a woman to ring me? I stopped myself from ringing him as it got later and later, and then her. Chas I could not go to a Doctor I was too embarrassed." I said.

"Nat I have no idea, why would a married man get a woman to ring his wife, Mat is a law unto himself. I know I will ring him, hang on," he dialed and it was answered after three rings "Hi Mat where are you there's a lot of noise, I wondered if we could meet for a drink?" he was talking I could just hear his voice "Okay some other time, is Nat alright?" more Mat's voice "Thanks, see you."

"He said, sorry but you were already out at a party, if you and he had known I would be calling, we could have got you an invitation. When I asked if you were alright? he said without hesitation you were fine and having a great time, perhaps you were drinking a bit too much, but that did not matter."

"I can't believe it Chas, he has changed since we married for some reason, it was as if we were now married he did not have to bother too much. He vowed he could not remember anything, and that it would not matter because it would not happen again," I said, "So are you staying in a hotel?"

"Yes I thought it for the best."

"Chas will you come and stay here I am so frightened," I am begging.

"Yes but I am not leaving you tonight, I will get my stuff in the morning, I will wait until he comes back tomorrow before I go, we do not tell him I was here when I phoned him, but you will say I turned up last night, then he will know I know, but not you," I made him something to eat, I was not hungry, I opened a bottle of wine and we drank it all, we sat on the sofa Chas had his arm round me.

"I will not let you come to any harm again," he kissed my forehead.

"I'd better make your bed up," I said getting up.

"I will help you, then I think we should have an early night," so we did just that, he gave me a swift kiss on the lips and we went to bed. It took me a while but I eventually went to sleep, until;

"Nat, Nat darling, wake up you were screaming, I thought Mat had come home and was attacking you, Christ you frightened me," he had pulled me up towards him, and was holding me close, gently rocking me "Darling are you alright can I get you anything?"

"No I am okay, I'll just get a towel."

"No I will get it" he said diving into the en suite, when I looked down I realised I was sitting there with my boobs on display, I started pulling at the sheets. "Too late darling I have already seen you, you really are gorgeous Nat, they are something you should be proud of, I could get lost in there," that made me laugh.

I told him about my nightmares, that they had started to get a bit better sometimes not even one a night, he said the same as Mat had about a Doctor, so I went though it all again. I slid down the bed and he lay on top holding me, I suddenly felt all safe again and I went back to sleep and did not wake up until 7am, there was no sign of Chas, I got up showered and dressed, when I got to the kitchen he was sat at the table looking out of the window.

"Morning my darling how do you feel? I'll get your tea?"

"Please Chas I feel quite refreshed thank you, when did

you leave? I am sorry about the nightmare and your disturbed sleep, I hope you are not having second thoughts about moving in?"

"No I will wait until he gets back, and see what he has to say, then I will fetch my stuff, but you know it is only temporary, when I find premises for the business and a flat or both together, I will have to go. I left you around 6am because you were sleeping peacefully," he said.

"Yes Chas I know you'll have to go sometime, but in the meantime I thought if you were here he would not misbehave etc. I'll do breakfast have you any requests," I asked.

"I will help, can I have scrambled eggs on toast, please?" he asked.

"Do you not want bacon or what? I have plenty," I said.

"No my darling, I really do not feel that hungry you filled me up last night," so I did his eggs, I had just one slice of toast but it took a lot of getting down.

At 10.30 am we heard the lift, then the front door, we were still sat at the table when he came round the door saying;

"Nat darling," and stopped when Chas came into sight "Oh I didn't know we had company, morning Chas."

"Chas came last night because he had not seen us for a while, so I asked him to stay, as you would not be home, he is in a hotel, so I told him we could not have that, he is going to collect his things and bring them here until he finds something," I knew I was gabbling.

"Morning Mat, you are one lucky bloke, got the most drop dead gorgeous wife, you stay out all night and she is not demanding to know where you have been. Where have you been Mat," he demanded.

He just stood there as if it were a natural thing "I went to a party, had too much to drink, I did not want to come home drunk so I stayed in a hotel where the party was, that's alright isn't it Nat?"

"No," I said "What would you do if I went out on my own, got a man to ring you and tell you I would not be home until the next day? You would find me and kill me," I snapped.

"Nat that is very different for a woman, it is different for men," he more or less leered.

"Why Mat you are still married to me, I don't know where you are? or who with? or even who you were fucking?" he did flinch at that.

"I am not having this conversation if you are going to be like that," he looked at Chas. "You're with me aren't you, it is different for a man?"

"How Mat?" Chas simply asked.

"It just is, I thought you would understand."

"Like I understand our last conversation Mat?"

"I will talk to you later, I am going for a shower, get me some breakfast Nat, eggs 2, bacon 3, sausages 2 tomatoes halved 2, got that I will have it as soon as I am showered, 30 minutes top."

"No Mat you get your own breakfast, if we are married, we do not stay out all night, you forgot you were married, I have forgotten we are married when you want food," I stood with my arms crossed looking at him defiantly.

"If that's the way you want it don't bother, I will have a shower and go out again, I know where I am welcome," and he stormed out banging the kitchen door behind him.

"I am not leaving you here, you will come with me when I go and collect my things, I think you did very well there."

Then the door flew open, Mat stood there naked and said "I have just thought you two were here together alone, did you fuck my wife bro?'

"No I did not," and he stormed back to get showered not waiting for Chas to say anything else.

"Chas was I seeing things there, had he got a love bite or a bruise above his dick also several on his neck?" I asked.

"Hard to tell it was one or the other, I'd say Nat he is playing away and I want to kill him," Chas was beside himself.

"Chas I know how you feel calm down, but please don't be in a hurry to leave."

Half an hour later we heard the door close and the lift start, I ran into the lounge and looked out, sure enough there he was, driving away, Chas was beside me.

"Come on let's fetch my things, tell you what follow in your car, then I need only do one trip, it's not that I have a lot, but I bought a computer and it is big, but I heard they are the thing of the future," So that is exactly what we did.

It wasn't until we got back I realised it was Monday and I hadn't even opened the post, but Chas said.

"Leave it today I will help you tomorrow, Nat I have to tell you something, I think I know why Mat is behaving irrationally, I think he is doing drugs again! When I think back that is how he was before when he drinks as well that is what pushes him to start behaving as he is, he becomes very unreasonable, unpredictable, he seems to crave sex but is very controlling, violent and rough as soon as you told me I realised, I should have warned you. I didn't think he would have cause to take them again, but something has set him off again. I have been racking my brains, I think that Max was one of his friends, he was the same as Mat was, they would egg one another on, also that Mick with the restaurant was the same"

"Here was I thinking it would be nice for him to get out a bit, I did not mean a bit on the side! You know the drugs, is it a white powder you sniff?" I said.

"Nat how do you know?" he asked.

"Because Mat put some out the other night, he said if I had some it would take the pains away," I replied.

"Oh Nat my little darling, you didn't?" I stopped him shaking my head. "Thank god. Anyway I rang my friend Rupert he is a few years older than me, but we have been friends for ever, I think he is a Lawyer I am not sure, he lives in Nottingham. We were around a lot together about the time Mat was doing drugs, so I phoned him and asked him if he could remember any of Mat's old druggy friends, Max and Mick both their names he came up with, along with Paul and Scot. I am so sorry Nat if I had known what was going to happen, oh god Nat I could have stopped this."

"How Chas? You were not to know he was going back to his old ways," I said, trying to smile.

"I have just thought you know Rupert, he came to the house a lot during the hols," he suddenly said.

"I know there were lots of your friends, and Mat's but I do not think I ever spoke to any of them, the trollop always kept me out of sight."

"I was meeting to give him some papers I want him to look at, I think I should ring and ask him to call here, because I do not want to leave you, you never know Mat may come home," he looked at me.

"Yes why not, we could open a bottle," I suggested.

"He does not need to stay."

"Well at least we could make him welcome, ring him," I said as I left the room. I had better look presentable, my trousers and top although a bit tight were okay, but I had better brush my hair and put something on my drawn face, a bag would be about right!

"Rupert said he would love to call and meet you, he does know about your problems."

"Did you have to," he stopped me.

"Darling I had to tell him something, because I wanted him to come here.

"Oh," I said.

"Excuse me you are wearing make up? Your hair is all brushed, you did not leave the room like that? I am not sure you should be making yourself even more desirable, I do not want you attracting any of the opposite sex my darling, if you divorce Mat I am top of the list," I was not expecting the next move, he stood up and took me in his arms and kissed me urgently, then softly, unfortunately I could not stop myself I kissed him back.

"Chas I should not have kissed you, I am sorry you'll be thinking I am a trollop like she is, was," I stammered.

"No way my darling, you would never be like her, anyway I am pleased you did kiss me, because it means I have a chance and the waiting will be worth it, I want to take you to bed, but I am not stepping that far out of line."

The bell rang, Chas went and opened the lift and he came in with a drop dead gorgeous guy "This is Rupert, Rupert, Nat," he said laughing, we politely shook hands.

"Pleased to meet you Nat, very pleased, I have to say I can see why Mat married you," I could feel my face going red.

"Wine red or white?" Chas asked.

We sat chatting for a couple of hours, that's when I eventually found my voice the time just flew and as he was leaving he said;

"Lovely to meet you Nat," he took my hand but kissed me on the cheek, I could feel myself blushing as Chas showed him out.

"Well that's it he's never coming near you again, he really fancies you and you looked somewhat over awed. Come on bed let's have a good night and see what tomorrow brings," Chas has taken charge "Night Nat," he kissed me on the lips but it was swift.

"Night Chas, thank you," I could not seem to sleep for long, it was sort of a nap, then I would wake up, everything went round, then I would nap again, this went on for several nights.

We did not hear anything from Mat, until he arrived at 11

am the next Monday morning, a week later, as though nothing had happened, I was in the office, Chas was in the spare room reading through some papers. He went straight into the shower changed and came back.

"Anyone for coffee," he shouted neither of us replied.

We heard him rattling round in the kitchen then he appeared in the office and closed the door behind him "Nat I am sorry, I have no idea what came over me, you know I love you, I only want to make you happy."

"Well you are not making a very good job of it, why? we haven't been married for five minutes, what's wrong with you? Where do you get to and who with? Why can't you be satisfied with me?" I said sulkily.

"It's just that I have met up with all my old friends, we are catching up that's all," he said.

"Do you think you can get away with that, what about the love bites and staying out all night, why can't you just go for a drink and come home," I waited.

"I haven't got any love bites, I do not go with other women, I love you Nat, you know that."

"Okay bedroom now," I said, I nearly raised my voice!

"What are we to have a morning of sex Nat, come on then," he grabbed me and pulled me behind him, just as Chas was coming out of the spare room, I shook my head and put my finger to my lips, he frowned. Mat closed the door and took hold of me, I pulled away.

"I do not think so, strip off now," I demanded.

"Nat what's got into you?"

"Strip off now," he began unbuttoning his shirt, so I grabbed the waist on his trousers and unzipped them "Off now," he did, but left his boxers in place, however his neck had three fading plus more new love bites, I got his hand and pulled him to the mirror "What are those then?" and whilst he was looking, trying to find an answer, I pulled his boxers down and yes it was a love bite not a bruise, fading, but it was there. "So what's that then, if you are not fucking around how do you get that lot, come on Mat I want an answer!"

He just stood, looking at me, "You know I love you."

"A bloody funny way to prove it," I snapped.

"Well you said you did not want me home drunk so I thought it best to stay away," he replied.

"Good one, so now it's my fault, Christ Mat I could kill you, and I started thumping him with my fists on his chest, which had no effect whatsoever, he grabbed both my hands in one of his and slapped me really hard across my face, I screamed and Chas flew in.

"What the hell do you think you are doing Mat?" he snapped he was red with rage.

"What? I am showing my wife who is boss, I am now going to fuck her, if you don't go you can stay and watch, she is not going to raise her hand to me, she should obey me, not ask stupid questions like a fucking stupid slut she is," he was gripping my hands they hurt.

"You are not touching Nat, especially with you like this, you are taking drugs again I can see the signs, I bet you had a snort after you came home? Let go of her Mat, now."

"She is my wife and I am entitled to do what I like with her, if I want to fuck her, I damn well will, piss off Chas pack your fucking bags," Chas did no more he took a big swipe at Mat, although Mat is a slightly taller, Chas is a lot fitter, his fist hit him on the nose, he yelled and let go of me, before he could do anything, Chas took another swipe and caught him some where near his left eye, he fell back onto the bed, blood pouring from his nose.

"Now Mat you get out, go and get yourself sorted, ditch the drugs and come home when you can treat our Nat, with some respect, and treat her gently like she needs and deserves, you have a very short memory Mat," with that Mat grabbed his clothes went to the en suite and then the door opened and he shouted.

"Look at my bloody face, look what you have done, I can get you arrested for that, you are going to regret this, when I come back I do not want to see you still here Chas, you are very protective towards that slut, I'll bet you are both fucking like rabbits, well you haven't heard the last of this and you, you dirty fucking bitch be ready because you are going to be taught a lesson in loyalty!" he was dressing whilst he was ranting, grabbed his wallet and jacket and slammed out, still holding a towel to his face.

All I said was "Loyalty?" I could not stand my legs were like jelly, I just wilted to the floor in tears.

Chas picked me up and lay me on the bed. "Nat I am sorry, I could not stay out when I heard him, I do not know what he has in mind, but we better drop the catch on the door in case he comes back soon, I don't know what I can say?" he leaned down and took me in his arms and cradled me "I think I have made it worse for you now, I am so sorry, I could not let him behave like that towards you."

"Chas please don't apologise I dread to think what he would have done to me, if you hadn't intervened," I said, through sobbing.

"I am going to ring Pa and tell him, no I will warn him about Mat, I will tell him a bit about today, but say you are safe as I am staying here anyway, is that okay?"

"Yes Chas and thank you," he went out and I could hear his voice but not what he was saying, but it was a long call, I just lay quiet, then my mobile started ringing, it was in the office, so I went to look who was ringing, I did not know the number so I answered;

"Hello."

A man's voice said "Mrs Cartwright?"

"Yes."

"You do not know me but is your husband there?"

"No I am sorry he is not, to whom am I speaking please?"

"Just tell him when you see him, if he ever does that to a woman again he will be sorry, and he will be minus his manhood," he said.

"Please who are you?" I begged.

"You do not know my dear, but if I were his wife I would be very worried for my safety, take care bye," and he was gone I just sat there numb. "Nat what has happened was it Mat?"

"No it was a stranger and I relayed what he had said, Chas I am so frightened, what did daddy say?"

"Darling show me your phone, let me see if the number rings a bell," but it did not "I assured him I would not leave you for a minute, he said if he comes back ring him," Chas said.

"That will be good what can daddy do on the end of a telephone," and I broke down again, I had a throbbing head, I could not think straight. Chas lifted me up and took me and lay me on the bed.

"Stay there I will make you a cup of tea and find something for your head," he quickly came back.

"Nat is there anyway, anyone could get up here, without a ladder of course, is there a way to your outside from inside the building.

"No, there is a flight of stairs that comes up into that black building, also a flight of stairs we can use if the lift breaks down, but you still have to get through the front door," I said.

"That's less to think about, can I get you something to eat?"

"No Chas I couldn't eat anything, I'll lay here for a while."

"Do you mind if I help myself?" he asked.

"Darling you live here just do it my darling, and thanks."

"I'll leave you in peace then," he left closing the door behind him.

After two more nights of my nightmares, Chas made the decision to lay on my bed with me, then as soon as my nightmare started he was there to wake me, and they were not so bad.

We did not hear or see anything of Mat for over a week, we had an early meal on Saturday, watched some TV and was thinking of turning in, when the front door bell rang, and rang, we looked at each other, it could only be Mat, no one else could open the lift doors.

We both went towards the door, when a mans voice shouted "Mrs Cartwright could you please open the door? this is the police," we looked at each other, I took the chain off and opened the door slightly, there stood two policemen, a man in a suit and Mat.

"Mrs Cartwright your husband has been in some bother, he said you would stand bail of £20,000.00," while he was talking the man in the suit answered his mobile.

I replied "I am sorry I do not have that kind of money,"

Mat shouted "You stupid bitch, it's in the fucking safe."

"It is not my money Mat, I cannot touch it,"

The plain clothes man interrupted; "Well," he said "That has all changed now, bail has been cancelled, we have proof of more crimes you have committed, Mr Cartwright, sorry to have troubled you, come on he is now under arrest, then he read him his rights," and they turned to go.

"Just a minute Officer, can you tell me what's he done?" I was very polite but I was boiling inside.

He turned to the two in uniform, with Mat handcuffed to one, "You go I'll be back soon."

"Would you like to come in a minute?" I asked.

"Thank you Mrs Cartwright," then he saw Chas.

"This is Matthews brother Charles he is staying with me,

would you like to come and sit down? would you like tea or coffee?"

"That's very kind but no thanks, I cannot be long. You want to know what your husband has been charged with. Well when we arrived it was for assault and attempted rape, this was two separate occasions. We thought there were other incidents, we have been trying to get some other women to make a complaint, anyway it was taken out of their hands because the hospital has now informed us, because they had two emergencies at A & E two nights running, and it looked too much of a coincidence from their injuries. It was your husband, how long have you been married Mrs Cartwright?"

"This September," I replied "But we had been together for a year before we married."

"Has your husband ever been a little bit shall we say rough with you?" Chas and I looked at each other and before I could say anything Chas said;

"Yes, he has and that is why I am here, because she is petrified of him coming back. He told him about the first incident when he was not here, then the second when he was, he told the police that he had hit his brother twice, because he was going to rape Natasha."

"Would you both be prepared to make a statement, you are obviously frightened of him, Mrs Cartwright, it would put him in prison for a few years at least?" he asked.

I am already trembling because I am upset, the tears are flowing, I looked towards Chas and he nodded, so I nodded and whispered "Yes."

"It is late now shall we send a car for you tomorrow," Chas interrupted.

"Can I bring her, also she had a mobile call from an anonymous man," and he told him what this man had said.

"Thank you Mr Cartwright, have you still got the callers number in your phone Mrs Cartwright?'

I said "Yes do you want to see it?" I asked.

"Yes please," I handed it to him and he noted the number, "If we can get some details from him, it will be more against your husband, he needs locking up and the key thrown away. We will see you both tomorrow around 10.30 shall we say?"

Chas said "That will be fine I will bring her, thank you and goodnight," he said and the door closed.

When he came back I was crying he took me in his arms and just sat and held me "Let it all out Nat we are going to have to do something, I know it's late, but I had better ring Pa," so after sometime he said "Stay there my darling, he came back straight away with a whisky glass, "Sip this, I will ring Pa from the office."

He returned and said "I have filled Pa in, I told him you were married, because it will come out sooner or later, and lets face it you have done nothing wrong, we are not related! I told him I would not leave you on your own, I would stay with you for as long as it takes. I then told him what the police had said, I am sorry darling but I told him about your two incidents with Mat. I am afraid he was in tears when we said good night. Darling can I get you something to eat, you are not eating enough to feed a sparrow?"

"No thank you Chas it would not go down, I am going to bed I doubt I will sleep, I have not been to sleep properly, I just nap and wake up."

"Sweetie here's me thinking the nightmares were getting better, but you haven't slept properly. Oh my darling," and again he picked me up and carried me to bed. "I will go and top your glass up and bring it back, you could possibly sip it, until it has gone, you might go to sleep then?"

I cleaned my teeth, brushed my hair and climbed into bed. "Here you are I have made sure everywhere is locked up, please try and sleep sweetie."

"That's what daddy used to call me Sweetie, Chas I cannot thank you enough, I do not know what I would have done without you, in fact I would have had no one and would have ended up how? I don't know because all this would have happened with Mat, and I would have just had to put up with the abuse," and the tears were falling again.

He took me in his arms again and gently rocked me "Well I am here, my darling Nat, I am going nowhere," he let me go, I slipped down the bed he leaned over and put his lips to mine, but swiftly moved.

"Good night my darling," he was going to get ready for bed, then he would lay on top of my sheet with just the duvet over him.

Everything was going round and round, I finished the drink then fell asleep. The next thing was "Nat, Nat please wake up are you alright, that was a bad one just look at you," he went to fetch a towel, and proceeded to dry me "Roll over let me dry your back properly," as I rolled, I was further away so Chas had to kneel on the bed, he removed the towel and started gently massaging my neck.

"Ooh Chas that is lovely, it feels wonderful."

"It feels fine your skin is as soft as silk, and you are doing things to me, I am not made of stone," he whispered in my ear. I turned round slightly, I had not realised the sheet was further down, too late my breasts were in full view "Christ Nat," was all he could say.

I felt an overwhelming surge towards him, I turned onto my back, now I was naked to the top of my legs. I slid my hand round his neck, he did not move or even blink, it was as though I had hypnotised him, I gently pulled his head to me, put my lips to his and kissed him very softly, then a bit firmer and then he was responding, he took me in his arms, held me so close, his tongue opened my lips and I responded to him. We lay on our sides, one of his arms was round me and had pulled my bottom to him and I could feel his erection.

"Nat I am so in love with you, I should not be here in bed with you," I put my finger to his lips.

"Darling I know it's wrong, because I am married, but you are so lovely and kind. I know how you feel about me, who is it hurting if we make love. Mat is obviously fucking around, so why should we feel guilty? I do love you, please darling I do want you, you cannot leave me now, please my darling," I am begging.

"My darling, I am aroused by you, I am nearly coming and I want to feel myself inside you Nat I want you so much," he kissed me again. Then his lips moved to my breasts treating them the same, I am nearly screaming, he caressed me gently all the way down my body.

"Chas please, please let me feel you inside me, my darling," he raised himself up and put his knees between my legs, he did not have to open my legs, they already were.

"Oh Charles I," I just trailed off I couldn't remember how to speak, the things he is doing to me, it was so different to Mat. His lips came down on mine, we kissed like there was no tomorrow. When I opened my eyes he was holding himself up on his hands, his arms were straight his head was thrown back, I have never seen so much pleasure before. I closed my eyes and let him keep thrilling me, it was different, so many things were happening to me, nothing I had experienced with Mat, a long time after, we both had an almighty orgasm, every nerve in my body was tingling, I was pulsating round him, I could not breathe, "Charles, Ooh Charles I love you so much," I realised in that moment, yes I did love Mat, but not in love with him, this is what I felt for Charles and I said aloud "Charles my darling I have just realised, I am in love with you, not just love you like a brother, I am in love with you and I don't want you to leave me ever."

"Nat I have known for a long time that I am in love with you, never in my wildest dreams could I think you could feel that way for me, I won't ever leave you my darling, I will never stop loving you. That was some orgasm you had, do you always have one?"

"I didn't know what was happening, it has never happened before, well not with his prick inside me."

I fell asleep, enclosed in his arms, we did not shower or anything.

Chapter four

I did not wake until someone was kissing me so I kissed back. "Morning my darling how are you?" Charles asked.

"I feel wonderful, I can't remember having a deep sleep like that for a long time, can we stay here all day?" I asked.

"Sorry my darling as much as I want you and want to make love to you, we have to get up, I have to get you to the police station for 10.30 and it is now just after 9.30. You go in the shower, while I make us a cup of tea, come on sweetie up you get," and he pulled me upright "Christ I shouldn't have done that, Nat the site of your beautiful breasts, look what you have done, he stood up showing me his big, very, big erection."

I was showered faster than I have ever showered, careful not to wet my hair, threw a bathrobe on and sat creaming my face and brushing my hair, when Charles came back, still as naked as the day he was born, but he was still quiet erect "Darling doesn't my new friend go down further than that?"

"How can he, Nat I can't stop thinking about us, when you took me in your mouth, that was something else," he brought my tea over "I'll have my shower now," and disappeared.

"Charles can you hear me?" I asked.

"Yes sweetie and why are you saying Charles all of a sudden?"

"Because when you made love to me, that is what came out I hadn't planned it, Charles seems so sexy so that is what I call you from now on, why do you mind?" I called.

"Darling you can call me what you want, but I have to admit when you say it you do make it sound sexy, as if we are still having sex."

"You know what I did to you, when I took you in my mouth, I want you to know I have never ever done that before. As you know I was a virgin until Mat and he was never ever able to persuade me as much as he tried, I could not fancy his in my mouth, now first time with you and I kiss you. Can I say something else, don't be cross with me but you are a lot bigger than Mat!"

He was laughing "Why would I be cross when you say something like that, it is a compliment, he has your name on now, it is you and only you. Nat you did not just kiss your new friend you actually took him in your mouth, which is what you would have done, if Mat had persuaded you to give him a blow job," then appeared at the door showered, shaved and naked. "I still want you so badly, Nat I can't believe I have actually made love to you, my wildest dreams have come true."

In minutes we were out of the door on the way to give our statements, we were taken into separate rooms, I gave my statement it was typed up and I read it and signed. I then asked "Did you manage to get hold of the man who rang on my mobile?" I asked.

"Yes we did, thank you because that is another claim against him. God knows how many women your husband has abused. I am sorry at this stage of the investigation I cannot give any details, but the man was ringing because of what he did to his daughter. I can say in every incident it is sexual with him, not just physical abuse."

I told him about the drugs and drink. I thanked him and met Charles who was waiting for me, he took me straight home.

As we arrived back the telephone was ringing, so Charles ran into the office and answered it was daddy, so Charles got him up to date on his eldest sons imprisonment and to date there were six woman he had sexually and physically abused, plus me, they could not give a trial date because they thought there could be a few more come forward. He would attend an hearing but had to stay in prison, bail would be refused on instructions from the police. He told Pa he would now be staying with me, Charles said Pa wants to speak to you.

"Hello daddy, I am sorry."

"Please do not say sorry, darling you have nothing to be sorry for, you are not responsible for your brother, sorry I cannot get used to saying anything else."

I could not speak, nothing would come so Charles took the phone from me. "Pa, Nat cannot speak, she is upset with everything that is happening. You do not know Mat and what he is capable of, poor Nat never stood a chance" he passed me the phone.

"Hello," I said through my sniffles.

"I am so sorry darling you are the last person I want hurt, I am so sorry my sweetie. Can you carry on the business for a week or so, when I knew what was happening I talked to Ernest and we decided to approach the 'Hotel conglomerate' to see if they wanted our remaining three hotels and they have agreed, we are talking terms now but we won't haggle, we will accept what they offer and then the paper work will be drawn up, can you do it on your own, until we can get someone in?" the phone was snatched from me again!

Charles was raging "Manage on her own, who the hell do you think has been running the company, I'll put it this way, the only thing Mat ever did was sometimes go to the bank for her, the rest my Nat did on her own, everything all the paperwork the lot, so please do not insult her and ask her if she can manage, she could do it stood on her head, sorry Pa but I am so angry about every aspect, poor Nat is at the sharp end," he didn't give daddy chance to speak he passed me the phone again.

"Hello daddy."

"Nat my sweet I am sorry I had no idea. When this is sorted it will still be split, but you will get Mats share, in the meantime darling please transfer £750,000 into your own account, note it as a bonus please. I will ring you when I have some news. What will you do about Mat, I hope you are not standing by him? You have had a lucky escape. If there is anything, at all I can do darling please ring me, I love you my darling never forget that. Bye sweetie," and he was gone.

Charles was still mad with daddy. "I hope he doesn't think £750,000 is enough, he would not have a business left to Mat," I was still sat on his knee and I turned towards him and he brought my lips to his.

"Oh Charles that really, really does help," he has made me start twitching down below.

"Do you want something to eat, I'm getting something we missed breakfast, although I am not complaining, because I would miss every meal if I was in bed with you," he smiled a lovely soft, kissable smile so I kissed him again.

"Charles," I said very quietly "Will it take you long eating your meal," and I kissed him again and whispered in his ear "Will it wait a bit longer I am so wanting you, Charles darling will you please take me to bed, I want you so much, you're so different to Mat."

He gave me a very long hard wanting kiss "Is that the answer you wanted my lovely sexy Nat?" he got up with me in his arms, I was not very heavy and he was strong, he carried me with ease.

We reached the bed and he lay me down, then his hand went up my skirt pulled my panties off, undid his trousers and was in me in a second. We both moaned together and our lips met, we were both hungry for one another. "Nat this is going to have to be fast and urgent, I was nearly coming before I got into you." It actually lasted longer than I thought, he was wonderful, it is so amazing the feelings he gives me, there are not enough words, we eventually both came together long and very loud.

"Charles darling please do not pull my friend out."

"Nat I had no intention of doing, I have now got to make love to you, we could be here all day! I realise now it wasn't food I was hungry for, it is you and I am still famished," we both laughed. Then his lips were on me again He did make love to me, it was out of this world it went on for ever he took me to the moon and back "Do you feel any better my angel?" he said kissing all round my face as well as playing with my breasts, he is doing things to me!

"Charles my darling I did feel a lot better, but you are now doing more things to me and if you really want something to eat, you will have to stop arousing me, you only have to touch me and I want you, why?"

"How do you mean why?" he asked looking slightly bemused.

"Why? when you just touch me am I getting aroused?"

"That is why us men caress certain areas of a woman's body my darling, but you know that don't you?"

"How would I know that Charles?"

"Say that again, my name," he asked.

"Charles," I whispered.

"God Nat when you say it is so sexy, you make it sound like you are caressing your new friend! it is the only way I can describe it."

"Well I am, Charles," I laughed "Anyway you did not answer my question, how would I know that I would be aroused."

"Well you and Mat were not celibate, he aroused you before making love or fucking as he called it!"

"Yes but his foreplay was putting his fingers inside me, for a second or do and ramming in and out fast then he would come. Not kissing my face like you are now, or when you are touching my breasts. My nipples went hard when he touched or kissed them, but it did not do anything down stairs and make me want him, like you," I said matter of factually "Most of the time he only fucked once, an odd time he might do it twice. Not like you, you can keep doing it, I want you to, I cannot get enough of you, whereas with Mat that never happened."

"I love you, you are so innocent, you can talk openly, other girls cannot until you get to know them, some a lot longer and you sit chatting about it as ordinary conversation."

"Well that did crop up with Mat, it is because I have known you for ever, and like I told him, we have seen one another naked, I know we are grown up and have more here and there, but it is because we were brought up together. Can I also say, I don't want you to get the wrong idea, because for a year when Mat and I were first together, he was so caring, he looked after me, even spoiled me, it all went wrong after we got married and met all his old friends. Also going back to being young, I can remember was I about nine, I walked in when you were in the shower, I got hold of my friend there and pulled him, I asked you what is was because I hadn't got one," I laughed loud and Charles laughed.

"I told you little girls did not have bits that dangle down there, then if I remember the trollop came along and slapped you hard across your face and your legs and told you, you had no right in when her son was taking a shower, she dragged you back with your hair, you did not cry or make a noise. Nat when I think what you went through with her, when I saw her do that to you, I stood and cried" and when I looked at him he had a tear thinking of that memory.

"Charles, I know what to do to forget terrible memories," I whispered.

"What Nat what would you do?" he had no idea what I was going to say.

I put the tip of my tongue in his ear and said "Put my friend in where he belongs, we can forget everything but the now, come on Charles I am sure we will forget," and put his lips to mine and he moved closer.

He was laughing "Well I don't know Nat, but let's give it a try," and he started kissing me and fondling me, he worked his way down my body with his hands. I am moaning at his touch, I begin writhing until he got over and between my legs and gently eases into me.

"If I died now I would be in heaven," I sighed.

"If you died now, I would have to continue until I come,

my luscious Nat," we could not help but laugh. We stayed in bed another couple of hours in the end Charles had to tell me, to get into the shower.

"Come on I will get the food, you go and get on with some work and if you do well I will give you a nice big erect treat," he laughed, I giggled and could not stop "Do you want tea or coffee now darling?"

"Tea please." We're so happy I didn't want anything to spoil it.

Two days later Charles said "Darling are you thinking of divorce?"

"Well I certainly don't want to be married to Mat so what do I do?"

"I will ring Rupert he will know" he went into the office and soon returned "Rupert said they have someone in Chambers who was very good at divorce settlements, he gave me his name and number, I have written it on your note pad, perhaps you could ring tomorrow and we could take it from there.

The next morning I rang and made an appointment with George Watson, for tomorrow at 11.30 am.

I did not sleep very well, I was tossing and turning, I knew I was getting very nervous. I was up at 6.30, Charles was fast asleep, I had a cup of tea, but did not want to disturb him, so I showered in the shower room. I dressed in a smart navy suit with a white blouse. I started cooking Charles breakfast and set the table for him, I knew I was not going to be able to eat, I was already shaking with nerves. I got a shock when Charles came up behind me, kissed my neck and whispered in my ear.

"Good morning gorgeous," he turned me round "Well who looks dead smart and very sexy this morning, why are you dressed and breakfast nearly finished, what time were you up? why didn't you wake me?"

"Err good morning my darling, I am up and dressed because I gave up trying to sleep at 6.30, I thought I may as well cook your breakfast for a change. Although when I gave up sleeping, I was so tempted to kiss you and play with my new friend, but I didn't think that would be fair, because you looked so handsome and peaceful, can I kiss you now?" and he took me in his arms and we kissed.

"Why did you not wake me with your nightmare?"

"That's because I didn't have one, I haven't had much

sleep, I could not switch off everything was going round. Then I began to wonder what happens when you want a divorce?"

"My darling why didn't you wake me, we could have done something to try and get you to sleep, you know we could have played cards or scrabble," his eyes twinkled when he is joking.

"Oh Charles I do not know what I'd do without you?"

"Stop it sweetie I am here with you, and it's where I am staying, I think you will find the sausages are done enough, is dark brown to black the normal colour?" he said as he lifted them off the grill, laughing all the time. "Come on lets get this plated and sit down," he said.

"No darling I am not having any, it is for you, I could not get one bite down, I will have something after I have seen George Watson, will you be coming in with me?"

"Of course you are my life and where you go I go, unless they say I am not allowed to accompany you."

We were there well before time but I was still called in dead on 11.30 and yes Charles was allowed in. I gave my personal details and answered all George Watson's questions, explained everything, details of what we knew from the police. Charles was brilliant he was able to add things I missed out. We left with the fact that it should be a fairly quick divorce, George Watson was claiming Adultery, Physical Abuse and Unreasonable Behaviour, he offered other reasons but we decided to go with those. Added to which because of his arrest and why, that will help. I was not claiming any settlement whatsoever.

When we arrived home, I was feeling not on top of the world exactly, but somewhat better than I had for a few days, Charles wanted to call for lunch somewhere but I just wanted to get home.

"Darling I will do us a quick lunch for now, and cook us a meal for this evening. I think you are wrong not claiming a settlement from him you deserve something you are too good, that is your trouble" and he took me in his arms and gave me the most seductive kiss.

"Charles darling can I have you for lunch? you have just turned me into a heap of wobbly jelly with that kiss, if you are going to keep having this effect on me, I think it would be easier for me to stay in bed. I really love you Charles, I really do, I love what you do to me and all the different feelings I get with you."

"I should not have kissed you like that, because you have

no alternative now but to go to bed, I cannot do anything with this erection, look what you have done," and there was the biggest bulge in his trousers. He grabbed my hand, we ran into the bedroom and that was it for the rest of the day, we broke for a sandwich over two hours later, then went back to bed, he did not cook dinner, he rang for a takeaway and we ate that and drank wine, then had and early night!

Rupert rang two days later to see how I had got on, Charles had a long chat with him. He informed him Mat would be serving a prison sentence, however, he would be out one day and I was petrified of repercussions from him. Rupert said he would make some enquiries, but would not say what? But would ring us in a couple of days, which he did and wanted to call the following evening as he had something to tell us.

So 7pm on the dot he arrived, he shook Charles by the hand, he took my hand but pulled me to him, and kissed me on the lips, "I am very pleased to meet you again Natasha."

"Come on through. Tea, coffee or wine Rupert, and stop undressing Nat with your eyes," the reply was totally unexpected.

" Well Chas you have got to admit she is one very beautiful young lady, she has a figure that is worth more than a second glance, in fact I can't think what Mat was doing playing away when she was at home waiting, he must be bloody mad, some men do not realise what a prize they have got, I tell you what if she was mine I would never get out of bed," he said as casual as you like.

I am blushing from head to toe and I know my mouth must be wide open. I know Charles and Rupert go back along way, I do not know what men do say.

"Rupert you cannot say those things in front Nat, she is not a worldly girl I think you have more than embarrassed her."

"Nonsense it was meant as a compliment, I will say this here and now, if I thought I stood a chance to take her to bed I would not hesitate, she is a very sexy, gorgeous, luscious girl, I would be only to happy to make love to her," I had to leave the room I did not know where to put myself. Charles came running after me.

"Darling please do not feel bad, you know he is right, any man looking, seeing you, would admit they would like to fuck you into the middle of next week," he laughed, I had to smile because it was my Charles saying it "You do not realise how beautiful and sexy you are, your figure is to die for, you do not get embarrassed, when I say these things."

"No darling that was because it is you, but I do not know Rupert, I don't know what men say to women? it could be the norm, but I have only had two men in my sex life and both are once my brothers!"

"Come on lets get some wine and glasses," as we re-entered Rupert stood up and said.

"Natasha I am so very sorry I did not want to upset you or embarrass you, I was only speaking my mind as any red blooded male would, what I said is true, it still doesn't alter the fact that I find you very attractive, given half a chance I would take you to my bed," I could see Charles holding his breath.

So I calmly said "Would you not take me for dinner first?" and slowly poured the wine, well it made Charles breathe, and they both laughed.

"Natasha if you said yes to me I would buy you breakfast, lunch and dinner for a month!"

Charles sat down "Now stop it Rupert what have you come to tell us?"

"Right back to business. Through the Police there is what they are calling a 'Witness Protection' it is for when people come forward with evidence to put criminals away, they give them a new identity and move them elsewhere. I have a friend Michael Roper who is the Chief Constable, I was telling him about you Natasha and you are frightened that when Matthew is released from prison what he would do, especially as he has said he does not want a divorce, so in cases like this, they do not stick to the normal rules, anytime you want he will see you and Chas, he will deal with everything, there will only be him and myself know where you go to, and your new identity, not even your family will know because the fewer who know the better. We would be doing it this way because he is a friend, otherwise someone of his rank would not be involved, but he is doing it as a favour for me. There is nothing to stop you telephoning your family, but you do not give anyone your new name, address and telephone number. Think about it and let me know what you decide?"

"Can I ask, nothing to do with this protection thing, but you said Mat doesn't want a divorce how do you know?" I asked.

"Because Nat, The Chief Constable himself made enquiries about Mat, he discovered when approached by his legal representative, telling him you wanted a divorce, he was like a maniac, he threw the chair he was sitting on, he attacked his legal man, it took four police guards to get him under control, all the time shouting about what he was going to do to you, shouting and ranting the most foul language, he'd never let you free, you belong to him, he would kill you first. The doctor was summoned and they put him out, in the hope that when he came round he was less volatile, just to be sure they handcuffed both his hands to the bed."

"Oh no," I am distraught.

"I do not think we have much choice Nat," Charles said.

"I wasn't going to tell you, I was going to tell Chas on his own, but as you asked, I thought we had better be honest and let you see what was in front of you," Rupert said very quietly "I am so sorry Natasha. Let me know what you decide, I will set the wheels in motion, it is a good idea,"   Charles shook his hand and again he took my hand but kissed my lips. "Let me know what you decide," and he was gone.

"Oh Charles what have I done," I could not stop crying, Charles led me to the sofa, and sat down beside me holding me close.

"Darling you have done nothing, he asked for it messing you around, thought he was being the big lover, but he is violent usually with the drugs and booze, but that just shows what he is capable of without either. I am so sorry my darling come on dry your tears, I think you have shed enough over that bastard!" he said it with such force, I looked up at him "Sorry sweetie but to think what he is putting you through, it is not fair. When you're divorced, will you marry me?"

"Yes Charles I have never been so sure of anything, I know now I was not in love with Mat, I did love him but as a brother. Also I think I was infatuated with him. Yes Charles my darling I do want to marry you."

The following day Charles rang Rupert and told we wanted to go ahead. Rupert said he would be in touch.

"Nat why do you not want to claim any settlement from Mat?"

"Because since I have been with him, apart from these past few weeks I have not spent a penny, this penthouse, legal fees, my car, my clothes, food everything he paid. I have a naughty plan," I whispered.

"Well Nat you do not have to whisper no one can hear you, what is your plan," Charles was whispered, we could not help but laugh.

"Oh Nat that is a lovely sound you laughing, come on the spill what's your naughty plan, knowing you it will not be very naughty."

"Oh yes it is Charles Cartwright, you see I do all the office work and I have all Mat's details of his two bank accounts, I have authority to work those accounts, all I have to do is pick up the telephone and transfer money from his to my account, that is what I am going to do. Daddy said when the hotels are sold I am getting Mats third share and when they wind the business up altogether, seeing as it will be me doing it all, I will get half and Uncle Ernest and daddy will have a quarter each. So I just have to work out what I will take for my inconvenience of marrying the bastard!"

"Good for you, I did not know you had it in you my love," Charles said kissing me, I give in to his kiss, we are really turned on, then the telephone rings. Charles always answers it now. "Hello Pa?"

"Oh no I am so sorry, when, where" daddy must be talking "Nat and I went last week we could see he was frail alright Pa let me know."

"What is it Uncle Thomas?" I knew by the conversation.

"Yes darling he died earlier today and Pa only just got home, so he will let us know the details."

"I am pleased he was in the nursing home, and he was not actually all alone as he was in that flat, that is one less complication."

Two days passed we heard nothing about Uncle Thomas's funeral or anything from Rupert.

Daddy phoned and asked us to meet at the families solicitor, they all had the same one for everything, could we be there for 12.30 tomorrow so we were. We all, well there is only us, daddy and uncle Ernest. We all said it was early for a Will?

We were called in to a very old office it looked like something out of Dickens, we were all seated and Mr. Haggerty spoke. "I am sorry to have got you here suddenly, however, we found on Thomas Cartwright's file, there is a letter which said to be read as soon as possible after he passed in your attendance. So you see me now opening the sealed letter" It was a big envelope out came two smaller envelopes, on one he read out "For the family and the other reads to be handed to the police as soon as possible on my demise". So with little old shaky hands he opened the first one and he reads;

"To my remaining family, I am sorry for any hurt and undue duress caused by my actions, but I could not let her carry on any longer, sometime after you threw the bitch out Lawrence, she came to me and started demanding money and different things, so I told her to meet me somewhere other than my flat on a given day and time, of course the greedy tramp was there thinking I was giving her more money, instead I demanded that she owed me a great deal and I would take her body in payment. For once she was not willing, I tied her hands and raped her several times and then took a knife and slashed her face and breasts, I was in full control although once I got going I was enjoying myself, I did gag her first because I thought she might make a bit of a noise, I let her suffer whilst I changed my clothes and bagged them up. Then I told her good bye you wicked apology of a mother, I hope Natasha has a happy life with you gone and I stabbed her, I wrapped her up in a lot of old sacks, shoved her in the boot of my car and drove to Wilford and dumped her on some waste ground near the Trent. I am sorry if you were all caused distress one way or another by her, but now my lovely family you are free, my love to you all especially my Natasha a truly lovely girl not just outside but inside x

We all just sat in stunned silence including Mr Haggerty, I was already gripping Charles hand, tears were running down my face, not for the trollop but for my uncle I did not realised I spoke "Poor Uncle Thomas I did love him," and they all looked at me, still no one spoke.

Then Mr Haggerty pulled himself together, we will send the other letter to the Police forthwith. I also have to tell you that he left instructions and whilst you were here together to read his will, it is very simple and easy "Whatever he has on his death is to go to Natasha, which as the sale of his flat has just gone through it will now be £988,965.73. Thank you all for coming if Natasha could wait I will fetch her cheque now, this amount is nett, all our charges have been deducted."

Charles waited with me I was shaking badly, he held me tight "Darling are you alright."

"I think it is the shock that Uncle Thomas thought of me, I am glad we kept going to see him, I told him I loved him, so he knew didn't he?"

"Of course my sweet, he is right you know, you are as lovely inside as well as out, that's why I am so in love with you."

We went outside Daddy and Uncle Ernest were waiting,

Daddy said he had to get off because he had another appointment, which was already set up before this happened. So Daddy kissed me and held me tight, then shook Charles hand but gave him a hug and whispered something to him, "I will let you know about the funeral arrangements, he wanted a cremation so obviously it will be at Wilford Hill, it is not worth going to the church first as there are so few of us, I thought I would take you for lunch somewhere afterwards."

Ernest and we agreed and parted saying we will see them there. Then we went straight home as we arrived the phone started ringing, so Charles grabbed it quick before the answering machine kicked in, it was Michael Roper and he asked if he could come and meet us, unofficially, so Charles said yes where or do you want to come here?"

Apparently he said he would come here, as it wasn't far but could he come today at 3pm, so Charles agreed. So we rustled up a bit of lunch together by the time we had finished we had not time to change so we were still both in smart suits.

Michael Roper was on the dot, Charles opened the lift door and showed him into the lounge, he was tall, but then he would be he is a policeman albeit of high rank, very smart in his uniform, nicely built, not thin but certainly not fat, very good looking, blonde hair, gorgeous deep blue eyes. I don't know what it is, as soon as I meet someone new of the opposite sex, I am scrutinising every detail about them? just lately the few I've met are all extremely good looking.

He came over and shook my hand, which he held firmly and looked straight into my eyes "I am very pleased to meet you Mrs Cartwright," he made it sound very sexy, with his deep, well spoken voice.

"I am pleased to meet you, I'm not sure how we should address you?"

"Michael will do fine," he replied.

"I am Natasha, this is Charles, Mats brother can I get you anything to drink tea, coffee or maybe a cold drink," I asked.

"I would love a cup of tea if it is not too much trouble Natasha," when he said my name, he made it sound like a caress.

"No we were about to have one, we haven't been back long, so it is no trouble," off I trotted, I could hear them talking but not what was said, I hope I am not missing anything, I had just loaded the tray when Charles came in.

"Let me take that darling," he said.

"You spoil me," he gave me a quick kiss. We went in and I poured the tea and offered him a biscuit which he refused.

Michael said "This is just an informal chat, as I think Rupert explained this is not part of my remit, but I thought it a good idea to meet you, see if there were any questions before we go ahead as Rupert said you wanted to do it and I think it is a wise move on hearing about your husbands threats."

I asked "How long will this take? I have to stay until I have wound the company up and there is so much to do yet."

"I see, I didn't realise you ran the company, I know of it, but did not realise that someone as young as you would have that responsibility, I do not mean that quite as it sounded, it's that well you are a very beautiful young lady and one associates business with older people," he laughed, I smiled, Charles was not happy.

"No, it takes a while to set up, normally when you are given your new identities we move you to somewhere further away, put you in a safe house, but Rupert said he thought you would prefer to select where you wanted to go, and move into a hotel until you found a property you wanted to purchase, is that correct?" he asked.

Charles said "Yes, that is what we would like to do."

"I see no problem but wherever you are going you must keep both Rupert, and myself informed, if you move that will also apply we need to have on our record any change for a long time, but it will only be the two of us know," he said. He went on to ask us personal information like date of birth etc. and they would try to give us a choice of names with people who died with a similar date of birth and we would be supplied with every document we needed to replace our own, even National Insurance number driving licence the lot. "I think I have all I need once we have some names and dates, I will let you know but you will have to come to my office for that, but do not worry you can go as soon as you are ready," he stood up "Lovely to have met you Natasha," and he shook my hand and looked me straight in the eye again, Charles showed him out. He was a bit prickly.

"Darling what is it, are you not happy with what we are going to do?"

"Yes I am happy with it, I will be glad when it's over, everyone we meet all seem to look at you as if they want to get into your knickers, I am sorry Nat but I am so scared of loosing you, as soon as we move away, I will keep you locked up with me, then I will be happy," he was deadly serious.

"But Charles my darling, I am in love with you, that is all I want you and like you, I will happy when we can move and get the divorce over so we can get married and live together happy ever after, as the saying goes. I do not want anyone but you my lovely, lovely Charles," and I went to him and kissed him, then I was in his arms again.

The following day Daddy rang to say Uncle Thomas's cremation would be next Monday at 11.00, we were to meet there.

It was a very cold, rainy day. There was only five of us, plus about six men who had known Uncle Thomas, it was a quick service and we were soon out, we decided not to go for a meal as Daddy made it clear he wanted to get off.

Uncle Ernest stood waiting, I wondered why, then as Daddy drove away he said "I wanted to tell you myself, now the business is being wound up there is nothing to keep me and Emily here, so when it is all finished we have decided, we are going to relocate to Canada, where Emily has an extended family, so I may not see you again, I want to wish both of you all the best in whatever you choose to do in the future," he shook hands with Charles and held me tight and kissed me.

"I will never forget you, Nat how you have turned out, after what you have been through, you are a wonderful girl," he said and left.

Charles hurried me to the car I was frozen, but what did I expect it was the beginning of December, it would not be long before Christmas was here. We knew it was just the two of us, daddy had told us they were off to America to be with all Suzanne's children, we've still only met her briefly.   We were happy, we did not want to go anywhere for our first Christmas.

The day after Daddy rang to say the conglomerate had offered one and three quarter million pounds, for the three remaining hotels, they had accepted and a bankers draft was on it's way to our bank, he instructed, I transfer half million into his and uncle Ernest accounts, I was to have the three quarters of a million seeing as Charles had said I was not seeking any money settlement from Mat! I told Charles I was not going to bother correcting him, to which Charles had said I would be very cross with you if you did, you have earned every penny.

I decided now was a good time to transfer what I was to

take from Mat seeing as he earned £450.00 per week plus expenses, against my £100.00 per week and I did everything, I did not bother taking into account his expenses, I worked out he should have earned £20.00 per week, so I transferred £27,000.00, I am listing it separately, I intend to leave an itemised note stapled to his bank statement, then a further £500,000.00 for taking responsibility of running the business, last but not least £750,000.00, for all the mental suffering and worry caused by his actions. Then £350,000.00, for lost interest, which I would have received if I had been paid, as and when!   I took the list I had made to Charles who is cooking dinner, he really does look after me, he looked in amazement and said, "Nat you keep amazing me, you have charged him over £1,500,000,00. I thought you were going to take possibly half a million, I hope you do not think I am marrying you for your money, because I know you had well over a million," he gave me a wonderful kiss, I obviously kissed him back, dinner was switched off we had other more pressing things to do, we eventually ate about 9.30.

The following week Michael telephoned, could we call that afternoon.

We finished the office packing. When we leave daddy was to have the keys, to collect everything. I had sorted the Inland Revenue, Customs and Excise, Companies House etc., to close the company, it would be finished before Christmas. Two and a half million and some oddments were left, daddy said three quarters of a million, to him and uncle leaving me with one million and the oddments plus petty cash. Charles was amazed what Pa said, it must salve his conscience.

We arrived at Police Headquarters and shown into a big beautiful wood panelled office, Michael stood and welcomed us, but showed us to some comfortable chairs round a table. He asked if we wanted tea or coffee we both asked for coffee, which he buzzed through from his desk and it arrived more or less immediately. "I have found two people with good date of births it is a brilliant match, first there is Elliot Windsor born 18/07/1974, registered in Leeds, and Samantha Pearson born 21/07/1977, registered in Hull. Charles you'd be two weeks older and Natasha you'd be twenty days younger. How do you feel?"

I said "Not keen on Pearson, I like Samantha, but I love Elliot Windsor it sounds upmarket Charles."

"I am happy with anything, you could have said John

Smith, I would have been happy, anyway you won't be Pearson for long!" Michael looked puzzled, then said;

"I am sorry I have to ask, how did you marry Mat and now you want to marry your other brother Charles, isn't it incest?"

We both laughed, then I said "I am not their sister, or I thought I was until I was sixteen, then I was told I had been left on the doorstep. Who told you we were committing incest?"

"It was Rupert he was quite vocal on the point, I am so sorry, please forgive me. So are you happy to continue with this?"

"Yes," Charles answered.

"Right we will get this started, I did forget one thing Charles you have qualifications do you not?" Michael asked.

"Yes I am a Chartered Accountant and Qualified Financial Advisor."

"We will have to change them, can you drop them in please? I think we have everything else we need. If you want to start looking where you might want to move to, that would be a big help, I suppose once you decide, there would be nothing to stop you looking for a property, as long as you remember your names! I estimate you could move in the New Year, if everything goes well, it could be earlier." He looked me straight in the eye. I faulted

"Yes, thank you very much," and we shook hands.

"Don't forget your qualifications Charles. If either of you have any questions you haven't already thought about, please ring and ask, see you soon," Michael said and we left.

"Wow," I said as we got into the car "Elliot Windsor I really like that and Samantha Windsor."

"Excuse me Samantha Pearson you are not married yet! I cannot get over Rupert saying that, he knows differently?"

The priority was to decide where we wanted to go, because it was not long until the New Year, we also had to start packing, I wasn't leaving anything we had brought with us, from Daddies.

We finished all the legal documents, all the paper work was filed and clearly marked in storage boxes. I packed empty files, stationery and office equipment, we were to take all that office equipment with us. Elliot dropped his Qualifications off at the Police Headquarters.

We decided we were not going to go mad with Christmas or cooking anything that took too long otherwise that would eat into or packing time, plus we needed plenty of time for our love making! Charles was wonderful he helped with everything, so instead of him insisting on doing all the cooking, I said we were to do it together.

We sat down with a glass of wine the day after we had our new names, we decided to look where we would like to move to? We decided some where near Melton Mowbray, it is not too far but when we thought we had better check with Michael, he said that was fine as long as we did not know anyone there, which we didn't.

Chapter five

The following day we drove to Melton Mowbray, it was a clear crisp morning, we had a wander round, found several estate agents looked what was for sale. We definitely wanted detached but not on a big built up area, something if possible a bit old cottage like. We came back with a number that could be possibilities, there was one that stood out a mile, although it did not have a garage or car standing on the property, but the estate agent pointed out the small front garden would be big enough to park two cars, if the fence, hedge and plants were removed. It was empty and there was no chain. We decided we would view that one, we made it for the following morning. As we pulled up it was even better than the pictures. It was fairly old built of stone with a door in the centre ground floor, it had a bay leaded window either side the door, two leaded windows above the lower windows and small one in the centre.

We were told five years ago everything had been updated, rewired, plumbing, heating, damp course everything you could think of. The whole was white ceilings, walls and doors, it was immaculate, to the right was a long through lounge, to the back were french doors. To the left of the hall a small room, we thought could be the office. Next to that one, was a beautiful dining kitchen which was an L shape, it went round the back of the hall, again french doors looking out onto a long garden, all neatly set out round a lawn, with shrubs round the boundary wall, there were no houses to overlook us.

There was a very large cupboard with coat hooks under the stairs in the hall, the stairs started at the side of the lounge door, up four stairs then turned left and that repeated twice more onto the landing. To the left the main bedroom mirrored the lounge from front to back, to the rear on the left was a big walk-in wardrobe. Opposite the main bedroom, was a good sized single bedroom, to the rear a fantastic bathroom, wet shower, corner bath, bidet, toilet and washbasin, a large airing cupboard, all tiled top to bottom in pale grey granite, the floor was white tiles, the units and sanitary wear, were all white.. Everything looked brand new throughout, it was immaculate. On the landing was a small window to the front, and access to a loft which had been boarded to use for storage. We were both in love with it.

We went back downstairs and the agent asked if we had anything to sell, which was no, then have you got a mortgage in place again no, we told him it is a cash sale, he seemed stunned so repeated the price £549,950.00, in case we were not aware, we told him yes we knew and we would purchase at the asking price, then without asking Elliot I said;

"As it is empty and we have the cash would it be possible to move in straight away? Even before all the conveyancing, paper work, stamp duty is done, we would give the vendor £300,000.00 now in good faith, we want to move as soon as possible. If we could get carpets and curtains fitted we would not have to put our furniture into storage and live in a hotel," Elliot had put his arm round me and gave me a squeeze of approval. The agent was once more stunned.

"It is not customary, but if you will excuse me I will telephone the vendor, he went out of the front door, closing it behind him. "My Samantha you have amazed me again, I could not have done that better, I do so love you," he took me in his arms and we were lost.

"Charles, Elliot you shouldn't have done that, you have set me off, I will have to wait," I stuck my bottom lip right out exaggerating a sulk. The agent came back, making me jump, Elliot laughed.

"Mr and Mrs Russell are more than happy with that arrangement," if we could go back to the office and we will do some paperwork regarding what you have paid etc.

We were shown into a rather grand office, "I will be but a moment." he said and was soon back "The temporary paper work is being typed out now, can I have your solicitors name?"

"Well we have not got a local one, can you suggest one here in Melton Mowbray?" Elliot said.

"Yes there is one, two doors down, 'Craddock and Spencer' they are fairly young only been here four years, I think they might suit you, with being young yourselves. Have you employment Mr Windsor?"

"I am self employed, I am a 'Qualified Chartered Accountant and Qualified Financial Advisor' Sam here is excellent with figures, we were going to run it together."

"Well that could not be better, that is the one thing we seem to be lacking here, there are so many small business's I am sure you will be a success. I can draw you up a list of where best to advertise, I assume you do not know the area," Mr Noble said.

"No we do not, that would be very helpful, thank you Mr Noble," Elliot said. Then there was a knock on the door and in came his secretary with some papers Elliot signed them and we left.

We went straight to the Solicitors and told the receptionist about our purchase and we wondered if 'Craddock and Spencer' would act for us, she disappeared and came back yes and showed us into another office. Later on the way home we were in very high spirits, we had put a deposit on the cottage, for which we had two front door keys. We had a new Solicitor Mr Alan Craddock and everything was fine.

We decided the following day to go and choose the carpets. We arranged to meet them at the cottage, the following day, and did the same thing with the curtains and cushion covers, the colour scheme was going to be the same through-out apart from the kitchen and bathroom. Pale blue carpet, with pale blue and cream curtains.

On the way back we purchased a 'King' size bed, a single for the spare room, a beautiful dressing table and matching bedside cabinets, a stool and two matching chairs for our bedroom. Then a small wardrobe, chest of drawers, bedside cabinet and chair for the spare room. We looked at suites it was difficult, we decided on three, two seated settees, with a couple of matching stools in pale cream soft leather. For the kitchen a table and four chairs, the wood looked almost the same as the hand made kitchen units, a small floral cottage style settee for the kitchen, the fireplace was still used for fires and we thought it would be cosy.

We called for a take-away and headed for home absolutely shattered but very, very happy. We decided we had earned an early night as we were in need of one another, I slept in Elliot's arms and did not have a nightmare, the next thing I knew it was getting light, and a certain someone still stark naked was bringing the tea tray into the bedroom, "Good morning my darling Sam, you are a very good girl you slept all the way through, I think that deserves a reward."

"Ooh, yes please Elliot," I am pushing the sheets down showing my naked body, my new friend reacted immediately.

"You brazen hussy, I meant you can have a biscuit with your tea, however I think your new friend has other ideas," I giggled.

"Have your tea first, now I have slaved over a boiling kettle to make it! I cannot believe all what we have got done, we will not have to store anything, I will ask when they come to measure up how soon the carpets can be fitted," he said.

"Darling I cannot wait to get into our own cottage knowing Mat will not know where we are, I can rest in peace," I said.

"R.I.P very apt, I don't think," I hadn't realised what I had said and it made me giggle again, until he dragged me down the bed and was caressing me, my mind was soon in over drive, he took me to heaven.

I stayed home packing, while Elliot met the carpet man, he said no problem, they could fit the day after boxing day. While he was there, he had arranged for the soft furnishing people to come, they said they could fit all the rails on 27th December and hang the curtains and the blinds on 28th December. When Elliot came home and told me I was ecstatic, we opened a bottle of champagne, and drank it slowly, then Elliot thought a siesta was in order, and finish the champagne off in comfort in bed.

Late Christmas Eve we had a call from Michael who said all the documents would be finished on the 30th December, he asked if we had any luck with a house, so Elliott told him everything and he congratulated us our success. He said he could drop round with all the documents late morning of the 31st that will be fine Elliot said.

We did nothing special Christmas Eve. Elliot said we were not doing anything Christmas Day, we woke early and Elliot fetched the tea. I gave him his Christmas presents, I had bought him a black Onyx desk set. A gold watch and gold cuff links engraved with E & S. I got the most luscious kiss. Then he passed me mine which was a Platinum fine chain with a single large diamond on and matching earrings, the chain was so fine it looked as though the diamonds were hanging in mid air. Then he said "Sam will you marry me?"

I frowned "You've asked me, the answer is still yes."

He produced the most beautiful platinum diamond engagement ring there was one large stone in the middle surrounded by two tiers of smaller diamonds, it glittered and shone, then the water works started. He put the ring on my finger, and that was it, we eventually got up at 11.30am. I was in heaven just the two of us, the heating was turned up full, it was windy, but we were cosy and warm. "Our first Christmas together, the first of many my love," then he kissed me.

"Yes many, I do love you Elliot," I keep saying it to remember it.

He went down to the cottage to let the carpet fitters in, his car loaded with boxes. He said they were getting on well, we did not have to worry about the key, the carpet people said they would give the soft furnishing people it, and pass to one another as they needed it.

We rang the furniture shop and asked when could they deliver, they said they had, had a cancellation for the afternoon of the 28th, so we jumped at that. We rang the removal people and they said they could do it, in the afternoon of the 29th seeing as we had not got a lot.

The following day we made several journeys in both cars filled with clothes and packed boxes, but we were exhausted. We picked up fish and chips on the way back, then took a bottle of wine to bed.

We were up at 7am on the 29th we made another journey each, put all the clothes on the rails properly, emptied some more boxes. Then went back to wait for the removal men, they were half an hour early, they were getting on well, I went down to the cottage and left Elliot to lock up at the Penthouse.

It was soon unloaded, the furniture was soon in place We had a quick meal but we were really shattered, so we decided our first night in our cottage was to be a nice early one. It was funny when we got to bed we were not as tired as we thought we were!

Elliot said "We have got to Christen this lovely big big, although why we needed a 'King' size, when a single would have been more than enough, we always sleep so close together," which made me laugh, which soon stopped when his lips were devouring mine. Yes indeed we did Christen it, in fact several times, I slept all the way through.

It was wonderful waking up fully refreshed in the peaceful, quiet that surrounded the cottage, after today, we had not got to rush anywhere, the days would be ours, to do as we wished. While I showered, Elliot cooked breakfast and then he went to get ready, we were meeting Michael with all the documents it was to be the last time at the Penthouse. He arrived dead on time. He passed everything to us told us to check all was in order, although he had gone through it all, but it didn't hurt to double check. We explained that we had now left here and spent last night in the cottage. We gave him the address and said if he was ever down our way by all means drop in. He said he would love to but he would ring first anyway.

Time soon past, it was April, we got such a surprise in the mail, it was all the documents stating I was now divorced, I know I was told it would be quick, but I had no idea it would be this fast. I was ecstatic.

"Tomorrow we go to the registry office and see what date we can get married?" Elliot calmly said.

"Really, Oh Elliot I didn't think it would be so soon, I cannot wait, my darling I love you so much."

"I thought for our two witnesses, I would ask Rupert and Michael because we have seen them a lot, then we could go for a meal."

"Later, he said he ought to do something about his business, we can't spend every day making love morning, noon, evening and night."

"I cannot see anything wrong with that, I love you making love to me, I love everything you do. I do not think anything should interfere with that. Especially now I know what it is like to have an orgasm every time" I was very serious, I am pouting my bottom lip.

"We'll see," he said, but he did have to laugh.

The following day we went to the registry office and they offered us Thursday 11th May 1995 at 1pm. Elliot rang both Michael and Rupert, they both rang back saying they were free and love to be our guests.

11th May arrived and it was a beautiful fairly warm day. I was pleased I had decided on a dress with matching edge to edge jacket in pale lilac, the dress was fitted with a deep V neck line, front and back, I wore a matching hat with large brim, white sandals and small clutch bag which I fastened a small bouquet of White Freesias on, the same for the button holes. It was quick we had no sooner in, then we were coming out. Elliot had booked a table at an exclusive restaurant for our meal, then we asked them if they would like to come back and see the cottage? By the time the taxi came, they were both plaiting fog!

"Well Mrs Windsor would you like to take your husband to bed and make love to him?' Elliot said kissing my face all over.

"Mr Windsor I would be delighted, I'll race you," I said rashly. He was up the stairs two and three at a time, and stood laughing at me.

"Come on old girl would you like a hand," and as I reached the top he swept me up into his arms and carried me into the bedroom, he gently stood me on the floor, took me in his arms and we were lost. I had no idea how many times we made love, when we were absolutely exhausted we decided we had better go to sleep and slept very late, it didn't matter the cruise didn't leave until Sunday, so we had a leisurely two days, I got as I did not make the bed it wasn't worth it!

We went on a two week flight cruise, it was wonderful we saw all different places, that I would not have seen but for our honeymoon, but the time flew by and we were soon on our way back.

We decided when we returned we would get the business advertised but agreed to work from noon on Mondays to noon on Thursdays, so we had a four day weekend. Soon we were receiving enquiries and it began to take off. Elliot went to visit his new clients, then I got stuck in with, what Elliot called the boring bit, but it was the important bit.

Soon it was our first wedding anniversary, then Christmas we could not believe how quick the time went by and another year gone, we were sublimely happy and another year got underway 1997.

February Rupert rang, saying Dennis, one of their school friends, wanted Elliot to be his best man in December when he gets married, he rang Rupert because he could not trace Elliott. Elliott said no, Rupert suggested he would stand in. So we were so happy.

It was already December, approaching the date of the wedding. Rupert rang, he was on big case in court and would not be able get to Scotland, he did not want to let Den down, would Elliot reconsider?

So he asked me and I said it was fine. He'd travel up the day before the wedding, meet for a few drinks in the evening, nothing heavy because he was marrying at 10am the following day, so there would be no late nights, especially as his father and future father-in-law would be there, then the reception and travel back late that afternoon.

On the day of the wedding, apparently Scotland was

having torrential rain, I was hoping Elliot would be alright, I rang his mobile, when I knew the service was over but before the wedding lunch.

"Darling I am a little worried, the radio says the weather is very bad, would you be better to stay another night and travel tomorrow in the day light? I am missing you," I said.

"Sam my darling I love you so much, I am missing you, so no I will travel as arranged, the rain has stopped, please do not fret and worry I will be safe, I will call you as I am setting off my love," he said.

"Elliot I hadn't realised how much I would miss you, I wish I had gone up with you, I could have found something to do, we would have been together, I do love you so much," I was whispering, I didn't want him to hear I was crying.

"I will ring you later, have got to go, I love you," and he was gone. I wandered around, I did some cooking and baking, I ironed to make time go. Later Elliot rang to say he was setting off at 3pm.

The telephone rang around 7pm "Hello" I thought it could only be a customer then a familiar voice said;

"Samantha, it's Michael, I wondered if you two wanted a visitor? I am on my way back from a conference, I'll be nearly passing your door."

"Michael how nice to hear you, yes by all means please call, the thing is Elliot is on his way home from a wedding in Scotland, I could do with some company, because I will not be able to go to bed until he is back safe and sound!" I said.

"Oh, are you sure it is alright then?" he asked.

"Yes please call," I replied.

"I will see you in about an hour or so," he said.

An hour and a half later the door bell rings, I go and open the door and there is Michael very striking in his uniform.

"Hello, come in," I say.

"Thank you, you are sure you want me here?" he said.

"Of course I do, I will not be going to bed until Elliot returns, and I cannot seem to settle, I have tried the television, reading, music, so I am glad of the company," I took him into the lounge.

"This is a beautiful room, you have got it perfect," he said.

"Do you want to take your jacket off, you would be more comfortable?"

"Yes I will if you do not mind, what time should Elliot be back?" he asked.

"Sometime around midnight, but you do not have to wait until he comes home, if you want to get off. Can I get you a hot drink or a cold drink?"

"I would love a coffee please," so I went and made him a coffee and had a fruit juice myself.

We started talking about this and that, he was very interesting to talk and listen to.

About 45 minutes into his visit the door bell rings, it makes me jump. "I assume you are not expecting anybody?"

"No, we do not have callers, we still only know you and Rupert," I look nervous, the door bell rings again.

"Would you like me to go?" he asks.

"Would you please," and he goes to the door, but pulls the lounge door to, so I can hear voices but not what is being said.

I hear the door close and he comes in, but I know something is wrong.

"What is it?" I ask.

He says "I would rather be anywhere than here at this moment" he sits beside me "There has been an accident," my hands tremble, I put one to my mouth, but cannot speak "I am so, so sorry about two hours ago Elliot was hit by an articulated lorry," he got no further.

"How bad is he can I go and see him?" I blurt out.

"Samantha, I am so sorry, he died instantly, they say the lorry did not brake when he got to the cross roads, he pulled straight out into Elliot, the lorry driver was doing over 50 miles an hour, well over the speed limit, Elliot would not have known anything," he says softly.

I am trembling from head to toe, I feel sick, I stare at him, then all I hear is a scream and I am sobbing. He takes me in his arms and holds me and just lets me cry and cry and cry. He is holding me close and gently rocking me. It seems like hours before I begin to stop. He lets go of me and goes over to the drinks trolley.

"Do you drink Whisky, Brandy or what?" he asks.

"Brandy please" I couldn't say not neat. He poured me a large brandy and a large whisky for himself, he passed it to me and I take a sip, he downs his in one.

"Take a drink Samantha darling it will help," I try a bit

bigger sip, it's hot and it burns "Do you mind if I help myself?"

"No Michael, please help yourself," then the flood gates open again, but he doesn't sit down, he takes his mobile out and then "Rupert, this is Michael, as soon as you get this please, please ring, it is urgent," then he comes back and takes me in his arms again.

"Samantha who is your Doctor?" through sniffles I say.

"I haven't got a Doctor."

"Have you not any medication on repeat, anything like the pill?"

"No nothing, I pay privately for a six monthly injection to stop me getting pregnant, but we do not have a Doctor, why," all through sniffles and sobs.

"I just thought your Doctor might give you something for shock or help you sleep, this is going to be a very trying time, you will need all the help you can get," he looked at me helpless "Can I get you something, I know I cannot ring anyone,"

"What about daddy will we not be able to contact him?"

"Well really no, because then he will discover his new name, also anyone he is with will find out, then we are back to square one and it will have been a waste of time, I am so sorry. Do you think you ought to try and go to bed and lie down," I get up and automatically climb the stairs, get ready for bed and lie down, my head is throbbing, I can't think, what will I do without my Elliot, my dearest darling Charles and then the water works start again. I suppose Michael knocked on the door but I didn't hear him, he brought the brandy and put it down.

"Try to keep having a sip of this, I will not leave you, but I want to go to the car and get my holdall, I will only be a minute."

Still sniffling and crying I manage to get out "Do you mean you are staying with me, you can use the spare room?"

"Yes I cannot leave you on your own, but I will be downstairs for a while as I have to make some calls, I have been away for three days and I will have to leave messages saying I will not be in the office Monday," he explains.

"Thank you," I sniff. I try drinking the brandy, I find I can take a bit bigger swallow, it goes down, how anyone can drink for pleasure is beyond me, it's worse than medicine. I heard him go out to his car and come back, I can hear him locking up, then he went into the lounge and I could hear his voice but not what he said. Later I heard him come upstairs, into the spare room then the bathroom, we do not have an en suite here, then he came out, went back into the spare room.

I could tell you when the wind blows and even an owl hooting. I lay and lay, I feel numb until the water works begin again and I try counting sheep, sipping the brandy and I just lay there, everything going round in my head.

I must have drifted to sleep, because the next thing I know, the bedside light is on and Michael is saying;

"Wake up Samantha, wake up," I think I must look like a blurry eyed drunk, my head is pounding, my throat is so dry. I'm sorry Samantha, I think you were having a bad dream you were screaming, I could not for the life of me think what it was at first," he was holding me in his arms, he felt nice and warm.

"I am sorry, they have come back, I haven't had one for 16 months, I thought I was cured," and I start crying again.

"What do you mean come back again?" he asks.

So I proceed to tell him the story, between crying which gradually stops while I am talking to him, he says nothing, just keeps holding me tight until I finish. I hadn't realised until then, he only had pyjama bottoms on.

"I am so sorry, you have had a rotten life and now this, it must have brought them back, is there anything I can get you," he is pleading.

"No thank you, I am sorry to have disturbed you, what time is it?" I ask.

"It's 3.25am, please you do not have to apologise," he said and went back to bed.

There was still some brandy left so as I went to switch the bedside lamp off, I picked it up and drank the lot which was well over a third full and it was a big glass, it was horrible. I slipped back down, everything is going round in my head, I start counting sheep again, but they were stubborn they would not jump over the gate, I must have dozed off again, until;

"Samantha, please wake up," it was Michael again. I am really sobbing.

"I am sorry," was all I could get out.

"Would it help if I stay with you, on top of the sheets but I can slide under the duvet, do you think that would help?" he asks.

"Please," was all I could get out. He got on the bed, I thought he was just going to lie down, but he pulled me towards him and wrapped his arms round me. I must have drifted off again,

I know I was exhausted. I awoke with a start because the telephone was ringing, Michael still held me as he did when I went to sleep.

"Bugger," he said and got off the bed and ran downstairs to answer the phone. I got out of bed, went to the bathroom, when I looked at myself in the mirror, I did a double take, I looked like an old haggard witch! Then popped on my robe and staggered downstairs, is this how it feels when you have a hang over, I felt rough.

I walked into the kitchen and put the kettle on. Then poked the fire alive, we leave it stoked up to last over night, then we haven't got to wait for it to come alive, we have central heating but we love sitting on the sofa together by the fire and watch the wind and rain outside, we, we, ooh Elliot, what am I going to do with out you, and the water works start full stream, I just sink to the floor and sob. I did not hear Michael enter, but I felt strong hands lift me up with ease and put me on the sofa, without a word, then he went and made the tea and brought me a cup.

"I have made it sweet and strong, which is what I should have done last night, but I was not thinking.

That was Rupert on the phone, he cannot get for a few days as he is in court and has other arrangements which he cannot get out of, I do not want to leave you on your own, but I will have to go and get some clothes and call in the office, but I want to take you with me I cannot leave you on your own. So will you have something to eat?" I shake my head "Well I will make you one slice of toast and I want you to eat it, please," I think for the first time since he arrived, I looked at him and he was looking me straight in the eye and I felt hypnotised "Please my darling please just try," he went over to the kitchen area and busied himself, he made me one slice of toast and cut it into small triangles and brought it over with a napkin "Please just try," he said and gave me the loveliest smile. He had made himself scrambled eggs on toast and sat at the table with it, looking at the morning paper that arrived earlier, he wasn't reading it, he was looking for something, then I realised what he was looking for, he found it and calmly ripped it out and put it in his pocket.

"What does it say, Michael?" I croaked.

"Nothing that you do not already know, I do not think you should read anything about it, that is an order Samantha," but he was smiling. I managed to eat all the middle, of the toast, but left the crusts and took my plate over to the dishwasher. "Good girl, now next time I see you, I would like to see something of the beautiful young lady you are," he gave me a heart melting smile, he was older than I am, but he was certainly fit and quite, no very sexy, although I should not have these thoughts but at least it is a distraction for a few seconds.

I went into the shower, wandered out as I usually do, naked to go and get dressed, I was miles away, I did not see Michael standing at the top of the stairs looking well, not actually shocked, more with pleasure.

"Well Samantha, I now know what beauty you hide under your clothes, I have got to say, a man would have to be made of stone not to appreciate what I am seeing. Christ Samantha, you really are gorgeous, you have certainly had a big effect on me," he said as he gazed into my eyes, because I was still wandering towards him, until I realised and stopped. He put his hand out towards me, took my hand and gently pulled me towards him, he put his arm round me and was devouring my body with his eyes. Without another word he held my chin and raised my lips to his, I did nothing to stop him, he began kissing me, the full kiss, I had no idea why but I began kissing him back. He pulled me in close and I could feel his erection and he was doing wonderful things to me, we were both breathing heavy. He lifted me and took me into my bedroom and lay me on the bed.

"Samantha I am so sorry, that was out of order, I am sorry, please forgive me," he was whispering and his voice was doing things to me.

"Michael, I know I should not have responded to you, especially with what has just happened, but I am not used to men as such, I have been married twice, but they were not strangers,as you well know. I have never been kissed by any other man, I could not help but kiss you back, because I liked what you did it is simple as that, I am sorry," I said.

"Samantha please do not be sorry, I loved that you kissed me, but I overstepped the mark, I am out of order, I am supposed to be a friend to you, not trying to seduce you," he looked full of remorse.

"But if I say you were not out of order, would that help you feel any better? please sit down," he did "Michael would you kiss me again please?"

"Darling I would love to but I know it is wrong, if I kissed you again, I would want to make love to you, and that would be totally out of order, I am a red blooded male, seeing you naked like this, it turned me on. Get dressed and I will go and get ready."

"Please kiss me, but please do not think me a hussy, I do love Elliot, I did love him very much, but I do not know anything really worldly, and you are really nice and," he put his finger on my lips which stopped me there.

"Samantha, you are really very unique, and far from being a hussy, you would not know one if you saw one, no my darling that is something you could never be," he took me in his arms and began to kiss me again, I returned his kisses with passion, I did want him, by looking at me, he was doing things to my insides. I was throbbing.

"Michael would you please make love to me, please?"

He was now kissing my neck and was slowly going to my breasts, his hand was gently caressing me as it travelled down my body, until his fingers entered me, I was wanting him so badly, I wanted to scream 'fuck me'.

When he did enter me he was so gentle and eased his way in, the feelings were out of this world, then he was pushing higher, I was writhing and pushing myself on to him, his lips were on mine, his hands were under my buttocks pulling me in to him and I was pushing as hard as I could, I could not get enough of him, we were moving together forcefully, fast, I was groaning, he was taking me up and up, everything felt exquisite, I began to feel I was going to burst, then we exploded together, every inch of my body seemed to be pulsating and throbbing, I could feel myself holding him inside me, I seemed to be squeezing and squeezing, with the pulsating.

"Samantha, you are one very surprising young lady, you are very good you react very well."

"Michael do you think so, is it not the same for men with whoever they are making love to then?"

"No my lovely, no you are all very different, but you are unique," and he kissed me again, very deep, I could still feel myself pulsating onto him "You know what you are doing to me don't you?"

"What do you mean?" I asked.

"You are massaging me inside you, I am wanting to take you again, I am sorry my darling but you are going to have to have me again!"

"Please don't stop," was all I said.

He took me twice "Please my darling go and have a shower or we will never get out, I must go to the office first now," so I did as I was told, in the shower, I broke down and cried and cried for my Elliot, I whispered to him to forgive me, but I thought it helped it took my mind of my loss, how would I be able to carry on without my dearest Elliot.

I dried myself, again I walked back to the bedroom naked and he was still lay on the bed "Christ Samantha what do you think you are doing, look what you have done to me," yes I could see he was throbbing and very erect, but he read my mind "No you don't my lovely," and he jumped off the bed and ran to the bathroom. So I had no choice but to get dressed, but first I changed the sheets and remade the bed.

It was a cold December day so I put a fine woollen dress on, it was closely fitted, it was well above my knees, so I put my knee high, high heeled boots on. I brushed my hair well, until it shone, but left it loose, then applied some make-up and my false eyelashes and perfumed myself head to toe with Chanel No.5, threw my short fur coat over my shoulder to carry it down.

I heard Michael on the stairs, but thought he had gone into the lounge, I was bending over putting coal on the fire to keep it going.

Suddenly there were two hands, on my hips and he was pushing himself onto my bottom "That was a very nice arousing sight as I came through the door, do you not wear panties?"

I stood up and turned round, he did not move we were so close he had a big erection "I have a thong, why don't you approve?"

"I approve very much, it is just unfortunate, I cannot give you my approval here and now, you can feel what you have done to me again, I cannot wait to get you back to bed and that is a promise, after what you have done to me, I want you more, you are very, very good, you are so experienced, you are so incredible! By the way you look very, very sexy with your short skirt showing your lovely legs and those boots. What can I say, I am all but drooling with almost seeing your delicious cunt."

I still cannot get used to men saying fuck, cunt and cock, I have always thought were swear words, it must be my sheltered life.

We locked up and we went to Nottingham Police Headquarters, as we travelled I suddenly felt depressed my Elliot, my darling, I would not see him anymore, the tears ran down my face, as we pulled into the car park, I dried my face and swiftly put my powder puff round my cheeks. I thought I would be staying in the car but he said I had to come with him.

We passed through a huge office full of men and women, I suppose all were police officers of different ranks, there were several wolf whistles, and one or two comments, but we kept walking Michael kept his arm round my waist, we left that office, and went into a small lobby with two doors, he unlocked the biggest door and it was the office I had been into before but I cannot remember the walk though that big office.

"I know where we are now," I said "I do not remember coming through that big office though?"

"Well you did not, you came the back way and up in the lift. I decided because you are so beautiful, and very young, that I wanted to show you off," he said looking deep into my eyes, he took me in his arms and was kissing me and I was kissing him back. "God Samantha I love what you do to me, I want to be inside you, you make me so hard with wanting you, I am tempted to have you here, but I must not this is certainly not the place." he had his hands on my bare bottom.

"I love being made love to, or having sex or being fucked, it does not matter what you call it I love it, so it's alright with me if you want to thrill me again. I know I sound terrible saying things like that, when my lovely darling Elliot has just been killed, but I cannot get away from the fact I love anything sexual," I looked at him wondering what he was going to say?

He said nothing, just pulled me towards him and was kissing me furiously, then he began to move away. "You are so tempting but we cannot not here, it would be totally wrong."

"I would let you if that is what you wanted to do, Michael you are so different to Elliot and Mat. I thought every man would be similar to them. I know Elliot was better than Mat, but you, I cannot describe how you make me feel, I only know I would be unhappy if you left, you are one hell of a man, I know you are older than me, but you are obviously very, very experienced, not only that you look good, tall, handsome, you have a fantastic sexy body, and the most wonderful deep voice, you know exactly how to make love," I then burst into tears.

He held me tight and let me cry, "I must be a terrible person to think of sex while my poor Elliot is dead, does that make me a trollop or a hussy?" I was sobbing, he still didn't say anything, he just held me tight, until I began to stop crying.

"First of all my sweet you are not a trollop, hussy or a terrible person, you are a wonderful, quiet girl, you have a calming effect on people, both Rupert and myself remarked on you to Elliot, you do not shout or raise your voice, you are a lovely, lovely girl. I do not think any less of you for what you let me do, if anything, I think it is helping because it distracts you from what is really going on, and that can only be a good thing, so please don't make yourself feel guilty, because if you are I am also, the way I feel about you is like nothing I have felt for the opposite sex ever. My wife Julia I love her but have never been in love with her and there is a big difference. Look the sooner I can collect some clothes and things from my apartment the sooner we can get back to your cottage, then if you like we can lock up and throw away the key until after the New Year, because that is how much leave I have informed them I am taking and if you want me to I will stay with you until then?"

"Michael you are so good to me are you sure, will your wife not mind?" I was looking at him in a different light, he is not a kind thoughtful man then?

"On the way back I will tell you about my wife and five sons," he said as if he was talking about the weather.

"Five children, five?" I could not believe it.

"Yes there is Michael junior, he was born in 1974, then twin boys Charles and John 1976, then another set of twin boys James and Simon 1978. Please darling do not ask any more questions, I will tell you on the way home, are you ready?" and we left his office but went through the other door and that is where the lift is I remembered now.

We were soon in the car, leaving the car park. We drove through Nottingham and went in an entrance I hadn't used before, but I knew straight away it was The Park where we had a Penthouse. "Do you live here?"

"Yes," he said as we drew up outside a beautiful big house, which had obviously been converted into flats or apartments. "Are you staying here or do you want to come up, but I will tell you now will we be in and out, there is no way I am taking you into my bedroom, not if we want to get you home this side Christmas!"

"I think I will stay here," I should have gone with him, as

soon as I was on my own my thoughts went straight to my Elliot, I really hoped he had not suffered, as the tears were rolling down my face, we did not have long enough why, why? we were so happy. I just let them fall and was diving in my handbag for some tissues when I heard the car boot open and slam shut, then he was sliding in beside me.

"My darling come here, he took me in his powerful arms and held me tight," until I could stop crying.

"I am sorry Michael," I said.

"Please my sweet you have nothing to be sorry for, I know how much in love you both were, how happy you were, I think you are doing really well and I am not just saying that. Come on lets get you home and see if we can find something to stop you thinking, not sure what but we can play cards or scrabble?" he gave me a sideways glance, that was something Elliot had said once and it made me smile.

"Right you want to know about my life and Julia my wife, we were at school together, we had to get married in 1974 when we were 20 because I got her pregnant, but we were happy and working hard because I was still at Hendon Police College, Julia was studying, she is now a Psychiatrist, but she travels around to various hospitals. Our children as I told you about quickly followed. She was never over the moon about sex and when she became fully qualified she was immersed in her work."

"Can I ask how did she cope with babies and work, it must have been hard?" I asked.

"Not really her family are very wealthy and anything we needed they would pay for including nannies. She did not have to look after the house, cook or clean. When she was at home she spent a lot her time with the children, of course when they were five they all started boarding school, so it was only at school or university holidays. We drifted apart, I said I didn't like that we were not having sex, I was not happy, she knew I was bedding other women, so Julia herself bought me that apartment and said do what I wanted, the only criteria was that I was home for most of the holidays as a family, and I didn't give cause for people to gossip about all the women I saw, but she would never give me a divorce, she was married to me and she liked to be seen with me when we go to these large evening functions and always she wanted me to sleep with her, but very rarely was there any sex," he took a deep breath.

"Was she not jealous then, I do not think I could share a man I was in love with," I said.

"My darling you would never have to share, because you like sex, why would a man look elsewhere, if he has you in his bed, I for one would not, we might spend a lot of time in bed but we would not need to look elsewhere, I know for sure I would keep you well and truly fucked, does that answer your question? You look so sweet, innocent and demur, you have that calming effect on people, but strip you naked and take you to bed and you turn into a wild untamed tiger, but then again who the hell would want to tame you, you are one wonderful surprising young lady," he smiled.

"So does she know you are making love to me?" I asked.

"Yes of course, I told her when I phoned, I said I was still here with you, although I told her it was unintentional, not planned. I have just realised do we need any shopping? because it is almost Christmas and the shops will be closed," he asked.

"I think we are alright, the milkman brings all different things so, I buy a lot from him, the mobile butcher will be round tomorrow, he sells vegetables. So unless there is something you would particularly like?" I looked at him he looked at me quickly, with a small boy like grin.

"Yes there is something I particularly like, but you are right here, my darling," he laughed, I laughed to.

"You say some of the most outrageous things, do all men say things like you do?" I am totally baffled and shocked.

"I do not think I am much different to any normal fit red blooded male, however young lady I absolutely forbid you to go and find out, at least not whilst I am here with you," he said still laughing, he was just pulling onto our front.

"Timed that right didn't we?" and he got out and retrieved his holdall from the boot. I have been that intrigued by what he was saying I have just released the uniform has gone, replaced with jeans that show his lovely little bum and fine turtle neck sweater.

Chapter seven

I unlocked the door, we went straight into the kitchen, I turned the thermostat up as I passed it in the hall. He left his bag on the stairs and followed me into the kitchen, without a word he enfolded me in his arms, his wanting lips were on mine and I was responding to him immediately "Samantha I want you so much, shall I make us a coffee, then I will take you to bed" he looked me straight in the eye and everything went south.

I replied with "I have a better idea let's have a drink of water and go straight to bed, all this talk of sex is driving me mad, one thrust and I will be coming," I smiled. He did no more lifted me up and carried me upstairs and stood me next to the bed.

"Do not move, do nothing, I will undress, then I want to lie down and watch you undress, although you can take your coat and boots off if you want," I did not need telling twice they were soon hanging up. He had gone into the spare room and came back naked with a growing erection, he lay back on the bed with his hands behind his head watching me.

I thought I would feel self conscious but I did not, it was quite arousing, I turned round and bent my knees for him to unzip my dress which he did, I slipped my arms out and let it drop to the floor, then purposely turned my back to him, bent right down with straight legs and I heard him almost growl with pleasure, seeing my bare flesh with just a thong between my legs, I tossed the dress onto a chair, I reversed back to let him undo my bra, he has done all this before he needed no prompting. I held the bra to me, turned back to face him, knelt on the bed close to him, took the bra off, offering my breasts to his mouth, which he took hungrily. I was driving myself mad with desire for him, everything was throbbing and pulsating I leaned back on my knees, he ran his finger down the thin piece of silk that disappeared between my legs, with one quick jerk it was down to my knees.

One minute I was kneeling, the next I am on my back, he was over the top of me, the thong was off flying through the air landing god knows where, then instead of what I expected, his fingers followed by his cock, he had his head between my leg. Christ I thought what is he doing and then I could feel his tongue doing wondrous things, his fingers gently massaging, but it was his mouth, lips and tongue, that were doing the most arousing things to me, I began to feel all the sensations, which are the same as when he makes love to me, the excitement I know he is going to take me to bursting, he is sucking hard, it is wonderful, then I have the biggest explosion of an orgasm, I am loud I am groaning, gasping, everything is throbbing, the pulsating is throughout my body, I lay moaning, his fingers are still inside me, he appears in front of me and his mouth is on mine. He is so wanting, his fingers are still inside me, they are working fast, then without moving his lips, he is inside me thrusting hard and fast, I do not know how he can keep the speed up, but he soon comes and I am getting close again, he knows so he keeps on thrusting into me until I let go. I am hanging onto him as if my life depends on him, I am still groaning and moaning.

"Michael, Michael," I gasp, "Michael," I try once more I cannot breath, I cannot speak. Then we are kissing as if there is no tomorrow. At the same time he is moving again, he has not withdrawn at all and I can feel him growing hard inside me. I am kissing him like mad, I still cannot speak, and then he said;

"I am going to make love to you now my darling I am going to take you slowly, but when I have finished with you this time, you will be up on the moon somewhere, you are so responsive, you are every mans dream, no wonder your brothers fucked you, I would not blame them, I am afraid if you were my sister I would have done the same," he smiled that melting smile.

"No, you have that wrong, they are not my brothers, I was left on the doorstep, I always thought they were my family, even though the Trollop told me I wasn't. Daddy had to tell me when I was sixteen because she had broken her promise not to tell me. It was a shock at first, as it was for my brothers, as I thought there were. But no it was not incest. I am not sure whether that made the difference or if we would have done it anyway," I stated.

I only had to look at his magnificent body and handsome face and I was wanting him. I said "Now what have you done, I am throbbing like there is no tomorrow, I cannot get over what you to do me, and what I do in response," he said nothing just the pace quicken a little, but he was kissing me all over, and fondling my breasts, I was writhing and pushing myself onto him, I could not hold still, I had my legs wrapped round his beautiful bum pulling him nearer to me. This went on for a long, long time when we both exploded together, very loud, very noisy and very long, we both lay gasping, trying to breathe for a long time, eventually he said;

"I think my darling we should have a shower before anything else, not that I want us to move from this position, but we have all the time in the world, I will not have to leave you until the 3rd January 1998, come on darling move it," he gave me a quick slap on my bottom.

"Right Michael Roper you may be bigger than me, but you are going to be sorry for that," and he ran into the bathroom shouting "Ooh I am scared," I ran after him, not looking where I was going, as I ran though the door it closed, Michael was stood behind it, he grabbed me and held me firmly in his arms, my arms were trapped down my sides I couldn't move, he was laughing.

"Now what are you going to do Samantha Windsor?"

"Not a thing I am quite happy here in your arms, I am all yours, you can do whatever you want with me," as I said that everything went south again, also a certain appendage reacted favourably to what I said, he kissed me and he grew to a full erection, I was rubbing it against me.

"Stop it my lovely, lovely Samantha, we are having a shower then we will have a drink and if you can live on love I certainly cannot, I need food to keep my strength up. I am sorry if I upset you, but Rupert told me they were your brothers, I assumed he was telling me the truth. I also have to say something my darling Samantha, I am so in love with you, I have never felt like this, I have been going with women for sex, there was no love, I just wanted to fuck, I would take them for dinner first, then fuck them, if they were not happy I just stopped seeing them, there are a lot more fish in the sea."

"And you are a great catch, who wouldn't want to go with you?" and we looked into each others eyes, we had to kiss we were both very aroused.

"Samantha what are you doing to me," he pushed me up to the wall and was inside me again and he was doing what he must do better than anything else in the whole wide world, that was fucking and he was really taking me high fast, very fast it was rough and furious it was lovely we both came again, I think we get noisier each time. As soon as we got our breath back he said;

"Get into that shower now you little nymphomaniac, you are making me worse than I usually am, we both have enormous appetites, I think this will be my best Christmas ever. My only regret is that we got together under terrible circumstances my love,

I will look after you, I will stay as long as I can, which if I had my way I would never leave you, I do love you my lovely, please get in the shower Samantha," I did as I was told, I was in and out quick, dried myself then wandered back to the bedroom naked as always. Michael got in the shower after me and I could hear him singing.

Without warning the tears were flowing, I just wilted to the floor near the bed, I sobbed and I sobbed I just could not stop, my lovely Elliot I would never have another kiss from him, we would never hold hands again, it went on and on.

I do not know how long I was there but suddenly Michael called upstairs "Darling where are you, I have made you a drink," and he came running through the door "My darling, I am so sorry I thought you were dressing, I went to make us a drink and find something for dinner," he picked me up and sat on the bed with me on his knee, gently rocking me as one would with a child, I felt safe again and his after shave was divine.

"I am sorry Michael, so sorry," I whimpered.

"Darling you have nothing to be sorry for, I think you are doing really well," then the telephone rang "I'll get it," he said and ran downstairs "Please come and have your drink."

I could hear his voice, but he had taken the call in the office and had pushed the door to. I put on a black lace negligee and wandered downstairs into the kitchen, picked up my cup and saucer and went and sat on the sofa near the fire.

He came in sat beside me, he took my hand "Darling when this all happened I told them who I was, I asked that they bring Elliot nearer to us, that was Nottingham, Elliot arrived today, we have to go tomorrow to identify him, then you can arrange to have him brought over here ready for his funeral," he kept looking at me and he could see my lip was trembling, I tried so hard not to cry but it was in vain, down came the tears I felt so devastated, Michael just held me, he didn't speak he just let the flood flow, after what seemed for ever, I began to stop but he held me close, he was warm and again I felt safe, it really could have been my daddy holding me.

The next day before we travelled to Nottingham, Michael looked in the telephone directory and found a Funeral Directors in Melton Mowbray and he spoke to them and explained, they took my details and Elliot's. Then we set off for Nottingham, it was bitterly cold. He knew where he was going I had no idea, he took me into this building and spoke to a receptionist, she phoned through to someone, Michael put his arm round me and led me through to a room. A man came in and spoke quietly to Michael.

Then Michael turned to me "Are you ready?" I nodded, my knees felt weak, we went to a curtained window as we looked the curtains opened, there was my Charles he looked as though he was sleeping, but it didn't help, I nodded again, but could see no more through the fog, which were my tears. Michael led me to a room, sat me down and held me close until I began to stop.

A young lady brought a tray of tea for us, Michael piled the sugar in stirred it and waited for me to relax a little, "Come on my darling drink this," he passed the cup which rattled on the saucer, so he took the saucer and left me trying to keep the cup steady and I sipped it, it was welcome.

"What happens now?" I asked.

"They will notify the Funeral Directors to come and collect him, they will take him to their place in Melton Mowbray and when he is ready they will telephone to let us know we can go and see him, then you can say your good bye. I know he wanted cremating so I gave them that information so they would be looking for dates as soon as I phoned this morning. I also rang Rupert, I am not very happy with him because he has not telephoned you once and he has been a close friend of Elliot's since they were very young.

We had just pulled out of the car park, waiting for a car to pass when it stopped "That's Julia I will have to have a word with her," so he pulled into the kerb, ran over to her car she was opening the window but he walked round and got in the passenger side. I watched at first she looked really angry but he stayed cool, Charles what have I got myself into, then the tears started, I rummaged round in my bag for a tissue to dry my face and blow my nose, I glanced across, she turned to look towards me but she put her hand up, waved and smiled at me. She looks really nice I cannot do this to her, I will tell him no more.

He got in the car and looked at me and leaned over and kissed me full on the lips, with his wife across the road watching, "Lets go home," he said, then put his hand up and waved to her and she smiled and waved back.

"I do not understand?" I said

"What don't you not understand my darling," he gave me that smile that would melt anything let alone my heart.

"You and your wife, she looked as if she was really mad with you, but by the time I had wiped my tears, she had turned and waved to me, then you both waved and smiled at one another, so I am confused."

"I told her quickly about you, how I first met you and Charles, then quickly what had happened, I told her I had seduced you and it seems to help. So she wished me a Happy Christmas and would explain to the family why I cannot be there, but leave out that I am fucking the poor girl, her words not mine," he said as calmly as you like.

"When I first saw her I thought she looked very nice and it was not fair what we were doing and I was going to tell you to go home, until she waved and smiled," I said.

"She is a good person that is why I love her, but I am not in love with her, there is a big difference however, I am in love with you my darling, are you still going to tell me to go home?" there is that gorgeous smile.

"No," I said and he laughed.

We were soon home, he drove over the speed limit all the way, but I suppose he can get away with things like that.

As he unlocked the door the telephone was ringing, he dived into the office before the answering machine kicked in. I closed the door as he was saying "I cannot see any problem with that, so tomorrow any particular time, yes, no that is alright I had forgotten it is Christmas Eve tomorrow, we will see you at 11 in the morning then, thank you, good bye," and he hung up.

"I gather it is tomorrow at 11am I will see my Elliot for the last time," and the torrents started again, I just sobbed and sobbed. Michael just stood and held me tight, he did not move or say anything he just let me carry on until I was exhausted.

"Darling I really think you should try to eat something, would you like some soup that should be easy to get down?"

"If it pleases you, but not a bucket full, I think there is some Garlic bread in the freezer, we could have that," I suggested.

"My darling that is a big leap, I would get you anything if you would eat, besides I need you with plenty of stamina, we cannot have you passing out amidst fuck, can we?" he said laughing, well I did laugh it was funny, I can just picture it. We sat at the table had the soup, then Michael made some ham sandwiches, I had cooked the ham while waiting for Charles to come home, I had made cakes and pies all sorts to keep me busy.

Michael persuaded me to eat one sandwich and told me, I would be rewarded in bed for being good and eating something.

He made coffee and we sat on the sofa next to the fire, we did not speak he had his arm round me, my head was leaning on his shoulder, I nodded off because when I woke up it was dark.

I turned to look at Michael he was asleep, his head had tilted towards me, he looked so handsome he was just breathing heavy, not snoring, his mouth was closed not like me, my mouth opens when I go to sleep, Elliot said I snored! I did not want to disturb him so I stayed still and must have gone to sleep again, because around 8 pm the phone woke both of us, "I'll get it my lovely," he went over to the phone in the kitchen.

"Hello" pause "Christ I thought you had emigrated, you have never phoned," pause "We are all busy Rupert," pause "Well I am staying with her for now, she cannot be left on her own would it be possible for you to stay with her for a few days after the 3rd?" pause "Well I suppose that is something," pause "Same to you," and he put the phone down and turned, I had been crying throughout the conversation, he rushed to me, took me in his arms and lifted me up, and carried me upstairs, went straight into the bedroom, he never spoke, just began undressing me, I stood and let him, whilst I still had my bra and skimpy lace briefs on I said.

"Sorry darling I must go to the loo and clean my teeth."

"That is alright I think I had better go and get my bag in and unpack, I will not be long my lovely," and he ran downstairs and went to fetch his bag from the car, then I heard him lock up, switch off the downstairs lights then it went quiet.

Shortly he came up stairs, I was in the bathroom removing my make-up. I heard a clink of glass, he has brought some glasses and bottle of wine up, by the time I was going into the bedroom he came up behind me and put his arms round me and snuggled my neck, when he turned me round he was gloriously naked and erect.

"I will go to the bathroom," he uncorked the bottle "While I am gone you can pour us a drink," and he was gone.

When he returned he smelt so sexy he had put some cologne on it was doing things to me, as he got into bed I leaned towards him "Hmm you smell divine," we sat and had a drink, then we slid down the bed and we made love, ooh how we made love, first it was quick and fast. When we were able to breath again, it was slow and mind blowing. We had numerous different positions, at half time, he'd said go and get on the bidet on your own and when I strolled out he was going in, he just stopped and gave me a long kiss.

We sat with another glass of wine, and talked, but his hand wandered, he was driving me wild, he gave me that wonderful smile, dragged me down the bed for, as he put it another session, then we slept a while, then we made love and that is how it went until morning.

"Come on Mrs-I can never have enough sex- Windsor, we have to be out by 10.45."he said laughing.

We arrived at the Funeral Directors just before eleven, I was trembling from head to toe, I had hardly stopped crying since I had, had my shower it was a waste of time trying to put make-up on. I was hanging on to Michaels hand as if my life depended on it, we were shown into a small dimly lit room and there was my Elliot in his coffin, but looked as though he could wake up at any moment, the tears were streaming and I went over and took his hand it was like ice "Elliot how am I going to manage without you, I love you so much, we have not had long enough," I bent forward and kissed his lips for a long time "I should be there with you, you should not be here it should be Rupert," as I said those words, I realised they were true, if he had gone my darling would not be here, I kept holding his hand I could not seem to let go, all the time the tears were streaming.

Suddenly Michael was at my side "Come on darling, we should go," he said quietly.

"We have only just got here, I cannot leave him all on his own," I cried.

"Darling we have been here for over an hour and a half, it will not alter anything if you stay with him all day, he is gone my love," he held me in his arms, I was heart broken, I just sobbed and sobbed "Say one last goodbye," I went back to him and kissed him on his frozen lips.

"I will see you very soon, my darling," Michael put his arm round me and gently led me out, he took me to the car, almost lifted me in, I was distraught.

We were soon home, he went and unlocked the door and came back, lifted me out and carried me into the kitchen, I was shivering, he went and closed the door and brought an envelope with him, someone must have put it through the letter box.

It took me a long time opening it I was trembling so much, it was a card 'In Sympathy' it read 'I am so sorry for your loss, he was such a very nice young man, you are in my thoughts Kevin the milk' that started the water works again, Michael could do nothing with me, he disappeared and I heard him on the telephone to someone, he was gone sometime. When he came back I realised he must have cried at some stage, because his eyes were red. He did not speak he made me a strong, sweet cup of tea and sat together on the sofa.

"What can I get you to eat?" he asked.

"Nothing, I think I am going to lie down I have a throbbing headache, do you mind?" I asked.

"Don't be silly, you have a lie down, have you got anything to take?" he asked.

"Yes they are upstairs," I said and turned away. Upstairs I filled a glass with water and took it with the tablets to the bed, I sat on the edge of the bed and tipped a hand full of tablets in my hand and started swallowing one at a time, anytime soon I will be with my darling Elliot, I had just taken the fifth when Michael came flying in.

"I was hoping I was wrong, Samantha that is not going to help," he said desperately.

"Please Michael, please let me be with Elliot," I am sobbing, "Please, please," he took the tablets from me.

"How many have you taken? tell me please otherwise I will have to force you to be sick," he was desperate.

"Only five," I sobbed.

"Are you sure?"

"Yes," and he held me so close.

"I had a feeling you were going to do something, with what you said to Charles, 'see you very soon,' I did not figure you would try now, my darling I am so sorry. I dare not leave you on your own now, you will have to come downstairs and lie on the sofa so I can keep my eye on you. Julia is coming down this afternoon, because I was worried about you and she will bring you something to help you," he said.

"Why? you should not have bothered her on Christmas Eve, she will be busy preparing for tomorrow," I sobbed.

"My lovely Samantha, if she was busy she would not be coming down here, she does not do any cooking, our normal cook has time off at Christmas, so Julia gets a caterer in to do everything, so it will not be a bother to her. Now go and wash your face change into one of your lovely outfits, put on some make-up and perfume, I will sit here and wait for you. Then you can come into the spare room while I change, then I will take you downstairs. I suppose it is a total waste of time asking you to eat something?"

"I could not swallow anything," he sat on the bed waiting for me, I put on what they call and coat dress, it does look like a coat, with cross over top and silver buttons, but the V is very deep and shows lots of cleavage and has a mini skirt, it is light navy, so I put on high heel navy sandals and lots of perfume and when I re-enter the bedroom he is stood looking out of the front window "Will that do?"

He spun round his face was a delight "Will it do? that has got to be the understatement, you look divine, that is the Samantha we all know and love, look what you have done to me again, come here," so I slowly walked towards him "I would like to bet you have one of those glorious thongs on?" when I reached him, he took my hand and put it on his erection I gently massaged it, "What am I supposed do with that," he said, but as he was talking, he had run his hands down each side of my body until he reached the hem and pulled it right up revelling me from the waist down, showing bare flesh and the thong. I smiled, he looked "A thong, they drive me wild with desire."

I was still gently massaging him while he was talking, he had not realised I had unzipped his trousers, I gently put my hand in and found his erection, I mean it wasn't hard to find, he wore boxers, plus he was big, very big.

It was then he realised I had released him, before he could say anything I went down on him, the first time I had him in my mouth and gave a hard, very hard suck, then I began to massage him with my tongue, my hand helped move his foreskin back and forward, he was moaning, groaning even growling, but I did not think it was pain, so I used my initiative and moved my mouth, lips and tongue up and down, he was gasping I looked up his head was back in ecstasy, then he started pushing himself in and out, he was right to the back of my throat, I wondered why I was not gagging, but I carried on for quiet sometime, until he said:

"Let go Samantha, I am going to come," I just carried on and I heard "Sam," that was it, he was pumping into me I just let him get on with it, until he stopped, I let him go, he put his hands under my arms bringing me up and his lips were on mine.

"Samantha did you know what you were doing to me?"

"No not really, I have heard about a 'Blow Job' I used to think it had to be blown, I have done it with Charles but not very often," he gave a loud laugh.

"Christ you are one hell of a young lady, that was brilliant what you did," he looked down my skirt was still up, showing my lower body and the thong "I love these," he said as he pulled on it and down it came, "You know you are one very easy to fuck young lady, I know that is what you want me to do, isn't it?"

"Yes, you know it is," I whispered.

"Ask me then, tell me what you want me to do to you, but we only have an hour before Julia arrives," he said.

"Why, how do you mean?" I asked.

"Why? because when you talk about anything sexual, you whisper and your voice is so sexy, so tell me what you want me to do to you."

"I want you to make love to me," I stated.

"Yes well we know that, but how in what position? come darling tell me."

"Michael Roper, if you do not fuck me pretty quick I shall be coming, without you, you turn me on just by looking at me, when you look me in the eyes I do not stand a chance, darling I need you now!"

He picked me up, dropped me on the bed, unbuttoned my dress and roughly took it off, as he did with my bra.

"Right Mrs Windsor you are now going to have it rough, if you are in so much of a hurry," he said.

It was still so arousing, he was thrusting right in and almost withdrawing and thrust in again, it went on and on, he was taking me up fast we both had very loud, long orgasm's, he dropped down on the bed beside me.

"I don't know what you do to me Samantha, you thrill me beyond words, I could stay in bed with you for ever and not get bored with you, I love you so very much," it did not come out as smooth as that because he was still gasping for his breath.

Eventually we had to get up because he said "Julia will be here in about twenty minutes, but you had better find something else to wear, I am afraid I have creased that one and you looked so young and sexy in it, you pop to the bathroom first," he said.

I redid my hair and makeup and chose a red mini dress, it was supposed to be what they call a shift, but unfortunately with me it was not loose it fitted across my breasts and skimmed over my hips, there was no cleavage but you could see my nipples bulging underneath the fine material, I put a red thong on to match.

Going down the stairs, rounding the last bend Michael stood at the bottom looking up, "Very nice, even sexier, I like the matching thong," I neared him, his hand slipped up my mini skirt.

"No you don't Mr otherwise, we will still be at it when your wife arrives."

"I knew you were a spoil sport, one fuck and that's it for a week," he kept his face absolutely straight, I was in stitches.

"I promise you as soon as Julia has left, I will be stripped off in seconds, and you can have me anywhere you want, as long as it is not outside it is too cold, you can do whatever you want with me, is that a deal?" I asked.

"Hmm I don't know I might not feel like it?"

"I'll bet you a million pounds you will. Michael I do love you, I do not know what I would have done if I had been on my own," and I gave him a quick peck and went into the kitchen.

"Oh I was going to lay the tea tray and you have done it, I will get some mince pies and some of the chocolate cake I made," I set another tray with the plates Christmas napkins.

"Have you made all that yourself?" he looked surprised.

"Yes I also made some steak pies, a Victoria sponge and some shortbread biscuits. It was while I was on my own, when," I couldn't get any further.

"Come on my lovely you were doing so well, here," he passed me a handkerchief, just as the door bell rang. I'll go he said, so I went to the door into the hall.

He opened the door "Hello darling," he said and kissed her on the lips and she reciprocated.

"Hello my love," she said. She was a bit taller than me slim with plenty of curves, he helped her off with her full length fur coat, she had a little navy suit on the skirt was just below her knees, plain box type jacket with a low front top underneath, showing plenty of cleavage, she looked nothing like a Doctor.

I stepped forward Michael said "This is Julia, and this is Samantha," I put my hand out I thought that is what she would do, but no she came towards me, put her arms round me and kissed my cheek.

"I am so pleased to meet you Samantha, I am sorry it is not under better circumstances. Come along darling close the door," she took my arm and led me into the lounge "What a lovely room."

"Please sit down I will make the tea," I said, Michael made to follow me "No you stay, I will bring it," so I made the tea, I could hear their voices, Michael took the tray from me and I went and fetched the other one and put it on the other coffee table.

Michael said "Samantha made all this," he sounded proud.

"It all looks good," she said. So I proceeded pouring the tea, Michael put the plates out, offering Julia the choice.

"I am going to be greedy and have one of each," she said laughing. Then she said "This is delicious."

"Thank you," I said.

"Michael has given me a quick synopsis of how he became to know you, and your husband and now how things are I am so sorry, you look such a lovely girl, we wonder why these things happen and if there is a god? but we have to muddle on, I know it is not easy, Michael told me earlier he was worried about you, and indeed he needed to be, but at the moment my love everything looks bleak, but you are young, eventually it gets a little better but only a bit at a time, but every little bit is really a giant leap. I have brought you some medication to help you, it is not a sleeping tablet but it is something to calm you, get you through this difficult period. Take one of these blue ones with food, then before you go to sleep take two pink ones. Please try to remember to take them as it is the continuity that helps, so they are in your blood stream, if you forget one please do not take two next time." Then she produced a little purple bottle, "Put a little drop on your hands and wipe them across your pillow, it is only Lavender but it is so relaxing, you need to sleep, if you can sleep you are half way there to coping."

"Now because it is Christmas, I was wondering if you would come over, say the day after Boxing Day, and stay a few days let me look after you, before you start over thinking, you will share Michaels bed no one need know, the others in the house will be Charles, John and James. The Grandparents are not staying any longer than Boxing Day afternoon this year Michael, what do you say? I am going to say something now, I assume Michael has been honest with you, I have never met any of Michaels bed companions and never wanted to, but you are different, you are so young, I want to mother you I want to look after you, please Michael do try to influence her," she said sincerely.

"That is very kind of you, Michael you should go, but I do not want to be anywhere but home until after the funeral," I got no further the flood gates opened, Michael was getting up but Julia beat him to it, she took me in her arms, and held me as I remember Great Aunt Celeste had done when I was young and upset, she held me gently, smoothed my hair with her free hand and gently rocked me, with a sh sh every now and again. I could not see Michael through my tears, but gradually they subsided, she had a tissue which she wiped my eyes and dried my wet cheeks, then gave it me one to blow my nose. "Thank you." I said.

"I do understand what you are going through, I know Michael will not leave you on your own, I would not expect him to, come on drink your tea, I can thoroughly recommend the cake and mince pies," she laughed as did Michael.

"Thank you Julia," he said very sincerely.

"I just want to help in anyway I can Samantha, I do not want you to think I am interfering," she stated.

"I know you are not and I know this is a first for you, but I cannot help myself, even though I did try very hard," he said.

"Darling I am not judging you," Julia said "Let me know when the funeral is please, I think Samantha ought to have some female support."

"Thank you very, I would appreciate it very much," I muttered.

"I had better make tracks, if there is anything I can do please let me know Michael?" she said as she stood up, we all did and walked towards the hall, she took me in her arms and said "I hope you find some peace soon, I am thinking of you," she kissed me on my lips.

They held each other he said, "I hope you have a good Christmas, please apologise to the boys and parents," and they kissed on the lips.

Julia replied with "I will do my best to give them all a good couple of days, don't forget as soon as you have a date let me know?"

"Yes, I promise," he replied opening the door for her.

"Michael, what a lovely person Julia is, I feel so guilty keeping you here and for what we are doing, I do not think we should go to bed together any more, I feel awful," I said through the tears.

He came towards me and wrapped his strong arms round me "My little sweet Samantha, you do not have anything to feel guilty for, Julia knows me and still loves me as I do her. She actually invited you to go and stay with me, in our house, even went as far as to say you would be sharing my bed, why should you feel guilty, it is not as though I am doing anything behind her back. Please try and relax probably when you start taking the tablets you will be able to cope a little better, it is still very early days. I do love you so much my darling," he said.

"I love you Michael," I simply said.

"You go back into the lounge and lie on the settee, I will rustle up something to eat, you have got to keep having something, so you can start your tablets. You can rest assured Julia will be telephoning to see if you are taking them, and check how you are feeling, if you do not take them, I will be in real trouble," he laughed "Go on and rest."

I must have fallen asleep, because he was waking me to go and eat, I thought I can't eat, but I will try. He had what he called rustled up a lovely meal, of Pork steaks, onion gravy, mashed potatoes, carrots and cabbage, he had even put it in serving dishes. He opened a bottle of white wine, set the table with napkins and even candles. I felt full up.

"Darling I thought you would rustle up egg on toast or an omelet, you should not have gone to all this trouble," I said.

"I want you to try and eat something, just try for me please, I want you to start feeling a bit better, but you cannot have the tablets without food, Doctor Julia's strict instructions, I will not be able to take advantage of your lovely body, do all the things I want to do to you, if you do not eat," he looked into my eyes, my insides flipped and I started to throb.

I was surprised how much I ate, I even had two mince pies which he heated up and poured cream on for me, he gave me a glass of water and the first tablet, I got up to clear the table.

"No my little darling, it will not take me long to get it all in the dish washer, now you can either go back into the lounge, or you can change into something more comfortable, then we will see what is on the Television for an hour or so, then my sweet we will go to bed, taking two tablets when you go to sleep!" and planted me a big sloppy wet kiss on my lips.

I decided to go and slip into something less formal, I undressed, decided to just put a black lace negligee and I must have fallen asleep, because when I awoke I was in bed naked, Michael must have removed my coat, he lay beside me fast asleep, he looked so handsome and peaceful, the small table lamp was lit on my side of the bed, a glass of water with two tablets, I eased myself up gradually, leaned on one elbow and took the tablets with a good drink of water, I quietly switched off the lamp, and slid back down the bed.

The next thing I know it is daylight, I am wrapped in Michaels arms as I am looking at him, his eyes flicker open.

"Good morning my sweet, you have had a really good sleep, I saw when I got out in the night, you had taken your tablets, that was a good little girl," and his lips were on mine but instead of continuing he stopped "I will go down, fetch the tea and I am going to do toast which you will eat my girl, if you know what's good for you, then you will be able to have your tablet.

Then because you will have done as I say, I am going to take to paradise. So while I am gone if you need the bathroom, trot along, I want you in this bed, still beautiful and naked for when I come back," he got out of bed, went downstairs as he was, gloriously naked and very beautiful.

We had a wonderful day, we got up for a quick lunch, went back to bed until around 4.30, we cooked a meal, sat and ate it with me in a flimsy see through negligee, he had a short robe on but did not fasten it, we cleared up loaded the dishwasher, then decided an early night was what we really wanted.

We made love several times, then he made me take the two pink tablets, I slept all the way through again, we did the same again on boxing day.

On the 27th we had tea in bed and made love, then we showered, actually got dressed, we were just in the kitchen when the phone rang. Michael answered it "Hello darling, did the two days go alright? - pause - good I am pleased. Well I think they are doing a lot of good, that night she actually fell asleep on the bed, before she had even took the two tablets, then the last two nights she slept right through, no nightmares, she seems, well I cannot say calm because she always seems calm, but more relaxed, and with having to have the tablets with food, she had begun to eat - pause - yes I will put her on," he held the phone "It is Julia."

"Hello Julia, is everything alright?" I asked.

"Yes my darling, thank you for asking, please do not worry about Michael not being here, I explained about you, all the boys sympathised. I am popping into work today, so I will have to go, bye Samantha. You are in my thoughts constantly," and she was gone.

The next call was the Funeral Director, Michael had answered the phone, he said "Yes that would be fine - pause - yes one car, what time? - pause - 1.30pm, thank you, bye," All the time I am waiting and begin to tremble "Darling sit down, you gather who that was, they have got a slot at 1.30pm at the crematorium on 30ᵗʰ December. They knew there would only be a few people, so managed to slot Elliot in, I am going into the office and try to get Rupert, he had better not say he cannot make it," he kissed me, sat me down and went to the office.

A long time after he returned "Rupert will be here and go in the car, I rang Julia on her mobile, her secretary said she would be able to come, she was going to tell her, she will ring later," he came and held me tight "Sit down my darling, I suppose it is a waste of time offering you a Brandy or something, I suppose it will be tea or even coffee?"

"Can I go and see Charles again please Michael, I must go please?" I implore him.

"Let me make you a drink, then I will ring to see which day and what time alright my love?" he said.

He came back with my drink, but went into the office to make the call. Then I heard the phone ring it only rang once, Michael must have picked it up, a short while later he came in," I looked up at him hopeful. "Yes my darling tomorrow afternoon at 4pm," I just drifted through the rest of the day, I had a throbbing head, so Michael put me to bed with the two tablets. I do not remember any more.

Thursday I cannot settle to anything, I cannot eat the smallest bit seems to stick, so Michael patiently sits and almost feeds me, so I can have the tablet.

Then we set off, to see Charles I want to go, but I don't want to go, when we arrive I ask Michael if I can go in on my own, he agrees, I go in, he still looks as though he is sleeping, I kneel on the floor next to him, hold his hand, sit and chat to him about all we had done, I waffled on for I thought a short time. I was alright at first then the tears started, I got up and leaned over the coffin so I was close to his face, I whispered to him how much I love him, and miss him, I keep kissing his ice cold lips, his eyes will open soon, then I can take him home, I am sobbing uncontrollably, a door opens and Michael appears.

"Darling come on it is time to go," he says softly.

I am hysterical "No, we have only just come, no he is

going to wake up, no I can't leave him on his own," I am thrashing about, I really do believe he is only asleep, "Please a little bit longer, we can take him home, please, please," Michael eventually manages to get both my arms in his hands. Someone else comes in as Michael is trying to get me to walk, I am pulling back, I am moaning "No, no no."

Suddenly I am lifted off my feet by two men, Michael still has hold of my hands, they carry me out I am struggling "No please, please I cannot leave him," they lay me on a sofa, an elderly lady comes in she says "Come along dear, we know it hurts, but we have to get you home because we have work to do."

Michael came back and thanked her very much, I let him lead me to the car, "Darling are you alright?" I nod.

We were soon home, he left me in the car while he put on the lights, came back, got me out and carried me in, closing the door with his foot and carried me upstairs into the bedroom, he put me down.

"Now my darling, I will find you a nightdress, wash your face, then get into bed, I will make you a small sandwich you have got to eat it, because I have to give your tablets, in a short while Julia will be here, she is on her way as we speak, please be a good girl. I know you are very sad and unhappy, but between us we will get you through this, because I will have to go to work on the 3rd January," he fetched me a lovely black lace nightie. I did as I was told, then looked in the cabinets for the headache tablets they were gone!

I was in bed when he came in with a tray, with a pile of sandwiches on, he saw the look of horror on my face, then laughed "It is alright darling, I am not expecting you to eat all these, I have brought mine up so we can eat together," he put the tray on a little table poured the tea, heaps in the sugar and stirred it, and brought it to me, then he put three little sandwiches on a plate and passed them to me.

"Please eat them, I found those shortbread biscuits you said you had made, I tried one, and had to have another they are so delicious, so I have brought some up and your tablets of course, but please hurry because I am supposed to make sure you have had them well before Julia gets here, if not you will get me into trouble!" he looked at me.

"Okay, you win," I struggled with the first sandwich but the second went down better, drank my tea so he poured me another.

"Can you not put so much sugar in please?" I asked.

"Right my love," and passed my tea over, I reached out, took his hand and kissed it and held it to my face, the tears started, "Please do not say you are sorry, it does not matter, I just cannot bare seeing you so desperately sad."

I did as I was told, tried one of my shortbreads, took the tablet and slid down the bed as ordered. The door bell rang. I heard the door open, Julia said something, "Michael I am so sorry, come and sit down, it does not make you less a man," and then they were too far away to hear.

I have made him cry, what have I reduced him to? he has been so good to me, I am crying for two, my Elliot and what is he my friend, my lover?

After a while I was dozing and I heard voices, I opened my eyes and Julia came in "Hello my love how are you feeling, truthfully?" she was watching me.

"I feel a bit better, I really thought he was going to wake up, I really did," the tears were streaming again. She came and sat on the bed, putting her arms round me.

"I am so sorry for you, I know it must be very hard for you, you are both so young, but we cannot alter the fact that he has gone, you could have stood there for months, he still would not have woken up, I am so sorry. I am going to give you an injection now, you will sleep for quiet a while, I have told Michael, so he does not worry about you sleeping too long. Do you need to use the toilet before I inject you?" she asked.

"Yes I should," she injected me in my bottom.

"There now lie down, I have asked Michael to bring you a glass of water, because you may wake up for a few minutes, and your mouth will be dry, so it will be there for when you need it," she tidied the sheets and made me comfortable, kissed me on the lips very softly.

"I will see you Thursday morning, have a good sleep darling," In a matter minutes I must have fallen asleep because when I awoke Michael was just coming in with a tray.

Chapter seven

"Hello sweetie how do you feel?" he asked looking concerned.

"I think I must have slept all night, I do not remember you coming, to bed." He laughed,

"Darling you have been asleep for two days. Julia is on her way, she told me to wake you, welcome back," I just looked at him, he came, took me in his arms and kissed me.

"But that's when," I could not say it.

"Here darling drink this and please, please have some of this buttered toast, because I have to give you another tablet that Julia left," I drank the cup of tea straight down, so he refilled it, I took another drink, then I nibbled at the toast eventually I ate a whole slice, and a half.

I was rewarded with a beautiful kiss, it really did start doing things to me, I was quite happy to kiss him back. Then he drew back.

"Sorry my darling as much as I want you, I am desperate for you, we are going to have to wait, go and have a shower, can I get you your clothes out?" he asked.

"No I can't think at the moment, perhaps the shower will revive me," I had a long shower, trying not to wet my long hair, I do not know where Michael was, he was nowhere in sight.

I went and dressed, I decided a little black suit I had never worn with a camisole top in black, I put 7 denier black stockings on, with my black stiletto shoes. Did my make-up, I felt very calm, brushed my hair, was contemplating whether to put it up as Michael entered in his uniform, he looked drop dead gorgeous.

"You have just done things to me, you look absolutely drop dead gorgeous, you are sex on legs in your uniform," I said dreamily.

"Thank you my love, I do not think anyone has ever said that before, perhaps you need your eyes testing," he said laughing "Please don't put your hair up, it is beautiful and makes you look very, very sexy, or are you wearing a hat?"

"I was thinking of doing but cannot make up my mind."

"Fetch it," he ordered "Christ Samantha, are those nylon stockings you are wearing, with that short skirt, you have just given me an erection, I can't do anything about it, Julia will be here shortly."

"Well because you have been so good to me, I will have to make a special effort later, let you take my stockings off," I said smiling.

"Ooh no sweetie strip off yes, but leave the stockings and suspenders on," he came towards me, took me in his arms "I do love you sweetie, I think whatever Julia gave you, and injected you with, has done you the world of good, I was so worried about you, when Julia came I just broke down," the door bell rang "That will be her now, come down when you are ready."

I finished getting ready, put the hat on, then went to join them. "Samantha it is so good to see you, you look, well stunning my dear," she came over and hugged me close, and kissed me full on the lips again, "The medication helped then didn't it, Michael was never off the telephone saying you had not woken etc. I told him you would sleep for a long time, but I know he was very worried about you, but you look wonderful now, absolutely beautiful," Michael came in with a he tray anyone want a sherry?" I took one.

The door bell rang. "I'll go Michael said this could be the invisible man," he went to the door.

"Julia I cannot thank you enough for all you have done for me, let's face it I was a stranger to you, and your husbands mistress, you are very special, and I will always be thankful to you," she was about to speak, but the door opened with Michael and Rupert following.

"Sam darling, I am so sorry I have not been able to get before now, but you know you have been in my thoughts, you still look as gorgeous and sexy as always," he took me in his arms, and kissed me full on the lips, I was shocked, I pulled away.

"Sorry darling it is too soon, I can wait," I stood helpless looking at Michael, then Julia.

Then Michael said "This is my wife Julia, Julia this is Samantha's Lawyer Rupert Russell-Brown."

"I am pleased to meet you Julia, another beautiful young lady, pleased to meet you," he leaned in and kissed her on her cheek, she pulled away, she did not look very pleased, Michael shook his head very slightly.

"Sherry anyone?" Michael offered, we all had one, and while Rupert was engaging Julia in conversation, Michael pulled me slightly away.

"I didn't know what you were doing for flowers, so I thought I had better order something from you, I hope I did right? I got a big spray that almost covers the coffin, in all white lilies, apart from one Red rose and wrote the message.

To my beloved Elliot, my first true love,
We will meet again one day Always Samantha xx,"

"Oh Michael what would I have done without you, thank you again, I must pay you all for all that you have spent on my behalf, including the funeral directors," I said.

"I won't hear of it, I really don't want to leave you on the 3rd but I have no choice, I can see what Rupert's intentions are, I have no claim on you, but you will be like a lamb to the slaughter," then the door bell rang, Michael left.

Julia had closed the curtains, I did not realise Elliot was here. Michael came back "Time to go," suddenly Rupert was at my side his arm round me.

None of us was happy, I stopped dead at the sight of his coffin, I felt my legs go, Michael grabbed hold of me, to stop me falling he carried me to the hearse, Rupert looked bewildered, Julia passed him, she got in at the other side of me. I could not stop crying, my head was pounding, the tears kept coming. I do not remember anything, the curtains started to close.

I heard "No, he's asleep he will wake up," Michael picked me up and carried me back to the car.

Next thing we are home, Michael takes me straight upstairs, puts me on the bed, then leaves, Julia is with me, she just sits and holds me.

"My darling will you have cup of tea?" she asks, I just shake my head.

"I just want to die, then I can be with my Elliot," I mutter.

"Sweetheart I know you are in pain, please come home so I can care for you, I will take time off work, I want you to be happy my love?"

"No this is where Elliot is," I say.

"I want to give you another injection," she said.

"Rupert said he would stay for a while," I said

"I'm sorry Samantha, but I do not care for him, I think what he would call looking after you, was having you in bed for his own gratification, I had to tell you how I felt, please trust me."

"Thank you Julia, I do trust you, he did offer," I said.

"Yes I know darling, I want you to reconsider coming with me, you will not be on your own, please my darling reconsider, it would make Michael happy, he is very worried about you, he is truly in love with you, I think you are a wonderful girl, bearing in mind all you had to put up with, you have turned out a credit to your father," she said.

"I want to stay where Elliot is, but thank you very much, you have been marvellous," she kissed me on the lips and left.

The next two days flew, I was eating, a bit, enough to take the tablets, I was sleeping through. Michael was so good he really did take care of me especially in the making love department.

The 3rd January 98, arrived, he had to go, he was worried because there was no sign of Rupert, we said a very long good-bye, he had loaded his car, closed the boot, all before Rupert pulled in.

He got out of his car, didn't even look my way. "You off now then, Happy New Year," he said. Michael drove off.

"Just timed that right did I my darling, have you got a kiss for Rupert then?" he walked towards me, took me in his arms, as though it was a normal every day thing with us, bearing in mind we had never kissed properly I was a bit wary.

He pulled me in close and looked at me "God Sam you are so beautiful, I think being a widow suits you," I gasped with shock, then his lips were on mine. I can honestly say that is the first time that I have been kissed and it did nothing for me.

"Come on lets get my bags and show me where our bedroom is, then you can cook me breakfast, I did not have time, I was up till all hours trying to finish some work at home, well not my home, I have a room with some friends, I always feel in the way, because they have not been married long! but I am hoping you will help me solve that problem?"

I took one of his bags and led they way. "I will leave this big one down here it is full of dirty washing."

Cook breakfast, dirty washing, there must be at least two weeks washing by the weight of it. This is going to be fun or not.

I followed him upstairs, he went straight into my bedroom, "This is my room Rupert, I will show you the spare room, you can put your clothes in there, I have not made my mind up yet what I will do with Charles."

"Well I can move them, it will only take a few minutes,

then I can put mine in with yours, find me some bags," he instructed.

"No, Rupert, you do not touch any of Charles's clothes, I am not getting him out of my life yet, if ever. You go into the spare room, I have made the bed up for you," I said in my usual quiet way.

"No Sam, not good enough, if you think I am staying here and not be in your bed, you have another think coming, you know how I feel about you, I truly love you, I even told you in front of Chas, that given the chance I would take you to bed and make love to you, there is nothing stopping me now he's not around."

I burst out crying, I can't take this.

"Christ almighty Sam I am only saying as it is, I want to take you to bed, I will make you forget Chas, once I have had you, you will be begging for more. So stop bloody crying I didn't think you were so sensitive, you never were with Chas," he snapped.

I wanted to scream, Chas is not here and that is why I am crying.

"Tell you what, I will go and unpack, you pop down and make my breakfast and then we will see what transpires, I wasn't thinking of reading or watching T.V for the two weeks I am here! Go on Sam run along, stop fucking crying like some spoiled brat!" That shocked me into stopping, I went down and cooked his breakfast, he came in and sat down.

"Sam you know the way to a mans heart this breakfast looks really good, are you not having any?" he asked.

"I had something earlier with Michael," I replied.

"Ah yes Michael, I bet he didn't let you say no to sex," he sneered.

"He did not force me to do anything," I wanted to add, I was up for it, but kept quiet.

"Sam I have got one or two problems, I thought you may be able to help me, I will pay you back with interest," I bristled for some reason. "You see I have got to have an apartment near to chambers, because when we are on a big case, the day does not end when court closes, we have all sorts of things that have to be dealt with by 9am the next day, when the case continues. I thought you could lend me the money, I need furniture, a new car, so I thought we could make it one big loan."

"So when you are in the apartment, would I come and be with you?" he threw his head back and laughed, I looked bewildered.

"Darling that could not happen, if you were there you would be too much a distraction, I would be wanting you in bed, so no I need it so I can work late, but it would just be for me alone. You know I want to win you round, I am so in love with you, I want us to get married and have children, if you are willing lots and lots of children, I think you would make a wonderful mother," he had took my hand and gently stroked it, I thought I could have been wrong he is sincere, I got up and walked round the table towards him, to collect the dirty pots, but he caught my hand and pulled me onto his knee.

"Sam I would never do anything to hurt you, I love you so much and I have been dreaming of what it would be like in bed with you, I want you so much, I would go down on my knees and beg you, if that is what you want?" he began kissing me round the neck and up towards my ear, he pushed one hand up my sweater, pushed my bra up and was fondling my breasts.

"Sam put your hand between my legs, feel what you do to me, I have got to see your wonderful tits, they feel big and soft and need my lips round them," he stood up with me in his arms and carried me upstairs and stood me by my bed.

Before I could draw my breath my sweater was up over my head, I had to lift my arms fast, then my bra which was not covering anything went.

"Sam Oh Sam, I knew they looked inviting when you are dressed, but in the flesh you are gorgeous, they are calling for my attention," while he was talking, my skirt went to the floor followed by my thong. He looked at it and said, "Do you wear thongs often, you dirty little bitch, that wonderful bottom all naked, for any man to slip his hand up and have a crafty feel of your cunt."

What is it with him, he starts to make me feel special, then he comes out with a statement like that, I must have looked taken aback.

"Darling it was a joke, if you were mine, you would not wear anything like that to go out in, they would be for my pleasure only, I will not and do not want to share you with anyone, I want you to be mine and once you have let me fuck you, you will not want any other man, I promise you my darling."

Christ I thought, I had better get this over and done with, I would not like to miss out on the magic of his love making, he has got to be really something to surpass my Charles, and even better still, Michael.

"Why are you still fully dressed, I thought you wanted to make love to me," I whispered.

He wasn't expecting that "It will not take me a second, but please do not move, I want a good look at your delicious body, you really are good enough to eat Sam, look at my prick, I'll bet you have not seen one that big," he striped his shirt off and his trousers and that was it, no under pants or boxers?

I wanted to laugh even Mat who was smaller than Chas and Michael, although Michael, was bigger than both, all were bigger in any direction than he was. I decided not to say anything, he thinks he is Mr wonderful, who in gods name would tell him that?

He lay on the bed, I am trying to get the throw from underneath him, "What are you trying to do Sam?"

"I am trying to get the throw from under you, get onto the sheets they are easier to launder,"

"My darling we are going to have some action are we?" I wanted to say I can't wait, but words failed me.

I slipped between the sheets, he threw the top one off, "I want to see that body not hide it," he then proceeded to kiss me, it wasn't so bad once I relaxed, but it was just a kiss, it could have been my daddy. He squeezed with my breasts in passing, then his fingers were straight in, as far as he could get them, then within a second, he was inside me thrusting away like there is no tomorrow, suddenly he is groaning, moaning and he is coming.

That really could be entered somewhere as a record, in my opinion even, Mat lasted longer than that, although I think they must have gone to the same school to learn foreplay.

"I am sorry Sam, I have wanted you for so long, I could not help myself, I promise it will be better next time," he said.

"Right," I said, but thought next time, not now then, so I started getting out of bed thinking, any second he will stop me, but no I went straight into the bathroom, had a shower, put a bathrobe on, went to get dressed, he was still in bed, fast asleep.

I did all the laundry, but did not know what to do for dinner, because I did not know what he liked. I got two steak pies out to defrost, he did not appear until 5pm.

He came into the kitchen "Hello my darling that is a lovely cosy bed, how are you feeling? Did the earth move?"

I cannot lie "Not really, I never got started, you were in and out and finished!"

"Darling, the one person I wanted desperately to impress, and I have failed, it will be better next time, I have been dreaming about you for so long, I think I was excited at having you naked in bed, it went a bit haywire. Is there a cup of tea going please? Can I sort out the loan you're giving me, I have seen an apartment, which I would love, the bedrooms only need beds, the kitchen is fully fitted and has a table and chairs, so I would only really need a suite and TV, so it will not cost much to furnish."

"You said bedrooms, I thought the flat was just for you?"

"Yes it is, it was a slip of the tongue," he replied quickly.

"So how much is the flat?" I asked.

"£600,000 it is a bargain," he replied.

"How much? for a flat?"

"Well actually it is a Penthouse, it will include all overhead expenses, I will pay you back, once we are married it will be as much yours as mine," he said.

If I am paying for it, it will be all mine! "Alright, give me the agent and I will go and look?" I replied.

Suddenly something I clicked, Penthouse, £600,000, only needs beds etc., sound very much like Mats?

"There is no need for that my darling, trust me I will draw up some paperwork, with what you have loaned me, it will be all above board, then of course there is the car, there is a rather nice two seater sports I have wanted, so tell you what make the total one million, that will be it, everything I need I can get, I have a few debts from previous loans to pay off, then we can start planning a wedding for next year."

"1998 has only just come in, so you are talking about next year 1999?" I asked. Wanting to get it clear in my head.

"Well yes, because I have a lot to do, I have got to start saving, I cannot have you paying for everything,"

Really I thought, you could have fooled me, but I let it go.

"There was another thing, I cannot keep travelling from here every day, it would mean spending the week in Nottingham, and only seeing you sometimes at the weekend, I want to be with you a often as I can, so I think we should look for something nearer Nottingham, and bigger of course."

"Bigger? Why, what's wrong with this?" I asked.

"Well we want children or don't you?"he asked.

He knew bloody different "You know I want children."

"Well if we move now into something bigger, then as the family grows we will not have to keep moving into something bigger, this way is more cost effective, don't you see?"

"Yes I suppose you have got something there, how big are you thinking?" dare I ask.

"At least six to eight bedrooms, we would want bigger rooms downstairs, because we would be doing a lot of entertaining, it goes with the job," he said.

Of course it does, but I do want children, he may not be an ideal lover but perhaps he has not had a lot of practice, who am I kidding?

"You could possibly start when I go back to work in two weeks, I thought instead of you cooking every evening, we could go to a restaurant, I do not want you slaving for hours, I want us to enjoy these two weeks together."

"Alright," I said.

The first night he made love, was no more satisfying, he did not even get me going! Over a few nights, he seemed to get into a different mood, he became a bit more thoughtful towards me, although if he found me crying, he would hit the roof, tell me to pull myself together, stop acting like a spoilt brat, or words to that effect!

So if I felt low, I would lock myself in the bathroom. I finished my tablets after four nights, I started with the night mares again, I think I frightened Rupert to death. So he made a decision, we would have sex, that is all it was, there was no making love. Then he would go to sleep in the spare room, with the door shut, so I did not disturb his sleep.

He used to like to go to bed around 9pm, so when we got home after eating out, me paying of course, we went straight to bed had sex, it was not making love, I got as I just lay there, he did not seem to notice, there was only one person in the room he loved, and that was Rupert!

Several times when I woke from a nightmare and went to the bathroom, the spare room door was not quiet shut, so one night I went in, the bed was empty, when I stood very quiet I could hear his voice he was on the telephone, it was around 12.30 to 1am, I crept down the stairs, I could see the light on in the office, as I stood he was saying 'It will not be for long my darling, you knew the situation, look what we will have in the end, you know I love you, it will not be for long. Did you check the penthouse is it still for sale, okay I will try to get her to transfer some money for a deposit, until I get back, the week after next. Good night sweet dreams I love you very, very much."

I flew up the stairs closed my door, stood with my heart pounding, I could not make head nor tail of that conversation.

The following morning he said "I have to go out, could you lend me some money as I am short this month? I think about £350 should do." I looked at him in amazement.

"It is a reasonable amount. When will you be able to transfer me some money, I want to hold the apartment until I can get back, I think £250,000 will be enough, transfer it into my bank account, I have put my details on the pad in your office, I would like to get everything sorted as soon as possible."

I said "When you come back, we will go into Melton to the bank, together and we will do it then."

He said "You have my details get there this morning, I am going to pay you back, it is all temporary, I thought you might transfer the lot it is not that you cannot afford it! I would like to bet you paid a lot to Mr. Plod and did not ask questions, you are like a prostitute in reverse, you pay a man to fuck you, you are pathetic, at least I am honest he isn't," he snapped.

"What do you mean? Michael has always been honest with me?" I asked.

"I'll bet he did not tell you what your daddy called you?"

"What has daddy got to do with anything?"

"He was disgusted with you, you turned out to be a prostitute like your mother, the Trollop only you seduced not one, but both his sons, she's a slut, a dirty little slag, you belong in the gutter, he never wanted to see you again, he is so ashamed," he sneered.

"You're lying," he cut me off, before I could add anything.

"Ask Mr. Plod if you do not believe me. I think you would let any man fuck you, you do not seem to be very particular, who's cock is slipping inside you, you really are a cheap slut." he turned to go.

"Stop now! Why would my daddy lie to Michael, also they did not know one another, they have never met?" I stood waiting. "Well I asked you a question?"

"How do you mean, your father lie, he was being honest."

"How do you know, you have never met my daddy either."

He just stood looking at me. "Right explain this then, Mr Lawyer. You see I have no brothers, I am not anyone's sisters, in fact I do not even know who my parents were. I was left on the door step and daddy took me in and gave me their name, but they knew nothing about me." He stood for a second, still did not speak, so I said, "You are a two faced liar," so he flounced out, without another word.

After he left I needed to speak to someone, I could not ring Michael at his office, so I tried Julia's mobile and she answered.

"Samantha how lovely to hear from you, how are you my darling?" I began to cry, I couldn't stop, "Samantha can you drive towards Nottingham? I will drive out, we can meet at that nice little cafe on the main road, can you do it?"

"Yes, when?"

"I will see you in an hour, please drive carefully my darling," and she hung up. I ran upstairs and changed into something warm as it was blowing gales. I arrived at exactly the same time as Julia, she ran to me, put her arms round me and kissed me on the lips she lingered a bit, the tears started.

"Come on lets find a corner where we can talk you go and sit down, I will get the coffee."

"Before you tell me what has happened, I may as well tell you, Michael has put his flat on the market, he has moved back home, back to his old bedroom, he is very down, I know he is desperately worried about you, now come on tell me."

So I started at the beginning of Rupert moving in, right from his bag of washing, the money, the house, the car, the apartment, his phone calls during the night, then what he said Michael had said my daddy had told him, I told her everything.

She was shocked "I knew I wasn't keen on him, but I would have never thought him this bad, does he know how much money you have exactly?"

"No I keep bank statements and the like locked up. He told me he has all the details about the accident and is suing the company for two million, but he seems to think if he gets any pay out for me, he will keep it and invest it on my behalf."

"Samantha I was so hoping I had misjudged him, I dare not tell Michael everything, he will go ape. I will get someone to do a bit of digging, what will happen when he restarts work, will he be coming to you?"

"No not until I move nearer Nottingham. Plus he is

supposed to be with me for two weeks, but he is never in. I was wondering because I do not need a job for money but I need something to get me out of the house, I saw an advert somewhere about hospitals where they have a League of Friends which is run by volunteers, then if he didn't come home, at least I would be doing something useful and get out meeting people. My nightmares are back only once a night, he sleeps in the spare room so I do not disturb him, that is how I heard his phone call. I know I do not love him, but I want children, he is happy with that, that is why we need a big house, so we do not have to keep moving," I said.

"Darling, think a minute, think what you overheard him say on the phone, he is not planning on being with you, let alone get married. Please do not, put his name on any property, it must be in your name only, darling why don't you give him his marching orders, come and stay with me, I want to look after you," she said looking deep into my eyes.

"I cannot be a burden to you, I have got to get used to Charles not being here. I do not know what I can do, because he said he will deal with all legalities, so my hands are tied," I said.

Julia gave a big sigh "I am so afraid from what you have told me, that if you buy another house, he will put it solely in his name and claim he paid for it. Look round by all means, but do not do anything in haste, bide your time don't let him hassle you, he thinks he is clever, but he is not going to bleed you dry, for his own ends. I have got his number and he is not going to fleece you to line his pockets, I have already got someone looking into Mr Russell-Brown," she stated.

"I go to the hospital in Melton Mowbray twice a month, I know they have a 'League of Friends' and always looking for volunteers, make some enquiries there, it is time you got out into the big wide world my love, I think the world of you, you are the daughter I never had. I do love you very much, I am here for you whatever happens please remember that. Please feel free to ring me even for just a chat and catch up, if possible in the evening when I am at home, but I will give you my office number, because if I am busy or not there my secretary will take a message and get it to me wherever I am. Take care my darling," she hugged and kissed me, I was full up when we parted.

On the way home I went into Melton, found the hospital and made some enquiries, yes they were desperate for volunteers, but no one was there that day, but they took my details and said someone would ring me, so I went home. Still no sign of lover boy.

He arrived at 6.30pm the following day, with the biggest bouquet of flowers "I am so sorry I got delayed, I hope these will help my tardiness," he put his arms round me and gave me his usual kiss. It was too late to go out for a meal, so I got something out of the freezer and did a quick meal, he opened a bottle of wine and lingered over dinner, he had changed, he suggested we take the bottle of wine to bed and finish it in bed. Which we did, I wanted to bring up about his lies, but thought better of it.

He was actually a little bit romantic, his kisses were more gentle, he began to arouse me with his form of foreplay, two fingers in and out a couple of times, oh joy! There was still a lot to be desired, but he actually made love (I use the term lightly) a second time, it must have seemed a marathon to him, but he rose to the occasion both times and yes I felt I was actually heading towards something? Not sure what, there's a long way to go before I get there!

His kisses were completely different, he was different. I wanted to ask him where he had been to make this change, but I didn't want to spoil it. I wondered if it was a guilty conscience. This continued until the end of his two weeks.

The very last night, I did actually feel as though I was getting as far as having a climax and I did! The earth didn't actually move! He looked surprised, I do not think he has fucked any girl who has actually had one! In fact thinking about it, he probably didn't know what was happening to me? He said he was loathe to leave me. I asked him to please ring regularly and he agreed, but he said he might be able to get away early Wednesday and if so he would get his secretary to ring me, but said lets not go out for dinner and waste time, he could not wait to get home because I excited him so much in bed and he wanted more. Now that was a shock!

I had been to the hospital, I was due to start the following day, Tuesday at 9.30 am to 3.30 pm. Then the same every day Monday to Friday.

I loved it I had a trolley to take round to the wards and side wards, it had newspapers, magazines, crisps, chocolates and sweets. I did very well, they were really pleased with me and I really enjoyed it. Rupert did not get home that Wednesday, I had not seen or heard from him since he left that day. I thought it funny because he wanted money for the apartment.

Julia and I spoke usually twice a week, but could not meet now I had my little job.

What I did not like was being on my own at night, I did not sleep very well at all. I had started double locking the front door, putting the bolts on front and back and the chains. I knew Rupert had a key, I didn't want him wandering in, in the middle of the night and frightening me to death.

I had never thought about my new diary for 1998 this year. So one evening I sat in the office and transferred everything from the old one to the new, although there was not much. But then I found I should have gone for my birth control injection on the 2nd/3rd January, it was now 27th, I had not been protected still I do not suppose it would matter.

The following day I rang round for a private Gynaecologist but could not get an appointment for two weeks, which I made for a Monday morning at 11am which was the 15th February.

I rang Julia, we had a chat I told her about the injection, but she thought I would be alright, but she said they will examine you anyway before they inject you, to check all is well, but I think you will be alright because you haven't had sex since he disappeared on the 18th January, so it was only 16 day window, maximum..

I loved my little job there was one lovely gentleman, he wasn't old, far from it. He was in a private ward and he called me his little angel, he was lovely, but he was dying, I felt so sad.

One Tuesday I was late getting round and it was nearly lunch time, his door was always open, "Here she is my little angel, I thought you had forgotten me?" he said.

"I could not do that Mr Saddler, my darling, is it your paper and sweets? You know you will ruin your teeth," he laughed loud.

"Yes my darling" then he spoke to a visitor who must have been behind the door "You look, if you do not think she is an angel, you will want your eyes testing," they both laughed.

As I went through the door it was pushed to, before I could turn a voice said "She is an angel, my angel," I turned and there was Michael all handsome in his uniform, we threw ourselves into each others arms and he whispered.

"My darling I have missed you so much," and then our lips met, ignoring poor Mr Saddler, who must have been gob smacked, we could not break apart, it was poor Mr Saddler, who spoke;

"Excuse me, do you two know each other then?" we had to break apart and laugh.

Michael said "Very slightly," I laughed, I couldn't remember the last time I laughed like that. "This is my wonderful Samantha, George is an old friend and colleague, we first met at Hendon and have been friends since," he said.

"She makes my day worth waking up for," Mr Saddler said "I miss her Saturday, and Sundays, "She is the best we have ever had, nothing is too much trouble, she is so sweet and charming and last but not least she always looks amazing, here's me wishing I was twenty years younger, fit and healthy of course, and all the time you know her, you always were a lucky bugger Michael," we both laughed but he kept his arm round me.

"Julia tells me things are not very good, she will not fill me in, but says you are not very happy, why didn't you call me?"

"I am sorry, I wanted to, but I did not like to telephone you at the office, and at first I didn't feel I had any privacy, he watched me all the time, sorry," I said.

"Do you get a break?" he asked.

"I have about 15 minutes for a coffee," I replied.

"How long before your break?"

"Well usually I have already had it, but I am late, I will stop when I get to the end of these private wards," I replied.

"I will meet you in the coffee shop, I must talk to you," he was so sincere.

"Alright," I said "I had better get on," So I finished that corridor, went to the busy coffee shop, I could see Michael already there with two coffees on the little table, I went straight over to him, as I neared he stood up, took my hands and kissed me full on the lips, in the front of all these people, then we sat down.

"It is surprising what a kiss from you can do, I don't mean sexually, but I have missed your kisses so much, they always make me feel better," he said "Tell me what has happened?"

"I haven't got time to tell you now it is too long, I have missed you all the time, not just in bed, but you always made me feel better and you took care of me," I said.

"Rupert wants me to move nearer to Nottingham, that is why he does not come home very often, because of the travelling.

Once I have found somewhere that is, I keep looking but when he phones me to see what's happening, I describe anything I think might be worth a viewing, there is always something wrong, mainly not enough bedrooms. Until then some evenings they are working till about 10pm, so he wants me to buy an apartment he has seen, for those nights when it is too late to travel home, " I say.

"For a start how bloody bedrooms do a couple need, okay I can see the travelling is too long when you have to do it twice a day, but bedrooms?"

"Well he wants us to have children, lots of children, I am all for that because that is all I want, but he wants six bedrooms minimum but eight would be ideal. He wants more room downstairs for the lavish entertaining we will be doing, it goes with the job according to Rupert."

"So who is putting up the money for this, are you going halves?" he asked looking worried.

"Well no, because he still doesn't earn a lot, he has debts from loans he has borrowed but cannot repay, he lodges in a room at a friends, but is not comfortable because they are newly weds and he spends most of the time, trying to work in a little room which he pays £100 a week for just the room, no meals," I say.

"£100 a week for a little room, he is having you on, I know the approximate salary he gets, even if he was paying £100 a week for ten rooms, he would have more than enough to pay what he owes and buy something in cash to live in," he sounded a bit put out "Does he give you anything towards the costs of living," he quizzed.

"No he has never offered, he is not like you, but when I think he does not pay for anything, if we go out, he holds his hand out for parking, he buys a different newspaper to the one I have delivered, and tells me each day he needs money for his papers and lunch, I did at first say I would do him a packed lunch, all I got was, you do not think someone in my high standing, is going to be seen with a packed lunch, no Sam you must accept who I am, and look up to me for what I am, if you give me £200 a day or if it's easier give me the whole lot on a Monday £1,000.00," I tell him.

"Apart from all that have you given him anything else?" he looked worried.

"When he went out the third day he was living with me, he said he was short this month, could I lend him something, when I asked how much he asked for £350, I got a bit stroppy he said you will get it all back, it's hard enough me having to ask but you make me feel very guilty, you know everything I have will be yours when we marry next year," Michael was visibly taken aback, he looked shocked.

"You are not seriously thinking of marrying that piece of shit are you?" he was shaking with rage and tried to keep his voice down and under control.

"Well he said he loved me, it is all he has wanted since our very first meeting, I know at first he was crap in bed, but after that day and the £350, he was very much changed, his kisses were different I actually had an orgasm."

"An? One! Samantha, what are you saying, you could have one or two before you got out of bed in the morning, you mean he is not as good as he brags he is. So what else money wise, come on the truth?"

"Michael I have got to get back," I had to get away I didn't want anyone to know, especially my lovely Michael, but he held my wrist tight "Well the morning of the £350 he wanted me to transfer some money to his account for a deposit on, well he called it a Penthouse, £250,000 I said we would go to the bank when he came home, but he said I had all his details in the office on my note book I did not need him, but I did not go by the time he came home it was too late," I said.

"So how much is this Penthouse and what else?" he demanded.

"£600,000 but he would only need to part furnish it, because a lot was fitted, then there would be fees etc., so he thought if I gave him £1,000,000 as one loan, that would cover everything including, his car and debts, he said he would sort the paper work and that would cost me nothing," he cut me off.

"One million? where the bloody hell does a car come in, tell me please, tell me you have not given it him?" he demanded.

"No only because he does not ring very often and when he does he is in a hurry, I fire questions at him so he never has chance to talk about money. Plus I have a feeling that the apartment sounds like ours, well Matthews," I thought I sounded upbeat.

"You do not give him anything else, I am going to have to do some checking, darling why did you not tell me? Julia is very vague, so I assume she does know something. I know you have to go but I promise I will ring you tomorrow evening," he said.

"Yes I promise I will not give him any more."

True to his word he phoned me, we had a long chat, he said he was getting someone looking into Rupert, but had mentioned it to Julia and she said she had been doing some checking and had already found out something, so leave it with us, I think Rupert will have some questions to answer.

The following Monday I went for my appointment and explained to the nice Doctor "I will have to do an internal, as I gather you have had intercourse since your protection wore off, go and strip your bottom half off behind the curtain and tell me when you are ready," I began to feel nervous I told him I was ready, he came round the curtain with his gloves on, switched the lamp on and shone it towards me, a few seconds later, "Yes, too late, I am afraid you are in the very early stages of pregnancy, I would say three weeks but you are definitely pregnant," he said.

"Are you sure?" I said grinning like a Cheshire cat.

"Yes, I gather you are pleased with the news."

"More than you will ever know," I thought a good job I had said Mrs Windsor when I booked the appointment. I will not tell anyone although I am bursting.

"Yes leave it for a few more weeks, will you be staying with me as your Gynaecologist?"

"If I may please Mr Croft?"

"It will be my pleasure, now let me give you another appointment, but if something happens ring my secretary, and she will give you an earlier one," he wrote on his card "This has all my details and my secretaries on and I have made your appointment for 11th April, which is eight weeks, so plus however far you are, I will be able to give you a date or an approximate date," he stated.

"Thank you so very much Mr Croft," I said.

"My pleasure," he said and I almost skipped away.

I was dying to tell someone but I do not want to tempt providence, I now had a pattern to my life, my little job I was still enjoying.

Monday, I went downhill when I got to Mr Saddlers room, the door was open but the bed was bare no sheets. A nurse was just coming along and she saw me and one look she knew, "I am so sorry Samantha he died on Sunday," I just broke down in tears, I could not wait to get home the first thing I did I phoned Michael he took a while but he answered;

"Michael did you know? Mr Saddler has died?"

"Samantha darling no I didn't, I was going to see him

tomorrow," I was in bits "Sweetie would you like to come over?"
"Would you please?" I asked.

Chapter eight

Two hours later he arrived, he took me in his arms and I sobbed, he was kissing my forehead and holding me close, I felt so safe. When he held me away, he had tears running down his cheeks "I have known George since we were seventeen, we have always been close and kept in touch, met when we had time I shall miss him so much. Can I make you a cup of tea?" he asked.

"No I will make it, you come into the kitchen, can I get you anything to eat, I think you have lost weight!" I said not thinking.

"That could be because I have been worried about the love of my life, I have missed you so much, you will never know, you still give me an erection just looking at you, I want you so badly, as soon as I close my eyes at night all I see is you. Julia has been brilliant she knows how I feel about you, she has been doing her best to cheer me up, but nothing works," I give him his tea and then we sat at the table, for a long time we didn't speak we really knew how we felt "So hows things with Rupert, have you given him any more money?" he asked.

"No because I have not seen him or heard from him, I cannot ring him because I do not know his office number and he has changed his mobile so I do not even know that number?"

"Well that is a blessing in a way," we sat and just chatted about things nothing in particular it was 7.30 and he had just said "I am afraid I will have to go Samantha, I really don't but," he stopped at the same time as I heard the front door.

Who came storming through the door but Rupert.

"Bloody good this is as soon as my backs turned you two are back together again, how long have you been here? how many times have you visited before? I'll bet you have been fucking behind my back, after everything I have done for you Sam, this is the way you treat me."

I stood, I think my mouth was open, I was just going to speak when Michael did.

"Don't you come in here making accusations that are not true, this is the first time I have called, it is only because Samantha was distressed over a death, I came to make sure she was alright, seeing as you cannot be bothered to come home, not even make a telephone call, don't tar everyone with the same brush. You low life playing on a young lady wanting to rob her of money with lies, where is it you live, ah yes a friends bedroom you rent for £100 a week, so who is the owner of that expensive apartment in Mapperley where you spend most of your nights? answer me that?" he was furious "And what is 'all I have done for you Sam' all what Rupert, you are a liar," he demanded.

"What do you mean?" I innocently asked.

"Nothing, your Mr plod has got it wrong, he is trying to turn you against me, I have been staying there while the owner is on holiday clever sod!" he snapped.

"So it's Mrs Russell-Brown's apartment is it? That would not be your mother, she has a big country mansion courtesy of your poor deluded father? She is far too young to be anyone's mother, why do you walk along kissing and cuddling, when you both leave in the mornings, you have barked up the wrong tree Rupert, you might be able to dictate and throw your weight around with kind, innocent Samantha, you think you are so clever."

"You can't talk to me like that, in my own house, I think you had better leave Mr Plod, I will deal with you shortly Sam," I was about to speak but Michael said.

"Your house, since when? you have not spent a penny while you have been here, Samantha has paid for everything, you belong in the gutter you are so low, I would not spit on you. You are also a bare faced liar, I have never met Samantha's father, let alone told you something he has said about her, and I will also underline, that you are out of order, telling people that she committed incest by marrying her brothers. If I hear any more, I will have you will be in court!"

I stood with my mouth open, I was amazed.

Samantha in the hall please," and he took my arm "Please darling do not stay here, come home with me," he was begging.

"Michael I do not understand was that true what you said? I cannot come with you I have to speak to Rupert urgently," I said.

"Yes my darling I would not lie to you, you can see he is only with you to bleed you dry, you do not give him any more money and what is so important?"

"I am sorry Michael I cannot tell you at the moment, I have to speak to Rupert," he gave me a quick kiss and was gone.

I went back into the kitchen.

"You must think I was born yesterday, you have been fucking around with him he is old enough to be your father," I opened my mouth to speak, he slapped me twice across my face. It was the shock and pain that made me just stand there.

"Yes you see you cannot deny it, you are a slut, who gets married to not one but two brothers only some little low life bitch, but I have to admit you are bloody good in bed and you are always ready and up for it," before he went any further, I swung my arm as hard as I could and slapped him across the face, his face was a picture.

"You have got it so wrong Rupert, I was willing to finance you with whatever you wanted, you could have had it all, I would happily given you the whole nine or so million. I have already told you, Michael has just told you, I do not have any brothers, I married brothers yes, but not mine," he was absolutely astonished when I said how much. He totally ignored most of what I had said.

"How much are you worth nine million or more?"

"Yes plus if you get damages, you said you loved me and wanted children, but you didn't want that did you, you would never have married me would you?"

"Sam darling I did not mean all those things, I was so mad when I saw he was here, I just saw red please forgive me, please, please my darling I will do anything just forget what I said."

I could not believe he thinks I could forget, "You changed so quickly, was it the thought of all the money you have just kicked into touch? I had something to tell you but I cannot contact you, so I have had to wait until you decide to honour me with your presence, I am pregnant with your baby, I know you said you wanted to wait but I forgot to have my injection which was due the 3rd or 4th January, but we both want children and this could seal our relationship," I said.

"A baby, a fucking baby, you stupid half wit, you bloody slapper, it's not mine!"

At first he was slapping my face, then his fists were landing hard on my face, then punching me anywhere, he banged my head against the wall, my head was ringing, he kept punching me in the tummy, then in his rage he took off his belt, and was beating me with it. Then he hit me so hard I fell down heavily against a solid wooden chair, then he was kicking me in my tummy and anywhere he could hurt me. All the time I was trying to get up, he was landing kicks and blows everywhere. I eventually managed to get up, took hold of the chair and smashed it onto him it was a solid wooden chair so it did not break, he sort of hunched up but it caught him across the left side of this neck and left ear but it shocked him and he stopped.

"That fucking baby is not mine, it's his or anyone you were happy to give yourself to, you can't wait to lay down a have a prick in your cunt, you have the audacity to say I am the father. I am not paying for you fucking around, I bet you do not know who the father is? I bet every night, it has been someone different, get rid of it now or you will never see me again!"

"That would be too fucking soon, get your fucking things, these locks will be changed, so do not try to come back. You think you are so good, you think women should fall at your feet, I have news for you a teenager could make love 100% better than you do. All you want, self gratification and that is it, a women is just for you to take, you do not give anything, she is not supposed to get pleasure, that went out of date years ago. This is 1998 and most women enjoy sex with someone who knows how to do it, you have not got a clue, I could give you the name of a good teacher," I could not believe I had said all that without him shouting me down, but that was just it, I was shouting and screaming for the first time in my life, my throat hurt, I was trembling.

I went upstairs with great difficulties, because everywhere hurt so much, I know I was bleeding, where his belt buckle had cut into my skin, but I was also furious. I cleared all his stuff out of the bathroom, I got all his dirty washing out of the laundry bin, stuffed it all in an old bag, went into the spare room, he was carefully getting his clothes out, folding them neatly, I just grabbed some and stuffed them in the bag with his dirty washing. Then the remainder I shoved into an empty case roughly which was on the bed.

"You can't do that, they will be all wrinkled." I ignored him, got his T shirts and sweaters out of the drawers and stuffed them in the same case, he was trying to lift things out and fold, I shut the lid quickly, all the stuff he had taken out, I opened the window and threw it onto the wet, muddy car standing below. I grabbed the rest of his stuff, he was trying to fold and stuffed it in the case, it was a bit full so I pulled things in and out, purposely unfolding his suits he had already packed.

"Now you can either carry them or I will gladly throw them out of the window and make sure the catches are unfastened first," he ran fast, like a scolded cat, not a word, not a sound then when he was safely outside, like a spoiled child, he turned, and shouted;

"You are going to regret this you bitch, I will be suing you, you are not getting away with this, I will take you to the cleaners, and show you up for the lying prostitute that you are."

I slammed the door shut, locked and bolted it and wilted to the floor, sobbing. I lay there for a long, long time. I switched off the lights and went and lay on the bed, I did not get undressed because I knew I was not going to sleep, I didn't know where hurt most from the beating. I think the bleeding had stopped, where the buckle of his belt had slashed me, but what did it matter, nothing mattered now.

Everything was going round, replay after replay, I went to the cabinet in the bathroom. Christ I have never replaced the tablets. I felt numb I could not think straight. I desperately wanted a baby, but not his, it was round and round, I was still awake at 6am, it was getting light. I went to the kitchen and made a cup of tea and just sat I could not think straight, I must have nodded off, because my head was on my arm on the table it was 9.30am.

When I tried to get up, I seem to have seized up, everywhere hurt, I had a job to walk, I was so stiff, any movement was excruciating.

I had come to a decision I knew what I was going to do. I rang Julia it was her secretary "Can you give Julia a message, I am going away and I want to thank her for everything, tell her I love her very much, it's Samantha."

So next, I rang Michael hoping he would not be in his office. He answered after the second ring. "Samantha I have been so worried are you alright,what happened?"

"Michael I am going away for a while, (I am trying not to cry) I want to say thank you for everything you have done for me, it is over with Rupert, he does not want me or our baby. I love you Michael, Good bye and I hung up.

I made sure everywhere was clean and tidy downstairs, although it took a long time, because of the pains through-out my body and head.

I went to the store of daddy's booze, found an unopened litre bottle of gin, went upstairs and began filling the bath, I went and tidied the bed, made sure everywhere was clean. I undressed put my clothes in the laundry bin, cleaned my teeth, the bath water is so slow, I ran some cold to fill it faster, but is would cool it too much, it had to be hot. I waited, then I stood in, but the water it was so hot, I was slowly lowering myself down, but realised I needed the loo, so I had to get out, then back in again, it was still hot! I gradually by letting myself down slowly, I got sat down. Then I could not open the cap of the bottle, so I had to get out again, dry my hands and opened it, then climbed back in.

I realised the phone had been ringing for ages, I forgot to put the answering machine on, but I wasn't going back downstairs. I took a sip of the neat gin, it is horrible, the tears started to flow, I just thought of Charles, and began sipping the gin, as soon as I swallowed it, I took another sip, it was fowl, I felt sick. Then I began to take a mouthful, then swallowed, I began to get used to it. I turned the hot tap on to fill the bath to the top, I did not want to fill it too full and wet the floor, the Gin was going down, I was going very fuzzy, I had ringing in my head. Charles I will be with you soon, I took two big drinks of the gin, I don't feel very well, I feel sick, my heads going round, everything is going blurry, I close my eyes, see Charles.

The next thing, I am choking, I am gasping for air, I am being sick, a fuzzy voice is crying "Samantha please, please darling breathe, breathe darling," I am lying on towels on the bathroom floor, I think Michael is holding me, I am face down I am sick again, he holds my head up them drags me with the towels out of the way, I am coughing and spluttering my head is banging, like someone is still hitting me, like Rupert did yesterday, then I begin to gasp and cry.

"Why didn't you leave me, I want to be with Charles, please, put me back," it didn't sound like me I was all crackly, my throat is sore, my left eye hurts, I can only see out of the other one. My whole body hurts, my face is covered with my hair. By now he is cradling me in his arms, I can just see his face is wet with tears, his phone rings, it must be on the floor he picks it up.

"No round the back, the stable door is open,"

In rushes Julia."Oh darling what have you done, why didn't you tell either of us,"

My throat hurts from screaming at Rupert, I cry, a croak came out. "I want to be with Charles, please." I cry.

"Darling it will not happen, there is nothing once we have gone, we are going to take you home, we will take care of you," Julia's face was full of concern, and wet with tears. "Have you any more bathrobes?" she asked. "God whatever happened to your face, she gently moved my hair, Michael her face is all battered and bruised, her left eye is closed and blackish purple, look at her neck," she moved the towels "Michael look at her body, she is covered in blood and bruises, did Rupert do this?" I nodded.

"God how did I miss those, all I thought of was getting her out of the bath and breathing again, I thought she had slit her wrist, there was so much blood. He is not going to get out of this, the bloody low life."

Julia left the bathroom and returned with two bathrobes she started putting them together one inside the other. "We cannot start trying to dress her, if we put these on, then wrap her in blankets, we will go in my car. Have you got any sanitary towels, not Tampax?" I shook my head "We will improvise with towels, is there anything here of value not locked up?" I shook my head, "Are your bank details locked up" I nodded, "You will not need clothes. Michael darling, you have had a shock, I will get you a little tot? you will not be driving."

"I think I could drink a bottle, if I hadn't thought what Samantha had said, I could have been too late, that's why I told my secretary to ring you, I got switchboard to ring here, to keep ringing in case Samantha decided to answer. Oh god," he hugged me tighter and kissed my forehead, he was really crying. I hurt, all of me hurts, there are pains everywhere.

"I got in because she forgot to bolt the top of the stable door to the bottom, if I had, had to break in I would have been too late," he was really crying. What have I reduced this wonderful man to?

"I feel sick," I croaked.

Julia grabbed a rubbish bucket, I was so sick, it went on and on until there was nothing left, she gave me a small glass of water, "Just a little sip," she said gently "I will go and get some blankets," she came back with two and some small hand towels. "Try to sit her up a bit darling, so I can slip the wet towels off and put the bathrobes on, I have some pins so they will hold the pad of towels between your legs, you know you have lost the baby don't you?" I began to cry and cry "Look at her arms, he must have he held her arms very tight to bruise like that, it's not just at her front but the back also, look at her tummy, God what has that bloody piece of shit done to you? he's an animal," she was furious.

I croaked "I am a murderer, it's all his fault," I cried.

"Just let us get you home," she wrapped the robes round me, I let out a cry of pain. "Sorry darling but I have to make sure you will be warm enough. I will hold her, if you stand up we will get her downstairs on the sofa, I will get you a drink, and come up here and sort out. Your sleeves are wet through, you had better slip that off."

"I have my overcoat in the back of the car," he said.

"I will get it for you, you get Samantha on the sofa." he gently lifted me, I cried out in pain, he carried me downstairs, as though I were egg shells, but I still hurt, he gently lay me down.

Julia came in and passed him a big glass of whisky. He sat on the sofa with me "My darling why didn't you tell me, you know I would do anything for you, I would have looked after you."

I took his hand and squeezed it then croaked "I didn't want any part of him, it would not have been fair on a baby. I didn't want to be a murderer, I didn't want to live any longer, I thought I would be better gone, no trouble to anyone any more," my voice gave out.

"Darling why is your voice so croaky and hoarse?" he asked.

I crackled, croaked and husky "I was screaming at him."

"Don't say any more, just close your eyes and rest."

Julia came in. "That is all done, I have thrown all the towels and things in the dustbin, I have cleaned the bathroom. Samantha darling will you please sip this water darling, just a sip at a time," she put her Doctors bag on the coffee table "Have you a sore throat?"

Michael answered, "She says she screamed at Rupert, I do not know what it would sound like? coming from someone who never raises her voice to anyone, I gather this is the result."

"Right Michael, how are you feeling? Are you ready for the drive home? Honestly? if not there is nothing to stop us, staying here, and travel tomorrow." she offered.

"No let us get her home, then take it from there, the problem is it will be left to you, seeing as I said do not call an ambulance, I want to keep this between us," he said.

"That is alright, the reason I was a while, I phoned my secretary, to get her to ring my appointments, and make new ones as soon as possible, if not she was to give them Franks number. I told her I would ring later to see what has been done, so no problem. I will take time off for as long as I need to, I want dearest Samantha to be well and fully recovered before I leave her."

Michael said "Just give me a few minutes, I need to make a couple of urgent calls before we leave," he soon came back.

"Michael, can you hold her up please, I want to give her an injection," Julia said.

"What kind of injection?" he asked.

"Like I gave her before, it will help her, feel a lot better."

"You cannot not until we get her home, I need her awake," then silence but I know they were mouthing something to each other.

His hands slipped under neath me, I flinched and moaned, my back really hurts, I let out a cry of pain, Michael had lifted me up in his arm, kissed me on the lips and carried me to the car, he slid me gently across the back seat. I moaned in agony, then he slid in, he held my head up and put it on his lap, Julia opened the other door and threw another blanket on me because I was shivering, Michael held me up close to his chest, he felt warm and I must have dozed off.

The next thing I was in bed all nice and warm, it was pastel pink and very pale green, there was Michael sat in a chair fast asleep, with a newspaper creased in front of him.

There was a glass of water on the cabinet, I raised up on an elbow and drank, I was so thirsty, I drank it all, lay down again. I hear a door bell ring, and voices, Michael must have heard, he suddenly opened his eyes, then he saw me watching him, he got up and came straight over to the bed, he knelt at the side, taking my face in his hands and giving me the sweetest purest kiss, "I am better now my Prince has kissed me," I croaked, he smiled at me.

"I have to leave you for a minute," he left the room, I could hear his voice and Julia's and another one, but I could not tell what they were saying, then Julia and a middle aged man came in.

"Darling this is a Doctor, he wants to examine you head to toe, because of your injuries, he will want to take photographs of you, do you think if I help you, you could stand on the floor, can I take your night dress off?" I nodded, held my arms up so she could take it off. I looked down and I had any old fashioned type sanitary towel hooked on a narrow belt round my waist. But I was bruised everywhere, some of my skin was cut and grazed and was covered in dried blood.

The Doctor started taking photographs of me from every angle, front, back, both sides, arms up, arms down, so he could photograph everywhere. Then all round my neck, close up of different angles of my face. Then he lay his camera down. "Can you sit sideways on the bed please?" he asked. Then he sat at the side of me. "Can I just examine your head if it hurts at all please let me know," he touch the left side.

"Ouch that hurts," I croaked.

"Yes I am not surprised, you have a large lump on the left side of your head," he said, "Were you struck on the head with an object?"

"No but he punched me with his fist, I fell and hit my head against a dining chair," I croaked.

"Can you tell me how many times he struck you?"

"No idea he seemed to have lost it, I thought it would never end, especially when he started using his belt," while he was talking Julia put my nightdress back on again, she sat with her arms round me holding me close.

"Have you any other pains? I have to know."

"My back really hurts," I replied. He lifted my nightdress and gently pressed, I let out a loud cry.

"What provoked him?" there was a tap on the door.

"Can I come in?" asked Michael

"Yes," the Doctor said. So I continued;

"A lovely man I knew had died, I rang (I looked up at Michael I did not know whether I should say it was him but he nodded) Michael to see if he knew he had died, I knew they went back a long way, he said he would come round, because I was upset,." I had to stop, I felt so full up, the tears were in torrents again, "I made him a cup of tea, we were sat talking in the kitchen, suddenly we heard the door and Rupert came storming in," I carried on and told him what happened.

"Thank you Mrs Windsor," he left the room with Michael.

"Can I get you something to eat?" Julia asked.

"No but I would like a gallon of tea, please," I was still very hoarse.

"I lay back on the pillows and closed my eyes, I was so tired but everything hurt, Michael came in and said;

"Can I come in? I have someone with me are you decent?" he came in with two men, "Samantha these are Police Officers, they want you to make a statement about Rupert, how you got your injuries, it will be recorded, typed up, then brought back for you to read and sign it, do you want me to go or stay?"

"Can you please stay?"

Then in walked Julia with a tray with tea, she poured it, left the tray close to me so I could keep filling it up, she popped out, then came back with another chair.

"Where do you want me to start?" I croaked.

"From when Rupert came home onwards, everything including if Michael here had said anything, any little detail you can remember."

"I have just told the Doctor everything," I said.

"Yes Mrs Windsor, we know but we have to get our own independent account, but we have been instructed to get this moving, like yesterday," he smiled. "Also with the Doctors report and photographs, it makes the case water tight, you cannot dispute photographs!"

So I went through it all again, I told them everything, I kept stopping for a drink, they did enquire why I was hoarse, so I explained, I frequently looked at Michael, he smiled.

When I finished "Could you please tell me what this is about?" they looked at one another.

"You know who the Chief Constable is?"

I said "Yes."

"When he tells us to move, we move, no questions. He has made a formal complaint against Rupert Russell-Brown, the complaint is Grievous Body Harm on you, his deception to get money out of you. We have to ascertain that facts. So have you any money Mrs Windsor? The Chief Constable, has given us details of his findings, whereby Rupert Russell-Brown told you one thing and the simple fact is something entirely different. So have you any money of your own and the approximate amount?" he asked.

"Yes I have some money, I think at present it is in the region of eight or nine million pounds, plus Charles had a million insurance, Rupert was claiming damages from the company of the driver who killed Charles," the tears were falling fast.

"Rupert told her, he was trying for two million, but whatever he got, he would invest on her behalf!" Michael said. "But so far nothing has been forthcoming."

"Mrs Windsor did he know what you were worth?"

"He knew I had something, but after he beat me, I told him to leave, I told him then, his jaw had dropped open, I said he could have had the lot, if I was married with children I would have been happy," I said.

"So as far as you were aware, he was definitely going to marry you next year?

"Yes'" I replied, "Because when he said next year, I complained it was only just 1998. He told me he had to save, that is why it would have to be next year," I stated.

"Well I think we have covered that, we will get back."

Michael said "You will have to bring it here to be signed."

"Thank you sir, we will see ourselves out, goodbye Mrs Windsor, you have been very brave," one of them said.

Michael came back to me, he took me in his arms and gave me one of those sweet, chaste kisses again, I kiss him back with passion, I feel him waiver but he releases me "No my darling I cannot if I do, I will not be able to stop myself. I love you so much. Please lie down for a while, the Doc will be in soon,"

"Who will be in soon?" Julia said as she came round the door "Michael get off that bed, you will hurting my little girl, how do you feel about that injection now Michael?" she asked.

"She will have to be awake to read the statement and sign it, tomorrow, so sorry no injection sorry Doc," he said.

"I will give you some tablets my darling," she said straightening my hair with her hand "I want you to have a good long sleep, it is the best thing for you, what would you like to eat?" she asked.

"Nothing, just a drink please."

"Darling you have to eat," she urged.

"Please don't be cross with me," I muttered.

"Darling I am not cross with you, I am cross however, with that bloody animal," she said.

"Excuse me Doc, you should not speak like that in front of your patient," Michael said, I actually smiled, she gave him a friendly slap.

He came back and gave me another kiss but this time it was passionate "I love you, please get better, I want you so much, I cannot live without you any longer," I of course kissed him.

"I have missed you so much, I want you as much as ever, I dream about you and the lovely things we do together, I will get well soon."

"I cannot leave you again," he said, as Julia came in.

"Are you alright my love, I think we will have an early meal tonight, then you can go and rest, you look all in," she kissed him softly on the lips, and he left "One big cup of tea and two tablets, I will bring a glass of water in, for if you wake up, but you should sleep all evening and night," she kissed me full on the lips and left. I drank my tea had the tablets and drifted away.

The next time I wake up, the curtains are closed and a small lamp is lit on the cabinet with a glass of water, I gladly drink it and must have gone straight back to sleep.

The next time I wake up, it was a bright sunny day, the sun was streaming in the window, in the chair sat Julia "Hello my darling are you with us, what would you like to drink?"

"My throat is still sore and very croaky, can I have a gallon of tea please. I've lost count what day is it?"

"Monday 14th March. I forgot, I am sorry, I went in your handbag and found Mr Croft's number, I explained you had, had a miscarriage, and you were not well, I would ring and make an appointment as soon as you are well enough to travel, as you are staying with me, we are not in Melton Mowbray. I hope you don't mind darling?"

"No I cannot thank you enough, I am so much trouble to everyone it would have been better to let me go," I said.

"We could not do that, you know how Michael feels about you, and I love you, as though you were my own daughter, you are so sweet and kind, you have been through so much in your short life," she smiled and sat on the bed, held me tight and kissed my forehead "I forgot I rang the hospital and told them you were quiet ill, and you would be back in touch when you felt better, obviously they knew who I was."

"You see I have put you all to a lot of trouble, I should go home now but I really do appreciate all you have done for me."

"I don't think so Miss, let me pop and fetch some tea, because Michael and I have been talking, I want to tell you what about," she left but was soon back with a tray, with tea pot and a heap of toast "Right cup of tea first, then toast and I want you to eat it up, I have put extra butter in the dish and marmalade to help yourself," Then the door bell rang and Julia went I could hear voices and she came round the door with one of the police that was here yesterday.

"Good morning, I was hoping you were awake, can you read this and if everything is alright sign it, then I will phone it in, they will then be going to arrest him and bring him in for questioning," he smiled.

Julia said "Would you like to come for a cup of tea, then perhaps she will be able to read it, with no distractions."

I read it very carefully, it was almost word for word, as I got to the end Julia came in the policeman "I have read it thoroughly, it is exactly as I said, do I sign here at the bottom?" I asked.

He came round "Yes please and can you please date it," which I did.

"Thank you dear, I will get off, I have to call in now, thanks for the tea Mrs Roper," and he was gone.

"Where's Michael is he at work?"

"Yes he has carried on, but I told him when I thought I could leave you in his hands, he has booked time off work, then I will go back and everyone will be sorted, by the way your bleeding has stopped now."

"Thank you for all you have done for me, but I could go home and leave you to get on with your lives," I said.

"Sorry you are too much in our lives, we both love you very much only I as a mother, with Michael it goes much deeper. No wonder men fight over you, your money does not help either, look at Rupert, it is obvious he had planned to relieve you of as much as he could." she said. "Really Michael should not be for you, as you know he is old enough to be your father, you need someone younger to take you out, show you the world. I have never been over the moon about love making, yes he is a very good lover, the only man I have had, but I just cannot get enthused, like apparently you can, you like sex!"

"As we are being honest, I knew I loved Michael, but I soon realised that I was in love with him, as I was with Charles. Yes I do like sex, and all it entails, the feelings, the excitement, there are no words as to how I feel when I have a man does that to me, although I have to say Rupert was only good, satisfying himself." I said, "Do you not feel any dislike or jealousy because of what Michael and me have done? I can't get my head round it, especially sitting here discussing things like this. You have been so kind, and well I do not know where to start, you are very special, but I have been your husbands mistress, you know he has had plenty of women, you suggested a flat of his own, if I was in love with my husband, there is no way I would want to share him with anyone, it's adultery," I say.

"Well, let me ask you something else first, has Michael

ever said anything to you about me in a derogatory terms?" she waited.

"No, never, if ever you cropped up he always spoke good of you."

"Precisely often when men have extra martial relations, they call their wives, pull them apart and basically make out they are a total waste of space, to ease their consciences. I know Michael would never do that because he does love me, I am in love with Michael and always will be, I could not give him all he needs, so as long as he does not brazenly flaunt women in public, and was home when the children were, I was quiet happy. But now all that has changed, he did not want to go back to how he has been living, because for the first time in his life, he is madly in love with you my darling." she stopped to drink her tea.

"That is what true love does, if he cannot have you, then he does not want just anyone to satisfy his needs. I do not want him to be miserable, because I know he will be, he is not used to the feelings he has for you, he has never known anyone like you, you satisfy him as no other has ever done. When he thought you were having Rupert to live with you, I thought he would go mad, it was torturing him, the thought of you with someone else. He said the very first time he met you, he admired you, the next time he fancied you, there was something about you, that drew him to you." She sipped her tea.

"He was not conscious of what he was saying, it was the afternoon we brought you back here, he had knocked a tumbler of whisky straight back at your house. Then after we put you to bed he sat drinking, he hardly ate anything, which is not like Michael, he likes his food, but he drank a bottle of whisky. He sat with his head in his hands and he sobbed, I have never heard such heart break, I sat holding him, he clung to me, that is when he said I cannot live with out her Julia, I am so sorry," he was so sad "Then he told me, what I have just told you, he rings incessantly asking how you are, I am surprised he hasn't rung at least twice, something big must have happened at work, that can only be a good thing, he will have to concentrate on something else,"

"So have you told him, what he told you?" I asked.

"Good heavens no my love, he would die if he knew he had told me all that, that is why I am telling you, because now you say you are in love with him, we have got to get something sorted, but you must never tell him about all this, you promise."

"Yes I promise, I never break a promise, besides, I treasure you as a friend, but you are more than a friend because I do love you very much, I think because I never had a mother, I think what you are doing for me a mother would do for her own?" I said.

"Yes it is not just that, I only have sons, I always wanted a daughter, then you, sweet Samantha turn up, turn not just Michaels world upside down, but mine, I would be happy if you came here to live with us,   Michael said it would not work, I have told him I will never divorce him, I would never forgive him if he left me, after all I have tried to do to keep him happy, all these god knows how many years," she sounded very bitter, that is a first!

"You see I love you, I want to look after you, if you and Michael were not together, I would have you here with me" I was speechless.

"I could go home, but I am seriously thinking of moving nearer to Nottingham, I feel so isolated out there, I do want to be your friend," or so I thought. "I want children, Julia, how do you think Michael would feel?" I asked.

"Michael would be over the moon, especially with you, he would be so proud to have you as a partner, he knows he would never be able to marry you, until I die that is!" she said so mater of factly.

"Please do not talk of not being here, how would you feel if I had Michael's children?" I quizzed.

"Lets put it this way, if I cannot have you, then I want you to be with Michael, because we would still be close friends, babies? I would be over the moon, however, I would look at them as grand children, but he would be their father, so what mixed messages would we be sending out?" just then the telephone rang and it made us both jump "This will be Michael."

"Hello darling have you been busy?" she asked "No she is awake she is on her third cup of tea and she has actually eaten three slices of toast, of course you can. Michael wants a quick word."

"Hello Michael," I said.

"My darling it is lovely to hear you, how are you feeling, truthfully?"

"I am not too bad thank you, I am wondering if this Doctor will let me go and have a shower, I dare not ask if I can get up, she is really strict," she sits beaming at me, Michael is laughing.

"Well I could be a bit late tonight, something big has come

up, but please do not go to sleep until I have had a kiss from you, my love. Can you put Julia back on darling?" so I passed her the phone, they had a quick chat and he was gone.

"So what are we going to do? Would you be happy if Michael lived with me, like he did in his flat, and came home to you when you have a night out. I would have to move nearer because of Michael travelling, also I would like to think we could see each other more, so would that be any different, to how you have been living? but instead of seeing different women he would be with me?" I suggested.

"Well we have to do something, I think when he comes home we tell him what we have agreed."

"You are happy with what I said?" I was a bit hesitant I was not sure what she was agreeing to?

"My darling I am more than happy, however, it did cross my mind at one point if we could share you? Now all the boys will be home for Easter so I have suggested we have a meal together, but you stay out of sight while Michael and I explain what is going to on, get their reactions, then bring you in to meet them. Then if they have any reservation or questions that we can get out of the way," she suggested "We always dress for dinner, so make sure you have something suitable for the evening, I am assuming you will be here, please I want you here?"

My head is reeling, share you? What? Why? Whoa! "I do not look forward to meeting your son's altogether, can I not just slip in quietly one day and be introduced as they happen to come home?" I asked.

"My darling no, it is better my way it gets everything out in the open there is no second guessing, we have always been open with the boys, they knew all about our previous arrangements, when they were old enough to understand of course, it is better then anyone outside the family cannot spring something on them that they were not previously aware of," she looked at me.

"Yes I suppose you are right," I replied.

"Darling you will be fine, we will sit either side of you. My only worry is the three eldest are older than you, the two younger twins are one year younger. Being so beautiful, I do not want them to start getting designs on you. If they are tempted, I will punish you severely. They are all randy little buggers, like their father.

"Come on lets get you out and find your sea legs, then

have that shower you are dying for." God did I hurt when I stood, but I'm not giving in. She has been saying some funny things, is it me being weird?

It was wonderful getting into the shower I stood for ages letting the water run over me, Julia undressed and came in the shower with me, I was shocked, but she said I will wash your hair, which she did, but when she had finished, she started massaging my body, paying particular attention to my breasts, I seemed to freeze, then she went down my body, she pushed her hand between my legs, I tried to move backwards, but I could not I was up against the tiled wall she was very close and said, "Darling do not worry I am only making sure you are nice and clean for my husband, did you think I was going to finger fuck you or were you hoping I would," she pushed her fingers into me, and was washing between my legs and my cheeks.

"Julia, please stop now, please," She held me to her very close.

"Please my darling don't be cross with me, I have over stepped the mark, I had to see if you were pliable, she got a towel and very gently dried my hair, she put a bathrobe on, then she took me into her bedroom, sat me down and dried me very gently "You do have a beautiful body. I wish I had a body like yours," she said.

"I cannot see anything wrong with your body, I hope I look like you after I have had five babies, I think you do not do yourself any justice," I replied. Trying hard to not antagonise her, I was not very comfortable with her being in close proximity now.

She then took out a new brush and comb and gently brushed my hair, it was divine, then she blow dried it and said;

"We could pop to Melton tomorrow and get some of your clothes and check everything it alright? If you are up to it that is? Michael has been a couple of times and left the heating on low." I agreed "Will you join me for dinner as Michael will be late," so I did.

I was surprised when we went into the vast dining room, the table was neatly laid out with two places, all silver cutlery, including several cut glass wine glasses. I did not eat much but she was pleased with what I had eaten. I keep forgetting that Julia does not do anything, it is all her staff's doing.

We went into the drawing room, she insisted I sit on the sofa with her, she put her arm round me and placed my head on her and I fell asleep.

Chapter nine

I woke up when the door opened and Michael came in, he looked very tired it was past 9.30 pm. His face lit up when he saw me sitting there "Hello my two favourite girls," we smiled he leaned over and gave Julia a kiss on her lips and came to me, but turned to Julia and said "Do you mind?"

"No, carry on, anyway I will have to go and put your dinner on to heat up," she said rising and went out.

He watched while she went and put his hands under my arms and lifted me to my feet, he stood very close, looking at me, then he kissed me very gently, then we were kissing very passionately, we were so hungry for one another "Samantha you do not know how I have longed to do that, I can't stop thinking about you, I find it even hard to concentrate at work," his lips were on mine again, "You are not going back to that room again, you are going to have to be with me, I have got to have you, feel the thrill of you," all the time he is pushing his erection towards me.

"Michael you are not the only one suffering, I have been going mad laying there, with you so close, I have been wondering when we can be together?" that was it, we hung on to one another.

"Can we not disappear now," I asked.

"No just a little bit longer, I have something to say, but I will wait until Julia is back," as he said that she came in, we all sat down.

"I have some bad news, I have had to drop the case against Rupert even though the CPS said it was water tight, because he has threaten to tell Matthew your name address, telephone number and anything he can think of, I cannot risk this, because I know what he is capable of, Rupert knows some pretty shady people, so I am hoping if I drop the case, he will not give any information to Matthew. The thing is I do not trust Rupert to keep his word, the C.P.S said I could drop it but he could still pass on what he wants. They are not taking it as withdrawn, to give me time to think, but I cannot possibly take the risk," he sat with his head in his hands, I wanted to go to him, as if she read my mind, she nodded to me and left the room, so I went and sat next to him, took hold of him, he turned and wrapped me in his arms, "I cannot put you at risk, it would kill me if something happened to you, through something I had done," he said.

"Darling, I know you are thinking of me, but it would mean Rupert has got away with it," he stared at me, then his lips were on mine kissing me with such urgency.

"I cannot risk it, my darling," come on I had better eat seeing as Julia has gone to that trouble heating it up."

"I was just coming to fetch you, do you want wine?"

"No, I will have some scotch later, I don't feel hungry."

"Just try a little darling, I have just got Samantha eating, now you are going to be a problem. So how are you fixed at work, will I be able to go back myself on Thursday? because I have to let my secretary know tomorrow, to sort out my appointments?"

"Yes, I just have some ends to tie up, then I can baby sit while you go back to your cushy job," he actually smiled.

"Samantha and I have been talking, I know we were going to talk it through together. Samantha will stay here until she finds a house nearer to Nottingham, then when she moves in, you go and live with her, exactly like you used to do when you had your apartment, but it will just be Samantha, our arrangement still stands," she said.

I said "I am sorry we have done this behind your back, but we were just talking, one thing led to another and that was it," I looked at him wondering what his reaction would be?

"I would have preferred us to live here together, and Samantha to sell her house, but this was Samantha's idea," she said.

"I must admit you have ganged up on me behind my back however, I have to say I think that is a brilliant idea, there is no way I would have wanted us to live here together, I do not think it would work. Anyway I want to have children as Samantha does, so it would certainly not have worked Julia."

"You know I will never, ever give you divorce, and Samantha does fully know this. You will never e able to marry,"she said it rather triumphantly!

"I know, I accepted that years ago, although I have never been in love before, I would love to marry her, I would not hurt you like that, because at the end of the day, you have been very good," he said. She looked towards me with a 'Told you so' look.

"While we are on the subject of changing things, I do not want to keep this name, I thought I could change it by deed poll, then at least Rupert would not know any more, I wondered how you would feel if I changed my surname to yours Roper?" I asked.

They looked at one another Michael was first to speak "I would be over the moon if you did, Julia?" he asked.

"It would be wonderful, it would make you closer to me," she said.

"So unless you suggest something different I thought Sophie Roper."

Michael said "It sounds perfect and suits you."

Julia had a tear running down her cheek "If I had, had a daughter that would have been her name, do you not remember Michael?"

"Yes of course, sorry I had forgotten," he said.

"So I take it that is what I will do, so from now please call me Sophie, when I meet your boys introduce me as that, they will never know anything else will they?"

"That is wonderful it makes you my daughter, is there anything else you want, because I am half way through a book and I must get it finished before I restart work," she said.

"No, you go, you know I have told Samantha, whoops Sophie she is not going back to that bedroom I want her with me!"

"Darling I knew that, that is why I had her in the shower, we shampooed her hair, so she would be nice, clean and ready for you, good night," she gave me a hug and kissed me as she always does on the lips, then kissed Michael.

"Don't forget you still have to get up for work, you must get some sleep. I know you have been apart a while, but you have to sleep, put your foot down with him Sophie," she left.

"I cannot eat any more, our bed is calling, making love to you is top priority, as far as I am concerned," he smiled. I cleared the table and was putting the dirty dishes in the dish washer, he came up behind me. "If you stay like that for another second, you will have me straight into you, you cannot bend forward like that and not face the consequences," I stood up fast, he added "Especially as you have nothing under that nightdress," he smirked.

I'm mulling over what Julia had said and done, do I tell Michael?

"You will have to catch me first and you have to switch the lights off," I said running towards the stairs. He was leaping up two, three stairs at a time, he caught me at the top, swept me off my feet and carried me to his bedroom.

"Let me have a quick shower, then I will be all yours," he was no sooner in, than he was out, I was already naked laying waiting for him "I have had that body in my mind for weeks," he wrapped me in his arms and just held me close to him.

"Let me just hold you my love," then he began to kiss me, that was it, the first time he entered me was exquisite, then he took me to heaven and back, we made love numerous times until we were exhausted, we had a quick shower, I went to sleep in his arms I slept all night.

The next morning Julia had to come in and wake us, she brought two cups of tea, because we had over slept, Michael would be late for work on his last day before his break, he jumped out of bed, straight into the shower.

Later Julia drove me to Melton Mowbray and helped me get some evening wear out, which we put on the back seat and filled two medium suit cases with other clothing and under wear.

The following day the roles were reversed, Julia went to work and Michael stayed home, we had a wonderful time mostly in bed, Julia seemed very happy now she was back at work everything was going well.

In the early hours on Sunday morning the telephone rang and startled us both, we were just resting after having climaxed.

Michael had to reach over me to answer the phone "Hello" he said in his deep sexy voice "Yes?" - pause - "When, where?" - pause - "Both of them?" - pause - "His what, wife?" a long pause "Do you need me?" - pause - "If you are sure, so have you got them?" - pause - "Right, well keep me posted, no problem you are just doing your job, good night," and he put the telephone down.

"Is there a problem?" I asked.

"No, not really, they were just ringing about a double murder, nothing to worry your pretty little head about," he said smiling. Taking me in his arms kissing me.

When I awoke it was broad daylight but no Michael, he will be here with a cup of tea soon I thought, I looked at the clock it was 10.10am, I was just wondering whether to get up when he came round the door.

"Good morning my love," he kissed me "I am so sorry I have to go into work, Julia will be home soon," he said.

"But Julia has only just gone back to work, why is she coming home Michael?" I asked.

"I did not want you to be here on your own, when I spoke

to her earlier before she left for work, she said she would come home and take you back to Melton again, to help you pack some more of your clothes," with that he left.

I went into the shower, as I emerged I switched the radio on, then I switched the hairdryer on to dry the bottom of my hair. I heard something about Nottingham, it caught my attention so, I switched my drier off and turned up the volume, the reporter was saying,

'Such a nice young couple, had only been married two years, attacked and died for a few pounds and some jewellery. They had been to a restaurant where it is said they were regulars, walking to where his car was parked, when people on the street said, they saw a man get hold of the Mrs Russell-Brown, there a struggle ensued, as her husband tried to get the man off. Two other men appeared, Mrs Russell-Brown was thrown to the ground with mighty force, when the ambulance arrived she was pronounced dead at the scene, the fall fractured her skull and she died within a few minutes. Onlookers moved forward to try and help, but one of the men, all were masked, drew a gun and threatened to shoot anyone who came nearer, there was a lot of scuffling, Mr Russell-Brown fell down bleeding from several stab wounds, the yobs, kept the onlookers at bay, but several people had mobile phones, and rang police and ambulances. Both died at the scene. Mr Rupert Russell-Brown who was a very well respected Lawyer, Mrs Russell-Brown was his secretary, was to take his silks, which is very rare for a man his age. He already received a considerable salary and was very wealthy, although friends said he was always ambitious and wanted to become multi-millionaire, he already achieved that!'

As I listened I felt the colour drain from my face, I switched off, I sat numb, just as Julia came round the door.

"Sophie, have you had the radio on? I can see from your face, Michael did not want you to find out until we were all together," she said.

"How could he, how could he, the way he slapped, thumped and beat me like some yob, the same as the yobs that attacked him, I do not feel sorry, he deserves all he got, she must have known what he was up to, that is why he made those calls around midnight and two in the morning, the pig," I couldn't say any more I just dissolved into tears.

"I am sorry my darling, I said there was something about him I didn't like, now this proves he was only after your money, and why he went crazy when you told him you were pregnant," she said.

"I think I am crying because I am frustrated, I want to hurt him the way he hurt me, the two faced lying bastard. What is worse they make him sound such a paragon of virtue," I cried.

"Well my darling, there is one good thing come out of it, he will not be able to contact Matthew with his tittle tattle," Julia said.

"I hope they really hurt him and he was in pain while he lay dying," I ran out of steam, Julia held me close.

It was late afternoon by the time Michael came home, I did not know Julia had already informed him that I knew about Rupert.

When he came in he rushed to me "Sweetie are you alright?" he kissed me.

"Yes I am not sorry he is dead and I hope he suffered whilst he lay dying," I said.

"Darling no one can blame you after what he did, but at least he cannot hurt you any more, I had a word with a friend at the C.P.S and he has put the file back, so it looks as though it was being looked into well before this happened, as it would have been if I had not told them to stop. Something can now appear in the media stating his crimes, so he will not go out whiter than white, so my love it is not what you know but who you know.

Mrs Roper you may go back to work tomorrow, we are having an early night tonight, because we are going to be up early and going to the Estate Agents to see what is on the market?" he stated, quiet pleased with himself.

"The boys will be home soon, it is Easter next week so do not forget our plans, I have asked them to be here on Saturday 9th April before 6pm, as we are having a family meeting before dinner, so that is when my darling you stay out of sight until Michael comes to fetch you."

I did not know, but Michael was not returning to work until after the Easter holidays, unless he was wanted urgently for anything.

We went house hunting at 9.30 the next morning, we thought we had done very well, and since we had been sleeping together again I did not have one nightmare, I still had not asked him about what my father had said, I did not want anything to spoil our time, it would not change anything, but I would like to know if Rupert made it all up?

We were lucky with the house hunting bearing in mind Michaels family home is at Edwalton, we found a perfect detached house on the outskirts of Tollerton, which is just down the road from Edwalton, well it sounded perfect on paper, we asked for a viewing and the vendors were in and about to go away for the Easter break, so we arranged to view straight after lunch.

It was a nice quiet road, only a few houses we drove up and down, the house was not visible from the road, because there was a high stone wall, with shrubs behind and the driveway although not long, it went in a curve so it was very private from the road, there was a large paved area for parking, there was a very big integral garage with rooms over the top, large bay windows downstairs and upstairs to the main bedrooms, there was a large enclosed porch to the front door and we rang the bell.

We introduced ourselves as Michael and Sophie Roper, they were an elderly couple Mr & Mrs Thorpe, they were wanting to move down south where their only daughter lived, with the grandchildren. It was a lovely wide hall, with a cloakroom and separate toilet. The large lounge was to the left which had been knocked through and incorporated the dining room, another thing I liked. The kitchen was very wide because it ran behind the garage, the fitments were a bit old fashioned but that would be easily rectified, it was big enough for a table and chairs and a sofa, but no fireplace never mind you cannot have everything. There was a very big garden, because it was a very wide plot on the garage side, it was well split up, into a terrace and various areas but sadly neglected, no problem there then. Upstairs there were seven assorted bedrooms, all were fairly big, and I must have en suite and walk-in, we could easily do that with out to much alteration because of the way it was laid out. Obviously the decor wanted up grading but that also would be quickly remedied, they asked if we would like to have another look on our own which we said yes. As soon as we were I said what I thought and Michael said he thought very similar.

I said "I cannot see any point in looking round more properties because it was more or less what I want, it is nice and private it is only down the road from Julia, I think it's just right, shall I put in an offer?" I was so excited I can't believe Michael will be moving in with me.

"Hang on my darling," he pulled me close and kissed me "What's this shall I put in an offer, firstly you go through the agent, secondly don't I have a say it's my money!"

"What, I thought I was buying it? I did not think you would want to pay anything, you already own one huge house," I stopped and looked at him he was smiling so nice at me "What?"

"My sweetie I cannot believe you, I still think I am dreaming, when I think I am going to be living with you, no my darling my name is not Rupert, I will be buying the house for us," he stressed.

"Why can't I buy the house for us? What am I supposed to do with all that money, can I give it to you?" I genuinely asked.

"Darling if I could marry you I would, I would buy the house for you. I am not poor you know," he added.

"Well I thought I could, well it doesn't seem right, I don't want people to think I am with you for your money," I sulked.

"No my darling, no one would think that for one moment, I know you want me for my body," we both laughed.

"Fancy you guessing my guilty secret," I laughed "I have had a thought you buy the house, I pay for all the alterations, decorating, carpets and furniture etc., etc. and for the garden, would that please my Knight in Shining Armour?" I was very close to him and I was very naughty and put my hand on the best part of his body, well I think it is.

"You can stop that right now young lady, if you get me going I will take you here on this spot, could probably give the vendors a nasty shock, but I cannot stop once I want you," he was laughing "Anyway, back to the purchase, I cannot let you pay because people could say the same about me, that I only want you for your money, they would be very, very wrong, it is definitely your sexy body, I want and at this present moment I cannot have you. Come along let us go to find Mr & Mrs Thorpe."

As we came downstairs they came out of the drawing-room, we all smiled Michael said "Yes we are very interested will it be settled fairly quickly or have you got to find a house down south first?" he asked.

"No we can moved fairly quickly because we are to go down and store everything and live with our daughter until we find something, have you to wait for a mortgage?" Mr Thorpe asked.

"No," we chorused and then I let Michael speak "No it is a

cash sale, we thought we would go straight back to the Estate Agent next."

"I suppose you are making an offer, if so why can't we sort it here and now that would save any delay, because we will not be back for two weeks, at least the wheels can be put in motion from today," he said "Come in, would you like a cup of tea or coffee?" we both refused.

Michael said "Would you accept £600,500?"

"I would, thank you very much, we have had a few offers, but people seem to want something for nothing now-a-days, I think the highest we have been offered was £400,000, we already took into consideration the decor and garden, it was valued at £700,500. we know it needs work, but it is a solid house, and it was rewired 2 years ago. We have been here for 35 years, very happy years, so we hope you have the same happiness as we have," Mr Thorpe said.

"Thank you very much, I am sure we will. I will ring the Estate Agent because he will want details of our Solicitor and everything, I will then ring my Solicitor, who is a friend and ask him to pull out all the stops, because we want to move in as soon as Sophie has done everything she needs to do, before we move in" Michael said.

"Have you nothing to sell then?" he asked.

"Herbert that is very impolite I am sorry" Mrs Thorpe said.

"It does not matter, we do have a house but we do not need to sell it first," I said.

"Are you from round here?" Mr Thorpe asked.

"I have lived many years in Edwalton, but our house is in Melton Mowbray, I work in Nottingham, hence the reason we want to move as soon as possible," Michael said.

"My wife was saying, while we left you on your own that she thought she knew you, but she cannot recall where she has seen you, may I ask what line of work you are in?"

Oh dear I thought, but Michael seemed n-fazed. "The Police Force actually," he replied.

"That is it, you are that lovely man, who was on the television a while ago, when you were telling people how to prevent crime, I thought it was very interesting," she said.

"Yes and if I remember rightly, you said he looked more like a film star that a police man," Mr Thorpe said.

"Stop it Herbert, you will be embarrassing him, Yes but

you are not just a police man are you, you are the top of the tree so to speak," she gushed.

"Now Mrs Thorpe you know why I am with him, he does not only look good, he is just as good on the inside," I said.

"We will not keep you any longer, thank you for showing us round your lovely house, good bye," and we made our exit.

"Sophie Roper, I thought I was going to have a heart attack when you said 'he is just as good' I wondered what you were going to say," we both laughed he put his arm round me and gave me a quick kiss.

"So I wonder what you thought I was going to say? would it be 'he is just as good in bed,' or I could have said 'he is the most wonderful, caring, loving man in the whole wide world and I am so in love with him," I had stopped walking, he stood in front of me, we were in each others arms, I knew they were watching out of the window, it is true.

"Come on my treasure let me get you home, but I must phone Colin my Solicitor first, he does conveyancing and all that crap they do, but a very close second, is taking you out of those clothes which are hiding your beautiful body, then we just might feel like making love, but I will not force you, I know you are not keen on anything sexual!" we both burst out laughing.

"My darling you know me so well," can you drive fast please.

When we were home I asked if he wanted me to make him something to eat and he'd said no, just you on a plate. Also if I wanted anything to eat, we have staff to do that, you are in Julia's domain now.

I went upstairs, undressed ready for him to finish his business. We had a wonderful few hours because Julia was working late and the staff were not on duty after 7pm tonight.

Off and on the news would state the police were not having any good leads to follow up in the Mr & Mrs Russell-Brown killings.

The day after the house buying I switched on the TV just in time for the news the news reader began saying:-

'Rupert Russell-Brown - An informant stated, although he had been tragically killed, it was unfair that the following information should remain unknown, in view of the seriousness of his crimes and especially as he is being painted whiter than white.

The information said regarding the Lawyer Rupert Russell-Brown, who was stabbed in a mugging in Nottingham a few weeks ago. It is alleged the C.P.S had this on their files sometime before his death, he had been arrested and charged with G.B.H on a young lady (who had Millions) and serious charges of attempted fraud against the same young lady, who is the widow of a friend of Mr Russell-Brown, they had been at school together. Obviously when he was killed this file was taken away from the C.P.S. But questions are now being asked as to why this was not made known at the time of his death. These are very serious charges against a man of his standing, also Mrs. Russell-Brown, was complicit, in helping her husband using his so called charm, on this young lady. The anonymous caller said 'What he put this young widow through was barbaric to say the least, she was all alone in the world, and pregnant by him, it was when she told him this, he savagely attacked her and left her severely injured from his onslaught, she had no family and he played on this for his own ends. It was totally by accident that his greed and brutality came to light. There is no doubt that he was the perpetrator because of one slight injury he received from the young lady, when she attempted to protect herself, she stood no chance he was a lot bigger than she was.'

The following day the newspapers were full of it, now every news hound was looking for a lead to find out who and where this young lady is.

After a few days it died down but neither Michael or Julia mentioned anything. I was going to say something then decided to leave it, I was glad it had come out because I did seethe when everyone without exception were saying how good he was, so wonderful, kind and would not hurt a fly.

Good Friday was coming up fast, I began to feel very nervous about the meeting tomorrow with Michael's sons, three of whom were older than I, the second twins one year younger. I do not know how it will go, I only wish it was not happening like this, but they assured me it's what they always did when there was going be to a change.

We had spent most of the afternoon in bed. We showered together, I loved that because he would soap me all over, he did not miss one inch, I just stood and let him do as he wished, of course it took fifty times longer than if I showered myself, but so what? Then he dried me with the same meticulous attention, we started kissing, which was fatal, but he remembered just in time. "You would have let me, you sex maniac," he said, laughing.

"Do you think so? because if I am, I am only what you have made me, you have made me want you more and more, it is because you are so good, I cannot see how Julia can resist you, but then her loss is my gain, I'm pleased to say," I kissed him on his growing erection.

"Oh no, you don't or we will never be ready, you do your hair and make-up while I get dressed, then I will go down, I want you to surprise me when you are dressed, or it may not be a good idea, because my antenna seems to get bigger, when he gets ideas about you," I laughed.

"Michael have I told you lately that I am so in love with you, also I would happily go back to bed with you, now!"

"You are a brazen hussy, but you are my brazen hussy, just remember, I have my name engraved on your ever open door, it also says anyone else keep out! My love I will keep you well fucked especially when we move into our new home," he disappeared into the walk-in, he was quiet a while, when he came out he seemed a funny colour, I looked at him in the mirror, I sat with my mouth open.

"Michael darling are you alright?" I asked concerned. I stood up hair done, make-up on but still naked.

"I had a bit of a funny turn, for a minute, I did not know where I was but I am alright now, my love," he smiled at me.

"I have never seen you in a dinner suit, I thought you were sex on legs in your uniform, but this Christ Michael, I am throbbing, you look so handsome and sexy, my darling I want you so much," I whispered.

"Look at my antenna, there you stand not a stitch on, and I am supposed to sit and discuss my future with my five sons, all I will think of is how long I can manage to wait, before I can have you my darling," he began to finger me.

"Oh yes Michael please," there was sudden bang on the door, we both physically jumped, a male voice said.

"Pa can I come in?" the door handle moved, we both stop hypnotised, even though we knew he could not get in, because Michael had wisely took the precaution of turning the key.

"I will be down in one minute," Michael shouted.

"Okay,"

"That was Charles, one of the older twins, we have always seemed closer than I am with the others, I don't know why. I had better go, lock the door behind me, when you can come down I will ring you, for your grand entrance and thrill me by seeing you dressed for the kill," a quick kiss as he turned to go, I said;

"Darling, are you sure you are alright?"

"Yes, my love, do not worry, see you shortly, he left, so I locked the door, just in case someone else decides to come in.

I finished my face, sprayed myself head to toe with perfume, then went to dress, I put on a full length coral dress, with deep V back and front, showing my cleavage, it fit like a glove down to my hips, then it went straight down to the floor, it had small beads scattered all over. I wore my hair down as instructed by Michael, what is it with men and long hair? I wore my long drop diamond earrings, Charles wedding and engagement ring on my right hand and no other jewellery, I wore a thong but I had to pack it for the time being, because I did not want a wet stain on my dress when I stood up, I put my high stiletto silver sandals on. I was just about to sit down, wondering, how long I had to wait, when the phone rang.

"Hello, that was quick?" I said.

"No my sweet we have not started, but they are all in just getting sat down, so I thought come downstairs, sit on the chair in the hall outside the door, then you can hear everything that is being said, I won't wait for you, because someone may come looking for me, I want to surprise them as well as myself, I love you with all my heart," so I made my way downstairs, sat on the chair, they all seemed to be talking at once, then I heard Michael.

"Come on boys catch up later,"- pause - "Right now we have some changes that you should be aware of, as usual we like to keep you in the picture, then no one from outside the family, can come and tell you something you do not already know," Michael said.

Then Julia spoke "I think before we start, I should tell you Pa gave up his apartment last January, he is living here because he wanted to make some changes in his life."

"It is about time, you are too old Pa, to be a Lothario any longer, it is time you faced your responsibility to my mother," I had no idea who that was.

Then Julia spoke "Thank you Junior, but your father has always took his responsibilities towards me seriously, your father has never, I repeat never done anything that I haven't been aware of. Also may I ask did you have such a terrible childhood, because of your father, did you ever want for anything, no you did not. Did your father ever neglect you in any way? no he did not, so, whatever we arrange in our marriage, it really has nothing to do with you, but we have always thought it fair to keep you all in the picture, but not asking for your interference, if you continue in this vein you will have to leave," I have never heard Julia sound so cross before.

Then Michael spoke "I am giving you the opportunity now, that if you do not want to know why we are having this meeting, you can go now," - pause - "Right we have someone we would like you to meet, she is going to become one of the family," I assumed he was getting up, as I heard a chair move, I would rather be anywhere than here right now.

Then Julia spoke, "You are going to meet the daughter I never had, she is very dear to me, she is a very good friend," the door opened and Michael was still sat at the table, it was Julia who came out, she took my hand and led me in, there were a couple of low whistles and one or two of them said something to each other.

"This is Sophie, I would appreciate it if you would please make her welcome, she will be staying here until the house is ready to move in to."

Michael said "Sophie is my new partner, she has taken our surname, we will be living together just down the road."

Straight away Junior jumped in "Well, we know why she is with our old man don't we, don't kid yourself Pa, if you had not got any money, she would not look at you twice, why would a beautiful young girl want you, it looks as though she has fooled the pair of you," whilst he was talking, one or two of the others were trying to stop him, but he carried on, both Michael and Julia were holding my hands, Michael was squeezing it.

Julia and Michael both went to speak but I stopped them.

"Let me please. Why would I not want to be with your father, he is a very nice, caring, thoughtful man, he is very good looking, and does not look anywhere near his age, why would I want his or your mothers money?"

"That is what girls like you do, get as much as you can, then run for it, you are a gold digger," junior said.

"Girls like me, what do you mean? I do not need your father or mothers money!" I stressed.

"I mean girls like you, who open your legs for any old fool with money, don't tell me you have your own?"

"Yes," I simply replied.

"Alright, as of now how much are you worth?"

"That's enough," Michael snapped.

I had to think a minute, because I had been told that Rupert had settled for a million and a half, although he had not told me, so I calmly said "No darling, I will tell him, well I have a house to sell and old jewellery but that apart, I would say roughly ten or eleven million" junior's face was a picture, the others looked surprised, one of them gave a low whistle. "Does that help at all?"

"Right, so have any of you boys anything constructive to say or ask?" Michael asked, I think it was one of the youngest twins said.

"Can I ask how old you are Sophie?" he asked rather shyly.

"I will be 20 in June," I replied.

"Have you been married?" asked the other youngest twin.

Michael jumped in "Yes and she is divorced, because he is now serving time at her Majesties pleasure," he went on with a brief narrative of everything up to and including Charles death, although he did leave out Rupert completely, he knew I did not want all my past repeating. Whilst he was talking, he took his hand from mine and slid it round me pulling me gently towards him. "Does that help boys? any more questions?" They all shook there heads.

Then, I think it was Charles who spoke "Well I tell you what, it will be a pleasure to see someone pretty besides Mum at the table, I get fed up with all your ugly mugs," well that got them roused, when it quieten he said "I for one want to welcome her, and hope we can make her feel at home, tell you what Pa, I wouldn't kick her out of my bed, so you better watch out, there could be some of my brothers who think the same as me," he added.

Now how wrong could I be, I thought that would provoke some response from Michael, but everyone laughed including me. Although when I glanced sideways, Julia was not laughing, I could see she was fuming and I know now why, it was because of what she said to me.

Then Michael said "You will have to fight me for her, then it would be only over my dead body," more laughter, now this is what I call a family, apart from Junior, I was not at all keen on him, yet he was the only one who was in the police force, not sure what his rank is, but he was what I would call a big head. However, Charles was lovely, he and John his twin looked like there father in every way, same beautiful blue eyes, fair hair, Michael did not look old enough to be their father.

"Right, I will go and see if we can eat now," Julia said as she stomped out of the room.

"My darling I am so proud of you, Christ that dress I am certainly glad I could stay seated, I was nearly coming when you came into view, you are simply the most beautiful girl, I love you with all my heart, but I will have to watch what Julia calls her randy little buggers, they are not made of stone, I think there will be some tossing off tonight after seeing you, their eyes went straight to your fabulous cleavage, I think they were hypnotised, I for one couldn't blame them, I am so lucky you could have anyone you wanted, but I have you, you are going nowhere, you are mine all mine," as we sat there in front of his sons, he kissed me quickly on my lips, I was actually blushing.

Charles was near to us, he leaned over to his fathers ear and whispered "Now lad if you are going to carry on like that, for gods sake get a room," which made them both laugh, I smiled because I could hear him, which I think I was supposed to.

Then Julia came in "Come along into dinner." We all went into the dining room, it was a round table, I was sat one side of Michael and Julia the other side, Junior sat next to her and there was a scuffle behind me, then Charles plonked down next me.

"It is only right I am next in line, so I get to sit next to Sophie, that's right isn't it Pa?" Michael smiled and nodded, it turned out to be a good meal, lots of banter between the siblings, the meal was good. Michael asked junior if he wanted the use of his apartment, he declined, but Charles and John said they would, as they were going to set up business in or around Nottingham.

Some of the boys decided to play in their music room.

"Don't forget it is, Easter Sunday, make sure you are up early enough to have breakfast before Church." so we said our good nights and went our separate ways.

As soon as we were in the bedroom I was in his arms, he was kissing me as if we had been apart for months and not a few hours, I was giving as good as I got "Quickly my darling I cannot wait another second," he undid my zip, my dress floated to the floor, leaving me in just my thong, "Bloody hell I like that, do you not wear a bra with that style of dress then? I love it stripped with one zip," he laughed as he was trying to get his cuff links off so I helped with his shirt buttons, belt, then the zip on his trousers, I gave one big pull the boxers and trousers were down.

"Come along slow coach," I said as I ran to the en suite "To answer your question no, no bra when dresses are low cut they have inbuilt bra's of a sort, it helps support and stops them drooping under the dress. I would have thought Julia had low cut evening dresses, the same?"

"Well yes I suppose she does, but she has never ever undressed in front of me," he said, his voice faded because he must have gone into the walk-in, then he came round the door, as I was sat on the bidet "I think you give yourself a thrill on there, you are always sat on it, I hope you are not doing me out of my job Mrs Roper?" he looked at my face, I was just smiling dreamily "I am going to call you that in future, because that is the one thing I want but I can never marry you, because of the promise I made to Julia, although I know she loves you and classes you as a very dear friend, her words, I doubt she will ever change her mind, that is the only thing that saddens me," he said.

"It does not matter, as long as I have you, and you give me lots of babies, I will be happy, I had already decided I wanted to be known as Mrs Michael Roper, after all it is only a bit of paper, being married has not brought me lasting happiness, so can you please stop talking and take me to bed and please fuck me!"

"My pleasure, my love," we were soon locked together going to heaven with the fireworks, the lot "I forgot I was going to bring a bottle of wine for us to drink," he said.

"Too late, you will have to make do with water, if you think you are going downstairs, leaving me here wanting you, you are sadly mistaken Mr Roper, shall I fetch some water? I do not want you dying of thirst," I said smiling.

"No not yet," he slid down the bed, he went down on me his mouth, his lips and his tongue, all around my clit and my happy spot, I cannot describe what he was doing to me, I had an enormous climax very loudly, but suddenly stopped.

"What is it darling you suddenly went quiet in mid flow?" he asked looking concerned.

"I suddenly wondered who sleep's in the rooms close to this, they can possibly hear me?"

"Oh sweetie I should have told you, where our en suite is one side of the room, the walk-in the other side, both have en suite's the other side of the wall, both rooms are empty because we keep them as guest rooms, usually when our parents come, like they will tomorrow, we put them in those rooms, so perhaps we could gag you whilst they are here, but this time it is only one night," he could hardly speak for laughing. "I am sorry I was laughing, but your little face was a picture, my love please do not worry when this house was built, it was built quiet sound proof, including between the rooms, so don't worry about making those glorious sounds you make when you have a climax, I don't think I am that quiet myself?"

We had a wonderful time until I was told at 1am I had to go to sleep, he wrapped his arms round me while we sleep, I feel so safe and comfortable, I still had not had a nightmare. I was woken up by someones lips on mine, I did not open my eyes, it began to drive me mad with want, so still not opening my eyes I said "Whoever you are please do not stop kissing me, but if you want to fuck me hurry because I do not want my lover to catch us," but then I spoilt it and laughed.

"My sweetie I have fetched us some tea, so drink it, then we can have a quickie, but we must be ready for breakfast around 8.45am otherwise my greedy sons will eat all the bacon and sausages, then we will have to wait," he said snuggling my neck.

"You really do know where exactly on a girl is the best places to arouse her, I am all but drooling my darling, thank you for that lovely session before we went to sleep, have you noticed I have not had a nightmare?"

"Indeed I have my love, you must be more and more relaxed, your subconscious is believing it."

"I think it is because I know I am safe in your arms, with your body wrapped round me, I love you so much," I said simply.

I got my quickie, then sent into the shower on my own, I managed not to wet my hair, then went and dressed. It was a bit over cast so I decided on a little cherry red suit, with a low camisole underneath of the same colour, then I thought if it is cold I would put my fur jacket on or just a three quarter winter coat with the usual stiletto heels.

As I came out of the walk-in Michael was strolling in all naked and lovely, I had to stop and kiss him before I put my make-up on. "Now Mrs Roper don't you start getting my little man excited, you know what effect you have on him," I slipped my hand down, just as he seemed to be waking, I held him gently and moved my hand back and forth. "What have you done you naughty, naughty girl, now I will be suffering all through breakfast," I didn't say anything, I kissed his lips, dropped fast, taking him in my mouth, before he realised what I was doing, now bearing in mind we had to get down for breakfast, I decided I would make it fast, did I make it fast? he was groaning and almost growling "Please don't ever stop," he managed to get out. It was quick he was loud, he was very loud, as he was coming he began to thrust into my mouth in a frenzy.

Here is me worrying about my noise, he sounded like a jet going over head, I smiled to myself, I think he liked that, when I had finished licking him he was dry, he brought me upright and his lips were on mine, now who's making who twitch? He pulled away and that fantastic smile was now sending me funny "You never cease to amaze me, you are one very sexy girl," he smiled.

"I have told you, I have never done it properly before, I am just a novice compared to you, I had better get my make-up on or you will be very cross with me," I said laughing, he disappeared in the walk-in. I applied my make-up including false eye lashes, I thought it was quiet suckle but it certainly did not look right with out those eye lashes," then from behind;

"Will I do Mrs Roper?" I turned expecting him in a suit, there he stood in his full uniform talk about drop dead gorgeous.

"Sex on legs, you gorgeous man, you have made me start twitching again, you should come with a health warning, then I would not look at you, Oh Michael what you do to me, no wonder you had so many women, I bet they used to fall at your feet, I know I could easily now, if we were not in a hurry," he stood and smiled.

"I cannot wait until we have our own house, you are simply the best, you tick every box, with what you say, your love making is second to none, you are truly one exceptional girl, I am so pleased you chose me to fall in love with, I will love you for ever, I will take care of you my love," he gave me a quick kiss on the lips.

"I knew I could get away with that kiss, because by the time you have eaten it will be refreshed, come on my darling let my sons see what a sex siren I have in my bed, I feel sorry for them, they will be thinking what they could be doing with you in their beds! Come my lovely, lovely Sophie" we went very sedately down stairs into the dining room, we were not the last Julia was not there and one of the two youngest twins.

"Good morning boys, are we all well?"

"Yes pa," was the chorus "Good morning, and good morning Sophie," it was as though it was well rehearsed it was lovely.

"Good morning boys, well young men," I stuttered. Michael put his arm round my waist steering me to the long side board.

"What are you having for starters?" he asked.

I whispered "I already had the best," he smiled.

"So have I," he kissed me on the cheek. I opted for fruit and fresh natural yoghurt as did Michael, then we sat down and ate, then we had almost everything, all kept warm on a long stand which held all the silver dishes with lids on, it was quiet impressive, then I followed with white toast, thick butter and marmalade. There was quiet a bit of chatter I just got stuck in with my food I was ravenous. Michael did not have any toast

"Can I get you a coffee?" he asked.

"Yes please darling," I answered.

Then Julia came in, I stood and said good morning to her, she gave me a big hug and kissed my cheek "You look positively radiant my darling, something or should I say someone agrees with you!" although she said it quietly some of the boys heard.

"Well we know what or who that is don't we?" they all cheered, I do not think I am going to get use to this, although I know it is meant jokingly, I just am not used to their openness.

Michael came over with my coffee, we both sat down "Can you lot just keep it down, Sophie is not used to us, but given time, she will give as good as she gets," he said pleading.

One of them said "Don't blame us Mum started it," So it all quietened down while we finished our breakfasts, I went and fetched my coat.

Then we all set off for church in two cars. Everyone seemed to know everyone else, we received a lot of looks and Michael whispered.

"I'll bet they are wondering which of my son's you belong to?" he put the tip of his tongue in my ear, now that would not go unnoticed because we were sitting near to the front, my mind is running riot.

Then when the service was over we started to walk out, Michael put his arm round me! Obviously he is not bothered what the congregation thought, but I did, I felt very self conscious, what were they thinking, with Julia there as well, as we left the doorway Julia was waiting for us, he kept his arm round me, she said; "I see you are sending out your signals Michael, I think you should think twice before you do things like that, I can see Sophie was embarrassed, are you alright my love?" she asked moving a strand of my hair, which had fell over my face, then kissed me, everyone was staring, I think I had better switch off when people are around, she is telling Michael off, then doing something equally embarrassing! "I am sorry I was sharp last night my love." she added.

We had not been back long when the Grandparents arrived, very soon after one another.

First was Michaels parents both tall, very serious looking, but seemed friendly.

Followed shortly after by Julia's parents both looked fairly old, lovely white hair, but they both looked quiet fragile, I would say they were a lot older than Michaels. I was calmly introduced as Michaels partner, I mean, elderly parents what would they think of me? All the boys were there as a welcoming party, they all kissed and hugged their grandparents, some of them took their over night bags and clothes on hangers, while we went into the morning room for pre-lunch drinks, we all sat chatting together, instead of small groups here and there it was all very civilised.

The rest of the day and Easter Monday passed quickly, everyone joined in playing cards or listening to music or in the entertainment room watching T.V.

Late Monday afternoon the Grandparents left, so we all did our own thing. I went sat watching the television with some of the boys, Julia disappeared, she had work to catch up on, we had an early night. After breakfast Tuesday all the boys left to go back to their individual homes. Julia was going to work Wednesday, Michael had the rest of the week off, so we were looking forward to some privacy, but unfortunately there were always staff around.

Michael had a call from Colin his Solicitor saying, Mr & Mrs Thorpe have the removal men in packing up for them, the property will be empty by next Monday, they are leaving the keys to enable us to start our work, so we can move in sooner than we thought.

He added if Michael wanted to transfer some thing extra, so I sent £250,000.00, which was on top of the original deposit, it would be a sign of good faith, although they said they knew they could trust us, they thought we were a delightful couple.

Michael said he had not expected it, he would have to get some of his investments sorted, however, that was my chance, I said mine was sitting in a bank account, so I had already sent it. He said that amount was not necessary, I said it only had to be paid once, plus they were doing us an enormous favour.

So Monday when Michael and Julia had gone to work, I telephoned someone Michael had suggested for the building alterations, bathroom and kitchen fitters, decorators and everyone we would possibly need.

My diary was full of appointments, I got on with things and work began to progress, I went to the house every day, in three weeks I could not believe how far they had got, Michael said he was not going to see it, he trusted me implicitly and wanted me to be happy.

Chapter ten

We moved into our newly upgraded and refurbished house in Church Lane near Tollerton on Thursday 19th June 1998, a week before my 20th birthday.

At 10am Michael was waiting for me at the door, as I pulled in he put the key in the door, flung it open but stood waiting for me, when I reach him he lifted me up and carried me over the threshold, and put me down, but held me close kissing me

"Welcome to our little love nest," he said between kisses "I want you to be happy for ever more here, that is why I left all the interior to you, I knew I could trust you, I knew I would be right, so Mrs Roper will you give me a guided tour? but please leave our bedroom until the last."

"I do not think I can last that long to get to the bedroom, you should not kiss me like that, you should be locked up for the things you do to me, I am throbbing fit to burst." I whispered.

"Darling please do not burst, what about all these wonderful new carpets," we were both laughing.

"Come on then," I said taking his hand. We went all round, he was greatly impressed with what I had done. When we reached the bedroom, again he carried me over the threshold and stood me beside the bed kissing me saying "This is where I am hoping to knock you up, as soon as you have given birth, I want you to be pregnant again, then hopefully no one will be able to take you away from me, I love you with all my heart, you make me so happy not just in bed, but I love being with you all the time," and before I knew it I was naked, he was undressed, I threw the quilt off and fold the top sheet down. That was it, the front door was left wide open, both cars were unlocked.

He began kissing me, his lips slowly went round to my ear, down my neck, to my breast doing the most sensual things with his lips, whilst his hand was doing equally melting things with my other breast, it was so arousing, I know I was sighing and moaning. Gradually he made his way downwards, fingering my clit and slowly slipping his fingers into me.

"My darling you are always so ready, you are every mans dream."

Then very slowly he slipped his rock hard erection into me and stopped. I could feel myself squeezing all around him.

"You are one amazing you lady, you fuck like someone

older with about twenty years of experience. What your cunt is doing to me is mind blowing, I am not moving yet, you are going to make me come, I can do nothing about it the way you control me. You are a first my love, Aha." He starts coming, then he really begins to move, really move, he is thrusting as high as he can get, he is taking me so high so quick, until I explode, I am sighing, he is grunting, groaning, moaning, until we both still.

The hours soon passed, when we looked at the clock it was 4 pm, we were taking another shower, which we had done several times, with the intention of redressing, finishing unloading the cars and closing the front door, we looked as though we were going to do it this time.

I was almost ready just brushing my hair, the door bell rang, a mans voice called "Anyone home," I have a delivery. "You go, I will be down and unload the cars for you."

I ran downstairs, there stood a young man with the biggest arrangement of red roses "Mrs Roper these are for you, be careful it is heavy, the florist said to make sure you fill the vase with water, because they have to empty it to travel."

"Thank you so much," I said trying to close the door.

"Here let me take that," Michael had come downstairs, I had not heard him, because of the thick carpet I had chosen "Where do you want it on the dining room table?"

"Yes please, is there a card, I do not know who would be sending me red roses?" I laughed.

"I think they may be from someone who loves you very much," I found the little card and read;

To my one and only true love,
You make the days so bright and happy,
My nights so full of love, you fill me with love,
I will love you for ever and a day. M xx

"Michael they are beautiful you are wonderful, I will love you for ever," the tears were in full flow, "Can I take you to bed to pay you," I asked kissing him.

"Normally I would not hesitate, but will you show me later, we really must get the things out of the cars and once everything is done, I promise I will fuck you day and night until you tell me to stop, or I peg out exhausted and dead," he laughed "You pop in the kitchen, put the kettle on, I will take everything upstairs, then you can sort out once we have had a cuppa, while I will sort out some food," he said patting me on the bottom.

So that was the first few hours in our new house, it did not take long to get everything sorted, he made a lovely Spanish omelette, it was huge, he had to cut it up to serve it had, ham, cheese, tomato and onion, we had brought from Julia's, well she did say to help ourselves to whatever we wanted, he opened some wine, we sat taking our time, enjoying our new kitchen.

Later he brought out a bottle of champagne. "I suggest we take it to bed and drink it, unless you think it too early for bed," he smiled that lovely melting smile.

"Oh dear Michael do we really have to, you know I hate bed, unless I am going to sleep," I said it without a smile.

"Okay we will go in the drawing room then," he took my hand, I thought he really meant it "It is alright my love, I have seen the panic in your eyes come on, bed, it has been so long, I do not know what you look like naked."

So that was the start of a lovely romantic couple of days, then Friday came, he had to go to work, he left fairly early as there were some papers he had left at Julia's, he would not let me get up with him he brought me a cup of tea to bed, kissed me like there was no tomorrow and left saying, "If I get a moment I will ring you my darling." I had one sip of tea and I felt sick, I ran to the loo, and was sick. Then it got me thinking I had not had a period since the beginning of April, no it was the end of March, so that was 2 months ago I wonder if I could be pregnant?

I rang Julia on her mobile, it went to her answering service, I just said 'There was no urgency, but if she did have a minute could she ring me.' I had just had a shower, got dressed when she phoned "Hello my darling have you packed him off to work, how is everything, are you all sorted and I miss you so much," she rattled everything off.

"Hang on, you are not giving me chance to answer, yes I am sorry to say he went to work today, I feel so lonely, everything is fine, yes everything is unpacked and sorted, there is just the garden to get stuck into now. I have rung you because I want to know living here, where would I find the best private Doctor?"

"There isn't anything wrong is there?" she asked.

"No, but I thought we should get registered, then if we need a doctor we will not have to start filling out all our details and things," I thought I had come up quick with that answer, I had not thought it through before I phone her.

"There is Doctor Knight in Tollerton or there is ours in West Bridgford Doctor Hudson, I have met both, they are very nice, although Doctor Hudson is getting on a bit, I think of the two Doctor Knight would be better, he is very dishy."

"Excuse me what would I want with a dishy Doctor? I have a very, very dishy Policeman, I am not about to look for his replacement yet," we both laughed.

"He was a very good husband and brilliant father, it was that I could not keep him happy in bed, he has a big appetite, I am keeping my fingers crossed, you can keep him satisfied," she did sound worried.

"Darling Julia please do not worry on that count, because he says it is me who is too demanding, he says I am his little sexy nymphomaniac, one of these days he will die from exhaustion," I laugh.

"I am really pleased with that, my darling, I love you so much, I am so pleased you are happy with my husband, I could not have selected anyone better than you, but it just shows how looks can be deceiving, you look so demur, so innocent, an untouched virgin, who would not know what a cock looked like, let alone have one inside you, sorry my sweet, I don't know what it is, but I cannot believe half the things I say to you, I never talk like this even to my closest friends."

"Julia I take that as a compliment, as you know I have never had a friend before, I do treasure you more than you will ever know, I really do love you Julia."

"Sweetie I will have to go, but I will drop in Monday morning about 10 as I am due in Radcliffe on Trent at noon, so we can have a good catch up then if that is alright?"

"That will be lovely, I will see you then, bye my darling."

"Bye sweetie, love you," and she was gone.

I found Doctor Knight's number, I telephoned, I explained we were new to the area. You can come in anytime to fill in the forms, however did you need to see the Doctor? because if so, you can fill the forms before you go in for an appointment.

So I asked when was his first appointment, she said today at 3pm or at 10.30 Monday? So I booked the one for 3pm was told to get there for 2.30pm.

I was there prompt, filled out forms for me and for Michael, I took them to the receptionist, a short while after she said Doctor Knight will see you now. I went in he sat beside a large roll top desk, he stood and shook my hand, Julia was right he is dishy but I am not looking for anyone I have my love.

"So you are new to the area, have you had any problems we should know about apparently, you were in West Bridgford?"

"Yes but I can never remember going to the Doctors, I have moved from Melton Mowbray. Mr Croft was my Gynecologist I had a miscarriage recently but did not go back to see him, as I was staying with some friends in Edwalton, but I think I could be pregnant as I have missed two months, but I was not sure how long to wait before a I saw a Doctor?"

"That is fine," he said "Get out of the bottom half of your clothing off, then hop onto the bed," which I did. Shortly after he came round the curtain "How long have you been married?" he asked switching on his light and pulling on the obligatory gloves.

"I am not married we are partners," I stammered.

"It is alright, I am not judging you, how old are you?"

"I will be twenty next week."

"Many happy returns for next week. Are you worried about being pregnant or is it what you want," he was very nice.

"I am desperate to start a family, I really want children."

"So when you lost your first, you must have been devastated, hence you want to know as soon as possible if you are again? Well yes you certainly are pregnant, but not far possibly 5 weeks, I want you to wait another 4 weeks, then come back to see me, make an appointment on your way out then we will know, but at least we have set the wheels in motion. Before you go, do you think you could leave me a water sample? it does not matter how small, but I can get that tested ready for next time," he passed me a little bowl "You have no other problems at all have you, anything I should know about?"

"No I do not think so, thank you so much, bye," I picked up the little bowl.

The receptionist must have known, because as I emerged she said "The toilet is down there on the right," There was a notice in the loo stating to leave the sample bowl on the shelf when I had done. I walked to her, she had some dates for 4 weeks ready for me to select one, I opted for 10am on Thursday 17th th July. I went home high as a kite.

I didn't want to say anything, I contained myself until we went to bed that night.

As we got into bed he said, "You are a wonderful cook my

179

darling, I know you are spotlessly clean, you iron to perfection, so I could not wish for any more, I have a cook, laundry maid, little scrubber, last but by no means least, I have my own sex starved nympho, who I can have anytime I want, she will let me do anything to keep me happy, my only problem is she makes me have her so often, I could be dead in a couple of months, unless I can be put on hold?" he kissed me, his face straight no hint of a smirk, I just melt and throb, I want him so much, but I wanted to say something, it gave me an opening with what he had just said;

"I am sorry I do not do put on hold, I will be withdrawing my services if you are not careful, however, I might just make an exception in your case, because you really are a good fuck, I would consider not making so many demands on your time, if when the time comes, you could promise to look after my baby," I looked at him.

"So, as long as I keep fucking you until I knock you up, then promise to look after the baby you will not be so demanding, all I have to do is knock you up?" he said "Can I start now?"

"Well you could, but I think you have missed that train!"

He looked at me, was about to say something, then his face lit up "Darling are you telling me you are pregnant?" I give a little nod "Oh my sweetie, my darling, my little treasure when?"

"Well, I have no idea, but it had to be over a month ago?"

He took me in his arms "My darling, sweetest Sophie, I did not expect it would be so quick, I cannot believe it, sorry darling are you happy about it being so soon?"

"Darling if I wasn't so desperate to have your baby, I would have had my injection, but I do want your baby, you have no idea how much, because it ties us together, I was never sure that I could keep you happy. I worried how you could settle for the same one all the time, when you had a varied choice, I want to be able to keep you with me always, I am so in love with you, I love how you keep me happy in bed, there is nothing better than feeling you my love inside of me," I said running out of steam.

"And there is something else my darling? I know what it is, but I want you to put it into words, before I say my piece, come on baby what else? or why else do you want me to knock you up?" he was giving me that smile.

"Don't smile like that, I am nearly coming, you are getting me so high, with your kisses, your smiles and just looking at me," I whispered.

"Come on baby I know," he said.

"How?"

"Because I am so in love with you, I do know you inside and outside, I don't mean just your body, although I do know every inch of that, come on darling, why else do you want the world to see that I have knocked you up, therefore fucking the arse of you," he said.

"I thought it would show all those women who you have fucked frequently all these years, who would have done anything to keep you, for themselves, that I am the one who has got the prize, the biggest, the best prize in the whole wide world, that is the reason why you want to knock me up, because of my age, being young you are telling them all that you are so good, you can start all over again but with a much younger model, that is also why you want to keep me knocked up, to show the world what we do, my darling I would be happy always being pregnant because I want to tell the world look I can keep him happy, I let him do what he wants, we are both happy and I am so in love with my Mr Policeman!"

His lips were on mine, we were both so wanting, the first time was quick it was rough, he was very rough, but I loved it, we soon climaxed. He did not withdraw, he then began to make love to me, after he assured me, that it was he who had the doubts that I would stay with him. Then we had a drink, and made love again, then we fell asleep exhausted but very, very happy.

The following Monday, I went down in my see through negligee that Michael insist I wore as often as possible, to get breakfast ready, he was a long time, I called "Michael darling your breakfast is ready will you be long?"

He appeared at the top of the stairs "I am on my way," as he neared I saw his face.

"Darling what is wrong?" I asked, I took him in my arms.

"I have had a funny turn, I could not remember where I was?" he said.

"Was it like the other one?" he looked at me a bit blank.

"Oh yes I did have one, but I am alright, come on I am dying of hunger, you work me so hard in bed, it makes me hungrier."

"What do you mean hungrier?" I had no idea.

"Well my sexy little thing, I am always hungry for you, not just food," I smiled.

"Come on darling eat, you are sure you are okay aren't you?" he just nodded, looked at me and everything was forgotten, except we both wanted one another badly. I had an idea while he was sitting eating his breakfast glancing at the newspaper, I crawled under the table from the other side, he was sitting perfect, I was able to unzip his trousers very fast, got out my little/big friend, he was in my mouth before Michael even realised.

"Fucking hell, don't let me stop you," I started nice and slow, then started building up, he was getting there very quick, he started thrusting into the back of my throat, I still do not know why I don't gag, all of a sudden he his coming, all nice and creamy, when he stills, I lick him clean, but leave him hanging out. Michael leans down and drags me from under the table onto his knees, but he opens my legs before I sit. "I am going to fuck you, so hard my little slut, so you will feel me inside you all day," he slips straight in, he holds his hands under my bottom and starts lifting me up and down, onto his big erection, he is thrusting really, really hard into me, I hang round his neck kissing him, our tongues deep in our throats, what this man does to me is out of this world. Eventually, I saw him off at the door, in a dream.

Julia called on her way to the hospital, I had coffee all waiting, I had made a sponge that I knew she liked, we greeted each other as though we had not seen each other for months instead of barely a week. She kissed me on my lips, for longer than was necessary.

"Do you want a look round first?" I asked.

"Of course, but," she turned me to face her and held me at arms length "Darling have you got something to tell me?"

"I wasn't going to say I wanted to make sure first."

"Oh my darling, you are pregnant, why didn't you want anyone to know, I assume Michael knows," she tossed her head as if she was mad with me.

"Darling I wanted to be absolutely sure, before I told anyone, you would have been the next, but please don't lets tempt fate, please keep it to yourself until my next appointment," I said.

"Of course my love, I half wondered when you asked about Doctors, so we have not any details yet?" she said.

"No I have missed two periods but I have another appointment on the 17th July," I said as we were walking round I had taken her upstairs first.

"Which room will be mine?" she asked.

"Why will you be staying? You only live up the road or are you thinking you will be drinking too much to be driving?"

"You never know, I just thought you might need me when the baby comes, when daddy will be at work, I just want to be a big part of your life, my love. Sophie you have made this house just perfect, this drawing room is out of this world, I think you had better come back and re-plan my tired old house."

We ended up in the kitchen it was a lovely day, I opened the newly installed french doors. I had the same installed in the drawing room, because there was a paved area all the way along the back, I would keep that although paved with something different.

"I can't wait to see what you have planned out in the garden, it is enormous, I thought you both said it was just a normal large garden? It is so quiet and peaceful, no one overlooks you, the view over the fields is worth a fortune, it will be wonderful for children, I say children, you are planning on more than one? However, you might not have much choice, Michael gave me two lots of twins and they are from his side," she said.

"I had never thought I some how thought it was your side, I want lots of children, I want to give them a real childhood one I never had," I had to swallow hard, a tear escaped down my cheek. She was on her feet and pulled me up towards her.

"Sweetie, I cannot imagine what you have been through, but that is all behind you, you have Michael, me and the boys, we all love you, unfortunately I think their love is totally different to the one I prefer them to have for you, but once you have had a baby, they will realise that their father is very serious about you," we sat chatting about this and that then she suddenly looked at her watch "Gosh I am going to be late the time has flown, I will ring later, there was something I wanted to discuss, I forgot, many congratulations," and she was gone.

I had just put the pots in the dishwasher when the telephone rang "Good morning my darling, how are you? I miss you, I don't like coming to work any more, I want to be with you."

"Hello my darling, I miss you to, Julia called, we forgot the time so she was going to be late getting to the hospital," I said.

"That has got to be a first, was everything alright?"

"Yes, the only thing she guessed I was pregnant but how? I did not give her a hint and she had not been here long?"

"That's Julia, she can spot a pregnancy miles away, it is

uncanny but she was always right. Was everything else fine?"

"Yes my love, she loved the house, suggested I redo hers. I thought you told me she had nannies for the boys? I had not realised the twins are your side of the family, but you are an only one?" I said.

"I was not, my twin brother was 3 hours younger than me died when he was 10 months old, I never knew him, I think that is why my Mother and Father decided no more children. Yes she never looked after any of our boys, as for changing nappies she would not know where to start! why did you say that?"

"Because she asked which bedroom would be hers? she said she thought after I had baby. I would want her to come and help me?"

"She never ever took any care of her own! Sorry I have to go another call is waiting, I love you," he was gone.

I was lost I did not know what to do I felt very restless, I went a walk all round the garden, decided I may as well get some expert in to put my ideas to and see what was feasible, I had the name of a young man, who was just starting out, I left my telephone number. I did some washing, pegged it out, then decided to do something ready for dinner, so that kept me busy. I sat at the open french doors and fell asleep, I was awoken by someone kissing me, there was my Michael kneeling in front of me smiling.

"Hi my lovely, you were well away, have you been doing too much? you must start to consider that little one inside you growing," he said.

"My darling, I missed you I felt very lonely, I have not been over doing it as you put it, I am a fit healthy woman in the first throws of pregnancy. There's millions of women work full time while they are pregnant, I wish I worked," I said sulkily.

"No, I had enough of Julia happy to give me children, only to have nannies and the like looking after them!" he stressed.

"Hey calm down, I have no intention of leaving my children with anyone, I am their mother, no one will look after my babies like I want to do. I want to give them the mothers love I never had, I want to watch them grow, enjoy everything little thing. That is why I am so longing for this baby," I said "Which made me curious about Julia, why would she want to come and stay here and help me?"

"You have lost me my love. It was the same when we brought you home, she stayed off work, she has never, done that for our boys. I am so sorry my love, I should have known, you are nothing like her, forgive me my darling please," he was very sad.

"Michael, there's something, you should know, I have kept putting it off," I went on to tell him about the shower incident, her innuendo's.

"My love please do not think any more about it, suffice to say, my wife is a law unto herself."

"Well I thought I should tell you. I could not stay mad with you who pleases me so much," I said "You don't have a minute to spare now? I desperately want you here and now!" I smiled as I said it.

"You are a very demanding, knocked up young lady, do I get to get out of this uniform and have a shower first?" he asked.

"Darling do you have to?" I asked.

His lips were devouring mine, he lay me on the sofa, in a flash his trousers and boxers were of, his hand went up my skirt, off came the thong, he waved it "My prize I think," he shouted "Let me get this cock inside you," I think his erection gets bigger, I moved slightly to accommodate him, I just closed my eyes to savour that moment when he first enters me it's indescribable, that's it he begins fucking me. Christ what feelings, he must be the worlds most experienced man in the fucking game, he takes me right to the limit then slows a little, he continues like that several times, when I do climax it is spectacular, we are together, we were very loud, kissing and holding one another.

He said "I have not finished with you yet, you are going to have to have me again, I hope you have not got anything in the oven? because after this, we're showering, you're going to have that mouth fucked."

"You know you can do anything with me, I will be very happy, I will do anything for you." 9pm, we were eating cheese on toast!

Saturday Julia rang, said she wanted to pop down to see us, she would be down in an hour. I had coffee ready, when she arrived she kissed Michael on the lips as always, then came to me giving me a lovely hug, whilst kissing me.

She told us, she was not going to be working on Tuesdays and Fridays, any longer, then if I wanted, we could spend more time together, I told her I thought it was a very good idea, because I was lonely during the day, Michael said it answered his prayers, because he thought I might start doing charity work again!

It was my birthday the following Wednesday, Michael gave me the most romantic card I have ever seen, a giant bottle of Chanel No.5, and he was taking me out Saturday for a special meal, which I was looking forward to. The postman brought more cards than I had ever had, all Michaels sons sent a card each, the one from Charles was particularly nice, it had not got a printed verse but wrote

I can not fault my fathers choice.
I hope one day to find someone as very special as you are!
'Many Happy Returns' All my love Charles x

I was touched it was so sweet, it brought a tear to my eye, Michael was not as thrilled.

Saturday we had a wonderful lie in, we spent a dreamy day together, until 5.30 pm, he said you had better get ready, I want you in an evening gown please my love.

I decided on a tight black lace long gown with a halter neck, rather a lot of cleavage was on show, also because it was so tight it accentuated my breasts, (it was not until I put it on I realised my nipples were a bit tender) the skirt was fitted tight, with a slit up one side well above my knee, I put my favourite stiletto sandals on.

As I was walking downstairs, he shouted "I am in the drawing room my pet," as I entered he stood in his evening suit.

"You look good enough to eat," I said.

"That is one hell of a sexy dress, I certainly do not want to eat you, but I will gladly fuck you, but we haven't got time because the table is booked," he came towards me "You are a dream, I have something for you," he held a small box, I opened it and there was a gorgeous engagement ring three very large clear sparkling diamonds, he took it out, took my left hand, slipped it on my third finger "I know officially we cannot marry but as far I am concerned, and the outside world we are, if I thought there was anyway I could marry you, making you mine, all mine I would, I would walk on hot coals if I could marry you," I was trying not to weep, but a lonely tear escaped.

"Michael you say the most unbelievable things to me, you surprise me you are so verbose, I know we will not ever be able to be married but in my eyes it makes no difference, I love you, I am so in love with you, I am yours, yours alone, you own me, that is how it is going to stay," and I leaned into him, rather a lot lower than I would normally do, showing him most of my breasts, then gave him a soft kiss on his luscious lips but moved back fast before he could get me in hold.

"You leaned down on purpose, I have got your number you dirty little slut, you wait until I get you home later, I will show you what dirty little sluts get, that my darling will be a first, I wish we were not going out now, I shall be drooling all evening, thinking what I am going to do to you. So tell me what are you?"

"I am a dirty little slut and I cannot wait until we get back, for you to punish me, I am getting breathless now. Can you ring and ask them to keep the table for another three hours, I will gladly go back upstairs and face my punishment," we are looking into each others eyes, then his lips are on mine, we are both wanting.

"My love I wish we could, you started this, now we have got to go out and act little civil human beings, instead of the over sexed fucking pair we are," we both laughed.

"Come along my love, you said there is a table booked," I suddenly remembered my lipstick, when I looked in my little mirror, there was none, I reapplied, then walked into the hall. He said;

"Just in case it gets a bit chilly," he wrapped a wonderful white fox fur stole over my shoulders.

"Michael it is lovely, but you should not spend all your money like this, you have already given me this beautiful ring, not counting the perfume," I said.

"When we get back, I want to see you in that with nothing else on, is it a deal?"he asked.

"So is this before or after my punishment? Anyway you know whatever you want me to do, I will always do without question, because I want to keep you very, very happy, and much to exhausted to look elsewhere!" I drooled at him, at the same time, rubbing myself up his growing erection.

"You do that once more, you will be stripped and I will be fucking you here in the hall, you really are turning into a little slapper, I am glad to say my little slapper, as well as my little slut, come on," he was really laughing, I followed him to the door, there was a big Rolls Royce parked and a chauffeur holding the door open.

"Good evening sir, madam" he actually saluted. Michael helped me in, then went to the other side and slid in. Then the chauffeur got in and we set off. Michael pressed a button and a screen went up in between us and the driver "Is this yours?" I asked.

"No I hire it when the need arises, I always get Grayson this driver, I thought you should go in style, you look like a Queen you should travel like one" he leaned over, gave me a quick kiss and blew down the front of my dress, which he has done in the past, at the same time, his hand had slipped into the slit, and his fingers were moving my thong to one side, I slid a bit further forward so I could feel his fingers slipping inside of me. He whispered "You are the dirtiest little bitch, you would let me do anything to you, whether we were in public or not, but I would not change a thing. I love you with all my heart," suddenly he moved his fingers and hand.

"No, darling please carry on, I love it."

He said "We are here, darling, come on take that wanton face off, I am as disappointed as you are, but I promise you later, you certainly not be wanting, first will be your punishment then I am going to fuck you silly," he was leering.

"You come up with the weakest excuses for leaving me panting for more," I leered back to him. "By the way, you have done that blowing on my breasts frequently, is there a particular reason?" I asked.

"Yes my darling, there is a particular reason, I know when breasts go cold the nipples always get hard and firm, when I do that it delights me thinking that I have just done that to you, have I or not? also depending what you are wearing, I can actually see them sticking out, thinking of them in my mouth," he said closing his eyes.

"Yes my darling they certainly do, always have when you have done that," I replied.

Grayson was out and let Michael out then Michael held his hand to me I took it and stepped out.

"I will ring when I need you Grayson, thank you," we went inside.

"Good evening sir" said a young man in evening suit "Your room is ready for you," we followed him, he opened the door and stepped into a dark room, Michael pushed me slightly forward, "Sorry sir someone seems to have turned the lights off," suddenly the room was lit up and a shout of   "Belated   Happy Birthday" all five of Michaels sons were there as was Julia.

Then I could not see anything for tears. Michael took me in his arms as the room fell silent "Come on sweetie it is supposed to be a happy night, we thought we would surprise you," he whispered.

"I am happy, it is that I have never had a birthday party before, but I am happy," I replied.

"Do you here that she is happy," a big cheer went up "My Sophie says she has never had a birthday party, so that is a first for us," They all came over to greet me, kissing me on the cheek, apart from one who kissed me on the lips, I knew who that was, it was lovely Charles, then Julia greeted me last, again she kissed me on the lips. I saw Michael watching her.

"I do wish Charles would not do that, I know he has always been close to Michael, but I cannot see Michael letting him keep kissing you on the lips and I do not like it! I do not want my son getting close with you!" Julia whispered to me. I was shocked by the tone of her voice, then waiter came in with flutes of champagne.

"Here's to my Sophie, to another five lots of twenty years," the chorus to Sophie went up.

Julia was still stood beside me, she beckoned to Charles "Why do you insist on kissing Sophie on the lips, you know your father will not let you keep doing it, I certainly do not want you to, you can do a lot better than her, I could not care less who your father has, you will stop kissing her," although she was whispering I could hear what she was saying, again her tone of voice told me that she was displeased.

"I am just marking my territory, I want Sophie as much if not more than Pa, if everything goes pear shaped as knowing Pa it will, I am first reserve I will be there for her!" he stood smiling.

"God forbid that anything should happen, but I will do all in my power to keep you apart, although Sophie has a mind of her own, I do not think she is too choosy in who fucks her," she snapped.

"Mother you are out of order there, anyway I thought you loved her, why should you say things like that?" he asked.

"Charles I do love her, I have very deep feelings for her, I want her in my life, you see darling you cannot help who you fall in love with but I will make sure she stays with me, you will never be any more that a relation of sorts, I will not let you, so drop it Charles, do as I fucking tell you," she was furious, Charles had glanced at me, he knew I had heard everything.

Michael came over "Come on lets get seated, I am

starving," Julia sat next to him, I was the other side, Charles plonked down next to me.

"I want to keep you near me, I love you Sophie but I can wait. I cannot weigh her up she says she loves you, but she will stop me if I get a chance?" he whispered in my ear, Michael didn't notice, Julia certainly did, she slowly shook her head at us and really glared.

"Please Charles stop it, it will never happen, I love your father we are staying together," I said pleadingly.

"You are a darling, you cannot trust people, I hope he does stay with you, he cannot help himself, it's impossible for him to be monogamous, he will cheat on you, you are not my mother, who let's him do as he wants, I will always be there for you my darling," while he his whispering to me, I am looking round the table but no one had noticed just Julia, Michael is talking to her, that's why she can concentrate on glaring at us.

I wish Charles had not said that, I feel like an accomplice however innocent, as we were getting ready to leave Charles whispered "Drop your napkin, I will pick it up for you, my mobile number is on a note, anytime if you just need someone to talk to please my darling ring me!" Then a bit louder he was saying;

"John and I are moving into Pa's old flat in the Park, so we will be a lot nearer then," I was complicit, I dropped my napkin, Charles bend down and handed it to me.

"Thank you kind sir," I said as he passed it with flourish, I could feel a small folded piece of paper. Michael came and stood with me while we were saying our good byes, Julia was hovering, the boys split up, they all kissed me good night on the cheek, Charles was last but he was talking to Michael, I heard Charles say, "Pa please don't hurt Sophie, she is so lovely she could have her pick of anyone, don't take her for granted," he was very serious. Then Michael said;

"Charles you may be my dearest son, I'll give you that you could be wanting to fuck her, but you will have to want on son, find your own, she is mine, you will never get that chance, we do love each other. Do not overstep the mark please son," he took hold of his neck, pulled him forward, kissed him on the forehead, "I love you, please don't disappoint me." I could not believe it.

Charles moved towards me I said "Goodnight," before I knew it, he had took hold of me, bent me backwards, his lips were on mine, it all happened so quick, I started kissing him back, then realised what I had done, it must have been a couple of seconds from beginning to the end, Michael was getting me back, upright laughing. "Well done son you have made your point."

I said "What's going on? I had to act as if I didn't know."

"It's alright my love, Charles and I are having a bit of fun sorry sweetie are you alright," but while he was saying that I could hear Julia saying;

"You really are pushing your luck Charles with both of us, you know she is pregnant, she says it's your fathers, I mean it stay away from her," she stressed, I could not believe what I am hearing, she says, I say it's Michaels, who the hell does she think is the father? I saw his face it was as if someone had hit him over the head I thought for a minute he was going to cry, instead he turned on his heel and left swiftly.

As he was walking away, I went towards the car, but as I turned expecting Michael to be behind me, she had pulled him to one side, was talking to him very fast, for sometime, he leaned in to kiss her. My whole being seemed to drop, I felt very down, what's happening I thought as I sat waiting. Michael and Julia strolled talking she had her arm in his she said   "Will we see you at church?"

Michael said straight away "I am thinking we would be better to go to Tollerton church it is only down the road."

Julia looked shocked "Oh, alright you didn't mention it before, it does not matter, I will see you Tuesday Sophie, I will ring you on Monday, good night darling," she leaned into the car and kissed me on my lips, Michael got in the other side and we set off on the short journey.

As we set off for home I said "Darling, what did Julia say to you, she seems to be dictating?" he didn't look at me, when he did he looked vague?

"Sophie I am not going to report back to you every time we say something to one another. If you know what's good for you, stay away from my sons, all of them. Try to keep your fucking legs closed," he really snapped. We were soon home, he got out before Grayson opened the door, Grayson opened my door, helped me out, I thanked him. When I closed the door, Michael was already going up stairs.

"Darling are you coming down for a drink?" I called.

"No, get up here now if you know what's good for you!" I

don't like the sound of that, one minute he's laughing, what's changed?

"Darling is there anything wrong?" I asked.

"I do not know is there, is there something you should be telling me?" he demanded.

"Michael I do not know what you mean, like what?" I asked.

"Like my son, are you leading him on? Julia said I had got to watch you because you making a pass at him, I am telling you, keep your fucking legs crossed when Charles, or any of my sons are around. You are mine and I have said before no one else is going to touch you. I will kill you if I see you rubbing your tits up against him, not only that you unzipped him and was massaging his erection!" he slapped me across the face "I told you, I love you, but you are turning into a slut, stop trying to get my sons into bed!" he slapped me again.

"What the hell are you talking about? I have never been that close to Charles, I love you, it is you I want, I don't know what has got into you? I didn't think you believed in hitting women!" I said through my tears.

"Julia said she saw the two of you in the hall, you had your arm round his neck, you were rubbing your whole body up against him, but he seemed not to like what you were doing, that he was clearly telling you, you were out of order, she said she heard him say, I would not do anything to hurt my Pa, you are with him, I do not want you Sophie. Then he moved out of your way and told you to leave him alone otherwise he would tell Pa what a little slut you are," I stood open mouthed my mouth was dry, I could not seem to speak.

"You see you are not going to deny it, so I take it that it is true, you are trying to seduce Charles, Julia said I should have known you were to good to be true. We all fell for your lies, the lies you told for sympathy. Julia did, but I am the biggest fool, even got you pregnant or is it even mine? Julia said you would let anyone fuck you, I dread to think, I have five sons, I bet you thought all your birthdays had come at once, she said you do not know what love is," he was staring, but did not seem to focus and he did not blink?

I found my voice "Michael, you know different to that, I do love you, I am in love with you, why did Julia say these things, she is supposed to be my friend, I did not see Charles in the hall, please where is this coming from. Please darling none of it is true, you know I am not like you say, please, please Michael, speak to me," he still stared at me, but didn't seem to see me? he did not blink, then all of a sudden, he threw my hand off him.

"Fuck you, Julia is right you may have money but she said you probably earned it opening your legs to anybody who wanted to fuck you! She said that's why you are so good in bed! Julia also said she did not want any of her sons having anything to do with you and I agree, I am going back to protect all my boys from you," that was it he stormed down the stairs, out the door, the car was driven at high speed, I was frightened, I stood for a while crying, as rooted to the spot.

Chapter eleven

Eventually I ran into the study and dialled Julia's home number, it rang for quiet a while before it was answered "Julia something has happened, why did you say all those terrible things to Michael about me seducing Charles, how could you, you know it's not true, I was never alone with Charles," I was stopped in mid flow.

"Darling mother is upstairs, this is Charles what are you talking about?"

"Can you please ask your mother, why she told your father I was trying to seduce you?" I am pleading, I am crying.

"Hang on, you, trying to seduce me? Well Soph I wish you were, hang on, Mother, oh there you are, what did you say to Pa about me and Soph?" I heard "What, what are you talking about?" I could hear she was getting nearer the phone.

"Sophie darling what's going on, I did not speak to Michael, he did a lot of talking, boring stuff, I kept my eyes on the pair of you, darling tell me what has happened and where is he now?"

"He said he was going to protect his sons, so I assumed he is on his way," then I told her what I could remember.

Julia said "Darling I would never say anything like that, I love you. Well, if he was on his way here he has not arrived, I cannot for the life of me understand, why he would say such things? I would never do anything to hurt you, you know that I love you as my own," I could hear faint voices "Charles says he has tried his mobile, it has gone straight to the answer phone, don't do anything I am coming, I will look after you," and she was gone.

In no time at all, I heard a car pull into the drive, I ran to the door it might be Michael, it was Charles and Julia they were having a blazing row, he was out of the car and ran to me.

"We have come the normal way and there is no sign of Pa's car, where the bloody hell is he? why would he make that all up. Mother is not happy with me either because I insisted on coming here?" Charles said.

"I don't know but he said some terrible things, he seemed to be staring all the while, he did not blink, he would not listen to me," We all went into the kitchen. Charles put the kettle on.

"Do you want a cuppa or coffee or something stronger?"

he asked.

"Tea please, let me make it," I was visibly shaking.

"No darling you sit down are you cold?" he asked quite concerned.

Julia said "I will have a large whisky, I can get it myself," then left.

"Why was mother so against me coming here to see you?"

"I don't know, but I know she spoke to your father, she pulled him to one side whilst I was walking to the car," I stated.

She came back with a large glass of whisky, so we stopped talking.

"I have just tried his mobile, it is still going straight to answering machine, where the hell is he, I am going to kill him when I get my hands on him, what does he think he was doing telling all those lies, I will try home, but I cannot see how he could have passed us?" we watched her "Sorry John, have I got you out of bed, is your father there? - pause - no it is alright good night darling. No he is on his own and although he fell asleep in front on the television, he would have heard him, anyway his car is not there, I cannot think where he is, darling you take your tea to bed, is a spare bed made up?"

"Yes I always keep one made up in case we have visitors,"

"Charles, I think you should go to bed, there is no point in every one losing sleep."

"Let me stay up, you go and sleep," he said.

"No he is my bloody husband, if I stay up I can play bloody hell with him, if he came in now I think I would kill him, for what he is putting me through," she ran out of steam. "Go up," she said "I will come and check you are on your own," we looked at one another, we both went upstairs, I showed him which bed was made up.

"Charles did she say what I think she did?" I asked.

"Yes darling, just ignore her, I am not quite sure what is going on at the moment," he kissed me goodnight.

I went into our bedroom, I do not know why, I will not sleep, I didn't, everything was going round and round, I kept looking at the clock 30 minutes seemed like 2 hours, the hours dragged. I decided to go into the office and look in his files to see if there was anyone's name or address, nothing. I decided to have a shower, get dressed and go downstairs, my waist was thickening just a bit, so it made the waist bands a bit tight, I found a dress that

195

was not too tight, and went downstairs, Julia was curled up on the sofa fast asleep, so sooner than wake her I crept silently back upstairs, as Charles emerged all fresh showered, shaved, in jeans and summer shirt over the top.

He opened his mouth to speak I put my fingers to my lips to stop him speaking too loud and waking Julia, so he followed me into the study and closed the door.

"Your mother is fast asleep on the sofa in the kitchen, I didn't want to wake her up boiling the kettle, Charles where do you think he is? I went through everything in here last night, to see if there was a name or address of somewhere he might have gone," the tears began to flow, he came to me and wrapped his arms round me.

"Have you had any sleep," I shook my head "You really should you are going to be no good if you are shattered," he turned me towards him "Please tell me again what he said last night," he sat me in one chair and pulled the other opposite me and took my hands "Come on try and remember from the beginning,"

So I thought, then began from seeing his mother talking fast to his father, then us setting off home, and everything until he drove off. Then added the innuendo's his mother had dropped. "The odd thing was, that although he was saying all these things he appeared to be looking through me, I didn't think until after," I said through the tears and sobs.

"Why would he make all that up, you don't think my mother could have said that to him, she was doing a lot of shaking her head and glaring in our direction, I am so sorry Soph. I should have not said anything to you, I was certainly out of order kissing you like that, I was just fooling around trying to wind Pa up, but, and it is but, I am sincere of my feelings for you, if I get the opportunity to get you away from Pa, I will, but I can wait. I have to get the business off of the ground so that will take a lot of time but I can live in hope," he took my hand up and kissed it.

"Charles the more I think about it, the more I think your mother must have said it to him, because he repeated what she had said, so why would he lie, although I thought me and your mother were close, I cannot understand?" I muttered. "There is something I think you ought to know, about your father, twice, that I know of, it could have happened before, he has had what he calls a funny turn, where for a while he cannot remember where he is, or what he was doing, it is only a few minutes, but he looks a weird colour for a time after, do you think he has had something like that, only longer? I think I should tell you something about your mother, I have told your father," so I told him about the incident in the shower.

"I don't know about Pa, sounds like there is something, has he been to the Doctors?" I shake my head, "Mother, I just do not know, she appears to think more of you, than she does her sons, she actually took time from work to look after you, when we were young, it was always Pa. Come on I want a cuppa, if we wake her up well tough."

We went down stairs, just as the door bell rang I looked at Charles I was glued to the spot. "It's alright let me," he opened the door and there stood two policemen.

"Good morning sir does a," out came the note book, "Michael Roper live here?"

"Yes that is my father, I am one of his sons," Charles said. "This is Soph, Sophie is my fathers partner,"

"Do you know where my father is?" he asked.

"I think they should come in Charles," I said as Julia came out of the kitchen.

"What's happening, where's Michael?" she snapped.

"You are madam?" said the first one, as they entered.

"I am Mrs Roper" she snapped. That raised their eyebrows they are totally confused. "My husband is Michael Roper," she snapped again.

I said "Come in here please, can you please, tell me where he is?" I am in tears Charles put his arm round me.

"I am not sure who I should be addressing, do you all live here?" one asked looking at Julia.

I said "No I live here with Michael, Charles and his mother live in Edwalton, but came down because I did not know where Michael was, please do you know anything?"

"Yes apparently he was heading for Melton Mowbray, he passed several cars at high speed, they all said he was well over the speed limit, he over shot the bend in the road, ploughed through the bushes and eventually hit a tree, he is very lucky, this was logged at 2am. He was taken to Melton Mowbray hospital, he has a broken ankle, sprained wrist, took a severe knock on the head and is covered in bruises and cuts to his face," he said.

The other officer said "Has he some connection with the Nottingham Police?"

"Yes of course he has, he is the Chief Constable, I hope he is in a private ward and not the N.H.S, he will be livid, if he isn't given the best treatment possible!" Julia was on a high horse, I had never seen her like this before, Charles and I looked at one another. "For the future he is my husband, as my husband you will address me, do you understand," they both looked shocked.

"Sorry Mrs Roper, we did not understand, anyway he is doing well and when the Doctor has been to see him tomorrow, he will be able to come home, but we will need to interview him, so do we come here or?" she stopped him before he could say anymore.

"No he is my husband, how many times do I have to tell you, he will be at home with me, and a team of nurses, to take care of his every need," she was dictating. I had, had enough;

"Excuse me," I said quietly "This is Michael Ropers home, here with me, I think Julia you should stop, take a breath, you are obviously in shock," I got no further.

"Shock," she screamed "How would you know shock, I am the Doctor here, if I say he comes home with me, then that is where he will be, he can come back to you, when I have got him back into perfect health, or can't you wait that long to be fucked!"

"Mother that is enough, don't you ever speak to Sophie like that again, officers this is where my father lives, when you need to speak to him he will be here," he was quiet and polite.

Without any warning she came over and slapped Charles across his face, with such force. He grabbed her hand;

"You will never do that to me again, get in the kitchen now, I am sorry Officers, if you have finished Sophie will see you out, I will take her to the hospital to see my father," he said.

I said "Thank you very much officers, I am sorry you had to witness this, I do not know what has come over her, she is not like this normally," I said apologetically.

"Good day madam," they said, and drove off.

When I arrived in the kitchen Julia was on the sofa weeping, Charles had the kettle on and was getting crockery out.

"Let me do that Charles, I think you had better take care of your mother over there, I have never been so ashamed in my life, what was all that about, I should think they went away thinking you were a mad women, you were definitely out of order there Julia, I thought you were my friend?" the tears were pouring down my face, as I made the tea, Charles had to carry it because I was shaking too much.

I went over to the sofa "Julia what is it, what have I done to make you so hateful towards me, to say that in front of the Police, I sincerely hope Michael does not find out, he will go crazy," I said.

She looked towards me, "You have no idea have you, you are so innocent. Michael will not stay with you, once he gets bored with you, yes he will keep coming home to you eventually, but you will have to wait, while he is fucking every woman that throw themselves at him, he cannot help himself, I don't doubt he loves you, but he cannot and will not spend all his time with you, I know, but what you have not got, is what I have, I have power over him, because we are married and at the end of the day he comes back to me, he will never let me down and he will never get a divorce, he will do whatever I tell him without question. I could not care less what he gets up to, it does not bother me one iota, it would never bother me if I never had him fawning over me again, because he is a typical man thinks with his cock. I do not need any man, you should have stayed with me Samantha I could show you real love," I tried to say something, but I didn't stand a chance, it was obvious Charles could not believe what he was hearing. "I cannot see you putting up with his philandering, I told him to go fuck, wherever he wanted, I even bought him the flat to get rid of him, he thought the world of me for that."

"Why did you call Sophie, Samantha?" Charles asked.

"I did not, I said Sophie! Where was I, oh yes, you have not got a chance, you can only offer him sex, he can get that anywhere a man with his looks and body. He is looked up to in the community, how can he stay happy with you, yes I have to give it to you, that you have a beautiful body, but he will spoil that making you pregnant. Now I suggest when he comes out of hospital you let me have him, I will make sure all the nurses, are beautiful, young and shapely. I will insist they keep him happy and will pay them extra each time they let him fuck them. I will let him know that this I have arranged specially for him, he will be more indebted to me," she sipped her tea as if she was talking about the weather. "You will never keep him, he will never let another man so much as look at you longingly, he would kill you first, you are his to do as he wishes. So I am now telling you, he will be coming to me, when he leaves hospital. Charles I forbid you to come here to see her on your own, you will never be alone with her!" she glared at me.

"Mother you did say Samantha!" he repeated.

"I will explain but not now I have something to say to your mother, Charles," I said, "You can talk until you are blue in the face, you will not change me, I am in love with Michael, I know I can keep him happy, I do not care what you threaten me with, I am having our first baby, I believe he will be a good father, I will give him the chance that you never gave him. It was nannies and nurses and everything run on a time table, you made sure they were always in bed before Michael came home, you made sure they were out of sight in a morning, it was the same at the weekends. Your boys did not know their father when they were babies, you made sure of that. I am sorry but I did not believe him, when he told me, but after your shocking outburst in front of the police, also what you have just enlightened me with, I choose make my own mind up, I sure as hell believe everything he told me. What is all this about Charles being forbidden to see me on his own, what the fuck does that mean?" her face was a picture.

"You dare sit there and tell me he has talked to you about me in derogatory terms, he would not, he would not dare, he only talks to others about me in the highest regard and love for me, he dare not do otherwise, he knows the consequences, you are a lying little bitch!"

"So how do I know about the nannies, timetables, things you used to plan, I am the one sleeping with Michael, so how else would I know, he talks a lot to me. Please explain what you mean by telling Charles he is forbidden to be alone with me?" I was really cross.

"Darling, you know I love you, when he has shown his true colours, you'll come and live with me, I will make you very happy, and show you what true love is, I have always wanted a daughter to love."

"I don't understand you Julia. Anyone want breakfast? Then I'm going go to see Michael. Charles you can take my lying so called friend home, I not think I could look at you again Julia, I think you are sick, very sick!" I left the room fuming, slamming the door as hard as I could.

I ran upstairs, made my bed, I also did something I have never done before I made the bed Charles had slept in, I have a feeling he will be disenchanted with his mother and seek his father out, or I hoped he would, I feel sorry for both of them. I brushed my hair, put on some make-up. I went into the office and rang Melton hospital, I was told he'd be coming out after the Doctors round tomorrow so can I go and visit him today.

I went downstairs, I thought they would be talking, but she was still sat on the sofa nursing another cup of tea, it looks as if Charles did her some toast, it had to be that way, she would not lower herself to do menial tasks for anyone let alone herself. "Charles, have you had any breakfast there's bacon, eggs, sausage there is plenty in the fridge, you cannot go home without having anything," I said quietly.

"I could not eat a thing Soph, it would choke me. I am going with you to see pa, she is going home in a taxi, it is on it's way," his voice went quieter "I have told them the address to take her to, not to take her elsewhere. Are you ready?" I nodded "Come on your taxi will be here in a minute, lets get rid of you!" I stood my mouth open "Soph, don't catch flies darling it is not very becoming," still she didn't speak, he picked her handbag up off the floor, pushed it into her hand but he did not look at her, she just ignored him, then as I was locking up, she called as she was closing the taxi door "Ring me darling if there is anything I can do, bye darling love you."

Charles and I stood looking at each other, in the end we shrugged. "We are going in my car, I do not want you doing more than you should. That was true that you are pregnant?" he asked as we set off.

"Yes, I am pregnant. Charles you know what I told you, what your father had said Julia had said, I do think she could have, but I cannot think why? Is that why your father behaved the way he did to me?" I asked "He seemed to be looking at me, but I saw nothing in his eyes and his pupils were very big?"

"Just think for a minute, I think what mother said about having power over him, she said if a man looked at you or whatever, Pa would blame you, is that not what he said he would kill you?" he asked.

"Yes but what if your mother, had said, what your father said, she has planted the seed, she admitted she has power over him, I know that as a fact, because your father said he begins to dread going to these functions, because she lectures him, that he must keep his arms round her, he must kiss her from time to time, and under no circumstances must he leave her side to talk to anyone else, he has to dance all night with her, he must hold her very close. He said she always insists they sleep together, although he admitted, he had never seen her naked, she has always undressed in the en suite and came out in a nightdress, even when they were first married. I honestly do not know what to think? I have to admit she was marvellous when your father rang for her to come and help him with me, she took time off work, yet she never took time off for her sons, I truly thought she was my friend," the tears were flowing again, Charles pulled into a lay by, he leaned towards me, pulled me to him and held me very close.

"Darling I hate to see you so unhappy, let's stop trying to second guess, let's wait until we get Pa home," he said.

When we arrived at the hospital, I found him lying down in bed, he seemed a bit groggy, Charles said he would wait outside for a few minutes, so we could be alone. I whispered "Michael darling are you awake," his eyes fluttered open, then when he saw it was me the smile lit up his battered face, it was covered in bruises, scratches and cuts.

"Sophie darling, tell me what has happened, all I have been told is that I was on the road to Melton Mowbray, I was speeding and lost control on a bend, went through a hedge and long grass which slowed me down before I hit a tree, but I cannot remember anything, why was I driving to Melton?" he looked at me pleading.

I sat on the bed, leaned over and kissed him on his lips, he kissed me back hungrily, he put his right arm round me "You look a wonderful sight my darling," he said,

"Charles has brought me he's outside, can I ask him to come in?"

"Of course," he replied, so I went to the door, he was talking to a nurse, but he saw me and I signalled to come in.

Charles walked in, "I was just saying to Michael we do not know why you were coming to Melton? you said you were going to Edwalton."

"Why would I be going to Edwalton?" he asked.

"Look darling, we have no idea, it is all a mystery to us, after you stormed out of the house."

"What do you mean stormed out of the house, why would I do that, had I forgotten something?" he obviously could not remember.

Charles went over and kissed his Pa on the forehead "Pa what can you remember about last night?" he asked. He looked puzzled.

I jumped in "What is the last thing you can remember darling? He was definitely thinking.

"Well we came out after the meal, were saying goodnight, Charles bent you over and kissed you full on the lips, I helped you up we were all laughing and then," there was a long pause, we were both holding our breath "Then I woke up here!"

"Is that it Pa?" Charles asked.

"Well I assumed we went home," he sounded very down.

"Can we leave it until we get you home, we can fetch you tomorrow after the Doctor has been round," in came Sister and another nurse, very young and pretty, "We're sorry, can you come back in two hours we want to run some tests, Mr Roper seems a bit vague as to how he got here."

"We will fetch you tomorrow," Charles kissed his father, I leaned over and kissed him again, the nurse coughed "I am sorry but we have to get on."

"See you tomorrow, after the Doc says you can come out."

"Come on let's take you home and put your feet up," Charles said holding me by the elbow. The car was warm, I was so tired, I dozed off as soon as we set off, the next thing Charles was saying "Come on, sleeping head, we're home."

He was so good, he made lunch and cleared away, then he cooked a very early dinner, he would not let me do a thing, we did not have deep meaningful conversations we just chatted, but he said I had to stop going over and over about Pa it was getting us nowhere.

I decided to try to explain about Samantha, but not the whole saga..

We decided an early night was what we needed so we were in bed before 10 pm. I must have gone to sleep straight away but something woke me, I do not know what it was, when I looked at the clocked it was only 12.45 am, I never got back to sleep again, everything was going round and round, in the end I got up at 5.30am had shower and got dressed went down, it was a beautiful day, so I opened the french doors in the kitchen and made a cup of tea, it went down like nectar and I must have nodded off.

The next thing is Charles speaking softly to me "Would you like another cup of tea?" I nodded half awake. I did not want any breakfast but he made me scrambled eggs on toast, I ate one slice of toast but all the eggs, which pleased him, he was more like a father than the son of my beloved.

I rang the hospital and was told Michael could come out, we could go now, so we were soon out of the door, but again I must have dozed, because next thing the car is in the car park, we are there. We did not see any staff, so we went straight to Michaels room, Charles was carrying some jeans and top, I had his boxers in my bag. He was sat on the top of a bed in a hospital gown, when he saw us his smile was lovely, I gently kissed him on his lips and he hungrily kissed me back.

"Michael I have been so worried," he held me close.

We had to borrow some scissors and cut the leg of his jeans, "We can get you some more," Charles started cutting.

"I have been so worried about you my darling, I love you and I have missed you, I have not slept at all," he clung to me.

"My sweetie, I love you more than you will ever know."

We soon had him decent and in a wheel chair, although he did object, he wanted to walk with his crutches, but we both told him to sit down and shut up. We had no problems getting him into the back of the car and stretching his leg out, I got in the front.

Traffic was light so we were home in no time, I had a job to keep my eyes open, I was so tired.

We arrived home, he went in on his crutches to the kitchen, the sun was streaming in, I opened the french doors and put the kettle on.

"Does either of you want a sandwich to keep you going? I will cook dinner later?" they both decided yes, so I made a plate of Ham and a plate of Roast beef with salad trimmings, Charles came and fetched everything, put it on the coffee table, while I made the drinks.

"Darling we need to sort out what happened, so can you remember any further than the car park, what did Julia tell you?" I asked.

"The last thing I remember is helping you up, we were laughing," he looked puzzled "The next thing I am waking up in hospital, like this, throbbing head, pains everywhere, I asked how I got there and was told I had driven off the road at speed, was lucky I was not killed, the hedge and field slowed me before I hit the tree."

"Hang on what about me and you getting home, what you said to me? Please darling, close your eyes, go back in your mind from seeing Charles kiss me, please darling," I am close to crying,

I could scream. He did as I asked he rested his head back, nothing, he sat for a while. "Well?"

"No sorry sweetie nothing, I just wake up in hospital, please tell me what happened, how did I end up in hospital please, Charles what do you know? please tell me, why is it blank?" he was worried.

"We are going to have to tell him," Charles wisely said.

So I told him from the point of laughing, then Julia talking to him, the journey home, what he said and did, then he stopped me.

"Hang on, you said I slapped you across the face? I would not darling, you know I would not hurt you for the world!"

I confirmed, then hurried on until he left me, driving away at high speed. I stopped he was unaware of anything, he was very upset by what I told him, Charles nodded to me. I continued until the police arrived, then Julia's behavior until now.

"Darling did anything ring a bell about you driving?" I asked.

"No, but what I want to know is 1. Did I really say that she had said that to me about you and Charles? 2. She didn't speak like that in front of the police? 3. Did she actually say that about having me home with her?" I could see he was livid. We both confirmed that what we had told him was exactly has things happened.

"Get me the bloody phone," I have never seen him so mad.

"Darling please calm down, who are you wanting to phone?"

"That bloody bitch that I married, she has gone too far now, although I do not remember any of this, but you said I had told you what she had said to me, yet she says she did not say any of that, also she denied the warning that you were to stay away from her son. I know who I believe, it isn't that dried up vindictive piece of shit I married, she has manipulated me all the time, I thought she was the best wife ever, when she let me do my own thing, but all along I have really been dancing to her tune and me a senior copper and I cannot see further than my nose end!" Charles passed him the telephone and he dialled.

"Yes can I speak to Mrs Roper please," - pause - "It's her bloody husband," Charles and I looked at one another, she had obviously come to the phone "Do not start asking me how I am, you two faced lying bitch, you have really fucked up this time Julia, we are finished. I am divorcing you, I should have done it years ago when I found out about your activities, but I kept quite, I let you get away with things because it didn't really bother me, it affected only me, but you did not count on the fact that I am truly in love with Sophie, I will stand by her and have listened whilst she told me of your outrageous behaviour in front of the police, you are nothing but a screwed up dyke, I knew you did not want me, but I put up with you, not now, you have hurt the most precious person in my life, my Sophie. You can say what you want to your lawyer it will not matter, because it is common knowledge I committed adultery, you knew so you were complicit in my extra martial relations. You have never been a mother, nannies and nurses all the time poor little buggers, then as soon as they were old enough it was boarding school, college or university, anything or anybody as long as the spoilt bitch does not have to do anything, only pleasure herself with her many lovers!" we could hear she was ranting, he calmly put the telephone down.

"I now know for a fact I will get my divorce, because she will not want anything to come out about her Lesbian activities, she will not want her pure name and reputation being spoiled. I know for a fact she will go for the easiest option to keep her private life private. Her parents have spoilt her for years, that bloody big house they gave us as a wedding present, they gave her a million pound for her to spend on her wedding, you see she wanted to keep me, because I was the perfect foil for her, that is why at the bloody functions she dragged me to, I was lectured on how to be the perfect, attentive lover and husband. I just went a long with it all it suited me, I could not have cared less, I was so brained washed, I even told you Sophie I loved her, she killed that after the last twins were born, I realised then she only wanted me to have children, she thought I was stupid, well I probably was but not any more. I now know she wanted you for herself Sophie all that 'I could bring you happiness,' she stated openly she was, well is in love with you, that is what is at the bottom of this, she wants to split us up because she wants you for herself. Look at her behaviour in the shower. I should have asked why she denied talking to me Saturday night, I should have pretended I knew," then telephone rang, he answered.

"Hi Graham what have I done to deserve this honour," whilst he was listening. Charles leaned over to me and whispered.

"Graham is a Lawyer as well as a close friend," he said.

"Christ she did not loose any time, let me get this straight, we are to agree on a divorce on irretrievable differences, so hang on is she not stating anything about my adultery?" he asked "I knew it, what a bloody fool I have been, I could have done this years ago, did you not know she is a Lesbian?" - pause - "No it is true she is," - pause - "No years ago, okay I will leave it with you," - pause - "She what? wants to make it quick, well report back to her daddies legal team I would be more than happy if it was done yesterday," he put the phone down, "Well did you gather," we replied together yes, he was really smiling.

He started dialling a number "Mrs Roper, her sodding husband. Tell me why did you deny to Sophie saying all those things Saturday night, surely you knew I would remember, you cannot deny you spoke to me." there was a long pause, I was holding Charles hand. "You fucking vindictive bitch, it back fired though, shows she is in love with me, as I am with her," he slammed the phone down.

"Well," both Charles and I said together.

"She thought I would believe her over you, my darling, she assumed I would want rid of you, she wanted to step in and take you, for herself. She had not envisaged me storming out and having an accident, and her plan not working." he said.

"Darling I am pleased for you that you are getting a divorce, but," and I looked at him "We should be looking at what has happened, the fact you remember absolutely nothing about coming home and up until you woke up in hospital, I cannot understand, you said you were going to protect your boys from me, does it not bother you the fact you were heading for Melton Mowbray? The hour or more of lost time? I know when people have an accident they do not remember from the impact, you lost an time before the accident?"

"Pa, Soph is right we should wonder, perhaps see a specialist?"

"Look I know you are worried, believe me I am, so let's give it a couple of days, see if anything comes back, then you can make an appointment via the doctor, okay my darling?"

"Yes Michael, I had better start preparations for our evening meal," I said getting up.

"No you are not doing that Soph, you did not sleep all night again, you should be resting in your condition, I will order and fetch a take out later," lovely Charles.

"I could not have said better myself, thank you Charles,

you really do care about Sophie, I am sorry while I am around she is mine, when I am divorced we are going to get married, you can give her away as a symbol that you will not try to take her away from me!" he was deadly serious, I looked towards Charles he was smiling at his father.

"Pa, I give you my word, I would never do that, I can wait, as long as you do not stop me from having any contact with you both."

"Don't be silly I would never do that, but I am very protective towards my one true love, she has made me happier than I thought I could ever be!" he said giving me that bloody melting smile, everything goes south, I want him on my own, I want us to make love, I am so needing him.

Then Charles spoke "You know I was moving into your flat with John, well he has moved Polly his girl friend in, taken the biggest room and I do not want to play gooseberry or listen to their loud love making, I told Mrs Roper I will fetch my things because as far as she is concerned, I do not want any contact with her, so I wondered if I could leave most of my clothes here, I will go to a hotel until I find a flat, the problem is I don't want to rent, so it takes a time for everything to go through, would you mind?" he asked.

We looked at each other I nodded "Son by all means bring your stuff here, but you can stay with us as long as you want, however, you may be walking from one noisy place to another, we are quiet loud, but if you have a room furthest away it could be better for you, son I am in love, I do not want to curtail our activities if you can put up with it, then it is alright by us, I know you would not sit and let the very pregnant future Mrs Roper wait on you hand and foot, like your mother does, while I am out of action," he said.

"Are you sure? Soph what do you say?" he asked.

"Darling I agree with your father, I would not like to think of you in a hotel all on your own," I said.

"Who said I would be alone, I know I am in love with you, but like mother said I am too much like my Pa, I do have his tendencies to like entertaining women a lot of women, I still would, I just would not be bringing them here, if they are not married, I'd go to their place, otherwise I would have a hotel room, so I will not be interrupting your night life because I will not be in every night!" he said smiling.

"Boys," I said "Do all fathers and sons have open relationships as you two do, are you the same with your other four sons Michael?" I asked.

"I do not know what other fathers, do but I have always had a deep affection for Charles from him being very young, I love my other sons, but with Charles I don't know, we can talk about anything from being young, I have always hugged him and kissed him. I am afraid I went over the top a bit when Mrs Roper told me to stop making such a stupid show of myself, it is not healthy, she forbid me to get anywhere near Charles, she thought I was a pervert. She threatened to have me sectioned if I touched his privates, I believed her because I knew she would, but after that I showed him more affection. I know I could leave you and my Sophie alone for weeks, you would not attempt to make love to her," he said.

I went over to him and put my arms round his neck, his poor face all scratched and bruised, I pulled his head towards me and kissed him, then he began kissing me with urgency. We wanted each other badly.

Charles coughed "Excuse me you sex starved pair, I am going to fetch everything from the house while she is at Grans, I will take the front door key with me, before I go Pa, let me help you get upstairs, I think it would be easier, to go up backwards on that big behind," he had to stop and laugh as I did "On the flat you are okay on your crutches, Sophie please take my Pa to bed before you both combust, come on Pa, Sophie cannot hang on any longer, there is nothing worse than making polite conversation, when you are in need," he said as we got Michael onto his crutches. I did not feel embarrassed by what Charles had said, it is obvious that yes they can and do talk openly together, I think it is lovely because that way any thoughts are out in the open, the only thing that did shock me, was that Charles would go with a married women, but then Michael did, so like father like son.

When we got to the top Charles said "Have a good session you two," he went downstairs laughing.

"Can you get it all in your car?" Michael shouted.

"Yes no problem, I sold all my rackets, clubs and sports equipment before I came back home, so it is just clothes, some keeps sakes and my 'Degree's' see you," the door slammed and he drove off.

"Come on Mrs Roper I am dying here," Michael said.

"I think I feel like Charles said ready to combust," I threw the quilt off, he flopped onto the bed, I got his jeans and boxers off much quicker than on, he got his own top off, I was soon striped, on the bed, he just grabbed me, pulled me so close and was kissing me with as much passion as I was kissing him, we were lost, some time later I went and made some tea and brought it back up to us.

I looked at his chest he was all bruised "Darling do you hurt? look at your chest," he looked down at himself.

"No, but my heart does, I am so sorry for what happened, I cannot believe I slapped you, and said those things, I love you so much, I have no idea why I was going to Melton Mowbray, I think I will ring the Doctor tomorrow, see what he has to say, thinking about it now in view of everything, as much as I try I cannot remember anything after laughing at Charles antic's with you," he said.

"I have thought of something, because you obviously were not yourself, do you think you were coming to me, in Melton Mowbray?"

"I see what you mean, I had forgotten we lived here, and transgressed back."

"Darling can I go and ring now, they will still be there, let me make the appointment now? Please, my darling, then when we have drunk our tea, you can have your wicked way with me again," I said very sensually.

"It doesn't matter whether I say yes or no, I will still have my wicked way with you, because that body is shouting to me please fuck me! okay you ring," so I crossed the landing, into the small bedroom we had made into a study, I made an appointment for 11 am the following day. I hadn't heard a car arrive or the front door, I am wandering back across the landing, when he suddenly appeared coming up the stairs. I stopped instead of keeping going, then;

"Pa will you get your naked, gorgeous, bit on the side off this landing pronto or I will not be keeping my word, Christ Pa keep this sex siren out of sight," he said ogling every bit of my body, even the larger than normal waist, I hurried back to our room, slammed the door shut. He was sat there propped up on his pillows gloriously naked laughing.

"Michael darling I am sorry I didn't hear him come I," he stopped me;

"Open the door a fraction" so I did.

"Son are you alright, have you been able to move yet?"

"Yes Pa, I cannot blame you for being in love with her, she is one of the most sexiest girls I have ever seen, even though you have knocked her up, anytime she gets too much for you, I can help you out, anytime day or night give me a shout, I do not mind putting myself out to help my old man, you have only just had an accident, I really do not think you should be getting too excited. Always glad to lend a helping hand, you lucky bastard!' Michael just lay there laughing his head off.

"I'll let you know, thanks son you are so thoughtful," I had to laughed.

"Excuse me you two, talking about me as if I was not around."

"Sweetie we know you are around, now close the door like a good girl, what did Charles call you a sex siren? Get onto this bed now," I fell into his arms "Sweetie it doesn't matter about Charles seeing you naked, I don't mind, so please do not feel bad."

Two hours later the telephone rang and Michael answered "No I am not knackered yet, so I do not need you now or later son thank you," - pause - "I think you could be right, he was laughing, Charles has cooked dinner, it will be ready in 20 minutes, he suggests, he bring mine up here and you can go down and eat with him, as long as you are dressed as you were earlier," he had a job to get it out he was still laughing, I had to smile.

"I will go and get a bowl of water, a face cloth and towel, you can wash your hands and face, but I will wash your little man," so we did that, although he was getting an erection because of the way I was washing him. I leaned down and kissed his little man, he quickly responded "That's ready for later," I laughed.

"I think I am going to enjoy being in plaster, if you are going to be doing that," he smirked. I ensured he was dry, passed his clean boxers.

"You know instead of that palaver putting jeans on, I could get you some shorts out, they would be easier," I suggested.

"Brilliant as well as sexy," I fetched some "You put them over the plaster, then I can clean my teeth on my crutches. Are you not having a shower before you go down like that," I just laughed, I had a cool shower it was so hot, I threw the windows open to let some air in, I found a loose sun dress and some lacy briefs, I didn't bother with a bra because my nipples were so tender, someone keeps sucking them and does not help.

"I have to get back on my feet I have a wedding to plan," he said smirking again.

"Anyone I know then?" I asked.

"What do you mean?" he was suddenly serious.

"I wondered who you were thinking of marrying, once you are free?"

"There is only one person for me the love of my life."

"Just one slight hitch there, no one has asked me to marry them," then we both jumped, there was a loud bang on the door.

"Dressed or not I am coming in," in burst Charles "I knew you were up, I came to see if Pa needed help coming down, I do not want this lovely pregnant young lady doing anything to hurt her baby."

"Charles you really are thoughtful," I said. We got to the top of the stairs, I held the crutches while those two larked about, trying to get Michael sat so he could slide down and he went down easily, I followed with the crutches. Charles had laid the table with glasses and napkins even some small flowers which grew through the weeds.

"Sit down I have got us prawns to start with," he had grilled gammon with new potatoes and salad for the main. "I haven't done a sweet because I found loads on tins with cakes and biscuits, all home made, so I thought we could have some with our coffee," everywhere was clean.

"Darling you are going to make someone a wonderful wife!" I said laughing "You should not have gone to all this trouble."

"I had to do something, the noise you two were making is very off putting, even with the radio on full blast I could hear you," he said laughing as was Michael.

Then Michael said "Sweetie he is joking."

"Oh right," I managed.

We had a lovely evening we sat out on the old paved area, drinking wine and just talking. We went to bed around 10 pm, I was all in, Michael said I had to go to sleep, I was to start looking after junior, then he said "As long as he does not turn out like the original one, god forbid there could not be two of them!"

We were up bright and early showered and dressed, when we arrived downstairs Charles had cooked breakfast for us and laid the table.

"Charles this is lovely but you must not keep doing this, it is my job," he stopped me;

"No your two jobs are to look after my baby brother or sister, the other is to be nurse to my Pa, you do those jobs for now and I will look after all the catering," he stated.

We went to the Doctors and went straight in obviously he knew me but had not met Michael, they shook hands, Michael gave him the letter the hospital had given him, whilst he read it, his nurse took Michael's Blood Pressure, Temperature, Pulse then left after passing the record to the Doctor.

"Your blood pressures high as is your pulse, but that could be temporary after the accident," he put his stethoscope to his chest and back "Right apart from your sprained wrist, broken ankle, have you any other pains, I can see you gathered quiet an array of cuts and bruises," he said.

Michael said "No not really."

"Well they did some preliminary tests and could not find anything untoward, perhaps if I see you say in two weeks, come before if you have any concerns, you will have your pot off in 6 weeks," then he looked towards me "How are you doing?"

"I am fine, however I am concerned about Michael," I went on to explain, "I wondered if we could see someone, I do not think I would rest until we have at least explored every avenue?" I said "I am worried, he's had two 'Funny Turn's, that I know about, where for a minute or so, he does not know where he is, and he is a funny colour afterwards, for a while Then about the incident before his accident, "Do not look like that Michael Roper, I am worried."

"Obviously typical man you were not going to say anything, you have a special young lady here," Doctor Knight said smiling;

"Yes I know, that is why I am here because Sophie insisted."

"I will contact Mr. Williamson his expertise is in Neurology at Nottingham, his secretary will ring you with an appointment, if we start from there then it will all be done at the hospital end, they will keep me informed," he said smiling. "I will see you at the end of the month does everything seem alright?"

"Yes thank you Doctor," I replied.

We had only been home an hour before the telephone rang, it was Mr Williamson's secretary saying "Next Monday 7.30am 8th July, Mr Roper does not have to bring anything, he will be here for at least 7 hours, so if somebody can drop him off, they will be notified when he is ready to go home."

"Charles said he would take Pa because he could get some things together for his work, call in on John to see how he was getting on, see what they were doing for an office.

Graham, Michaels friend and lawyer came to see him regarding the divorce, it will be fairly quick, there is no finances to arrange.

Charles and John decided they could use the spare room as an office, John's side of the business could finance all over heads. Charles was still looking for a flat to purchase.

Charles took his father to the hospital, and he gave them his mobile number for later He rang me at 3pm said he was bringing his Pa home.

I had washed, ironed, cleaned, cooked and baked to make the time go faster and as soon as I heard the car I was out of the door, as Charles helped him out of the car we were kissing as if we had been apart for months. He looked exhausted he said he'd had electrons or something similar stuck all over him, he had been x-rayed and examined top to bottom. They will send the results to Doctor Knight.

Doctor Knight rang about ten days later, said no need to go and see him, they could not find anything whatsoever, obviously his loss of memory was the contributing factor for his accident. If anything happened to Michael no matter how small, we had to go to see or ring Doctor Knight immediately.

I went for my appointment with Doctor Knight, and was told I was carrying twins, I was over the moon, he said I think I am safe in saying around the 9th January 99, Charles had insisted on driving me, he would not take no for an answer. Michael was getting fed up of not being able to do things because of his pot, I had told him I was happy he could still make love to me, that was all that mattered!

Michael was sat outside reading when I got back he came in, Charles was putting the kettle on, I buttered some scones I had made, we sat round the table, just chit chatting then I said "I have something I think you should know."

They both looked at me alarmed "No there is nothing wrong it is just that you will have to get used to two babies I am having twins!" Michaels face was a picture, I got up, went and sat on his knee "I guess you are not mad with me landing you with two instead of one."

"Darling I just didn't think you would have twins, my clever little girl," he said kissing me, as I got up Charles went to shake his fathers hand and congratulate him and kissed him on the forehead, I was just going to sit down and Charles said;

"Congratulations Soph, I get two more brothers," he gave me a swift kiss on the lips. "We'll have to take care of you now, there is two."

That was what he did I got as I was not allowed to do anything it was frustrating, Charles even drove us to hospital to have his fathers pot removed, he was given exercises to get the movement in his ankle and foot going again, he was very dedicated, two more weeks Doctor Knight said he could start driving and go back to work, so that was one down.

After Michael had gone back to work, I said, "Charles isn't about time you dealt with some of your enquiries for work, I love you to bits but I would like to get myself organised, I cannot because you stop me doing things."

He replied "Yes I agree, it is just I like to look after you, because I knew Pa could not, I will start work, I must look in earnest for a flat."

"You do not have to rush, it's pointless if you are not sure, we both love having you here, please do not think I am trying to get rid of you, but I have got to get used to coping myself."

So he did start work. Then I missed them both there was no one to have a laugh and joke with. I was kept busy making tea and coffee for the gardeners. They started with the patio all the way along the back, the new pavers which were natural stone looked very good, I had asked they widened it a bit more. They constructed a beautiful pergola over whole, with it being south facing, when the climbing plants grew over it would give dappled shade. The rest of the garden was being made into several different areas, made private with screening of various flowering shrubs and all joined together with a winding path that went from one to the other.

I was 21 this year but I demanded no party this year but I had cards, presents, flowers and lots of visitors.

Everything seemed to be going smoothly as we were nearly at the end of August I was getting fat! Michael had no after effects whatsoever.

Charles was getting very busy, he is a Chartered

Accountant and a Financial Advisor, which was a coincident because my Charles who I had married was. I told him I knew all the basics, if he wanted I could do that for him, but instead of just bringing me the books and all the requisites, he brought the lot and we set up his office in Michaels study. Which I pointed out to Michael I did not want, I did not want him to think I had encouraged him to be back at home full time. Michael said it made sense we worked together.

Chapter twelve

The first week in October, Michael came home from work mid morning, I heard his car draw in, "That is Michaels car, I hope he is not ill?" I went as fast as I could downstairs as he was coming in the front door.

"Darling are you alright?" he stopped me.

"Yes my darling, I have come to tell Charles," he stopped, Charles was on the stairs. "Lets go in the back," so we followed him "Charles son, your mother had a severe stroke and died."

"Well I am sorry she died in those circumstances but I cannot be two faced Pa, lets face it she was never a doting mother, it was always someone else, we all saw more of you and did loads of things with you. Look at her jealousy of Sophie. I have had no contact since that night of your accident. Please don't think I am hard!"

Michael said "I have telephoned the others, but I didn't want to do that with Charles, I rang her parents, they asked if I would do the all the funeral, neither of them are in the best of health, they had her late in life, they are well into their eighties, I hope you don't mind Sophie, it is for her parents not Julia."

"No darling what can I do?" I asked.

"You can put the kettle on for a start. The gardens coming on, it will be lovely for somewhere for the twins to play in safety," he came up behind me and nuzzled my neck "How's my gorgeous mother to be then?" I turned and we kissed.

"Come on you two, I thought we were having coffee? it doesn't matter carry on I will do it," he said. So we did carried on, just stood in the middle of the kitchen kissing like a pair of teenagers.

I helped Michael with what I could for Julia's funeral. Her parents were lovely even though they couldn't get over their daughter dying before them, I was worried about going with Michael with me being pregnant, but he assured me they were nothing like their daughter.

The funeral was getting close, I had to get something to wear it took me ages to find something, but I hoped Michael would say it was alright. He said I could wear a sack bag and would still look perfect, more so when I was naked, he could see, what started as a small bump now looked like a huge volcano ready to erupt, because like he had said before he never saw Julia naked, He did not want to see what I had bought he knew he would like it.

The day of the funeral arrived we three decided we would spend the night before at Edwalton, then later on Junior, his wife and the youngest twins all said the same thing because of them travelling, so we had a house full, they all slept in their old rooms. We were in Michaels old room I'd said it was like old times. The rest of the family were to meet at Edwalton, we had hired Julia's favourite caterers to do the catering

We rose early Michael came out dressed in his uniform "I am waiting here," he sat on the bed whilst I went and got dressed having done my hair and make-up already in the bathroom.

As I got dressed I had second thoughts "I will be a while that dress and coat I think is all wrong," I called.

"What do you mean it is all wrong? I should be the judge of that, come out as you are now," I came out and stood, he took one look at me and said "Fucking hell Sophie, it will more than do, just look what you have done to me!" he pulled his jacket up showing his enormous erection, come here my gorgeous Sophie "Don't you dare take that off, you have got those fine black stockings on," he made one dive for me before I could move, his hands were up the skirt of the dress, gently stroking the gap between the stocking top and what should have been my panties but it was a thong."You drive me mad with want, you sexy little slapper! my little slapper!" he pulled the dress down, stood looking taking in the length of the dress, which was above my knees, the neck was not showing any cleavage but the way the material was cut, it fitted under my breasts with small pin tucks, they looked enormous, the tucks allowed the dress to flare out over my baby bump, the matching edge to edge coat had the same neckline and three quarter sleeves. I turned to the mirror on the wall to try the hat on, he was behind me rubbing his erection along my bottom, so I pushed back onto him. I twisted my hair round my hand and plonked the black hat on my head.

"What about that shall I have it on or off?" he looked up.

His eyes said it all "Yes, oh yes on, Christ Sophie I am so wanting you," So I turned round to face him, gave him a very soft kiss, I did not want to smudge my lipstick but he had other ideas, his lips were on mine, his tongue was doing things to me, his hand had drifted up my leg again. We both jumped as the door opened quickly and Charles said, "I was just coming to see if," and he stopped "Aw come on you two, you are worse than kids in a sweet shop."

"Don't blame me son, it's this sexy siren here, I have never felt like this about any other girl, I am glad you came, come in and shut the door, I was going to make an announcement to the others, when we are together, but I have decided, this is not the time or place, so my darling, dearest Sophie, will you marry me on 20th October?" I was gob smacked, Charles just stood beaming.

"Well I do not think I have any appointments, so I could possibly make it, what time?" I did keep my face straight.

"I have not the foggiest idea, I was so busy thinking it will not be long, but it is in my diary, can I get back to you on that small point?" he was smiling that all melting smile.

"I cannot wait my darling," he was kissing me again "And my answer is yes, please, incidentally when did you arrange the wedding?"

"When I went to register Julia's death, I thought I may as well kill two birds with one stone," he laughed.

"Can I be the first to congratulate you, you have got to be the luckiest man alive, to have my Sophie all to yourself. I hope it is not too much for you, you are not as young as you were, I don't want you keeling over with a surfeit of sex, will you go steady with him, he is the best Pa a lad can have," he hugged his father, they kissed on the cheek, I was almost in tears.

"Charles that was a lovely thing to say, I mean the bit about Michael being the best Pa," he came, kissed me briefly on my lips "Will you still give me away darling?"

"I would deem it an honour, although I would rather keep you for myself, however if it had to be any other, I am glad it is my Pa," he said "Now come on the others are down, but no one else has arrived, I suppose you'd better go put some lipstick on Soph, you look as if you have been snogged by someone cannot imagine who?" so I did as I was told. Then we walked down stairs together me in the middle and my two favourite men each side "Tell you what Pa, Your sexy wife to be has really good dress sense, she has legs up to her arm pits," we all laughed, until we arrived in the drawing room, all Michaels sons were there and someone was answering the door bell.

Julia's mother and father came slowly in, Michael went to them and then all the boys followed to greet their grandparents, Charles stayed with me. "Did Pa tell you they are having the Will reading here after the wake, bet I am not mentioned.

A waitress was bringing round Sherry I took one, then Michael brought Julia's parents to say hello and Charles kissed them both. I went and sat down with them as others began to arrive, I did not know any of the couples who came in, Charles was in deep conversation with his Twin, Michael was playing host. There was another Police Officer arrived I think the same rank as Michael, he didn't introduce anyone to me because I was keeping Mollie and Henry amused.

Then it was time to go, Michael helped Henry and Mollie up, whilst Charles helped me up, Michael said the five of us were to travel in the first car, as there were two others, they seated six. It was a service at their church followed by a burial, at Wilford Hill. We returned to the house. There were a lot of people at church, we assumed a lot were work colleagues or old school and university friends, it was announced that all were welcome after the burial.

It all went well in church and at the grave side, Michael had his arm round me, letting everyone know I was with him, the obvious baby bump were the results of his sperm! Well they were his exact words.

We all went back to the house there was plenty of room for everyone because it was a big house, the buffet was huge in the dining room, Michael and Charles agreed that I must be seated so we went into what they used to call the snug, which was as big as anyone else's lounge, we sat together, Michael said he specifically did not want to get into conversations with her friends, we could not blame him.

"I think when I found you heaven must have been looking down and decided to send me an angel," he gasped.

"Hardly, I do not think an angel would do what we do, she certainly would not let you do the things you do to me, my darling sex addict," he laughed "I love you so much Michael," I said.

"Pa, my Sophie gets more and more beautiful she keeps surprising me talk about sex on legs, she maybe one very much knocked up young lady, but she keeps doing things to me that should not happen. Sorry Pa but we do say it as it is," he laughed.

Michael said "What the fuck do you think she does to me," we burst out laughing, every body in the room turned and stared at us, Michael said "Come on Charles we will go and get some food, we will bring you something and extra for the twins," all three of us were smiling.

I must admit the food was very good, everything went very well, then people started to drift off, one by one the boys came in and joined us. A woman put her head round the door and said "Michael we will take Julia's parents home it is on our way," so Michael jumped up and went to say his good bye to them.

When Michael returned he was accompanied by a tall grey haired man and introduced him as "Julia's Lawyer Frank Barlow," he sat at a small table, he ran through the preliminaries. The Will was dated July 1988. Then he began with the main part;

"1.To my five sons I leave the house and contents - which are to be sold and the proceeds divided equally between the five. This is gross any fees and costs must be taken from my estate.

2. I leave one million pound to my friend and partner since 1979 Glenda Marshall, I could not have got through life without you.

3. I leave one million pound to my friend and partner since 1982 Christine Thompson, you were truly my rock through all the up's and down's.

4.The remainder after all costs, fees, taxes etc., are paid I leave to Michael my husband, thank you for everything, I am sorry I could not be a true wife which you really deserved.

The house without contents which was purchased 1974 for the sum of One million pounds, has been valued at today's market price at Four and a half million pounds plus the contents which contain a lot of Antiques and Original paintings which at a rough estimate should sell for another two million pounds plus, which should when divided maybe One million, three hundred thousand pounds to each, but could be more.

Now bearing in mind it was only the three of us who knew of Julia's proclivities, as soon as Michael showed Frank Barlow out and returned the other four sons all started talking at once. "Boys, please let us have an orderly discussion, if you want to speak stick your hand up." of course all four hands went up "Eldest first come on Junior what do you want to know,"

"Well" he said "I think we are all wanting to know what our mother was playing at, she has left two friends one million each? and what did she mean friend and partner, was she in a business we did not know about, or are you as much in the dark as we are Pa?" and they other three are nodding in agreement.

"No I am not in the dark, although I did not know any of

her friends, that was a separate life your mother had. They were her friends for many years, no she was not in business with anyone, you must know in today's world what partner means, until we marry, Sophie is my partner!" he stood holding his breath, he was right, they were all shouting one against the other.

Then Junior stood up "Pa are you saying our mother was a Lesbian!" he almost spat the word out, it was so quiet you could hear everybody breathing.

"Yes," he simply said.

"How long have you known Pa?"

"Well it is neither here nor there, but a long time."

"Look boys, I am sorry, it was not the thing a father can tell his sons, that is why, despite my life style encouraged by your mother, I always took you on holidays, I was always home at term holidays, I was always there for you boys at all times, I know a father cannot be a substitute mother but I did my best," I could see he was really trying to hold it together. I felt for him I was not sure if I could do anything, then Junior said.

"Pa we are not criticising you, we all know what a great father you were, and yes, you were always there for us, even when we were ill at home, you always took time from work to be with us, we are all in agreement that we had the best father any sons could and can have."

They all got up and went to him, hugging him, I had tears pouring down my face, I was transfixed by the love and warmth they showed their father, they openly kissed him. I thought back to that first evening I had met them all, they were not the same that night, I think they reigned in their emotions when Julia was around. Charles sat with his arm round me holding me close.

I whispered to him "I think you ought to tell your brothers about your father memory loss, we should not keep something like that from them, but tell them they must not let him know that they know."

"I cannot see why, it was just something that happened."

"Please darling for me,"

"Okay I will," then we heard;

"Boys you are killing me with kindness, look what you have done to my Sophie," he came over and sat by me, took me in his arms and kissed me in front of them all "Boys I am asking you, if you will all please help me celebrate, marrying the only woman I have ever been in love with, on the 20th October this year? You may think this is sudden, but somehow she got herself pregnant, and is having my twins, well that is what she tells me, she could have a cushion up her dress, she knows I am such a good catch!" That caused cheers and lewd remarks but we were all laughing and enjoying ourselves.

I said "We will be able to put you up at the house for the stay, please if you have girl friends they are invited to. I don't think we are going on honeymoon, I think we have already done that, been there and got a baby bump as a result, I do really love your father, I will do my best to always keep him happy."

I am not sure who said it but one of them said "In that case you won't be seeing many rooms in your house, apart from the bedroom," they all cheered again.

So I thought if you can't beat them join them "Well what can I say I am all for that," the noise the five no six, because Michael joined in, was deafening.

"Can I just make some amendments to your statement darling, none of us will be staying at our house, we will all be at the hotel the day before the wedding, we will have a meal and a few drinks the night before, we will be having the Wedding Breakfast there after the registry office and a meal in the evening and stay overnight, then we can all have a leisurely breakfast together, before we go our separate ways. I am not having you sweetie cooking and looking after our sons prior to the wedding, do you agree boys," a big chorus of yes went up.

So they all left to get ready to go their separate ways, we three were staying another night to make sure everything was all ship shape, we also decided we had better empty any food, cans and the like left because it was going to be put straight onto the market. So Michael and Charles had obtained boxes, filled them then when the car was full it was taken down the road to our house, this we did until we knew everything was sorted.

Michael had prearranged with the cleaners to come in and strip the beds and clean top to bottom the following week, so I was to be there to check everything was done and pay them for the last time.

Time was getting close to our wedding. Through going for my regular health checks with the midwife, I had got friendly with two other girls, Amanda and Jane, we used to call for a coffee on the way home, I had said I was getting married but wondered what to wear. Jane said she knew a woman who was a brilliant dress maker, you give her a design she will measure you, tell you how much fabric you need, she will make it one in a week, so that is what I have done. She even made suggestions for the material something light and floaty, if I bought a hat the style I wanted she would cover it with the same material, she lined the coat to make it warmer with it being the end of October, I decided on very Pale Blue, in a fine Crepe de Chine. I was beginning to panic, but everything was done on time.

19th October the weather was cold but it was sunny, so we packed what we needed, I had my dress and coat in a special bag on the hanger. It made deciding what to take a bit of a nightmare, because tonight and after the wedding breakfast we would be dressing for dinner, so I took an easy option, I had a long black maternity skirt in very fine velvet it was fairly tight round my legs but had a long split up the side to the top of my leg, I had bought two glittering maternity evening tops, although both revealed a large amount of bare breasts, Michael would like it.

We dressed, the top for tonight was halter neck with very deep v at the front, it had a black background with gold, silver and bronze sequins making small leaf designs all over it, obviously loose so the twins were not squashed inside! Michael's face said it all, "My sweetie I think we ought to delay going down look at your beautiful tits, they are calling out for my attention," he was almost drooling.

"Michael you see my breasts every day, so what is different when I am dressed and you see just part of me?"

"My sweetie I cannot explain, you look so desirable, I don't know it is something I cannot put into words? you just look so sexy, I am so in love with you I just want you more and more."

I sat on the bed "Come here," I said, he walked to me, looking puzzled "Darling I am not going to hurt you, I hope the feeling I am going to give you has the opposite effect. Please darling get your little man out now, all the way come closer," I put my lips on the very end gave him a kiss, then I leaned nearer to him and sucked him into my mouth, the lovely growling, groan I heard was all I needed, but I didn't want us to be late, so I thought I had better make it fairly quick, it didn't matter because he was so aroused, it wasn't long before he was forcing himself to the back of my throat, the noises, it really did sound as if he was being tortured, and in agony. I made sure he was all clean and dry. "You can put him away now, but I look forward to seeing him later, I really feel like a good session are you up for it Mr Roper?"

"You are very demanding Mrs Roper knocked up to, are you sure you will be wanting a session, I thought knocked up lady's did not want much sex, I thought you would be going off me, although I hoped only temporary, I think you are more demanding if that is possible! Come on my darling let us go and meet the family."

We met in the lounge bar for pre-dinner drinks, Junior introduced me to his wife Jackie (short for Jacqueline) they had been married for 20 months, John was with his partner Polly who we knew, James introduced us to his girl friend Andrea and Simon was with Emily. They all obviously went for tall, slim well endowed girls, I say girls because we are all about the same age.

The evening went very well there was lots of banter between the boys and their Pa, there was a small group started playing music in the open end of the dining room, people got up and danced, so we got up and danced, all but Charles, so Michael told him to dance with me for a while to give him a break, which I know wasn't true, he like me felt sorry for Charles.

It was a slow dance, Charles pulled me in closer so my bump was as close to him as I would get "Darling I hope you will be happy when you marry my Pa, you may be well into your pregnancy, but you look good enough to eat, tonight is no exception you always look sexy."

"Darling you say the nicest things to me, you know I am very fond of you, no that is wrong, I do love you, but not as a lover, I can see why you and your father are so close, there is something about you that makes you so loveable," he drew me even closer and kissed my neck.

"You always smell divine, this is our last dance I will take you back to your Groom to be when this ends, thank you for the dances. I have told the boys about Pa just to let you know I have done as you wished," he said.

"Thank you my darling," we walked back to the table, where most were sitting down. When we had finished our drink Michael said "If you do not mind we are going to retire now, it's a big day for us tomorrow, so we will see you at breakfast, don't forget we are getting married at 11.30," we wished them a good night, as we turned to go Charles said;

"Hang on a minute Pa, you should not be sleeping with your wife to be tonight, you should not see her again until you are at the registry office," they all joined in "Yes it's bad luck," and all that sort of thing, then Charles got to his feet with his room key in his hand, we were all waiting to see what was coming. "Here's my room key Pa, I think you should sleep in my room tonight, as I am giving you the bride tomorrow, I do not mind putting myself out and bunking up with her, I cannot do much harm she is already pregnant, in case you had not noticed!" everyone in the room turned to look at us because they made such a lot of noise and cheering.

They were expecting Pa to say something, but I got in quick "Charles darling you are very thoughtful, that is very kind of you, whilst I have no doubt your Pa would take you up on the offer, I cannot put you to all that trouble and inconvenience because you would not get much sleep, if you were with me because, I left a pause and they were wondering what was coming especially Michael, because I snore!!" that was more noise, Michael grabbed me and kissed me to loud cheers and we wished them goodnight.

As soon as we were in the room "Christ Sophie I wondered what you were going to say there, I have got to admit you were brilliant with my sons, have you enjoyed it?"

"No! I left another pause, he was looking shocked. No darling because the time would not go fast enough so that we could be alone again!" I sighed, he took me in his arms and kissing me with passion, we were undressed, I had my make-up off, cleaned my teeth sat on the bidet and was on the bed, before he had even cleaned his teeth. He seemed to be a long time, when he did come out of the bathroom he looked grey and unwell. My heart sank "Darling are you alright?" I asked getting off the bed going towards him.

"I had a bit of a funny turn, I went dizzy, for a few seconds I did not know where I was," my heart almost stopped, then it was beating so loudly I thought he would hear it.

"Darling come, lie down," I held his hand and led him to the bed "How do you feel now?" I asked, "Shall I get a Doctor?"

"No I feel better now," but I think it shook him up, he was very quiet.

"Darling, I think we should go to sleep, you are possibly over tired?" he agreed, I switched off the lamp, he didn't turn to kiss me or even speak, I waited but then I realised he was breathing deeply, he was asleep. It wasn't black in the room, there was some light coming through the curtains, I picked up my mobile and took it into our sitting room, closing the door behind me. I dialled Charles mobile after a while "Charles I whispered I am frightened, your father has just had a funny turn," he stopped me.

"I will be right there," he said, I unlocked the door, then realised I hadn't got anything on, I went quickly into the bathroom and grabbed a bathrobe, went to Michael he was sound asleep breathing deeply, as I went into the sitting room Charles was just closing the door quietly.

I told him what had happened "I have just been and checked, he is asleep," I just broke down he stood and held me close.

"Let it out darling, I hope that this funny turn is just what it was, I am sorry you are having all this. I think tomorrow you ought to ring the Doctor, no forget that I will, it will be easier for me, I will explain exactly what you have told me, he did tell us if anything, no matter how small, I will take it from there, will you be alright or do you want me to stay in here? I do not mind."

"No it might make him cross if I have told you, you have been put to a lot of trouble, I will take my phone to bed, hopefully I will not need to use it. Thanks for coming," he took me in his arms, hugged me, then his lips were on mine, I kissed him back.

"Charles I am sorry I should not have done that," I said.

"Darling it was a very chaste kiss, try to get some sleep my darling," and he left.

I went to the loo, slid slowly into bed, I turned on my right side to face him, he was on his back still breathing deeply, I put my arm over his chest, closed my eyes, everything started going round and round I think I fell asleep through exhaustion.

When I awoke it was just beginning to get light, I was on my left side, with Michael snuggled up to me, both his arms were round me, his right leg was over mine, so at some stage he must have woken up, moved me, I could feel his warm breath on my neck, I was so comfy but I needed the loo, so I began to slide slowly towards the edge of the bed "Where are you going?" he asked.

"I was trying to get out of bed without waking you, sorry but I really do need the loo," so I slid out fast, well as fast as I could to the bathroom, plonked on the loo "That was close I only just made it, darling how are you, how do you feel?"

"I am fine, why did you let me go to sleep last night?"

"I did not have much choice, as soon as you were in bed you lay down, next minute you were fast asleep, I did not even get a kiss!" I said as I was coming out. He was already out of bed, met me more or less at the door, he took me in his arms and gave me his melting kiss.

"I am sorry darling, I do not know what happened, I felt lousy but I feel really fit this morning, any chance of a marathon?" he asked.

"Darling what day is it?" I asked.

He stood and looked at me as if I was talking double dutch "It's Thursday."

"Any particular Thursday?" I said looking at him.

"Is it the one where I get to marry you?" he was laughing.

He was having me on, but I really did not know I was petrified if he said he had no idea, "No because we have to have breakfast I think I will have it up here to save getting dressed to get undressed, if you want to go and join the boys, it will be fine because I must try to look my best, I do not want my groom to have second thoughts, so I am sorry as tempting as you are, as wanting as I am, someone has to be realistic," I said.

"I see now, you really are not what you led me to believe, that was to fool me into marrying you, I can see it all now, we get married, then it will be once a month if I am lucky, well it is too late now for me to back out, I will go and have my breakfast with my sons, they will sympathise with me," he looked all sad, even the bottom lip was out.

"I can see you are not in the police force for nothing, fancy you guessing my guilty secret, I am truly sorry I have been forcing myself to let you make love to me all the time, I cannot see why anyone would want to keep doing things like that, it is so boring, so do you still want to go ahead with the wedding, I will try a little bit harder if it will help? I tell you what, after I have had the twins in January, I will let you have your wicked way with me once a fortnight! that should please any man?" I even managed to keep my face straight. He just stood and said nothing, but I could see a twinkle in his eye, he grabbed me, his lips and tongue were doing lovely melting things with my insides, I was throbbing, I was groaning, my knees were going weak, he held me upright, then he stopped, I looked at him in amazement.

"Now Mrs Roper to be, first I will order your breakfast

then I will get ready, have my breakfast with my sons, leave you to relax and get yourself ready for becoming Mrs Roper at 11.30 today, alright?"

"Darling you cannot go now, you have me nearly melting, my legs are weak from wanting you, just a quickie my love, there is time for that."

"My darling you are now ready for me, by the time we are married, had the Wedding Breakfast, you will be dragging me to bed," he then lifted me up and carried me gently to the bed he placed me down very carefully, as we were still naked, he was on the bed, was entering me, I just let out a sigh.

"My sweetie, your face was a picture, you don't think I could wait that long for you, I missed last night altogether, I know time is short, so I won't say we will satisfy ourselves because it takes us a while, but just a quickie for the time being, I love you so much, in a few hours you will be mine, all mine," his lips were on mine, we had a nice slow making love session.

Then it was all rush, I had my breakfast, Michael showered and shaved, put some jeans and a top on. He took his uniform to Charles room, so he would not see me until I arrived at the registry office with Charles, the others were to be there waiting

It was a lovely sunny day, Charles and I were to travel in the hired Rolls. I had just finished getting ready when there was a knock on the door, I opened it and there stood Charles, he looked drop dead gorgeous in a Navy suit, white shirt and navy tie, he came in "I knew you would not disappoint me my darling you look ravishing," his look was not what it should be "Come here," he held my arm, come close to me "You can scream and shout as loud as you like, but I am going to kiss you for the last time before you marry my Pa, please darling kiss me back," his arms went round me, I did not have chance to think, let alone speak, his lips were on mine, at first I did nothing, then he became urgent, I could not stop myself, I gave in to his kiss, his tongue was in my mouth, I retaliated, I know it is wrong but he was lovely, maybe I am a slut, but I couldn't stop myself.

"My darling that will keep me happy for a long, time I am so in love with you, I will keep an eye on you to make sure everything is alright, please do not have silly thoughts thinking you are a slut, because my darling you are not, I know you are in love with my Pa, this is our own secret. Come on don't stand there looking all sexy, if you do not move that dress will be on the floor."

"Charles you would not dare," I said, moving fast into the bedroom to put my coat and hat on, oops nearly forgot to repair the damage his kiss done, I emerged round the door, I knew he had not realised he had my lipstick round his mouth "Come here let me get rid of the evidence," at first he looked puzzled, then the penny dropped, I carefully removed the lipstick, he was looking straight into my eyes, it was uncanny "Darling," I stroked his cheek with my hand "It is just like looking into your fathers eyes, when I look at you."

"I must start looking for a flat and get out of the way, I cannot keep doing this, please don't feel guilty about kissing me, I think no less of you, in fact I admire you more, because I was the one pushing you. Pa said the other day please do not rush to leave I love having you with us, I know Sophie has no objections, I know she loves you as much as I do. Unfortunately he does not take into consideration my feelings for you, he does know I have told him often enough," he now had his arms round me again, I was so close when suddenly someone decided to play football

"What was that?" I took his hands, placed them both where little things kept pushing out.

"That my darling is your brothers or sisters playing," he stood ages mesmerised pressing his hands on my bump.

"Sophie that has got to be the most marvellous experience in the world, a little unborn baby moving around inside his lovely mummy."

"Come on Charles we are now going to be late.

We hurried out into the sunshine, there was the car with white ribbons and bows on the handles, Grayson waiting to hold the door for me.

"May I wish you a long and happy marriage Miss."

"Thank you Grayson, we are a bit late can we go a bit fast." I asked.

"I will do my best Miss," he replied.

We were two minutes late, so that wasn't too bad. There was a big crowd outside from the previous wedding having photographs taken, it was mad, confetti blowing all over us eventually we managed to get in, Michael was looking worried until he saw us hurrying in and he broke into a lovely smile.

"You look beautiful, why are you both covered in confetti?"

Charles said "We were not going to tell you, but we have just got married, sorry Pa."

I said "Charles behave yourself, we got stuck in the crowd outside, I think they have just got married. You look sex on legs in your uniform. Hello every body," They all shouted back then a door opened and a voice said.

"The Roper wedding next," we went in, it was a bit dull and dark but it did not matter at least we got married, were soon out and on the way back to the hotel, my husband took me in his arms.

"You must be the most beautiful bride in the world, I love you now and always will do, I hope we have a very long marriage my darling, I will never let you down," he kissed me just as the twins decided to play football again, his hand went to my tummy and sat, just like Charles had earlier mesmerised "They are my babies in there my clever little wife." he had tears in his eyes.

"Yes, not so much little though! Darling you have made me the happiest girl in the world, my sexy hunk of a husband, you realise after we have had the wedding breakfast you will have to take me to bed, I am so wanting you. By the way how do you feel?" I asked seriously.

"Darling I am fine, truly I am," he said kissing me again. Just as we arrived at the hotel.

We had Champagne waiting for when we arrived, then had a wonderful four course meal, everybody was relaxed and in good humour. Then as the evening meal was not until 7pm., it was left to them what they wanted to do, we already knew what we were going to do, so while they were sorting themselves out, I said "I feel sorry for Charles he will be on his own."

"Sweetie please do not worry if I know my boys the two lots of twins will go playing cards, they play poker or brag. Michael and Jackie will go off and do their own thing, Polly, Emily and Andrea will be left on their own, so they will do something together, what do you want to bet Mrs Roper?" I looked at him, "Well?"

"How will we know?" I asked.

"Boys and young ladies can I have your attention for a moment, have you all made up your minds what your are doing. Come on Mrs Roper what are you going to bet?"

"I don't know, a million pounds!"

"What's all this Pa?" Junior asked.

"My wife and I have a bet on, so can you please, do not talk all at once, tell me what you have all decided to do until dinner?"

"What's the bet Pa?" John asked.

"One million pounds!" Michael said squeezing my arm, there was a whistle from one of them.

"I'll speak," it was Charles "Junior and Jackie are going to do something together, god knows what, us twins are going to play cards in my room, the girls are going off to town to shop. Well who said what Pa?"

"I said exactly that, so Mrs Roper you owe me one million, so do you want to pay with cash? or would you like to pay me with your body?" one of them shouted straight back.

"Give him the bloody money," needless to say that produced the usual round of laughter and cheers.

"Not quiet so fast, you did not say what we had planned, so you have only answered part of the bet," I said.

"I think I had better take you out of earshot for my reply Mrs Roper, bye all see you later, this way Mrs Roper," Michael said laughing.

One of them said "Be careful Pa, we all know what you are, try not to knock her up!" we left them cheering. I waved to them.

We had a lovely afternoon in bed, then the meal was very good and they were all in a high spirits, all night we danced a lot until my feet were killing me. Charles managed to say he had rung the Doctor, he said to keep him informed for anything no matter how small. Then at midnight I was glad to see my bed, the twins were really going at it, I began to feel not ill, but not right, so I was told I had to rest and go to sleep, but we made up for it in the morning, were all down for breakfast early, then all went our separate ways. With the promise that we would see them all for Christmas, we booked the hotel and rooms while we were there, then headed off home.

As we arrived home Charles said "I had better get packed," we both stopped and stared at him.

"What do you mean packed?" Michael said.

"Well I knew you were having two weeks off work, that you had decided not to go away, if you had been going on a honeymoon, I would not have been going with you, so I thought I would get out of your way, so I have been in touch with some of my friends Mark and I are going for two weeks from today to Gran Canaria, leaving you to do whatever you want to do on your own. You will be all on your own, I cleaned out the stone shed at the bottom, there are power points, while we were clearing out Grans, I brought things for the shed. There's three nice collapsible garden chairs, a small coffee table, a lot of big breakfast cups, teaspoons a few empty biscuit tins, a dozen or more assorted packets of biscuits, three containers for tea, coffee, sugar and have left enough to last for about a month, also an extra large electric kettle. I also found a plastic washing up bowl and left some washing up liquid so you need not be bothered whilst you hibernate on your honeymoon!"

"Well son you sure thought of everything, I never gave it a thought but it was a good move," Michael said.

"You did all that without telling us, even going on holiday, I hope you have a good time, thank you so much my darling," I said going to him, I took his face in my hands, kissed him on the lips, he reciprocated, I looked at Michael, I thought, knowing how Charles feels about me he may not like it, but he just smiled.

"Do you want me to help you pack darling," I asked.

"Yes mummy of course I do, I have never packed a case in my life, my mother always spoiled us boys by doing everything for us!" Michael laughed.

"Sorry darling, I did not think, but what's this mummy?"

"Sorry have I missed something? have you not just married my father? so if you did, I am sure it was you, that makes you my mummy," he said with such a straight face. Michael could not stop laughing.

"You have a point son, however just because your biological mother did not prove any good, please do not think you are wanting to start from scratch and want breast feeding!" he said.

"Pa I never thought of that, I don't suppose there is just a possible chance, it would give her some training for when my brothers are born."

"Charles any training my wife needs, I'll do the teaching, there is not enough for two big boys!" Michael said laughing. I stand there amused. Michael took me in his arms.

"You are one very special girl we all love you, all my sons have said the same, I already knew Charles did," he kissed me.

"I think that is my cue to go and get started," he ran upstairs two at a time as always.

"My darling how are you feeling, I am very worried about you?"

"I have told you I feel fine, really fine, I seem all refreshed well rested, but then I need to be because we are going to be very busy for the next two weeks, you will not need any clothes, it will not be worth you getting dressed, you will have all my attention, I will even put the answering machine on, so we do not have to answer the phone, would that please my beautiful wife?"

"Indeed, I cannot wait, I seem to have been short changed for the past two days," I pouted.

"You short changed, me you mean, I have had to pay 7/6d for you, I haven't even had a farthings worth yet, I shall be wanting my money back!" he raised that one eyebrow.

"Sorry I don't think they give refunds you are stuck with me."

"My darling I am happy with that, there is nothing I want more than to be stuck, up you, that my darling is what we are going to do, I thought I would try and make you pregnant, do you think it is too soon?" he laughed.

"Well I am not sure we have only just got married, I think we should wait a year or two," I said just as Charles came in.

"What are you going to wait a year or to for then?" he asked.

"Your father wanted try to get me pregnant, I said we should wait a year or to, what do you think Charles?"

"I think you should wait you don't want to get knocked up too soon, people will think you've been fucking you out of wedlock," we all laughed.

"Right so let's end the comedy, Charles what are you going to have to eat? what time have you got to leave?" I asked.

"Darling you are not getting me anything to eat I can get my own, in fact let me get you both something to eat, you go, put your things away and I will get us something to keep us going, I will be leaving around 2.30pm because I am meeting Mark half way, now get lost you two, but do not be more than 20 minutes, so do not think of getting into bed for session, you can wait until I have gone!"

So we went upstairs, I got changed into a loose maternity dress, but I was told to try to wear and bra at all times and to have a maternity girdle on, because in both cases it saves your muscles taking all the weight, therefore stretching, you more than you need be, plus, I know this, it was more comfortable, so I do not think Michaels latest idea will be much good. I shall wait and see, I was just brushing my hair when he came out in jeans and tight T shirt. "I am so glad I married you, you really are sex on legs, just look at your fantastic body," he came up behind me where I was sat, pulled me up to him and locked me in his arms and kissed me in that all consuming way that he did, I just melt.

Then we heard "Come along you two I have to get my lunch, time is getting short," Charles shouted.

"Just hold where we were, we will restart when the little brat has left," he laughed. We went downstairs and had lunch, I said;

"Leave everything Charles I will clear up you go, get your case."

He ran upstairs and we heard him moving about.

"Darling run upstairs, get some fivers out of my bag to give to my son," I laughed as did Michael.

"No need sweetie I have some here to give him," he replied. Then we heard him coming down, so we went into the hall "Have you got everything?" Michael asked.

"Yes Pa, please do not ask the next question, because yes I have my passport," he laughed. "Well gotta go, bye Pa look after my gorgeous new mummy," they hugged, then kissed on the cheek "Bye mummy please go steady with my Pa, he is not as young as us," he put his arms round me, gave me a hug, well as close as he could get, then kissed me on my lips, I kissed him back.

"Bye son take care of yourself, please do not do anything your father would do!" I said laughing as Michael handed Charles some money.

"That's right mummy spoil it before I have started, I don't want this."

"Darling all little boys have to have ice cream money," I said as he got in his car and was gone.

"Darling I like the way you have started calling him son."

"Well if I am mummy then he must be my son."

"I do not think it will be Charles on his own, I have a feeling it is something they have cooked up between them we will wait and see."

We cleared up Michael said "I will put the pots in the dishwasher, you go up stairs, I want you naked, so that I can admire what I have paid 7/6d for!" he gave my bottom a gentle tap

"Off you go Mrs, my Mrs Roper," he smiled.

We had the most romantic two weeks that I could ever have imagined he was so gentle with me, he was so thoughtful, when the twins decided they were going to play football, he had his hands on my huge bump, on more than one occasion he was in tears, it was a shock "Darling," I asked "What is it?"

"I did not think I could ever be this happy, I am part of your life, we do everything together, I can hold you when my babies are kicking you, that alone is wonderful, I have never had anything like that experience before, you make my life so complete thank you my darling. You do not stop me looking at you, you do not stop me kissing you and most of all you do not stop me making love to you. I am so very happy my darling, I am so in love with you, I never want anything to change."

Eventually when we came up for air "Michael it is you who have made me happy, I wish I had found you before," I said "Can I have a lot of babies please?" I said kissing him all over his face.

"How can a man refuse such an offer, my darling you can have as many as you want, although after these twins, you might decide you do not want to go through it all again?" he looked at me. "Darling, I want whatever you want, I know I will always be happy with you, despite what everyone has kept telling you that I will not be faithful, I will have no need to have anyone else, you fulfil me in every way and I want to keep you safe and happy," he said kissing me again, so we slid back down the bed and carried on where we had left off.

We marvelled at how well they were getting on with the garden, but as Charles said we would not have to make tea and coffee, he had even ordered an extra pint of milk each day from the milkman and told the men when they arrive to take a pint off the door step as they passed, he had organised it to perfection.

He was enjoying his holiday plenty of sunshine, girls and night life and needless to say lots of ice-cream, he rang every other day to check we were alright and keep us up to date. I knew who he was really checking up on, he was worried as much as I was.

He arrived home in the early hours of Sunday morning, we did not hear him, we were wandering down to have breakfast Michael starkers and me in a very see through negligee, we saw his holdall with his washing in, we soon turned round and went back into our room and redressed just in case he got up.

Michael said the twins needed a cooked breakfast, he was cooking, so I set the table, put the toast in the rack, with butter and marmalade, I did not think I was hungry until the bacon was cooking, I wanted to help but was told to sit down and shut up, he was making me laugh and suddenly we heard "Can't a chap get a good sleep here, you are worse than teenagers with all your noise you two," Charles came in.

"Darling you are back, my you are well sun tanned, look how it's bleached your hair, come here," I put my arms round him and hugged him to me and then we kissed on the lips.

"I have missed you so much, mummy and you Pa," he laughed.

"I suppose you want some breakfast do you son?" he asked.

"Yes please Pa, the smell drifted up, is there enough?"he asked.

"Of course because I have catered for three, if you let mummy sit down, set a place for yourself at the table," he came sat next to me, Michael was whistling to himself.

"Has he been alright?" he asked I nodded, the collar on his shirt was turned up, I automatically leaned over to straighten it, before he realised. He caught my hand and shook his head, while his father was busy, he turned the edge down showing the biggest love bite.

I said quietly "You have been getting a bit of exercise then, not been laying around all day," I laughed, wondering if Michael had heard me but he was concentrating on what he was doing.

"There was no one, who came anything close to you, so I just closed my eyes and thought of you, it worked," then a bit louder he said "How is the garden going, did I save you getting out of bed?"

"Yes son," Michael said "That was very thoughtful of you, we have a fantastic two weeks on our honeymoon, I am looking forward to going back to work tomorrow for a rest, your new mummy is very demanding!" he said with a straight face.

"There you are I knew I should not have gone away and left you on your own, I could have lent a hand, you know give you a break, I would have been happy to sleep with my new mummy, while you got your breath back, I did warn you, you are not as young as you were, but you would not listen," another straight face.

"Excuse me, when you have finished my lovely new son, your father would give you a run for your money any day, possibly leave you standing," I said.

"Ah yes mummy dearest, but I was not talking about his daily run, I was talking about the exercise, you persist in making him have, against his will I might add, in bed," another straight face.

"It is alright son, I have managed, but it will be a relief to go to work. Now it is all ready but instead on putting it into servers come and pick what you want."

"Come on old girl, let me give you a hand, Pa you are feeding her too much, look how fat she is getting," he really did help me.

"Thank you darling, I am struggling a bit, I am alright sitting down but the twins get in the way when I try to stand up," I said.

The breakfast was delicious, we spent the rest of the day lounging around, Charles regaled us with what they got up to whilst away, we had an early night because like us Charles had not had much sleep the night before. Michael had said he didn't really want to go back to work, I'd said don't, we have enough money between us you could retire, when the twins come you will be able to help me and be a proper daddy, but he went off Monday morning, he rang me at least five times every day.

they took off, all lights flashing, any cars that were around moved out of our way I did not look at the speedometer I knew it was fast.

"This is more like it, hang on my darling we will soon be there," and we were. There was a male nurse waiting with a wheel chair for me, although I said I was able to walk, I was told by a very panicky husband "Just sit down and shut up, do as you are told," he was smiling but was hanging on to my hand as if his life depended on it.

"Darling you are squeezing my hand so tight, are you alright?"

"I am now we are here, how are you? how are the pains?" he asked.

"Coming thick and fast" I replied I wanted to scream out but thought don't be a baby.

I was taken into the labour room, undressed and put in a gown and a cap to hold all my hair together, then my pulse, blood pressure everything was checked, when they had finished, I was given an enema, shortly after that had worked, I was put on a trolley with a pillow under my head, they let Michael come and sit with me, he had a gown on, I was given a button, I was to press every time I had a pain which I did, Michael sat at the side of me looking very worried. "Darling this is a first for me as much as it is for you are you alright, can I do anything?"

"Yes my darling, you hop on here and give birth, I am now dreading it, if these pains are anything to go by." Then a big one came and I was told when they lasted to keep pressing the button, in rushed a team.

"Time to get you into the delivery theatre, you coming Daddy?"

I did not give him the chance to answer "Of course he is," I said and screamed as another one came. The over head lights were blazing down I was now hanging on to his hand, they put like a big cage over my lower body covered in a green sheet, the same as the gowns and caps we were wearing, including Michael. So neither of us could see anything because Michael was sat on a chair.

Suffice to say, I am not about to give you a blow by blow account of the events that followed, it is enough to say there was a lot of groans, moans, pushing and screaming! but eventually on the 27th at 5.30am we had twin boys, they were identical, both weighed 5lb 10ozs, we were given one each, they looked lovely, tiny fingers and toes, everything was where it should be, we both cried. After I was stitched and taken to my room, the boy's would be brought in for their first feed.

I told Michael to go home and get some rest, I must have fell fast asleep, the next thing I knew they were bringing the twins in, they gave me one at a time, so they were both feeding together one on each breast, it was a wonderful feeling. "How will I cope when they are bigger?" I asked.

"Do not worry at this stage, your home midwife will answer all your questions, just relax and make the most of this time," nurse said. She came back later, took them back to the nursery because they had both stopped sucking and were fast asleep. I fell asleep again and was awoken by a nurse coming in with the biggest bouquet of Roses, she put them on a cabinet and passed me a little card.

To my adorable wife and mother of my twins boys,
I love you so much, thank you for bringing me to life
I Will Be Yours Always Michael xx

They brought the twins in again both were crying, the nurse gave me the first, then put the other one on my arm so I could lift him to me, she just had to help him get my nipple they were soon happy, she said she would come back. She had no sooner gone, than she was back with two vases of flowers, passed me two cards, one from Junior and Jackie and the other was from James and Simon all sending their love.

The door opened again, in came Charles holding a big bouquet of Lilies and Pink Carnations, the nurse followed him "Shall I take them and put them in a vase?" he turned and said;

"Yes please," he came and looked at the twins as they were suckling. "What a beautiful sight you are, how are you?" but before I could answer, he kissed me on the lips, so I kissed him back, but it went on for a while.

"That was a long one? Bring that chair over darling, when did you get back? You were supposed to be going a New Year Party? Have you seen your father, well you must have done that is why you are here, is he alright?"

"Bloody hell Sophie, where do I start to answer? Well I thought you deserved a nice kiss, I love you so much Soph. Yes Pa is alright. I must have got back around 7am, I'd had a short text in the night from Pa "Twins on the way," so I had to come home, Pa came home around 8.30, he was so over come by the birth, as we hugged he burst into tears, he was really crying, I already have five children, but this is the first time, I have actually been involved from beginning to end, Sophie is one wonderful wife she makes me so happy, but it was definitely a wake up call, with what she went through to give birth, but at the same time it is like a miracle, then we were holding them, we both cried," he said "I was so touched Sophie, I have never seen this side of Pa, because he was never given a chance with our mother, we all have a lot to thank you for, you have made us a proper family, they all said they will be around a lot more," while he was talking they stopped feeding and were asleep "Can I hold one," he asked, so I said;

"Take one of them," he leaned over, and as he took him obviously my nipple slipped out of his mouth, Charles was looking at my breast as if mesmerised, so I moved the other one away, so I could fasten my buttons up again "I suppose you will get used to them darling, there is a lot of feeding to do, I would not dream of asking you to leave, besides you have seen all of me naked, I do not mind if you don't," I smiled at him.

"Sophie I may have seen you naked, but I will never get over seeing any part of you naked, you have such an impact on me, in other words you always give me an erection, I like it, so it doesn't bother me when I see you, because I like what you do to me, but my darling it is our secret, I would do nothing to hurt Pa. He hasn't had any other turns has he?"

"No darling I am pleased to say," then nurse came in and Michael.

"Hello son, getting your hand in I am pleased to say," then before nurse could get any further "Hang on a minute, can I hold my son, I passed him to him, but he leaned over and gave me a delicious kiss, hi my darling how are you feeling?"

"Tired, sore and very happy," I smiled.
Nurse said "I will leave you for a while, but not long I have to get them changed." I looked at my two favourite men and babies.

"You have one each, I think we ought to decide on names?"

"Darling, I thought we had, this one with the blue band is slightly older so we agreed on Elliot Charles" the delight on Charles face was unbelievable "The turquoise band is Felix Michael, which is mine but the other way round," Michael said.

"I was not sure if you'd, had second thoughts," he sat on

the bed laid Felix down, took me in his arms, we had a lovely long romantic kiss.

Charles said to Elliot he was holding, "You will have to get used to seeing our mummy and daddy in one another's arms they really do love each other," we ignored him, the door opened and nurse came in;

"Can I have our twins back?" she asked.

"Yes sorry nurse, I can tell you their names now, the blue band is Elliot Charles and the turquoise is Felix Michael."

"Good we'll put their names on their baskets, do you want anything?"

"No thank you I am fine, apart from when can I have a shower?"

"Leave it until after lunch, if Mr Roper is staying he can stay with you make sure you are alright for your first one," she answered.

"Yes I am not going anywhere," Michael informed her.

They let me go home the following Friday, 2nd January 1999, it became a bit hectic, all the family wanted to visit, the twins came without girl friends and stayed three days, Michael and Jackie came and stayed four days, John and Polly always seemed to be here, Michael and Charles did all the catering and shopping, I just made them lists. They changed the beds as they needed doing, washed and ironed, I was in charge of the twins, I fed them with Michaels help, when his two weeks were up, he returned to work, then Charles helped me, he was as attentive as his father, anyone would think they were his.

The garden was completely finished by second week in March, they had, had a few hold up's with the weather, it was frost or snow or blowing rain, we walked round one sunny morning, when it was finished and it was going to be beautiful once everything started shooting, because the shrubs and trees, would not grow to more than ten feet, and were all mature when they planted them.

Each day Charles and I went for a walk with Elliot and Felix, I think people who had not seen us before, thought we were a couple and Charles said please do not point out their mistake. We decided to have them Christened in April, but Michael was adamant I was not doing the catering, so I did a 'Julia' and got caterer's in, it was a bit of a squeeze to put them all up over night, because the twins brought their girl friends, so there were 11

243

adults, but Charles slept in the office on a fold up bed. We had a good time all of us.

The twins were growing fast, they were identical to Michael, he said it was like seeing Charles and John again. I missed April, May and then June, so I went to see Doctor Stuart Knight, who had become a frequent visitor, with his wife Annabel but she preferred Bel, to see the twins and had become good friends.

He said "Yes you are pregnant, but isn't it a bit early did you not use any contraceptive?"

"No we want a lot of children, I was hoping I would get caught sooner than this!" I replied.

"But the twins will only just be a year, when this one or these depending on whether you are caught with twins again, how will you cope?"

"I did not think, but other people do and I have got Charles he is brilliant with the twins."

"Yes Sophie, but you will not always have Charles one day he will find someone, he will leave you to make a new life, anyway what's done is done, if you are happy I am, can I tell Bel, I know she will be over the moon, I'll bet she will be telephoning you if I know her."

When I returned Charles was waiting, "Why did you not tell me where you were going, what is so secret Sophie?"

"Darling I only went to see Stuart, I didn't want you to worry."

"Sophie are you pregnant?" he asked.

"Yes but you have spoiled the surprise now, I wanted to tell you both together, so stay out of the way when I tell Michael, I do not want him thinking you know something like this before him."

"Sorry Sophie, I know you are happy, I am to," he came, took me in his arms, "I am sorry, I spoilt it for you, am I forgiven?" he kissed me for a while, I tried not to respond but I failed miserably. "One day Sophie you will be having my baby, and that is a fact."

"Charles darling please do not go there," I said.

It was not 5pm, I heard Michaels car pull up, but he did not come in, so I went to the door to see where he was, he was sat in the car with his head in is hands, I shouted "Charles somethings wrong come here," I ran to the car as Charles reached the door, I opened the car door and Michael looked a very funny colour he seemed dazed.

"Let me get him out Sophie," I moved to one side, Michael still hadn't spoke.

"Michael, darling what is wrong?" he managed to walk with Charles help, we went straight into the kitchen, I ran, got a glass of water, he took a big gulp, "Darling please what is it?" tears were streaming down my face, he was struggling to speak then he said.

"I do not know how I got home, I have no idea how I drove, or when I left the office?" Charles and I looked at one another.

"Darling tell me precisely what you do remember prior to being here in the car?"

Well Mary, (his secretary), had asked him if he wanted anything at 3pm, I asked to a cup of tea, my jacket was on a coat hanger on the door, the next thing, I see is the empty cup and crumbs on a plate, I have my jacket on, my brief case in my hand with my car keys, then the next thing I am sat out there in the car," I flew to the telephone told Stuart, Michael had lost time, I gave him a quick run down of what happened.

"The ambulance is on it's way, Sophie love try to keep calm, I am on my way," I ran back and opened the front door, within minutes Stuart was here, he came straight in Michael was quiet lucid now, so while he checked him over I said to Charles.

"I am going in the ambulance you will stay with the boys won't you?"

"Sophie it is no problem I am always with them, they will be fine, although I would rather go with you," he ran upstairs to fetch some trousers instead of leaving Michael in his uniform.

"I do not know how long we will be you know where everything is, I will ring you as soon as I know something."

We heard the sirens, it was one mad dash, we were in the ambulance flying towards Nottingham. I did not feel very well myself, but sat holding his hand, because he wasn't laid out on a stretcher, but he was hooked up to a machine that monitors the heart, then I heard the medic who was in the ambulance with us say to someone on the radio E.C.G, well I knew it was something to do with the heart. In no time we were there, they rushed him in to a cubicle, I was getting violent pains in my tummy the medic who had come with us was just leaving.

"Are you alright love?" he asked.

"I have violence pains," I nearly screamed with the pain.

"It is probably shock, are you having your monthly."

"No I am pregnant, just over three months," he held me nearly carrying me, I suddenly felt wet and there was blood running down my leg. "Oh no," was all I said, he had seen it at the same time.

"Can I have a hand here," he shouted, a nurse looked down, he said something to her, she took me to a toilet, pulled my blood soaked panties off and sat me on the loo.

"You are aborting your baby," she said, "I will stay with you, then we will see what's, what, how far were you?"

"I only went to the Doctors this afternoon just over 3 months," tears were streaming down my face.

"Is it your first?"

"No I have twins, they are just six months."

"It has got to be the shock, you came in with the ambulance, is it your father?"

"No it is my husband Michael, do you know what is happening?'

"No sorry, I was not with that team," she turned and pulled a red cord in the corner of the loo.

"Did you pull the cord," a voice said, the nurse with me opened the door, she whispered something to the nurse who had come to the door .

"Do you want me to bag these up?" as she held my blood soaked panties, I shook my head, so she put them in a sanitary bag and put them in the bin, soon the second nurse came back with a bowl, gauze and various items "Stay here while I clean you legs, then put this belt on and we will put a towel on, I have some paper knickers for you.

"That is very kind of you to go to all this trouble" I said.

"It is all part of the service which you get when you are private," When she had finished, I thanked her and went to find Michael.

He was not in the cubicle, so I had to ask and they showed me where he was, he was lying in bed but he still looked frightful colour.

"Darling how are you, what have they said?"

"Not much they are keeping me over night again, I was worried where did you get to?" he asked.

"I was took short I had to go to the toilet."

"Sophie I will ask you again, where were you? the last time I saw you, you were with the medic from the ambulance, there seemed to be a problem he shouted he needed a hand, come on darling what's going on?" he looked worried.

"I did not want to tell you, you have enough on."

"Sophie you are making me worry now please, darling please tell me, are you ill?" his eyes are pleading.

"I went to see Stuart today, to get him to confirm I was pregnant, I was just over three months," I just burst out crying.

"Darling, what is it?" he asked looking worried.

"I have just lost it, they said it could be with shock, but I have not seen a doctor," he raised himself up, took me in his arms that made me worse.

"Darling I am so sorry, that is my fault."

"No, Michael it is not your fault, it would have happened anyway."

"Stop it, you just told me the nurse said it could be through shock, or wasn't you intending saying that?" I just let him hold me, and someone came into the room.

"Mr Roper, you are supposed to be laying down, not having a cosy up with your young lady," I do not think she approved.

"Sorry nurse, but I was trying to comfort my wife, she has just lost our baby, as far as I am concerned she is my first priority, so do not come in here dictating to me," he was so cross.

"Sorry" she said, and left.

Next to come in was a Doctor, nurse had obviously told him what had happened. "Now Mr Roper we want to run some more tests, would it be possible Mrs Roper if you could leave for a few hours?"

"Yes," I said, Michael gave me a lovely kiss, "I will come back later."

"No you will not you go home, rest Charles will take care of the twins, I will ring you, I haven't got my mobile," so I gave him mine.

"I will ring anyway later," I said, I left and asked if they could ring for a taxi for me which they did and I only had to wait five minutes, so it wouldn't take long to get home, because it was around 7pm so traffic was light. Then I realised I had not contacted Charles.

As I was paying the taxi the front door opened as I was walking towards the door, "Please Charles do not shout at me, I have not had chance to ring you, I gave my mobile to your father," that is far as I got, I just broke down he grabbed hold of me shut the door with his foot.

"Darling what has happened, how is Pa," he was holding me close.

"I have lost my baby," was all I could get out. He picked me up and carried me into the kitchen.

"Darling come on tell me, the boys are in bed, they have been no trouble, come on please Sophie, tell me what happened?" so I told him everything, "I am so sorry darling, I know how happy you were, but there is plenty of time. Oh yes John popped in so he knows about Pa, so no doubt he will have told the rest so we will probably have a full time job answering the phone. "Food come on?" he asked

"I will just have cup of tea, then shower, the nurse was very good, but I will be happier when I can have a shower, I only have paper knickers on. I will go and kiss the boys, thank you my love, I do not know what I would do without you, I do not think I want you to go anywhere else, we are just one family, you do more than your fair share of everything, I have come to rely on you. I told him what Stuart had said earlier. I was thinking of that as I was walking home, I would be very sorry if you did, but I cannot expect you to stay forever," I looked at him.

"I do not want to go anywhere, I do not want any other life than the one I have here with you, when I went on holiday, it was the biggest mistake I had ever made leaving you, but it would not have been fair."

"Yeh like your father and me had never slept together before."

"No it wasn't that, I was sorry you were not around, two weeks have never ever gone so slow I missed you so much." He took me in his arms. "I am so sorry about the baby," I thought he was going to let me go, then his lips were on mine, I tried to pull away, but he was strong, his tongue was in my mouth, it had started doing things to me, I gave in and kissed him hungrily. "That's all I wanted to know."

"What do you mean? I couldn't stop but I didn't want to."

"You kissed me the way I wanted you to. Do you want your tea now or after your shower," then the telephone rang.

Chapter thirteen

Time soon passed and Christmas was coming fast, we had received five Christmas cards all with Mummy & Daddy on, which we both laughed at, so we all met Christmas Eve at the hotel, we went our separate ways on boxing day morning, it was a wonderful Christmas, all the boys and partners said they had thoroughly enjoyed it, which pleased us greatly but especially me. I was huge so after Christmas we just relaxed Charles went down to stay with Mark his friend Boxing Day evening, they and four others were meeting up at a big New Years Eve party somewhere.

When we went to bed that evening I seemed as though I could not settle. The twins were really moving about, in the early hours, I had pains I woke Michael, I think the twins are wanting to be born.

He was out of bed like a shot, on the telephone to our Gynaecologist Mr Harlow, who said to bring me straight in as long as the pains had a good interval in between, he waited on the phone with me to time them, while Michael went in the shower and dressed, so I passed the phone to Michael then went into the shower myself, I shouted another pain and straight away my waters broke, Michael relayed it, Mr Harlow said to set off as soon as we could and we should be alright.

Then Michael started to panic what if I cannot get you there in time and wondering if, this and that, "Darling please stop, Mr Harlow said it would be alright, I am just popping some clothes on, you get my case that is packed," by then I was ready, we set off at high speed, it was 1.30am little traffic, it had not been frosty so we were safe "Darling please slow down, I do trust you we have plenty of time."

"Sorry sweetie I am not risking anything, I want you there as soon as possible," we had just past over Trent Bridge, a police car came out of nowhere "Bloody hell," Michael said and wound his window down.

"Sorry sir, I didn't know it was you, you were clocking it."

"Yes well you fucking would if your wife was in labour, I have got to get her to the Private Hospital on Mansfield Road, before she gives birth, unless you want to play midwife and deliver twins?"

"Follow us sir," he ran back to the patrol car and driver,

"I will go and get in the shower." I went to see my babies they were fast asleep and adorable little chubby cheeks pink and warm. He had even remembered the baby monitor he was worth his weight in gold.

Michael was sent home the following evening, Charles went to collect him, they still could not find what was happening, he did not seem to have any after effects, but he seemed to get tired quick, especially when he was at work, he had been back now a couple of weeks, although I know he loved his work, I did not even mention my thoughts to Charles, I hesitated before I said anything to Michael and was mulling it over for a while, then I asked him.

"Darling would you consider finishing work? We have more than enough money between us. Please it would be lovely to have you home all the time, it would give us longer for you to get me pregnant, so that has to be a bonus,"

"I am not old enough to retire I am only forty four," was his excuse.

"It does not matter about your age, what does matter, is that I keep you here with me as long as I can, I do not like these funny turns you have, I worry about you, I just wondered, if it is stress that comes with your job, darling I want you here, I want you to enjoy your twins, I need you to make more babies please darling. I love you so much, I want you as long as possible with me," I wasn't sure that I was getting anywhere "Please darling, please consider it?"

"Consider what?" Charles said.

"Sophie wants me to finish working," he simply said.

"That is brilliant Sophie, so when are you going to finish?" he asked.

"I cannot say I am not tempted, especially when put so sexily by my wife," he proceeded to tell him what I had put forward, he stopped and looked at me.

"Sorry Pa, I think your wife has some very valid reasons, I for one would be happy for you to be at home, because if you got bored you could do bits in the garden, trimming etc. We could possibly go for a game of Golf when the weather is good, but I doubt you would have much time on your hands, knowing your wife's appetite for all things to do with sex. I think the twins should have lots of sisters and brothers, I know if I were in your shoes, I certainly would not be leaving my sexy wife to go to work, better to fuck the work and stay home and fuck your wife," he said I was smiling.

"Charles you certainly do have a way with words, I could not have put it better myself," I said, laughing.

"Okay then I will do it," he just looked at us, I think we were both shocked into silence. I put my arm round his neck, was kissing him all over his face until our lips met and we just melted together.

Then we heard "Don't think you need me, I will go and see my baby brothers."

When we came up for air, "How long do you need for notice?" I asked.

"Well in my position usually three months, unless it is on health grounds but this will not count, because the Doctors have not suggested it."

"Leave it with me," I said.

I phoned Bel "Could ask she Stuart to ring me when he has time?"

Before I left the study the telephone rang, it was Stuart, "Hello Stuart, I am sorry it was not urgent, I did not want to interrupt you," I said apologetically.

"No, problems darling, I have just seen my last patient, it's not Michael, is it?"

"Yes, but not what you are thinking, I have persuaded him to give his notice, to take early retirement, but he would have to give three months notice, unless on health grounds," I went on to explain my all reasons.

"Darling, you are a special young lady, no problem, I know the Specialist will agree. I will see if I can contact him, leave it with me. I will ring you when I have news."

Two hours later Stuart said, yes they agree, if someone wants to go over after 3pm today, there will be a letter waiting for collection. Charles did not need telling twice, he went and was back by 4pm. With the letter for Michael to take to work the following day.

They said they were sorry to see him go, but health had to come first. He finished work on the following Friday 7th July 99.

It was lovely not having to get up and rush for Michael to go to work although the boys usually woke at 7.30am. Charles usually fetched them in to him and he gave them a bottle, then he decided to move their cot in with him, he had plenty of room, he started to put them in bed with him while he gave them their bottle, then they got as they all went back to sleep for an hour or more so we all had a lie in. I still breast fed them at night before they went to sleep, but now they were bigger they were happy to wait their turn because there was either daddy or Charles on hand to entertain them.

Both Michael and Charles had started playing Golf, something they had done years ago, in fact all the boys did at one time they told me, of course once John found out he went as well, although they said they felt guilty leaving me, I said go and play because usually Polly came, she was only a year older than me and we had become very good friends, she said they were hoping to get married next year but they didn't want a big do, her mother had other ideas, they lived in Chester and wanted it up there because most of their family were up in that area, so she had to go with the flow because mother was footing the bill.

She also said her mother wanted her home for Christmas but she said she had already accepted our invitation.

We put a big Christmas tree up for the boys with lots of lights on, although they were in to everything, they had been crawling since they were almost eight months, once or twice Elliot had pulled himself up and tried to do some steps but his brother used to crawl over to him and knock him over, they both used to sit and laugh, it was infectious we all laughed.

I thought I had better decide what we would take for the boys for Christmas away, as usual Michael played with his boys and Charles came to help me. I was feeling low because I was still not pregnant, he knew there was something wrong, he asked me but thought it was Pa?

"No darling I am pleased to say he is well, I'm still not pregnant Charles, I thought I would be before now, it's months since I lost the last one," I was close to tears.

"Come here," he folded his arms round me "Have you been to see Stuart or at least told him your worries?"

"Look well if I can't have any more," I cried.

"Now you are being silly, it might be Pa, you have had him fucking you day and night, he could have run dry," he could not help himself he had to laugh, I had to smile.

"That is not funny, if that be the case, I shall have to bring on the substitute," I said, with a hint of a smile.

"Substitute what bloody substitute Sophie?" was he cross

or joking, I never knew with either of them?

"There's only one substitute," I said looking at him.

"You mean you would have me make love to you so you could tell Pa you were pregnant?" he sounded displeased.

What have I said, it was only a joke, I tried to speak. "No I would love to fuck you, but while Pa is around, I wouldn't as much as I love you Sophie, you are Pa's, if he cannot get you pregnant then tough luck Sophie sodding well live with it!" and stormed out, I heard voices, the front door slam, his car start up, gone!

What have I done, I only meant it as a bit of fun, I have really put my foot in it, I was in bits I sat and cried for a long time, then Michael was at the bottom of the stairs, "Darling how long will you be? shall I bath the boys?"

I managed to say "Yes please," that means he will be coming upstairs so I ran to our room, washed my face in cold water, then sat on the loo for a few minutes, until I heard the twins giggling, so I flushed the toilet and went to see what they were up to, they were in the bath with dozens of ducks and boats floating.

"Hey there's my boys," I said.

"I thought you had got lost, Charles said he had forgotten he had to pick something up, said sorry he had to leave you to it."

"Well darling in normal families the mother has to cope, I have got two full time helpers, I am lucky," I knelt down at the side of him and tickled their little chubby tummies "They are adorable Michael, thank you so much," but a tear escaped and he noticed.

"Sweetie what is it? tell me, you're obviously upset about something?"

"Sorry I am being silly,"

"Alright Mrs Roper, so lets be silly together, come on my darling what is it?"

"I thought I might have been pregnant by now, nothing has happened, look well if I cannot have any more?" I had to let go and the tears came both boys were sat looking, he kissed me.

"Darling it may not be you, it could be me, have you thought of that?" I shook my head "Come on lets get the boys out, we will talk in a while," here you take Elliot, I will have Felix, we had discovered that Felix had a very small mole under his left foot.

I dried Elliot and started to breast feed him until he went to sleep, I laid him in the cot, fed Felix "Can you feed me later?" Michael said kissing me, I kissed him back wanting more of him, then Felix was asleep, I laid him next to Elliot in the cot, they were always together side by side.

Michael took my hand and led me into our bedroom and closed the door, he sat on the Chaise we had in the bay window, "Come on darling," so I sat at the side of him, the water works were in full flow again "Sweetie why did you not say something before you have been bottling this up, I will ring Stuart tomorrow and tell him we want a chat," he kissed me, then he kissed me deeper, one thing led to another we ended up in bed. He still thrilled me beyond words, we lay with Michael holding me close. "Are you feeling a bit better?"

"Not altogether, I said something, in a joke to Charles, he made it sound terrible, he has never ever been cross with me before he has always laughed knowing I was joking, only this time he it took it serious and I have made him hate me," the tears were flowing fast.

"My darling, I do not think Charles could ever hate you if he tried, I am not going to ask you what you said, I know you would tell me, but it is between the two of you, when he returns I will have a word, then the pair of you can sort it out, go and get in the en suite on your own, I want no distractions, then I will go put dinner on, I know it is all ready it just wants cooking."

"Michael there is something I have been meaning to ask you for a long time, did you ever know or speak to my father?"

"No sweetie, why that is a funny thing to ask? I do not think I ever met him."

"Sorry it was something Rupert, said that my father had told you something about me," I looked should I have left it buried.

"No darling, knowing Rupert he was winding you up, is that it?"

"Yes thank you darling," I said and went and sat on the bidet it saves getting wet through all over in a shower, I came out nice and dry and crossed to the walk-in and got dressed, I put a polo neck sweater on, it was a bit tight and some tight jeans. Michael was still lay on the bed and said;

"You are a very sexy little slut! If I hadn't got to slave over a hot stove, you would be in here, you would have to have me make love to you, which I sincerely would love to, look," there was his little man standing very big and straight, so I started to walk towards the bed "Oh no you don't Charles will want his dinner when he gets back."

"Yes, but I am only your slut!"

I went in to check on my babies, I sat looking at them and wondered what they would be like when they got bigger, what would they do when they were young men.

"Sophie," it was Michael, I came out of the nursery.

"Yes."

"Come on down dinner will not be long, Charles has come back, he is in the drawing room," he kissed me when I reached him "Go on sweetie make your peace."

When I walked in he was looking at the Christmas tree, he knew I was there "Charles please forgive me, it was a joke please Charles," I walked towards him, touched his arm, he turned to me, just stood and looked at me for some time, but it wasn't the glare he gave me earlier. "Charles please forgive me, please I cannot bear for you to be cross with me," I said, a tear or two were making their way down my cheeks, he still said nothing just took hold of me hugged me close to him.

"No darling I am the one who is sorry, I knew you were joking, how many times have we joked before, it was, no I have to be honest, I wasn't mad with you for what you had said, I was so bloody fuming with myself for my thoughts. I was not honest with you, you see it was not as I said it, it was the opposite, I was mad with myself for thinking it and took it out on you, you see I would take you to bed and make love to you, as often as I could, as often as I could get away with it, but I know it is wrong because it would kill Pa if I did, and that is why I was cross with you, because it is exactly what I want to do with you. I cannot take girls out any more because they are not you, so I will wait and if I die without you so be it, you cannot choose who you fall in love with, and I love you it is as simple as that. Even if I can't fuck you, I want to be with you, I want to stay in yours and Pa's life! Come on my love dry your eyes, tell Pa it was all a misunderstanding, leave it at that okay," I nodded he kissed me again, I kissed him straight back and he kissed me again very deeply and I returned it. "That will keep me going until Christmas under the mistletoe, have you got any yet, if not that must go on the top of the list," we were talking all the while we walked towards the kitchen.

"What is on top of the shopping list then?" Michael asked.

Charles said "Mistletoe Pa, I want a kiss from your wife, a proper kiss so please be forewarned Pa,"

"I will make an exception, but it is only you, the others can have a peck and like it, those lips are mine," he said laughing "But occasionally you can borrow them, until you find someone of your own, but do not try to find another Sophie because there is only this one, you will have to lower your sights son. Look how many years it took me to find the girl of my dreams."

I went up behind him, put my arms round him and pressed very close to him, he turned round "Now press those wonderful tits against my chest where I can feel them, Christ have you seen that sweater she has on."

"I have indeed Pa, she should be locked up flaunting them in that tight sweater, no wonder we have to limp round having those pointing at us," and they both laughed.

"Shall I go and change I thought it was a bit tight?" I said.

"Don't you dare Mrs Roper, you are bringing one old man and one young man a lot of pleasure isn't she son?" Michael asked.

"Definitely, if you had made her change. I would not speak to you again," they were both laughing, so I walked sticking my chest out further.

"Careful babes you'll be giving Pa a heart attack," still laughing.

"I gather you two have sorted out your misunderstanding, I told you both I did not want to know the why's, but you see what misunderstandings lead to, never leave one unresolved, because they build and build until it is too late to go back," he smiled at us both.

The next day they went shopping they returned with the biggest bunch of Mistletoe Michael said "I think Charles means business Mrs Roper, so you had better be prepared for a marathon kiss," we all laughed Charles went to hang it in the hall.

"I think I will wait until the day before Christmas Eve because we will not be here after then," he said, I for one believed him.

The following day the twins were having an afternoon nap, Michael was in the study, making some telephone calls to some of his old friends, I was just walking out of the kitchen, Charles was heading my way "I was just coming to fetch you Mrs Roper," he said taking my hand.

"Why where are we going?" I asked.

"Just here," he said making sure we were under the

Mistletoe.

"I thought you said we were," I got no further his arms were round me, his lips were clamped on mine, my hands crept round his neck pulling him into me, I gave as much as I got, he was really doing things to me, he dropped his hand down to my bottom and pulled me in to him, so I could feel his erection, I did nothing to stop him, it went on and on, I know I was moaning, eventually we had to stop for air. We just stood together, my legs were like jelly, I was holding onto him to steady myself "Charles I am sorry I should not have let you do that but I couldn't stop you even though I know it is wrong."

"Darling I am the one to blame, I also know it's wrong but I have already told you I need your lips however, I seem to need them more often, but I would never take it any further, even though I desperately want you, I would not hurt Pa, please do not blame yourself it is me, I think no less of you and it is only a kiss after all," he said.

"But that is it, it isn't just a kiss, it was like making love with clothes on," he laughed.

"Sweetie that's a new one, but when I make love to you, I can assure you there will be no clothes in sight," he gave me a swift kiss and ran upstairs two at a time.

It must have been over an hour later, I was just going into the kitchen and Michael was coming downstairs, then Charles came into sight "Would you two like a cup of tea or coffee?"

"Hang on there," Charles said "Pa can I claim my kiss under the Mistletoe?"

"Son I did not know you cared that much for me, you know people will talk," Michael said, I burst out laughing as did they "Yes son be my guest," he took my hand "Now Mrs Roper this is your lucky day, you get to be kissed by my wonderful son, there must be hundreds of girls out there would happily change places with you, so make it good."

"Thank you Pa," Michael went towards the kitchen.

"I will put the kettle on, you have 10 minutes maximum," he laughed.

I looked at Charles "Come on Mrs Roper pucker up," again his lips were on mine, he did not hold me the same as earlier, but his kiss was the same, as was mine but we stopped before it was too long "Pa I really enjoyed that do you think I can have another one?" Michael came to the door, one eye brow raised.

"I think you are asking the wrong person son, should you not be asking my wife?"

"No, for that reason, she is your wife, and I do not want to be thrown out on my ear," Charles said.

I said "What about when we come back in the New Year you can have one then before we take it down."

The next morning Michael rang Stuart and explained what I thought was a problem, he would make some enquiries at the hospital to see what he had been on because medications can often affect a man temporarily, he would see us both in the New Year.

Chapter fourteen

Christmas was almost here. Christmas Eve we left for 'The Manor Hotel, it is only about 10/15 minutes from home. The decorations were beautiful as always, very tasteful, the twins did not know where to look, as normal Michael and Charles carried them, I was the spare part, but they explained one day I will be pregnant so they were in training.

Our suite was always the same, because of the very large drawing room, where we all gathered. Charles wanted the twins in with him. I said to Michael, I think he feels a bit out of it in a single room, so that is why we did it, plus Michael said it doesn't matter how much noise we make, trying to make more babies.

We had a wonderful time, the twins really made it completely different, everything during the day revolved around them, until they went to bed. Christmas Day evening Jackie announced she was pregnant, she had been given 10th June 2000. Then Junior said they he was taking a higher rank and they were moving to Carlton near Nottingham in February, so we had an excuse for more celebrating.

So all in all we all had a good Christmas, Simon and James with their partners asked if they could come to us for New Years Eve, so Junior asked if he and Jackie could come, so it looked like instead of us seeing the New Year in, in bed making babies, we were having a party because, John and Polly said they were not doing anything!

Boxing Day morning we were all having breakfast together and Polly passed us all an envelope, we all sat and looked, I knew what it was, "Open them then," she said and yes they were Wedding Invitations for 21st August 2000, 11.30am at St. Jude's in Chester followed by the reception at 'The Hilton Hotel' in Chester. So it was congratulations all round John asked Charles to be his Best Man? and Polly asked me if I would be her Maid of Honour? I was full up, we both accepted and I said to Michael looks like you will be on child minding duties.

Then Michael said "I will make the room reservations at the Hilton, then we will not have far to stagger and it is my treat," so they all cheered.

"You are a lovely, lovely father, but more than that, you are a lovely husband, you are one in a million," I said and kissed him, forgot didn't I that got a loud cheer, Elliot and Felix looked round they did not know what it was? but they both started making a loud noises.

"No my darling, I have the very best wife anyone could have, look how you have brought me and my boys together, we are one very big happy family and it is growing. Sorry darling that was thoughtless."

The twins took their first steps whilst we were there Charles and Michael were sat apart and put Elliot on his feet while he held onto Michaels finger he did a step or two while holding on, then he let go and he walked on his own to Charles, we all cheered and he stood holding onto Charles leg, bopping up and down, then Felix was wanting to go down, so they did the same only from Charles to Michael and he did it the same as his brother.

"That's it there would be no stopping them now. It looks like time for a big play pen," I said, Michael agreed.

When we left with them, we were loaded with Birthday cards and more presents for the twins 1st Birthday.

They all left shouting see you New Years Eve, I told them I would cook lunch, then have a buffet in the evening, then we could pick as and when we wanted to eat. I genuinely meant that I would cook and do the buffet, but Michael said no you do a 'Julia' so we got the caters in, which left more time for other things as Michael put it.

New Years Eve morning they all arrived, after lunch we all went to the park, there is a lake with ducks and swans and we had taken some food so the twins could throw it to them. We did not bother with the push chair there were many willing arms to carry them and they could see more. They were fast asleep, as we made our way home.

The party had started early so the twins were still up, when they went to bed we played some party games and did some silly things, but we all laughed, we drank and ate plenty and when it was midnight, we all sang auld-lang-syne and kissed everyone, for a new millennium.

We hadn't told the family, but we had a firework display in the garden just after midnight I was full up, in fact I could not stop the tears Michael took me in his arms "What is it sweetie?"

"I don't know, I think it is because, we have a lovely happy family, something I have never had, there are so many of us together having fun and it is genuine."

We had some more drinks, then we all began to flag, so the girls helped me clear glasses away, Charles was filling the dish washer, the others were clearing up and in next to no time every where was tidy, not clean but tidy and one by one they were going to bed.

Michael said "I have to go and have a sit on the loo, but I will use ours, if are you nearly finished?"

I said "Yes I will be a few minutes, be undressed, on that bed naked and waiting."

"Yes my love anything you say my love," he gave me a very wanting kiss and was running up stairs.

I switched off in the kitchen, after checking everything was locked, I went into the lounge because there was a table lamp left on, as I walked through the door it was pushed to, two strong arms were round me, one straight onto my bottom pulling me into him and Charles lips were on mine, I just melted and gave as good as I got, in fact I was pushing myself on to his erection, we stopped for a second then he whispered "I am sorry darling, after watching your lovely curves all day, I just had to kiss you," his lips were back on mine, it went on for a long time. When we parted, he said you switch the lamp off, I will wait until they're all in their rooms, and come up. Good night, Happy New Year for 2000."

"The same to you my darling, I do love you Charles," I switched the lamp off and walked up stairs, I need not have rushed he was still in the en suite, so I went into the walk-in and got undressed, I came out just as Michael came out of the loo.

"Are you alright darling you have been a while?"

"Yes I am fine, I decided to go and look at my babies my darling before Charles came up, I just stood for a while looking at them, then I realised I still needed the loo," he got into bed.

"I have to do my face, this will keep you going," I put my bare breasts into his hands and kissed him, I only meant it for a second, but we could not part, then there was a tap on the door, I grabbed a bathrobe and opened it, it was Charles in just his trousers "Can you come Felix is crying and I cannot stop him,"

I turned "I will go Michael. I love you so much, I will be quick," as I went to the other end of the house, yes I could hear both of them crying now.

"Felix must have woken Elliot," he leaned in, passing him to me. "He started it," so I sat on Charles bed and tried to shush him, but he was having none of it, so I put him to my breast and he soon stopped, so I let him suckle until he was asleep, Charles was still holding Elliot he had stopped crying, but as soon as I put Felix down he cried, with his hands out to me, I sat down again and put him to the other breast.

"Pop along, tell your Pa, I will not be long," off he went but soon retured.

"He is fast asleep, so I covered him up and just left your lamp on, so you could see your way in," he said.

"I wonder why Felix woke up, he woke Elliot, they should not be in here with you, you should not be caring for them, it is not fair on you," I said.

"Darling I would be happy if they woke every night, I get an extra chance to see your beautiful breasts, it's a treat for me."

"But you have seen them dozens of times."

"Nevertheless my precious, I could never ever get fed up of seeing them, ask Pa he will tell you the same," he did something he has never done before, he snuggled my neck and slipped his hand on to the vacant breast.

"Darling please don't make it any harder," but it didn't stop me leaning into his snuggle.

"It isn't sex, I am only holding it so it does not droop, I am a live bra," I had to laugh. Elliot was asleep, so he took him from me and I turned to go, pulling my robe round me, he grabbed my arm,

"Not so fast you have to pay a fee to enter my boudoir, I will take it," his lips were on mine again, but he moved the bathrobe away so my bare breasts were on his chest "Oh yes," he said, then was kissing me again, after some time I said;

"Charles you are getting very naughty, it has to stop, we are going to get caught," I said giving him a quick kiss and heading for the door.

"Mummy if I am naughty, do you get to spank me, please," I couldn't speak, I left his room.

Now back to Mr Sleeping beauty. I took my make-up off, cleaned my teeth and went to get into bed, I normally would not wake him, but it was New Year and New Century, and he hadn't made love to me yet, I walked round to him, and sat close to him.

"Wake up sleeping beauty, I need your little man, and kissed his lips," nothing so I kissed him again nothing, his face and hands didn't feel as warm as normal, so I slid my hand under the sheets to where his hot legs were, but they weren't, I looked back at his face, I realised I could not hear his breath, I put my now shaking hand under his nose nothing.

"No, Please no, Michael wake up, Michael please, please Michael," I heard this awful scream, I didn't realise it was me, Junior came flying in, he was in the next bedroom to us "Please, please wake Michael," then all the others came running, Junior shook his head at the others.

"No, no, no not my Michael, no he is asleep," someone takes hold of me and lifts me, from where I am sinking to the floor. "Please I must stay with Michael, please put me down," I am crying and sobbing and struggling.

I hear Charles say "Take her to my room with the twins."

"No please I must be with Michael," I am thrashing around, then there is two of them trying to hold me, they put my on the Charles's bed.

"Shush don't wake your babies," I realise it was John and Simon who have carried me, I continue to cry, but stop shouting, Simon left and a few minutes later Charles comes in.

"Charles please let me go back to Michael."

"Darling, I am sorry you can't, you have to be brave my love," he came and sat and taking me in his arms.

John said "I'll go and put the kettle on, did you say the door is open?"

Charles said "Yes, Stuart is on way, as is the ambulance and I will ask Stuart to give you something, do you want to sleep here I will go elsewhere."

"No I want to go downstairs," I am still crying, my head is thudding. "Charles why, why has Michael gone and left us? please are you sure he is not asleep?"

"No my darling, this shows there was something, when he had his 'funny turns' but he did die happy Sophie, you brought him more happiness in the short time you were together, than the rest of his life put together."

"Why when I find happiness with someone are they taken away from me, is it because I am bad, am I always going to bring someone bad luck, it has to be me."

"No it does not and please do not think like that Sophie," it was Stuart our Doctor "I am sorry, I could not help hearing what you were saying. My darling it is just one of those things, they happen. This is going to be a very trying time, I know you have Charles, the rest of the family will all be around whenever you need them, you have Bel and me, you have other friends, you will not be on your own. We all love you and understand how you are feeling. I am going to give you some tablets, these white ones, one with water when you go to bed. The pink, one twice a day with food, you must eat, your sons need you, you have to be strong," Stuart spoke very gently.

"I will make sure she takes them with food, even if I have to spoon feed her like I do with the twins," Charles said.

"Yes, I know you will, she is very lucky to have someone so close keeping an eye on her," he said "I am so sorry for your loss Charles, it is always a shock," I will pop in later tomorrow to see how you are going on Sophie," he kissed me and shook hands with Charles "I will see myself out."

John put his head round the door "He's gone, do you want anything to drink Sophie?"

"Thank you, no I will come down," I said getting off the bed, Charles was putting his dressing gown on his bare top.

Everything seems a blur, I do not think anyone went back to bed, next morning they were leaving because they were to go to work on the 2$^{nd.}$.

I think for several days I slept most of the time. I seemed to wake up in time for someone to force feed me, then have another tablet, it must have been the tablets that were making me sleep. Charles was brilliant with me, John and Polly decided it was easier for them to stay with us, they were both self employed, so it did not matter where they were, it made everything easier for Charles, because I was no good to anyone. I became more aware after about five days and actually was doing things for my twins.

The funeral was arranged for Thursday 14th January, 2000 at our local church for 10.45am, the cremation to follow at 11.45am at Wilford Hill. We had no idea how many people there would be, numerous people had telephoned home regarding Michael, so we decided to hold it at the Manor and book a room then when the twins needed a nap it was easier. Although one or two said the twins should not be there, I said they are his children and I know if I had died Michael, would have brought them to mine.

Charles said Stuart had telephoned he wanted to come to see us, when he arrived Polly brought coffee into the drawing room, the twins were having a nap, which made it better "I have brought the Pathologist report on Michael, the cause of death was a

'Subarachnoid Hemorrhage' in his brain which is an 'Aneurysm' which burst, it does not entirely explain the Funny Turns he had."

"Would he have any pain?" I am trying to hold it together.

"It is unlikely, it could have happened anytime, but you spoke to him about thirty minutes earlier, he did not say he had any pain did he?" I just shook my head, the water works would not stay back any longer, I got up.

"Excuse me," and ran out, Charles was right behind me.

"Darling, there is nothing to be ashamed of in grieving in front of others, come here," he put his arms round me "I am here for you, I will look after you, you know that, I love you so much, it breaks my heart to see you suffering."

"I'll go and sit with my babies, please give him my apologises." I went and sat watching them sleep, all the innocence in the world, I wonder what will be in store for them.

On the Monday Charles took me to see Michael, I would never see him again, it brought it all back to me from when Charles died, he did just look as if he was asleep, I kissed his frozen lips and held onto his hand, talked to him thanking him, for all the happiness he had given me and our twins, I rambled on and on. Charles just sat to one side, didn't speak, it was not until I looked at him I realised how hard it has been for him, after all he was not just my husband he was Charles father.

I went to him and knelt in front of him "Charles I am so sorry, I am so selfish thinking of me, he was your father, I have left everything for you to do," my tears were still in full flow and for the first time, I saw tears start falling from his eyes "Darling," I got up as he did "I am sorry, what you must have been going through," I held him to me, he just let go he really sobbed, it was heart wrenching. I gave him a large handkerchief and he dried his face and blew his nose.

"Sophie I am alright now and please do not start beating yourself up about everything, I was happy to know that I could take care of you and the twins," he gave me a swift kiss.

The day of the funeral arrived I was a lot more in charge of myself, it did shock me when I thought of how all the boys had rallied round me, and taken care of everything, me forgetting it was their father.

It was a bright sunny, cold day I decided on a black trouser suit with my black mink, full length fur coat and hat, which Michael had bought for me but the obligatory stiletto heels, I needed them because the boys all made me look like a dwarf even though I was 5"6" they were all 6'2" plus. All Michaels sons were in the first car with me and the twins, I had Elliot and Charles had Felix. I had a bit of a wobble when I saw his coffin in the hearse, covered with just the one wreath from me of 4 dozen red roses, and small one with Yellow roses from the twins, the request was no flowers, donations were for charity. As we arrived and were getting out of the car, they were lifting Michael out six handsome Police officers in full uniform carried Michael in with ease, I did not know them, that made the tears flow. When we walked into the church it was full, they were even standing at the back, you do not know how many people you know until you are dead!

It was a beautiful service John read a lesson, Junior gave a eulogy about his father, from them being young, and said it took his Pa to find me before we became one a big happy family. The family were indebted to me for bringing him the happiness he enjoyed until his death. We ended with Jerusalem Michaels favourite.

Then it was off to the crematorium for a brief prayer, but when the curtains started to close and he was going out of sight, that is when it hit me, someone took Elliot from me and Felix from Charles, Charles put his arm round me to help me out. Junior and John went and had a word with many people who were there, inviting them back for refreshments.

The Hotel was packed, numerous men came to me and said what a wonderful dedicated man he was. He was respected by all including criminals. All the faces were one blur there were so many of them.

Charles came and said the twins were getting a bit tearful and thought they ought to have a nap, so Charles took Felix and collected the key from reception and I followed with Elliot they had been fed as well as feeding themselves.

He opened the door and went in, I took my coat off, it was so hot everywhere. We took their coats and hats off, I said they would have to be changed first, but even though they were tired, when we lay them next to each other, they would smile and make noises to one another Charles said "I may as well do Felix I can do this blind folded now," I laughed.

"I think I will give them a little drink, they may sleep quite a while, they can always stay up a bit then when we go home," so I undid my little jacket "Can you unfasten my bra please before you pick him up."

"My pleasure Mrs Roper," he smirked, I just looked at him and he gave me a swift kiss, I lift my bra up releasing one breasts and whilst I was getting Elliot sorted Charles released the other one.

"Look one out all out!" he laughed.

"Darling you sound a bit like your old self, thank you for everything," he held my face between his hands and gave me a full kiss, I just closed my eyes, it could have been Michael. Elliot was asleep, so I lay him in the cot and Charles passed me Felix, before I could do anything Charles gave Felix my breast.

"Just thought I would help," he said, Felix went to sleep quickly, Charles took him and laid him down at the side of his brother and covered them up.

I was struggling to try and get my bra back on "Hang on Mummy where's mine," I laughed "I thought you were joking?"

"Darling where your beautiful breasts are concerned I will never joke," he knelt in front of me "Can I?" his lovely eyes it is like looking at Michael.

I shrugged "If you want," he put his mouth to one of my nipples and took the other in his hand, he began to suck very gently, but it went straight down below, now why does it not do that with my babies, a little whisper said "Oh Charles," I felt very weak, He was gently pushing me backwards. He released my breasts, his lips were on mine, my arms went round him holding him close, he was rubbing his erection onto me.

Then we both stopped we heard the lift "Could be someone looking for us, quick put my bra on for me," he did he made sure my breasts were in the cups. He pulled me to my feet just as there was a tap on the door, I pull my jacket round me Charles opened the door it was Jackie.

She stepped in and whispered "We wanted to get off and someone said you had brought the twins up here. You are looking much better Sophie you even have some colour," Jackie said, I heard a cross between a laugh and a cough from Charles. I walked to the lift with her and left Charles bringing up the rear.

There were still quite a few people here, I went to the table where we were sat with the boys and partners "Before you all go, can we please sort out either a Saturday or Sunday for you to come over for lunch, I need to see you altogether, so out came diaries then Junior said "If it will keep until February we will be in

Carlton then, so we will not need to come and stay," he said.

"Good idea" I replied so it was decided the 7th February which is a Saturday, they all agreed "Do you want any help when you move, is there anything we can do from this end?" I asked.

"We will phone you and have a chat," then it was good bye, we had a drink, I had Brandy and lemonade it was big, I said to Charles "I hope this isn't all Brandy?"

"It is only a triple but plenty of lemonade try it," so I had a sip, I nodded, he winked at me, so I did a Michael and raised an eye brow, which made him laugh, they all turned and looked at him and he said "What?"

The reception came and said there were baby chuckles and noises coming through. So they all told us they would wait until we fetched the boys down, then they would be off. We got in the lift and as the doors closed Charles stood in front of me and said "When we get back John and Polly are going home," he was standing so close. We went into the boys, who were stood up jumping up and down in the cot, they were having a great time, until they saw us, then there little chubby hands and arms reached up to us. "Mammamm," Elliot said "Did that sound like Mama to you?" I asked Charles.

"I think it is close," then he put his arms to Charles Dadaddddd, I think the world stopped.

Charles said "You cannot blame them, they saw the same face whether it was me or Pa."

"I suppose you are right," I replied. We went down to the others, they all made a big fuss of the twins, then we all went our separate ways.

We were soon home we took the boys outdoor clothes off and plonked them in the playpen in the kitchen, where there were plenty of toys for them to throw around and play with, while we got ourselves sorted out. Then we went and played with the twins until they looked tired so we took them to bed. I decided not to bath them, just changed their nappies and gave them a drink, but I did it on my own, Charles had disappeared. I decided to change and be comfortable. I had another silent weep.

When I went downstairs, I realised Charles had cleaned everywhere up, put glasses and pots into the dish washer, he had got change into his jeans and tight T-shirt.

"Darling I wondered where you were, you should have left it for me, you really do too much as it is."

"I thought while you settled the boys, if I did this then we could have the rest of the evening to ourselves," he replied "Can I get you a drink of anything?"

"No thank you, I feel half squiffy as it is, with all that Brandy, you have whatever you want," I said.

"No I am not bothered, like you I think I have had enough," he said "I want us to talk before we go any further."

"Charles what is it we have to talk about, you have me worried?" I tried a smile.

"I have to get something clear, before we go any further, how do you feel about me?" he asked.

"You know, I love you very much," I replied.

"Yes, but is it me or because you think I am my Pa?"

"No I do not think you are Michael, you are two different people how could you be him?" I was confused.

"Sophie you know how I feel about you, I have made no secret of my feelings, do you think sometime you could feel the same way about me, I know you were in love with my father, do you think one day you could be in love with me in the same way?"

"Charles, you have no idea have you? why do you think I let you kiss me like you did? Yes I was in love with your father, but you see I was falling in love with you, as much as I tried to stop my feelings. I did not want you to just kiss me, I wanted you to make love to me, but I would never have done that because of your father, but I could not help the way I felt about you. I began to wonder if I knew what love was? because I had heard it said in the past, that you cannot be in love with two people. Also what would you think of me, if I had let you make love to me, when my dearest Michael had just died, it makes me look like a slut, a slapper or whatever the name is. All I know is my feelings for you were the same, you turned me on as much as your father. Does that explain anything to you?" by now he was very close to me, he had wiped my tears away whilst I was talking, he just sat looking at me.

"Sophie you're not saying that?"

"I cannot believe you said that!" I couldn't look at him.

"Sophie I am sorry, but it's been going round and round in my head, I had to say something, I am so sorry, but I cannot believe what you have just told me. I could not have hoped for that in a million years, all I could see was that it would not be appropriate for me to stay here alone with you, I thought you would be telling me to leave."

"What is it with men, they seem very clever, then they come out with something stupid like that, me tell you to leave?"

"Sophie," he came closer, just brushed his lips across mine, then his arms were round me, his lips were devouring mine, his tongue was doing magical things, it went on and on until we had to stop to breathe.

"Charles, you have frequently told me you want me, I am equally wanting you," I simply said.

"Oh Sophie," was all he said, he swept me off my feet and was carrying fast up stairs.

"Where are we going?" I asked.

"To my bedroom," he replied.

"What's wrong with the master suite?" I asked.

"I didn't think you would want me to completely take fathers place."

"You are saying father and Sophie why? Anyway you aren't taking his place because I was married to him, you are just a bit on the side!" I tried not to laugh "The bedding is clean."

"First of all father sounds more respectful, and Sophie sounds as sexy as you are, I have been saying it for a while now, I am happy to be your bit on the side, but not for long. As long as I am fucking you, what the hell. I am marrying you as soon as is deemed to be respectful to my father, I am not asking you Sophie, I am telling you, you have no choice, even if it means locking you in. In fact you will stay in this bed and never leave it until you are pregnant, I will have you tied to it, so I can take you any time I want you. Do you understand Mrs bit on the side Roper!" He had stripped to his boxers, while talking, then began undressing me.

"Can I correct you on a little point, you do not have to tie me to any bed, I will happily stay there, you can fuck me 30 hours a day if that is what you want, ME beg you to stop, I do not think so, I only beg for more, I do not care how many babies we have, I am in love with you, now and for always. However, it will be my fourth marriage, I am still only 22, do you not think you should heed the warning signs?" I looked at him waiting.

"No I am not going anywhere, we will grow old and grey together," he picked me up and carried me into the master suite. He stood me down, kissing me, then he moved away "Please do not move, I want to eat you with my eyes, just check you are the same as my memory remembers you," he soon had his boxers off.

I stood enjoying the view, "I thought your father had the best body and biggest cock, but you far exceed anyone, you have the most magnificent appendage, it's all mine! only mine?"

He began to walk slowly towards me, he did not blink, or say anything, it seemed to be in slow motion. His fingers lightly brushed my breasts, my nipples stood to attention immediately. Then he closed the space between us, wrapped his arms round me, his lips lightly brushed mine, then they were taking possession of me, I just melted, the kiss deepened, our tongues were entwined, I heard a groan, I hadn't realised but it was me.

He gently lifted me onto the bed and followed me down, "I love you so much, Sophie, I have been longing for you, I cannot believe I am here with you, both naked," he began fondling my breasts, he was kissing round my ear, his hand slowly made it's way down my body, I am so wanting, I can't hold still, his fingers were caressing round my clit and happy spot, then he slowly slipped them inside me, I am writhing.

"Charles, please," he stopped me by kissed me.

"Sh, baby, don't rush, when I first enter you, there will never be that feeling again, that very, very first time."

I gave a little giggle "Darling we even think alike, I have been saying that for years, it can never be repeated, please let me have that feeling, now."

He kissed me, as he was placing himself over me, he kissed me again, the full works, he was gently lowering himself, I could feel his erection rubbing along my clit, I moaned, I looked into his eyes they were looking into mine,

"Please do not close your eyes, when I enter you, please keep looking into my eyes," I did as I was told, although when I felt him just beginning to enter me, I really wanted to close my eyes to savour the whole sensation. He was just easing himself in, so slowly, I wanted to push myself onto him, but I let him do it how he wanted, I have got to say, the sensation was out of this world and looking into each others eyes, was something I could never put into words, in that moment, I realised how much I loved him, he was thrilling me as no other had before, he parted his lips and lowered them onto mine, once our lips were locked together, he then started to move, long full length movements, almost out and then to the very top, it was so gentle, he kept it like that for a long time, slowly taking me up, until after a long time, he really began to move, we were going up together, he kept taking us both up, and up until we could not hold any longer, we let go together, the orgasms, were spectacular, my whole being, was throbbing and pulsating, I was milking him, it went on and on, we were moaning, groaning and gasping for breath. He was holding me tight, he rolled onto his side, while we were still locked together, but facing each other laying down, he was kissing me with such passion, I took everything he wanted to give, eventually, we began to get our breath back.

"My darling, that was fantastic, you are so receptive, you are one very, sexy girl, you really know how to make love, I have never had anyone, who could make love, like you just have. No wonder my father was happy with you."

We lay for a long time, locked together, we both must have gone to sleep, still locked together. I was awoken by a certain someone, drawing me to him, and locking me in his arms. As I opened my eyes, his lips were just taking mine, I closed my eyes, with a loud sigh.

"Charles, I am so in love with you," I sighed again.

"Mrs Roper, I feel exactly the same as you, you were fantastic last night," he said, brushing his lips across mine.

"I am wondering, can we do it again, it might have been a one off, I want to be sure." I whispered.

"Don't think so, listen," baby talk, mammmm, ddaddda.

"You are going to wish I didn't have a lot a baggage."

"Never, I love them as my own, shall I go?" he offered.

"No, I'll go."

There they were side by side, holding onto the side and jumping up and down. "Stand still," I said, I unlocked the side, then I tucked one under each arm, and ran with them, to where Charles looked as through he was having a peaceful moment, not any more, I thought, as I dropped them onto the bed, beside him, they were crawling all over him.

"I will have a quick shower, then," I stopped.

"What is it darling?"

"I have had a thought, we could put them in the shower," I got them ready and stood them on the floor, I ran in, had a shower, then called to them, they came running in to me, I had lowered the head and turned the water down, they loved it running in and out, I grabbed one, soaped him well, then picked him up and turned him in all directions, he squealed with delight, so I repeated it with the other, they loved it running in and out, then Charles joined us.

"This sounds like fun," he took me in his arms and melted me with his kiss. "I shouldn't have done that," we both looked down at his erection. "My own fault, I know what effect you have on me, I have been living with a permanent erection, for months," he laughed, so he started washing himself. I put some soap on my hands, took hold of that erection and started massaging him, pushing his foreskin right back, holding it there, with one hand, while fingering the head, he gave a low growl, just like Michael, his head was back, eyes closed. "Can we stay like this all day, Sophie, you have no idea what you are doing to me," the boys were sat on the floor, while the water slowly kept them wet, they had ducks trying to float, so while they were occupied, I slipped down his body and took him in my mouth, and slowly very slowly sucked, while I was still holding his foreskin right back. He was gone in ecstasy, he soon let go, "I can't stop myself, ooh my darling Sophie," he was pushing himself to the back of my mouth, I realised his skin and let him do what he wanted to. Eventually he pulled me up towards him.

"Sophie, you are a very exiting, surprising young sexy lady, I love you with all my heart." his lips claimed mine, one hand at the back of my neck, holding me close to him. His other slid down my back to my bottom and was caressing in between my cheeks, until his finger slowly slipped inside and was gently moving it in and out. I heard my breath catch, I was beginning to really breath heavily, all the time he is kissing me, then his new erection has slipped between my lips and is massaging my clit with it. We are so wanting, then someone lets out a little cry and brings us back to earth with a bang, Elliot has rolled over and cannot get back up.

We decided we had better get us and the twins dry, we didn't put anything on their feet, because they were still running in and out of the wet shower floor.

We were soon dressed and giving the boys their breakfast, while Charles made us a cup of tea. Suddenly he said "Look, look," he was pointing to the windows, it had started snowing, we pulled the baby chairs in front of the window, so they could eat their toast while looking at the snow. They were enthralled. We put the playpen in front of the french doors, so they were playing and watching the snow. We sat eating our breakfast in peace for once.

The boys soon, got tired, "It must have been all the

running in and out of the shower," I said, as we carried them upstairs for a nap, they lay down and were soon fast asleep, I stood looking at them, tears running again.

Charles came round the door, took one look at me "I thought so, please don't hide from me, I do understand, I think you are doing well," he said holding me tight. "I know what will take your mind off your grief," he took me along the landing to the bedroom, he led me to the bed, threw the covers back, undressed me in one second, then himself and we were back in bed.

"I want to finish what we started earlier," he held me the same, his finger in my bottom, slipping in and out, his cock really massaging my clit, but he would not let me move, so he was not inside me. His lips devouring mine. "I am not going to fuck you, my cock will make you come without entering you, the only thing inside you will be the finger, plus one. He slipped two fingers inside. He was right, what he was doing to me was getting me very aroused.

"After you have come, I will really fuck you, then later, you are going to have this beautiful arse, well and truly fucked. Sure enough I climaxed, I was very loud, while I was still in the throws, he slipped inside me and was really going at it, he was hitting the spot every time, we both climaxed together, we were very loud. True to his word he did take my mind off Michael. It was the same with Michael, when Charles was killed, he soon knew how to help me.

"Sophie, I cannot believe my luck, no wonder my father never looked at a another woman once he found you, he didn't need anyone else. All the girls I have been with only want it a couple of times, maybe again the next morning. That is all I have been used to, I think all my birthdays have come at once. You have let me do what I want with you, as I think you did with my father.

We were there for quiet a while, then we heard baby gurgles and laughing. "I'll go," he said.

So I went and sat on the bidet.

"Where's mummy," I could hear Charles, suddenly the door was opened and Charles shouted "I have found mummy, I have heard about that thing from my father, he said you were always on it."

"Well it's easier, I like to be clean but not shower."

The snow kept coming, it was really thick, the boys wanted to go outside, so Charles said he would take them, I got them dressed in little wellies, thick coats and hats and mittens. They built a snowman and threw snow balls, they really enjoyed it, but then it was getting really cold, and was snowing again, so they came in for their tea, they were all in.

While I finished our dinner, Charles took them upstairs to get them ready for bed, then they came down to eat and have a drink, they were falling asleep as they sat in their chairs, so we put them to bed.

The tears started again! "Darling," he said, holding me.

"Michael will never see them grow up, I really loved him," I sobbed.

"Come on darling, let us go and finish dinner off, then we could probably have an early night, I know I am exhausted," he laughed. He cheered me up. We had soon eaten, Charles, left saying, upstairs as soon as possible please, when I turned he was gone. I went up to the bedroom, as I walked through the door, he took me in his arms "Darling I cannot wait any longer, I have to make love to you, I know you don't really like anything sexual, but could you please try for me?"

"Tut, do I have to? can you not wait a week or two," I really did well, keeping my face straight.

"Well if you just get into bed, perhaps I could help myself?"

"Oh alright then, give me a minute," I went into the bathroom, cleaned my teeth, sat on the bidet, while I undressed and appeared shortly after, naked.

"Christ Sophie, that sight has got to be worth ten million pounds at least, come here my love," I walked to him, he gently lay me on the bed and that was it, he made love to me again, as he did earlier, with two fingers and his lovely big erection.

"Darling, would you please get up on all fours?" suddenly a night mare came back to me, the first time was Mat and the following consequences! This will be different this is lovely Charles, try it and see. I did not speak I just got up on all fours.

"Christ Sophie you are hard work, trying to get you to do something. I am going to say it again, no wonder my father did not want any other woman, and he has left you for me. I must be the luckiest bastard in the whole wide world. I will love you for ever, I am besotted by you, I am beguiled by you, I just want you all the time."

I was still on all fours he slipped under me and pulled me

onto him, and kissed me, then rolled me over onto my back.

"I thought you wanted?" he stopped me.

"Yes my darling, I do, but there is a slight difference between two of my fingers and my little cock. I have to just do a bit of preparation, a man cannot just go charging in, can you hang on for a short while?"

"Yes," I lay watching him, he was getting something out of the bedside drawer. He was fiddling with something, I could not see.

"Right, my little sex addict, see this," he held a shiny round, chrome like thing, about 10" long about 1" diameter. "Look it has little holes in," it had all the way round, top to bottom. "This is a lubricant, I will insert this into you, when it is in I press the bottom, all the lubricant will come out. Then I get you in the mood for me slipping inside you. Have you not done this before then?"

"Not making love in there."

"What other way is there?" he looked at me. "No, don't tell me, you were forced." I nod. "Sorry we will not do that."

I stopped him "No, I want you to because you are making love to me, I want you to do whatever you want, I love you and there is nothing I wouldn't do for you, because I know I will love anything you do to me, please Charles."

"Darling are you sure?" I nod. He rolls me over pulls me onto my knees, but leaves my shoulders on the bed, he starts caressing me and stroking my clit, slipping his fingers inside my cunt, straight onto my happy spot. While he is doing this I feel the cold of the chrome on my opening, he slips it up into me, very slowly, every so often he must let a little of the lubricant out, to help it go all the way up, he twists it round, I groan. He pulls it out slightly and pushes it right in again, and twists, I let out another groan, he whispers in my ear, "I gather you like that?" I nod.

"Sorry my darling, I cannot have an object doing me out of fucking the arse off you, because I think you are ready," as he says that, he must have pressed the end, releasing all the lubricant. He withdraws it, and says "Right, my little slut, all fours please," his erection starts very gently to go in, then starts to push himself in, he feels big, bloody big, but it doesn't hurt, I realise I am pushing back onto him, it feels tight, but I know he is going to take me up. Soon I have all of him inside, he just gently draws back very slightly, but pushes himself back in fast, he continues like that, then begins to move as normal, but not too far out. He moves his hands to my breasts. Christ what he is doing with my breasts, nipples and my arse it's wonderful, he does not let up he keeps up all the thrills, he knows I am getting close.

"Babes let go, come for me, let it go," it tips me over the edge and I have the most noisiest, groaning, grinding, grunting, orgasm ever. He is the same. My legs give way and we fall flat on the bed, with Charles on top of me, he lifts slightly taking his weight on his arms.

He begins kissing me round my ears, he twists my head round so he has access to my lips, while he is kissing me, I am suddenly moved quickly, he is laying on his back, with me laying on top of him, lips still together.

"Mrs Roper, I am so in love with you, you amaze me. I want to stay in bed with you for ever, I would never get bored."

"What did you say?"

"I want to stay in bed with you for ever, I would never get bored, why?" He sees my lips tremble. "Darling what, I am sorry, I did not mean to upset you."

"That is more is less word for word what your father said," by now the tears are falling. "You are one person, you are your father and your father was you," I say through the sobs.

"In that case my darling, you do not have to grieve, we are just one person," I know he was trying to make me laugh but fails.

We slept quiet late, the twins were nearer to us, I had, had Charles move the cot back into the nursery, through my sleep, I could hear them playing and giggling, in the end I had to get up, so I went into them and four little arms were held up to me, they always stand still now, while I drop the side and then picked them up one under each arm, and took them into Charles, who was just opening his eyes. So I drop them onto the bed at the side of him, they were climbing all over him giggling.

"Good morning my darling," I said to him and kissed him, the twins thought that was good and tried to kiss him.

"Come here you little sex addict," he said, and pulled me down to him and kissed me, a deep kiss and I kissed him back, the twins were wetting us through, trying to kiss us both.

"Will I be able to have a replay, or would you rather leave it a while."

"No way, I am ready now." one eye brow up. "Come on you two nappies off, then shower," they were soon in the shower.

Charles said "Sophie I feel wonderful, I have never had

such a satisfied feeling before." he laughed "God, I must have died and gone to heaven, you are one very amazing girl, my love. I have just thought are you on any contraception?"

"No, why would I be? I want babies, not stop having them! Although if you are going to keep doing it up there, I will never get pregnant!"

"Well what if you get caught?"

"What about it?"

"Well people will talk," he said.

"I am hoping by the time I am pregnant and it shows, people will know we are together, the family at least, I am not ashamed of loving you, I am not ashamed of letting the world know you are fucking me, in fact I want to shout it from the roof tops, you are so wonderful, I am so in love with you Charles," I felt a sudden pang, I could feel the tears building.

I went into the bathroom, "Can mummy have a shower, please," I moved the shower head, so I cold have a quick one, they stood watching me. I was soon lowering the head for them, they and they loved it, I saw very little through the tears.

Charles came round the door "This sounds like fun again," he joined us, I rinsed the boys off by picking them up, holding them upside down and making sure the was no bubbles anywhere, they just kept running in and out. I still cannot stop the tears.

Suddenly he grabbed my arm and turned me to him "Darling I am sorry, I thought you were doing well, but you have been hiding from me," he took me gently in his arms "It is alright, it is early days, you are coping magnificently, but please don't keep hiding from me, he was my father, I do understand," I just stood and sobbed, he just stood and held me close, the boys were stood watching and Charles said "Mummy is not very happy that is why she is crying, we will have to make her better, they just stood looking up at me, I bent down to them and they put there arms towards me I put my arms round them both and kissed them, they started laughing, it was forgotten, they began running in and out of the shower again.

I started to shampoo Charles "You do the top, I will do the interesting bit," I was caressing him more than washing, the boys suddenly stopped, they looked at their little men, then at Charles, one of them came and pulled him "No I said you cannot do that you will hurt daddy," I said, but he was getting harder.

"Will you stop that Mrs Roper, otherwise the boys will not

get any breakfast, you will get fucked so behave yourself," Charles switched the shower off, I slipped a bathrobe on and took two bath towels, threw one to Charles he was putting a bathrobe on.

We dressed them and gave them their breakfast. I said "Are we getting dressed? I wondered if you can think of something else we could do naked?" I just smiled. So Charles made our tea, as I was stood making the boys drink, he came up behind me and put his arms round me, snuggling my neck, I go all wanting, for the want of a better word. I turned to face him and put my lips on his and kissed him, we were soon back in our little world, until the boys started making noises, from their high chairs.

"Look what you do to me you sexy thing."

I said "I really do love you Charles, No I am in love with you."

"My lovely Sophie, I am in love with you, I just hope I can make you happy, as my father did."

"Darling please do not refer to your father as a comparison, what we had has gone, he took it when he died," the tears are coming, I tried to ignore them "You are a new chapter in my life, what we have got is our own, not the remnants of what your father left, so please my darling, you are making me happy, it's a pity I cannot spend all the time in bed with you, because when you are making love to me the tears do not come, so we know the answer don't we?"

"I would be more than happy, but darling, one of us has to live in the real world and there are two adorable boys here need us. I think of them as mine, in fact I have been with them more than my father was?" he said. "I will be the only father they remember,"

"I know my darling, I want us to be one family, and I am very much in love with you."

Chapter fifteen

Charles still had some accounts so I helped him finish them. We decided not to take any more clients on, we wanted time together, we didn't need the money.

Graham, Michaels Lawyer telephoned to see if Charles was still with me? we arranged for 12.30. that afternoon.

Graham arrived on time, we were all ready. I put the kettle on, Charles went to answer the door, with two little ones trailing behind. When they came into the kitchen Charles was carrying Elliot and Graham carrying Felix, I said we could go into the drawing room, Graham said we will be fine here.

The twins were put into the playpen, when I had made coffee, I took them a biscuit each, we sat round the table, first of all Graham took two envelopes from his brief case, your father Charles, Michael, Sophie left these with me to give to you." We could see our name on the envelopes in Michael handwriting. "I have come to read you his last Will, I will not read the jargon, it is straight forward, he left eight million to Charles, the remainder of his estate, not including this house which is yours Sophie, I have done a rough estimate, including investments, it will be in the region of nine or ten million."

I sat I could not speak "But what about his other sons?"

"This was what he asked me to do, although we have been friends for donkeys years, it was not my place to question his bequests. I do believe there is a large amount coming to all the boys from Michaels and Julia's parents. Everything they have will be going to all his sons, Michael was aware of this, that is why he felt he could leave you financially covered, also there is a two million Insurance, which will come to you Sophie when they decide to pay out. Plus you will get something from his Police Pension. I am sorry I cannot stay any longer, I am so pleased to have met you Sophie, I was at Michaels funeral but there were so many people there and you were obviously very upset, I did not want to impose. I will let you know when everything is transferred to you."

"Wait, you are wrong, Michael would not let me buy the house, he bought it," I said.

"Yes, but it was put straight into your name on the purchase," he replied. I could not hold back, the water works were at it again. I tried to say;

"Thank you very much," but it was all wobbly, shaky and sniffles, "I am sorry," I said.

"Please do not apologise, I do understand. Also for what it's worth, you made Michael extremely happy," Charles showed him out.

Charles came back and took me in his arms, that made me worse, he just stood holding me close, the boys were both stood looking up at us "Come on my darling, look at the boys, they are wondering what you are doing again," he lifted them out, I was sat on the sofa, he put them with me, they were getting tired they had been awake since around 6am.

"I think we should take them up for a nap," so I went to pick them up, one under each arm.

"No love, let me carry them they are getting too heavy?" He took them from me and we ran upstairs, the boys chuckling away.

"In we go have five minutes, then after, if we can get through the snow, Mummy and Daddy will go to see the ducks," they both lay down on their own. I wish Michael could see them, the tears flowed again, I went and sat on our loo for a while, but they would not stop.

Suddenly Charles came round the door, "Come on my darling please don't keep hiding from me," he held me close, walking me towards the bed and we sat down.

"I can seem to go ages then something sets me off, why?"

"It is early days my love, but please do not keep hiding away," he said and kissed me, then he kissed me again, each time it was a bit longer, until he had pushed me back onto the bed, then we were kissing, tongues entwined wanting each other, his hand went up my skirt, he roughly pulled my thong off, he knelt up unzipped his jeans and out popped his big beautiful erection, he pushed my skirt up and thrust inside me "Oh yes," I said.

"Oh yes, my angel, I do not want you to hide when you cry, because I know now how to stop you, I have never wanted anybody as much as I want you, as often as I want you."

He started to move very quickly, it must be something men are born with this ability to move so fast, he was taking me up fast the thrills and feelings are something no words can describe, then we start having an orgasm together he is thrusting hard, I am throbbing and pulsating, when he quietens and slows, that is when he feels me 'milking him' "I love what you do to me, the problem is you make me want you again," he whispered, putting his tongue in my ear, he knows I go weak. "From now on every time you hide from me when you cry, I am going to start punishing you, only thing I have to find something that will not turn you on."

"Right, why is it a problem you wanting me again? I cannot see any problem, the boys are having a nap, I could not care less, if we have nothing ready for lunch, I would rather you fuck me than eat any day, I love you so much Charles, please take me to heaven again," as I say it I know I can squeeze him harder so I do.

"I don't stand a chance do I, you make me want you so much, who wants food anyway?" he started again "I am telling you now, I am really going to fuck you, no making love, I want you to feel me up to your tonsils my darling. I have said it often in the past, anything to do with sex, you love, I am pleased it is me that has you, you will never have anyone else, because I am with you for a long, long, time, my darling," all the time he was just moving very gently and slowly, but when he stopped talking that was it and did he fuck me, Oh yes!

We lay a long time gasping and trying to breath, we just lay in a crumpled heap, bedding all messed up, my skirt up round my neck somewhere, we just lay in each others arms. "Come on my love, let me take you into the shower because I can hear two little voices chuckling and playing, before long they will know their tummies want filling," He was right, as we were getting dressed, we could hear their little tones change before it became a cry. Charles ran into the nursery and came back with one under each arm, it really made them laugh.

"Where's mummy find mummy," he said, they started running round the bedroom, then went in the shower but decided they were more interested in wanting water, so I called out. By this time I was ready to go down stairs.

We carried them downstairs they really wanted to try to walk down, we kept saying when they are bigger, we made sure the gate at the bottom and top were locked.

After we had fed them, we got ready, and went for a hike through the snow, it was lovely now the boys could walk and run because it tired them quickly. We could not bring the pushchair, so we had to carry them back.

"It's alright them sleeping now, but when we want a peaceful half an hour they will be awake again," Charles said.

"Don't tell me you are thinking if we were at home, we could be trying to make a baby or two," I looked at him, he gave me the biggest grin "I thought they were my thoughts?" I said.

"Not any more my love, you have changed me completely, making love to you, comes first, second and last. By the way why did you want to see my brothers altogether?"

"Because your father had told me that I was to get a lot of what he had, I didn't want them to feel I had taken what was rightfully theirs, so I decided, I am going to give them a cheque each for one million, I have that sitting in the bank, growing doing nothing. So I thought I would make them a gift."

"You are the most generous person I have ever come across, my father told me lots of things you did, you said to get rid of the money, you used to make him laugh when you did things like that."

"Did he tell you much about me and him?" I asked.

"He frequently talked about you, especially when I moved in with you both, he told me you were the best thing that ever happened to him, he said from the first time he met you, he was drawn towards you, each time he saw you he realised his feelings were more than sexual, yes he said at first that was what he thought of, having you in his bed, but gradually he realised he was in love with you. Something he had never experienced in his life. He always seemed to be dreamy when he talked about you. You are calm, or well until you are naked, then in bed you are a wild tiger, no one would believe you are the same person."

"Darling that last bit, has someone said that to you?"

"What do you mean, has someone said it to me?" he asked.

"Did your father ever say something similar?"

"No my darling, that was me, why do you think he would say that?" he looked curious.

"Because he said more or less exactly the same as you."

"Honestly?" he asked.

"Yes darling honestly. This is getting eerie, look what you said in bed," I said.

"Well we both can't be wrong, it is eerie we both think the same?"

"Well, you look identical, so other things must be the same," I said. We were home, they were still fast on. I went and locked the door again, as I turned Charles took me in his arms and kissed me, I returned his kisses "I love you so much, I am going to tell the family when they come for lunch in February that we are going to get married, I am not pussy footing about waiting for what everyone calls a reasonable period of mourning, you could be mourning for months, even years, I want us to get on with our life together and hopefully have more children."

"Wow, is that a proposal then?" I asked.

"No I will propose to you when you are not expecting it."

"Right," I said. I looked at the table and saw the two envelopes still unopened "Charles why do you think we have both got a letter from your father?"

"If you read it you will find out," he replied.

"No I will wait until the boys are in bed and it is peaceful," as I said that two little heads popped up "Peace has gone."

So we played with them for a quite a while, Charles was wonderful with them, they had a great time, while I prepared dinner and made the boys tea. We got them ready for bed together, then I gave them a drink and they went happily to bed.

We had dinner then we went into the drawing room and took the letters with us so we sat on the longest settee, at each end and opened our letters I did not know what to expect, I opened it carefully and read:

My dearest wonderful loveable Sophie,
You are reading this because I have gone, not that I wanted to I wanted a lot longer with you, you made me the happiest man in the world, I found true love with you, I was in love with you and you made a world of happiness for me, even brought my sons closer to me. You now have our twins and I will never see them grow up but I know they will be loved more than most boys, I have left you well provided for, I do not want you to keep mourning for me, you are too young, you need to live but I need to know you are not open to anyone who will only want to relieve you of your money, so what I am about to advice, tell, ask and beg you, is coming from the bottom of my heart and I do mean sincerely.
I know of a truly wonderful and decent young man, who loves you in the same way as I do, he is in love with you, he has stood by and suffered watching us being in love together, yes I do know because we have talked, also I allowed him to borrow your lips from time to time, it gave him some hope my darling, he would look after you the same way as I have, he would not want you for your money.
What I am asking is, would you please give him a chance to love you openly, it would make me so happy if I thought you were together and he was bringing my boys up as his own, if you tried, I truly believe that you will love him, because as you have said many times we are one person,

one older and one younger, but we look the same in every way, yes I have filled out over the years which everyone does, but I started out exactly the same as my Charles, I have always loved him more than the others, I don't know why because John is his twin, but I cannot explain it, when he told me how he felt about you, I could feel for him, because I was attracted to you from the first time we met, each time we met, my feelings changed, until I realised I loved you, but then it wasn't just love, I was in love with you as I know my Charles is.

Thank you my darling for making my life so different and making me so happy in every way, my love will never die Michael x

I am sitting sobbing I cannot move, what a wonderful letter for Michael to have thought he might die and leave this, how did he do it, he was thoughtful to the very end. Charles was now sitting beside me, he was in the same state as I was, we just put our arms round one another and sat crying. Eventually when we were able to put a couple of words together I said "I want you to read what your father has written to me."

"Yes you should read mine, I think they are probably similar, but I think we ought to have a drink first, sit quiet for a bit longer, do you want a Brandy darling?"

"Yes please, shall I get it?"

"No I'll get it," he brought me the biggest goblet I have ever seen, he had a large whisky tumbler, full of neat whisky.

"Are you trying to get me drunk Charles Roper?"

"No my darling, I know I can have my wicked way with you either way," he smiled, we sat for at least an hour we did not speak, we just sat as close as we could. Then we exchanged letters.

My dearest son Charles,
We have always been close right from you being young, I could never understand why, but since my Sophie came into my life and made me the happiest man in the human race, we have been even even closer, we were always honest with each other, in recent years we became even closer not like father and son, but very close friends, I have treasured what we had. I have been so lucky there are not many men who have a relationship like we have had and still did until now, I didn't want to go, I wanted longer with my Sophie, but someone above took pity on you son, they decided I had to move on, however, I have had more happiness with Sophie than I had, in all the rest of my previous life before her.
I know how it feels to be in love son, I told you Sophie was the first and only girl I have been in love with, I did not have to watch her daily with another man, like you have had to suffer with us, but you decided you

wanted to stay with us and love her from the side lines, well you do not have to do that any more, I have made the way clear for you son. Please do not wait, please show her now how you feel, do not bother what people think, it is your life please live it with my Sophie. I know you will treat her well, look after her and bring my sons up as your own, that is if she will have you? I have no doubts, I am certain she will love you, otherwise she would not allow you to kiss her, I know she felt guilty that is why I did try to openly let you do it, so she did not feel as guilty, it was only a kiss.

She is a truly remarkable girl, I know for sure she will love you in return, she has such a lot of love to give, she will never let you down, she will give you lots of children, she wants to give children the love and family. She was sixteen before she discovered that her father, mother and two brothers, were not her biological family, she had been left on the doorstep Mrs Cartwright broke her promise and told her, in a terrible way. Yet she has turned out this beautiful young lady, she is calm and has that effect on all she meets. My wish for you is a VERY, VERY LONG and happy life together and every night please give her one kiss from me. My wonderful son, I have loved you so very much, now please love my wife for me. Your father & friend x

"Charles," I sobbed "There could never be another man like Michael, I wish we had, had the chance to say goodbye, there is so much I wanted to tell him," the tears where just flowing they would not stop, Charles was exactly the same as me, then the door bell rang, I could not go. So Charles dried his face although the tears were still flowing. I could hear a voice, as Stuart came in.

"What ever has happened, what is it please tell me?" I just shook my head I could not speak. Charles was a bit better than me, he showed him his letter, which he read, it was unbelievable, he had tears streaming down his face. Charles poured him a large glass of whisky, he took it gladly.

"I have never ever experienced anything like this before, to think he wrote this, how did he manage to do it, he was a wonderful man, I gather this is true Charles?"

"Yes, we have read each others letters, we are already sleeping together, I made my feelings very clear, although Sophie being Sophie, felt guilty because Michael had recently died, but making love to her stopped her grieving for the time we are together, so I keep making love to her to save her distress."

Stuart laughed "Let me be the first to congratulate you, you are both very unique people, you are obviously meant for one another," he said cheers and had a long drink of his whisky, "I came for two reasons, I enquired at the hospital regarding Michaels medication, yes there is frequently side effects in both men and women, they loose their fertility for a few months, depending on how long they were taking the drugs, so I thought it would put your mind at rest Sophie, because I think you thought it was your fault, so who knows there could be the sound of tiny feet in the not too distant future. The other thing is in this Magazine there is a wonderful tribute to Michael?"

"Thank you Stuart that was a nice thought. How is Bel she hasn't been too well has she, is she alright now?" I asked.

"She will be in six and a half months time," he did not get any further, I got up and kissed him.

"She's pregnant, I am so glad Stuart, I know you have been trying a long time, I think she began to think babies were not going to happen, give her my love," I said.

"Thank you my darling, at least that has took you out of yourself for a while. How are you sleeping?" he asked.

"When I have someone at the side of me I am fine, but on my own the nightmares return, but I have Charles now at the side of me, so I really do not want to sleep too much anyway," I said, not really thinking. They both laughed.

"Well I am certainly pleased you are on the up, Bel said she will ring you and come for coffee and see the twins," he said.

"Anytime tell her."

"Well I better be off, it will take me longer to go back, I think I will be a going sideways, I should not have had all that whisky," he got up, kissed me and Charles showed him out.

"He's not a bit like a Doctor is he, I am pleased about their baby, I forgot to ask the date although he said six and a half months, so that will be around September," I said.

We decided to look at the magazine together, there was two full pages in 'Tribute' to Michael it was very interesting and enlightening, he did not ever say much about his work, there were some photographs at various Seminars or Presentations. There were some of the funeral, one showing the Policemen bearing Michael into the church, a very clear one of me and Charles with the twins, then one of all five of his sons, I do not remember that being taken, but then I cannot remember much at all.

We had been in contact with Junior and Jackie, Charles had been over to the house to let various people in. The day of their move was suddenly here. I did a big bake the day before. The following day we loaded up Charles car and we went over when we knew the removal men would be gone.

They were genuinely pleased to see us, Charles helped Junior, No, I have to remember, now Michael has gone, he wants us to use his name, moving furniture into place, I helped with emptying some boxes, we thought it a good idea to take the play pen, it worked the boys were quite happy playing. Jackie was getting a good big baby bump "Are you having one baby or are they twins?" I asked.

"God no," she said "I do not think I could cope with twins, one is enough thank you," she laughed "Although Elliot and Felix are adorable, just like the pictures, I have seen of Charles and John at that age, it could be the same babies."

"We won't hold you up any further. Have you finished work now, because at one stage you said you were asking for a transfer?" I asked.

"No Michael, put his foot down, he wants me at home, so I did not argue, because I really did not want to return to work while baby is very young, after seeing you with yours, I made my mind up I was going to be a stay at home mum, although he seems to think we are having a house full of babies, I think he will have to rethink, a couple will be enough for me," she said laughing.

Don't forget Saturday the 7th, it has flown if you want to pop in anytime, we would love to see you," so we loaded up the boys and drove home.

"Sophie I think we ought to do a 'Julia' for the 7th or even go to the Manor, it is a lot of work for you, I will help obviously but do you need the extra work?" he asked.

"Darling, I have been cooking since I was three, Great Aunt Celeste taught me, I do enjoy it, so until we have more babies, let me do this, I want them to see that I looked after your father, not just in bed, well and now taking care of you in every department," I smiled at him.

"Alright just this once, I have thought about things, whilst I do not want them to see our letters, I am going to tell them what father had said, I am telling them that I am enjoying fucking you at every moment I get," I stopped him there.

"Charles you cannot say that," he now stopped me there;

"My dearest darling Sophie, I was just winding you up, I thought slip that in and see if you noticed?" he smiled at me, it was that same melting smile Michael had. "No, I am going to tell them we are an item, if anyone has anything to say, we do it like we always have as a family, then there are no doubts whatsoever, while we are altogether alright my little sex pot?"

"Sex pot that is a new one?"

We were soon home the boys were looking tired, so we gave them their tea, Charles had a play with them, I had made a meat and potato pie for us so I put it in the oven, with a dish of leeks in cream sauce to keep warm. I washed them and put clean nappies on, Charles was amusing Elliot, whilst Felix had his drink, Charles was saying to Elliot;

"Now I do not want you to drink all mummies milk will you leave some for daddy?' Elliot was laughing and talking his baby talk, it was lovely to hear. While Daddy took sleeping Felix, Elliot stood in front of me, watching everything with interest, then with his little chubby fingers he took my nipple in his hand, and tried to reach up to put it in his mouth, just as Charles turned round.

"Yes son, it has come to something when it's self service, look watch daddy," I just sat wondering what he was going to do, he got down on his knees next to Elliot, and said "Look," he took my nipple in his mouth, so Elliot tried it, so I leaned slightly forward to make it lower, he got my nipple in his mouth "Good boy that's my Elliot," he was so pleased, he started doing his bopping up and down and laughing but lost my nipple, he looked at me as if to say where as it gone, his lip started to tremble.

"No my sweet come here," I got him on my knee, my nipple in his mouth post haste, and he smiled round my nipple.

We were getting very organised with the twins and fitting in making babies as often as we could. I could not believe some of the things he did, but I loved everything he did to me.

Soon it was Friday the 6th February the day before all the brothers got together again. We had been shopping on Thursday and then Friday I got all the vegetables prepared and the large joint of Sirloin Steak done. I had made an Apple and Gooseberry Pie and a Lemon Sponge pudding for dessert so they could be warmed up while we ate the main course. I wasn't sure what they all liked or disliked so for starters I did Melon cubes with blue berries or Prawns with celery in sauce. I laid the table when the boys were in bed.

Charles helped me do a quick clean round afterwards.

That morning, I left Charles with the twins showering.

Everything went according to plan, the meal was all ready, put into serving dishes and kept on a special heat in the big oven which was specially for that purpose.

I changed, Charles was waiting to check before I went down. When I emerged in a very tight, V neck top, showing rather a lot of cleavage and tight trousers. "Bloody hell, Sophie, you could give a monk an erection, you are beautiful, I think all my brothers, will be feeling randy looking at you. Yet you look like little Miss I am still a Virgin," we both laughed.

We fed the boys early before they all arrived, they would be sitting in their high chair and see what we were doing, knowing them they would want to be given more food. Charles is absolutely marvellous with them, anyone who did not know would think they were his own, he put their little wellingtons and coats and took them into the garden for an adventure.

When they returned they had big chubby red cheeks, they were given a drink, we were just going to sit down as James, Andrea, Simon and Emily arrived they were going to stay over night, seeing as they have the further to travel. We took them straight up to their rooms, of course the twins had to come with us.

"Come down when you are ready," I said, just as we got downstairs the door bell rang, it was John and Polly the twins ran straight to them because they knew them very well. They were closely followed by Junior, no Michael, Jackie, she was getting very big.

"Are you sure you have not got twins in there?" I asked.

"Christ do not ask her that, she will have a hissing fit," laughed Michael "Everyone's asking her the same thing, she is not however, she eats enough for an army, she is always hungry," we all laughed.

"Poor Jackie," I said "Come into the lounge Sherry or Martini's?"

The others had come downstairs and joined us. I tried to ask which starter they wanted, it was hard work because the twins were getting all the attention, I got there in the end. We all had another drink and went to the dining end, it is times like this that I would have like a separate dining room.

It was still my fathers very large oval table, when all the extensions were pulled out. I put Charles at one end, the boys next and I was next to them. I cleared the plates, Charles came into the kitchen with things we did not need. Then the main was taken in when everyone had filled their plates and Charles had taken the wine round, I decided this was perhaps the moment to explain.

"I invited you here for a reason, it is regarding your father, I do not want you to think that because I have been his more or less sole heir, it is to the detriment of yourselves," someone started to say something but I hurried on, "I do not want you to think that I have taken your inheritance, to this end each of his son's, will leave here today with my personnel cheque for one and a half million, this is not your fathers money, that will be a long time being sorted out, this is from my own money, I want to do this because I want to keep you all as close friends." Oh no, my bottom lip has started to tremble, I looked at Charles, he did his one raised eyebrow, with a big swallow I carried on "You are all very dear to me, I want us to all stay as one happy family that we became while your father was alive." I could not hold off any longer, the water works were in full flow, I wanted to leave, Charles put his hand on mine and held me down.

Michael began speaking, "I think I can speak for my brothers, we do not expect this Pa explained to me last year, that he wanted to leave you comfortable, we would eventually get their parents inheritance, or it could have been the other way round. I do not think we can accept this Sophie, we all love you to bits, you made our Pa so happy and brought us all back together again," the brothers all agreed with this.

"I am sorry but I really do want to do this, it will help you all, it is a gift from me, that is why it is out of my own money, Charles knew what I wanted to do and he," he stopped me there;

"I knew what Sophie wanted to do, this is the kind, generous person she is, I think it would be wrong if you refused it, I am sure if you did, you would get it one way or another, if I know my Sophie, she will find a way, so please accept it with the love it is being given," he said.

Then Simon said "What are you going to do now Charles? did Pa leave you this house, if so, will that mean Sophie has to move or what?" he asked, all heads turned.

This was the moment I had been dreading "No the house is Sophie's, unbeknown to her, father put the house in her name, even though she wanted to purchase it with her own money. So no, Sophie will not be going anywhere and neither will I."

I thought everyone would start talking at once at this point, but it was a stunned silence, even my twins were sat looking at everyone. "I want to explain, something we were unaware of before father died, he wrote two letters for when or if he did, Graham, father's solicitor brought them round to us, one for me and one for Sophie. Father has known for sometime, that I was in love with Sophie. So in his letter to me, he asked that I wasted no time in making my true feelings for her clear, as more than anything he wanted me to bring his twins up as my own, he knew I already loved them, I did take care of them a lot of the time, he also knew I would take care of her for him, he said a lot of other things, but that is the main thing I wanted you to know," I couldn't speak to save my life, Charles squeezed my hand.

"As you see my Sophie is in no fit state to speak at present, so I will tell you what I think she wanted to say. In her letter from father, he explained about my love for her, and that he approved, his dearest wish, was that as soon as possible she give me a chance to love her, to marry her and continue to look after her and his twins, then extend the family further, he knew that is what she wanted a large family," he looked down at me I was looking at him, he leaned down and gave me a quick kiss on my lips. "He also said, he knew I was not like some outsider who would only want her for her money. Who'd want her bloody money, with a body like that." they all cheered in agreement. "I think by now you have guessed, I did make my feelings quite clear to her and whilst she was very reluctant to move on, she felt guilty with father only recently dying, I pointed out what he had said in both letters, that he approved, it was his dying wish. Eventually, I was able to make her see that she was doing no wrong, in fact she has made me the happiest man in the world. I have now become her bit on the side until we get married," that made them all laugh, so the twins joined in. "We are not bothered what outsiders think, we have clear consciences, we want you to be happy for us, there is nothing in this whole world would keep me from her bed now, I am in there to stay, I am so in love with her. I think she might care a little for me in return, even if she only wants me to 'knock her up' I will add, that there is no one like her, I can see why our father loved her so much, he never looked at another woman once he was with her, she is one very remarkable, beautiful young lady, I say a silent prayer to my father every night, thanking him." by now Charles had tears running down his face, we clung on, to one another.

They all started talking at once, so the twins joined in, I

thought I had better start clearing everything away, Charles told the girls to sit down they were our guests, he came in loaded and started stacking the dishwasher, whilst I took the dishes and serving spoons and desserts in "Please help yourselves, then you know how much you want," and went to see if Charles needed a hand "Are you alright there darling?"

"Yes it is full, so I thought I may as well set it going, are you alright my darling? I am so proud of you."

"Thank you darling," he took me in his arms and we had a beautiful kiss, then it went deeper, his hand were on my bottom pulling me it to his erection, I even pushed myself towards him harder, he felt so hot through his shirt.

"Darling you are not only hot, but your body is like a fire, have you got a temperature?" I genuinely asked.

"No temperature, it is just you, you are so hot and sexy you make me boil," he said "I want you, can we slip off now for a quickie?"

"I think they will miss us, come on my hot, hot slave," I said, holding his hard big man "He is not such a little man now, is he, he is a gigantic, huge, beautiful cock," then I lowered my voice "And what I want is that cock in my cunt."

"I love it when you talk dirty to me, tell me again," he was kissing me and I was loving it.

"We wondered where you two were?" we both jumped, we did not hear anyone come in, it was John, he started walking back laughing, as he entered the dining end he said "We should have known, they were nearly at it in the middle of the kitchen, I don't know these young ones today, no respect!" it got a very rousing response from the brothers.

We walked in, whilst they were all saying different things, the twins thought it lovely they were shouting and banging their spoons on their trays.

"Well I have got to admit Sophie, has a lot more colour than earlier, I do not think we should stay late, they will be wanting an early night, I should think any time now," it was Michael, so another round of innuendos and cheering.

Charles said "Boys, can we set a better example to our babies, they will think you are hooligans, I know you are but," he was drowned down again, so he sat down and looked at me, no one was really taking noticed, so he kissed me full on the lips, that made me worse.

"So," John shouted "When do you think you will be getting married then?"

"We have not really had time to think, everything is moving so fast, do I take it you are all coming then?" it was yes's and nods all round "Well I want it as soon as possible, but we are not having a big one, we do not think we will tell the grandparents, they are not very good any of them at present, so besides us, we have two friends we would like to ask and that will be it, I am not bothering with my friends from school, I know they will understand. "It will be at the registry office and a meal at probably the Manor again. No presents, whatsoever, I doubt we will go away because of our twins, we will get married and lock the doors for a fortnight in bed, just get up occasionally to feed the kids and go back to trying to make some more," that started them off again.

"I will bring coffee down the other end or does anyone want tea?" all wanted coffee. They all said they would help clear away, they took the table down, and everything was ship shape. The boys were nearly asleep on their feet, but they were not giving in while there was so much attention on them, soon everything was done in the kitchen, Charles carried the big tray with everything on, the girls started getting the tray unloaded.

"We are just taking the twins for their nap, we will not be gone too long," so I picked Elliot up, was about to pick Felix up as Charles came in;

"No you stop doing that they are getting to heavy, we will only be a minute," we changed their nappies, put them in their cot and that was it, they closed their eyes and were gone.

"You didn't say you had increased the money for my brothers, I don't mind, you just didn't say? That was a wonderful meal here's a little thank you," he kissed me and kissed me, we could not stop, I was pushing myself onto him. Darling I would dearly like to stay here for hours but we cannot we have guests," he said.

"Sorry about the money, I really did forget. You go down first then, I will clear the nappies up and nip to the loo," I said he gave me a swift kiss, then ran down the stairs, I decided to go back and look at the twins Elliot was a little restless so I lifted him out and lay on the single bed with him and I must have fell asleep.

The next thing Jackie's saying "Sophie would you like a cup of tea?"

"I must have fell asleep why didn't Charles fetch me," I said, still holding Elliot.

"He came up over an hour ago and said you were asleep, so we left you, until we made a cup of tea. "Can I hold him," so I passed him over he was half and half and drank my tea.

"That was so welcome thank you, how are you doing?"

"I am fine, I am getting a bit apprehensive about the actual birth, people have been saying such terrible things about the pain, I am beginning to wish I wasn't pregnant," she was almost in tears.

"Darling do not take any notice, you will always get people giving you the worst case scenario, I am not saying it is painless, but once you see your baby it will all be forgotten."

"I am so pleased you are with Charles, you make a lovely, really lovely couple, do you really want more children?" she asked.

"Yes I do, I want a house full, I want to give them the love of a real family. I love everything sexual, there is nothing like it in the world do you agree?" I asked he, Felix was awake, just looking as if to say I am here.

"Well once I am in the mood, but he really has to work at it to get me going, once it happens, yes it is good, but I do not always have an orgasm, do you?" she looked dubious asking.

"Look you can talk about anything to me, I won't say anything to anyone, but yes always, it is very rare I do not get there. There was a guy, Michael discovered, he only wanted to relieve me of my millions, he thought he was gods gift, I had the pleasure of telling him a teenager had more idea of making love and foreplay than he did."

"So you were not married to him?"

"No, he was my then husband's friend and Lawyer, when he was killed in a car accident, he thought he would relief me of my money," I replied.

"So how'd you meet that hunk that was my father-in-law?"

"Did you think that as well? he was really lovely. I did not see the age difference, because he did not look anywhere near his age," I went on to tell her everything from how I knew Michael and Rupert because of my ex in prison etc., etc.

"The others don't know do they? because my Michael has never said anything about his father, the first they knew about you, was apparently you were already living with him at their home with his mother, and you were introduced as Michaels partner, I think my Michael felt a bit ashamed, he did not know you, and accused you of wanting his father for his money, didn't he?" she looked at me.

"Yes I soon proved him wrong. There was something about Charles that separated him from his brothers, he was very nice to me from the beginning, when I told Michael senior that I liked him, he then told me how close they had always been. He ended up staying with us, we had some really good times, the banter between them was marvellous. They looked like one person only one older and one a younger version of the other. That was something Michael put in his letter to me, that I would have no problem with loving Charles because they were to all intents and purposes, they were one person," suddenly the tears sprang from nowhere.

She got me to sit on the bed at the side of her, she put her arm round me, the twins were very good they sat on our knees just watching us, "I cannot imagine what you are going through, you do put on a brave face, but it suddenly cracks, that's when we see you are heart broken, but I think with Charles at your side you will be fine, we gather you have been to bed together, is it hard knowing how much you loved Michael, and suddenly he is gone, now you are in bed with Charles?" she looked at me "I am sorry I should not have asked that."

"Don't be sorry, if you want to know something, you do not find out if you do not ask. I took some convincing but Charles kept repeating what Michael had put in both his letters, that he wanted us to be together as soon as possible, that I should not be feeling guilty, when I did first sleep with him I must admit, it helped me because I didn't break down while we were making love, Charles said that helped. We make love every night, not just once and go to sleep, once we start we cannot stop."

"Oh," she said.

"Sorry have I shocked you?" I asked.

"Not exactly shocked I just thought things like that happened in books or films, not really true to life?"

"No darling, it does happen in real life."

"Do you mean you have sex, more than once every night?"

"Yes, and in the morning, and in the afternoon when the twins are asleep, I honestly can never get enough until we are exhausted."

"So is this with just Charles?" she asked.

"No, his father was the same, as was my husband Charles," I decided not to speak of the rat.

"Sophie, I have never had a conversation like this, even when I was young and had a best friend, thank you Sophie," she said, as Charles came round the door.

"Come on girls, we thought you had got lost, where's my little chubby boys then, he took them from us and tucked them under his arms and they squealed with delight. We stood up she put her arms round me.

"Thank you Sophie for being honest with me, I will treasure it, I hope we can be good friends," she said.

"I hope so to," we walked downstairs arm in arm.

I made them all tea, Jackie and Polly came in to help, I got all the cakes and scones and biscuits I had made, we set it on the table and told them to help themselves. As we were finishing eating, John said "Sophie which caterers did you use for the food and cooked meats, I have never tasted anything so good?" they were all nodding and agreeing.

Charles said "The caterer's none, my Sophie would not let me get anyone to do what she said she could do equally as well. She loves cooking, her Aunt taught her from when she was three years old," They all sat amazed and were congratulating me on how good I was.

Then they all thanked us and said they had, had a good day. It was kisses and cuddles all round, when we went back in James and Simon said they had decided, as it was not late they were not going to put us out and stay, they had decided they would drive home. The girls were upstairs getting their things together, we tried to persuade them, but they said no it was not fair on me and we had our hands full with the twins, so we waved them off.

Chapter sixteen

We sank on the sofa together with the twins climbing all over us. Charles said "Let us see if there is anything on the television to keep the little imps quiet for a while," low and behold there was a 'Tom and Jerry' on they sat mesmerised. "You were upstairs a long time after Jackie took your tea up," he said;

"Yes she was asking about giving birth and the horror stories she had heard, so I tried to put her mind at rest," then I told him everything we had discussed, I left nothing out, including her saying she hoped we could be friends.

Charles said "Monday morning we are going to the registry office, I need to find out when I can make you mine, so put that in your diary Mrs Roper, I do not want you to forget."

"As if I would forget that we are going to be married."

We put the twins to bed and decided because I had a throbbing head we would have an early night, even though I had nodded off I was shattered, by the time we had tidied up and put the dishwasher on again, sorted a load of washing out ready for the wash, it was 9pm when we got into bed.

"Now Mrs Roper, we want none of your wandering hands all over me, I do want you to go to sleep, I really do, you are looking very pale and you have dark circles coming under your eyes, come on slide down, I will just have my nightcap, turn your lamp off, I have in built radar where your breasts are concerned."

"Darling I know you have your mouth full, but when you have finished, would you tell me, why when you are suckling does it make things happen down below and I want you, but not when my babies do?" I asked and I waited, he was doing things to me "You are going to have to do something if you do not hurry, I am really wanting you."

"Tell you what, be a good girl, go to sleep then I will give you a good fucking tomorrow morning, because we should be awake before the boys, is it a deal?" he asked.

"I suppose so," I said sulkily.

"Let me kiss those lovely pouting lips," it was lovely kiss.

"Turn over like a good girl. Cuddle up close, I'll keep you safe."

I had a wonderful nights sleep I felt really refreshed, I had already been in the shower before the boys woke up, Charles was just lay in bed doing nothing, so I dropped the boys on the bed and that was the end of his peace.

"I will get their nappies off and you can take them in the shower, I gave him a big kiss. I will go and put the breakfast on, would you like me to bring you a drink up? my little sex machine."

"No, my darling I will come down for it."

Monday at 11am we arrived at the registry office. We were given Friday 2nd April at 3.30pm., we were very happy.

As soon as we got home we rang the Roper boys, they all said they would be there and were happy for us. Jackie said she was not very happy because she would still be pregnant and probably as big as an elephant by then. We said we were sorry but that was the earliest date we could get and we certainly were not going to wait until she had, her baby, she then laughed and said it would possibly cost us more because Michael had said she was eating for four.

We rang the Manor Hotel and booked the meal for twelve adults and two children, we would call in to select the menu. I had rung Stuart and he said they would love to be there, then asked him if he would give me away, he said he would be honoured.

The weeks were flying by, we are now in March I must decide what I am wearing for my wedding, the fourth one, please god make it my last I cannot keep doing this!

We managed to get the accounts done Charles had taken on, we made a great team, he went to drop two off at the business's and run through one or two things with the clients.

He had only been gone a few minutes when the telephone rang, I answered but no one spoke. I walked into the kitchen when it rang again, I answered, no one spoke and it happened twice more, it was a bit spooky.

I had just put the boys in bed for their afternoon nap when the door bell rang, I opened the door, there was nobody there? but as I closed the door an envelope dropped out of the letter box, the envelope was blank. I walked through to the kitchen, sat at the table and opened the envelope, I took out a single piece of paper, all it said was:-

I've been watching you, I will take one or both your boys if you do not follow my instructions, do not tell the police, you have not got your Mr Plod to help you now!!

I just kept reading it over and over, my hands were shaking, Mr Plod that is what Rupert called Michael, but Rupert is dead, I then ran and bolted the front door and put the chain on, I went out of the back and locked the gate and bolted the back door. I could not stop the tears, I rang Charles, but it went straight to answer phone, so he must not have a signal. He was late he said he did not think it would take long, but it was now 4.45pm. I decided to close all the curtains, fetched the boys into the bedroom with some toys. When there is banging on the front door, the bell is being pressed as though someone has their finger on it, the boys stopped and looked at me, then I hear;

"Sophie where are you, I cannot get in darling is everything alright?" I flew downstairs, with shaking hands removed the chain, then unlock the bolt, he nearly falls in as I open the door "Christ Sophie what's going on?" I slam the door to put the chain on, pull the bolt over again. My hands are shaking, if fact my whole body is shaking, my face is wet with tears.

"Sophie my love was is it, what's happened, I turned and he saw my face?" he looked up and there were two little figures just stood at the gate, their little arms came out "Sophie please."

"You fetch the boys down, I have something to show you," he was no sooner up than he was down again, with a giggly boy under each arm. He closed the door, I told him what had happened, and this, I pushed the note into his hand, he read it, "What's or who's Mr Plod?" he asked.

"That was what Rupert used to call your father, but Rupert is dead, Charles who is it, they must have been watching the house, saw you go out, because it all happen a few minutes after you left, I tried calling you but it went straight to your answer phone."

"Sit down darling let me make you a cup of tea, I'll give the boys something," he busied himself and brought me my tea, but my hands were still shaking, I had a tidal wave on the go, he put the boys in their chairs and gave them some sandwiches.

He went to the telephoned "Hi Michael we need some help," he proceeded to tell him what had happened "Are you sure, alright then see you about 7.30 tonight. They are coming over tonight as you heard, do you know anyone who would want to harm you or worry you, think darling," he said "I suppose it is useless asking you if you want any dinner?" I shook my head, "I will have some of this soup you made, is that okay?"

"Of course it is, Charles I cannot think of anyone who would," I stopped "No, no it couldn't be?"

"What is it, have you thought of someone?" he came and stood close to me and gave me a kiss "Come on."

"Well, but I don't know how he could have found me, he is in jail, I thought my tracks were well covered by now," I said.

"Darling who?"

"Well the only person I know is my ex, but he's in prison, how would he find me!" I am half thinking and half talking.

"You mean, Matthew your ex?"

"Yes, but he is in prison," I replied.

"Darling how long did he get, because with good behaviour?" he looked at me.

"I cannot remember I think your father told me, I think it was five years in 1995," I replied.

"Yes but that was 95, it is now 2000, so at least if he was sentenced in 95 it is five years ago, they kept him in prison whilst awaiting trial, didn't they? so that would reduce the sentence he had to serve, with good behaviour he could easily be out now!"

He ate his soup.

"I think when they have eaten, I will go and put their pyjamas on, then they will be ready for bed but can stay up until Michael and Jackie come," I said.

"Excuse me since when was I, it is always we, we do everything together, the way I like it and the boys do."

"I just thought you have been out on business I'd help."

"Darling you do help, I would never have got all the accounts done if you hadn't helped me, you did 75% of the work, made it easier for me, you know I appreciate it," he said. He stood up and took me in his arms, his lips slowly taking mine. I just melt.

I feel a lot better now, thank you my love."

"I promise tonight, we will have a marathon session," he cleared the table and lifted the twins out of their high chairs.

We got them ready for bed, I tidied myself up "I think I had better put some make up on I look like an old hag," I said as he came up behind me and snuggled my neck.

"That is one thing you will never be and old hag, but will you change for me please, I want you to put something on with a lot of breast on show, even better if it is short, you will drive me mad, I love the things you do to me, the waiting is something else. I like you to show plenty to any of my brothers because I have got the best prize, their girls pale into insignificance at the side of you. Also Michael really fancies you," I turned to him and gave him a deep kiss, I led with my tongue, I was really pressing into him, my hand was on his erection making it bigger.

"Right, Mr Roper your wish will be carried out to the letter, you are sure you do not want me to come down in my tiny bikini, the one with the thong?"

"I have never seen it, you can put it on one day for a surprise, what other sexy things have you hiding in your wardrobe, Mrs Roper?"

"That would be telling my love, look these children are running riot, but at least you took my mind off the problem I now have."

I did my make-up, brushed my hair, looked what would attract my brother-in-law to be, I selected a little black dress it was very short, no quite a mini, but the whole dress was very tight, it had a deep V, there was a lot of breast on show, I put on my bright red heeled sandals. The long drop diamond earrings, with a matching pendant, the bottom just disappeared into my cleavage. My other Charles bought me. Charles in the kitchen with the twins, I walked round the door "Will this do," his look said it all.

"Christ you could melt an ice berg looking like that, I want to take you here and now and I think I will," as he said it the door bell rang "Shit, bugger and anything else," he said, I laughed.

Michael and Jackie were dead on time, we went straight into the drawing room and put the television on for the boys, it did not matter what was on they sat entranced, but we kept the volume down. Charles said "I will make the drinks, unless you want something stronger?" Michael asked for neat whisky, which was what Charles was having, I said Brandy and lemonade, Jackie wanted tea. So he went and put the kettle on, whilst I started telling them exactly what had happened, then showed them the note. I think Michael was taking it in, but he was looking first at my breasts, then his eyes wandered down my body to the short skirt showing a lot of leg.

Charles came back with the tray with Jackie's pot of tea, milk and a plate with some of my home made shortbread's.

Michael said exactly the same as Charles, he also agreed with Charles that he could be out long before now, he would make enquiries but needed some details, I dithered so Charles knowing what I was thinking jumped in, and held my hand saying "He was

301

her husband Matthew Cartwright, she divorced him when he went to jail for rape and GBH, I think it was eight women, it was 1995 when he was convicted," he said.

"Okay I will see what I can find out, who is he referring to as Mr Plod?"

"That was your father," I replied.

"How did he know my father? Why would he? Well it looks like he wants to black mail you, why? has he got a grudge against you?" I went on to tell him everything about Mat and me."I will make some enquiries, see if I can find out if he is out on Probation, if so we can find where he lives," he said.

"He had a Penthouse apartment in 'The Park' but I am not sure whether he sold it or not, I can write the address down if it is any help," I said.

"Yes anything will help," he said. So I popped into the kitchen and got it. When I walked back in Michael could not take his eyes off me, Charles was watching him, with amusement.

"So how did he know my father, were you having an affair with Pa whilst you were still married to him?" he asked, looking at me a bit suspicious.

I then went on to tell him about how I met his father and Rupert, and the witness protection. Then how he was with me when Charles died, I told him the lot.

"So when did you actually start sleeping Pa?" he asked.

Charles jumped in, "That is neither here nor there, it has nothing to do with her ex. The only thing we assume that before Rupert died, in a mugging attack. We think he may have indicated to Matthews Solicitor that father had helped her and his brother, because Rupert always called him Mr Plod, that is we think the connection. Sophie changed her name several times, so Matthew could not have possibly known his ex had married our father."

"So why now? and how has he found her?" he asked.

"Hang on, I brought a magazine to show you, the one I showed you Michael of the 'Tribute' to your father, I thought you might like to read it, but look," Jackie said as she was turning pages over, "Here look there are several photographs, three of them show Sophie quite clearly, could he have recognised you from that, have you changed much?"

Charles said "Stuart our friend and private Doctor, brought one round for us, but it was a different magazine because ours has two of Sophie."

"So have you changed much, when did he last see you, 1995?" Michael asked.

"No, 1994 around October, I am not sure," I replied "So that is about four and a half years, but I do not think I have changed, I look the same, apart from I had a hat on for the funeral," I was getting a bit nervous, Charles could see the change in me, came closer and put his arm round me.

"Have you got enough now Michael, anyone would think you were a copper!" Charles said and they all laughed but me.

"Just one thing, I just thought of, is there any chance he would have a photograph of you?" he asked.

I could feel the colour drain from my face "Oh I never thought of that, yes he would, because when I packed everything. I took several locked boxes with his bank and personal stuff in, to his Solicitor and there was a scrap book. I did not know what else to do with it." I held on as long I could, but in the end the tears were falling fast.

"Come on my love, I will not let anything happen to you or our twins," who were still mesmerised by the television "Wherever we go and whatever we do we will all do it together, come on love," he said kissing me on the cheek.

"I am sorry Sophie, I do not want to upset you, it is the last thing I want to do, you were so good with Pa, we all owe you. Leave it with me darling, I will see what I can find out. Of course he could have hired a private detective and given him your photograph long before Pa's funeral. Although look in the note he says 'You have not got Mr Plod now,' so it could be from the magazine." Michael said.

We switched the television off and the boys looked around as if to say where has it gone "It has gone to bed now," Charles said to them, so they decided to investigate Michael and Jackie, they saw her tummy and stroked it, that made us all laugh. Eventually after the brothers had, had another whisky, they decided it was time to go home, I said I must put the twins to bed.

So it was kisses all round, Michael actually held me and pulled me in to him, I could see Charles over his shoulder, he winked at me, Michael kissed me on the lips and whispered "I am so sorry to upset you love, I would not hurt you for the world, I love you," and they were gone.

As Charles locked up, he said "You have a new fan, my big brother is fancying you, mind even the toughest man would be hard pressed not to think of you sexually, looking like you do, any other woman would look cheap and easy, but you my darling are all class, Miss Purity, I am still a Virgin. He took in every inch of you in with his eyes, but kept going back to your breasts, I could read his mind, he was undressing you, he actually had an erection, because I have never seen his trousers bulge like that before and when he stood up he repositioned himself."

"He told me he loved me? We have to get the boys to bed come on," so he picked them up under his arms, then they start giggling, it was a wonderful sound "I had better change their nappies," so I got everything out, but because my skirt was tight I had to haul it up, so I could get Elliot across me knees "What?" I said because Charles was just looking.

"My darling, I am not complaining, but you may as well have taken it off because I am going to have to unzip you so you can, flash your gorgeous tits at me and give the boys a drink," he was almost drooling "Anytime soon that naked body, will be rubbing up against me," I changed Elliot's nappy.

"Shall I do Felix?" I asked.

"No love, I will do him but turn round let me unzip you," so I did, he pulled it down with the hem and held it while I stepped out which just left the thong "Just look what you have done to me," he pointed to his erection.

"Let me see to the boys and then I will give you a good seeing to," he burst out laughing, they are usually his words

"Elliot is really sucking tonight, I think he is thirsty, I never gave it a thought, put Felix on my arm and let him have his as well," we managed it but Charles supported Felix just in case.

"Darling why do you want me to flaunt my body in front of your brothers, I do not mind I quite enjoyed it watching Michael."

"I have told you, especially Michael, because he always thought he was better than the rest of us, he would brag how many girls he'd bedded and what lookers they were, I have to admit Jackie was, as were my other brothers girls, that was before you came on the scene, because you are beautiful, have a gorgeous figure, you have this lovely soft, relaxing voice everybody always seems so relaxed with you and your calming ways. They all knew from father you were good in bed, never refused him anything."

"Hang on," I said "Do you mean your father used to tell you what we did in bed," he cut me off;

"No not like that, but he was very verbose about you, how he could not fault you in anyway. He stressed that now he had found you, he would not need to look elsewhere, because you fulfilled him in every way, we knew he had a big sexual appetite, that was why he had an apartment, and lived away from mother. We did not know until years later, she had actually bought him the apartment, so he could do what he wanted to do, we now know why, she was a Dyke. That is why she accepted you into our house, I think, no I know she was hoping you would turn to her, because she never ever took time away from work, to look after us when we were ill, it was always Pa who did. Also I heard her say more than once she could make you happy, and how much she loved you," he leaned over and kissed me.

"Take Elliot darling he has nodded off," I lifted Felix off while I turned him round, he did let out a shout he was soon back to it.

Charles came and sat back on the bed with me "I was thinking I might just drop a hint or two about how Pa was right, you did not refuse ever, you are the best thing that ever happened to me, it is true though, would you mind?" I shook my head "At first I wondered how I would feel, knowing what we do together you did with my father, then I realised if you had not been with him, I would not have known you, so I say a little prayer most nights thanking him for bringing you to me," and one tear fell.

"Darling don't start me, I love you so much. I thought your father was the best, he was, but I did not know you sexually, as a lover you have surpassed all my expectations, the best man, the best lover and the one with the biggest cock and I love everything about you, like Jackie has said we make a perfect couple. I just cannot stop wanting you. I love some of the things we have done together, you really excite me," he started those melting all consuming kisses, I think poor little Felix had been asleep ages before we realised "Charles please get me pregnant, I want your babies."

"My love, I am doing my best, we cannot spend much more time in bed, it is hardly worth getting dressed as it is, try to relax stop thinking of babies, you see I will have you knocked up in no time."

It's March and I still had not decided what to wear, when I marry again! Charles said "Get a long dress, then it would come in useful, for our formal dinners."

My brothers think I should not be here over night, so Polly is coming to stay here and I am going to John's, John is to be my best man, although I don't think it matters because there will only be a few of us, but you do have to have someone to give you away?"

"I have already asked Stuart and he said he would be honoured," I said. "I also asked Bel to come with me for my dress."

We went off to town, I was lucky the second dress I found was beautiful, it was cream very fine lace, full length, tight fit to below my hips, then straight to the floor. The lace fitted up to my neck and down my arms to make three quarter sleeves, but unlined from part way up my breasts and down my arms. I bought a cream silk tie and handkerchief for Charles who had a brand new light navy suit he had never worn. Cream Carnations for the men, pale pink freesia for the girls.

We hired the Rolls for me and Stuart, Bel drove herself, Polly and the twins to the registry office, as usual it was a quick service and then to the Manor for snacks and Champagne, the meal was to be at 6pm.

We all enjoyed ourselves, the boys had a nap soon after we arrived, as usual it was a full time job with them feeding themselves but Charles and I shovelling a spoon in, in between.

We all had a lot to drink, we left at 8.30pm the boys were all in, we came home by taxi, they were asleep when we got home. We locked the door and went straight upstairs to get the boys in bed. I took my dress off first which left me with just some little lace panties and strapless bra, which matched my dress. Charles had gone to the loo, so I got the twins ready for bed, they didn't wake at all.

We had a wonderful first night as Mr & Mrs Charles Roper, with Champagne breaks and we all slept late.

Michael informed us that they now knew where Mat lived because he is out on probation. He had sold the penthouse whilst in prison.

We kept everywhere safely locked and bolted, the twins were never out of our sight.

We had a very comfortable relaxed life, it couldn't get better than this. We had no more notes through the door, the summer was lovely and warm, we spent a lot of time in the garden.

Jackie gave birth dead on time she had a girl 9lb 10ozs

she said never again! We went over to see her regularly with the boys, they could not get over a little baby they stood looking trying to understand what it was, it was quite funny really.

The garden was becoming established, everything was healthy and growing, it was now impossible to see each section until you got there. The last one at the very bottom of our land with the big stone building which we now used to store garden furniture, and toys.

It was a Tuesday in late July a lovely summers day. Me and the boys were down at the very bottom of the garden. I had just come out of the shed, when something fell hard on my head, it was a heavy bang which stunned me, at the same time a hand went over my mouth, then someone put tape over my mouth, I tried to scream but nothing would come through, a bag was put over my head and tied round my neck, they were working fast. They tied my hands together in front of me, then my legs were tied at my ankles, then I was roughly lifted. I could hear a lot of rustling leaves, they must be taking me through the shrubbery into the field, they were running fast, I could only hear the thud of feet on the dry earth. And I heard my babies crying in the distance and Charles calling my name, I was roughly thrown into a car, I assumed it was a car because the sound of the boot lid being slammed down, it started, it was going fast, I was rolling back and forth, side to side, I was hurting everywhere.

The journey seemed endless? Eventually the car stopped, two people got out and slammed the doors, then feet walking away, I was still there bound and gagged, then nothing, everywhere hurt. I don't know how long I was there it seemed for ever, I had stopped myself from crying because if tears started then my nose would run, then what, so I steeled myself and waited. There was a road nearby because every now and again a car or lorry would go by, I started counting the cars to pass the time. Then it dawned on me, that at least they had me not my babies, please Charles find me, I was praying as I had never prayed before.

After what seemed an age I heard feet, but again no one spoke the boot opened, it must have been raining, because I only had a sleeveless top on and I could feel it on my arms, I was roughly man handled out and they ran with me until I heard a door slam, then everything stopped. I heard some other feet, I was stood down but leaned up against the wall, a door opened and closed, then someone lifted me over their shoulder. I was being carried up some stairs, another door opened and a door closed, then another, my hands were untied, so someone must have been in front of me, so I started lashing out in all directions, I came in contact with someone once or twice, until I was whacked across my face "You fucking bitch, yer gun ta regret that," he slapped me across my face again, my head rattled, I knew when he spoke it's not Matthew? I was sure he was behind this!

He put a set of handcuffs on each wrist, attached each one to something, I found my left one was attached to the arm of a small chair, I could just get my hand up to my face, I was roughly pushed into it so I was sitting, the other was on a longish chain I could hear it, then it was attached to something else I did not know what.

Then I heard cutting and the bag on my head was moving, as it was being opened, I saw a ceiling light, which was on, something else was put over head which covered my eyes and nose, it left my nostrils and mouth clear, a straw was being push in between my lips "Ya bera drink it, it's watta, it's all ya gerrin," that is a Nottingham accent? Then I could feel he was putting cuffs on my ankles, he removed the rope, he moved my legs showing me that I could move with very small steps. "Yer close ta sink n'bog, ya'll ev plenty a time ta find ya way,"

I thought he was going to go but I could hear him breathing, the next thing is I feel his hands on my breasts "Yea is right ya ev gorra good pair a jugs, pity," he said "I bera not fuck ya," he left I heard him run down the stairs and the door slam, then nothing.

A long time after the door opened, I do not remember hearing a door or footsteps, someone came in they did not speak, pushed a straw to my lips, it was tea it was sweet and tasted foul but I drank gratefully I said "Thank you," hoping they would take pity on me, instead he slapped me several times across my face and left, I heard him go down the stairs, but no door slam?

I stood up and swung the chain so I could grab it in that hand and work my way along, it was attached to a pipe under the tap, so that is the sink, a wall was to my right, I had to drag the chair with me, so I eased round to the front of the sink to the left and my hand was on the top of the toilet cistern and the handle flush and I found the lid, it might not be clean, I tapped round the wall at the other side of the toilet and it was a corner and yes on that wall was a toilet roll, I ripped some off and lifted the lid pulled my panties down, put two strips of the roll on the seat then gently lowered myself with one hand the other was stretched out attached to the chair, I had a lovely long pee, flushed and put the lid down, back to the sink, there was a bar of soap on the sink so I washed my hands, wiped them round my mouth while they were still soapy, because my lips felt sticky from the tape. I rubbed my hands on my skirt and sat down again and waited. I started to feel funny, not very well, I feel weird and woozy, my head was swimming, it is spinning round, I feel sick, I must have been given something to knock me out.

I was still here in the same position when I awoke, I listened and I could hear distant music, but I think it was drifting in from somewhere outside. I must have passed out again and when I came round again, I sat pondering, my headaches and I am still nauseous, then I must have gone again, I lost count how many times I passed out and woke up? I have no idea how long I had been here, but my head was throbbing!

I decided to find out if there was a window, or if I could get to the door but it was wall all round the sink and toilet area, I couldn't get anywhere near the door or the other wall. I began to wonder what my fate was going to be, lets face it I had just got married again, so now I suppose it is my time to die, I knew I was going to cry, but I could not because this thing that was over my head, was rubber or something because it was tight over my head and face my eyes were closed tight.

I went to the loo again, so I have been here a while, to need to go again! I pulled myself together, if someone has decided I was going to die at least I had to try and do something not just sit here and wait my fate. I moved as near to the sink as possible, making the chain loose and dragged the chair as close as I could, it tilted over but I wanted my left hand as close to my right, I bent over to my left, put my thumbs under this mask thing, it was so tight nothing happened, maybe if I did it the other way from the back, it had to be a bit easier because of all my hair, I twisted my head to the left, because that hand could not move as much, I realised there was a chunk of my hair missing, I felt again, yes there was a piece missing on the left side am I the ransom, is the hair proof they have got me, come on Miss Marple's get on. So I got my left thumb hooked under neath it, then my right as far round as I could reach, nothing it did not move at all, I pushed and pushed for a long while, but nothing.

I sat, I felt really tired and weak, I must have gone to sleep or passed out. But I was still sat there, I think I passed out again. I suddenly thought wet hair, if I wet my hair it will flatten it, so I struggled to the sink, found the plug and it started filling the sink, I let it fill to the top, it was a bit over and was dripping on the floor. I struggled, turned round not quite all the way, this bloody chair I thought, and kicked it, that was a mistake, it really hurt my ankle, I think it is bleeding? It also hurt my wrist, I think it could be more blood. I waited a while for the pains to ease then started with my right hand slopping the water onto the back of my head, it was slowly getting wet, it was very slow   but at least I was doing something, I had to keep resting. Turn round, drop your head in and ladle the water with my right hand, yes, it was happening my hair was getting wet, but at the same time the rubber was gradually filling up, it was heavy there was a lot of water, if I could keep my head upside down and push my right thumb under? I lifted my head above the sink, it moved with the weight and my thumb, it was only a fraction but it did move and a bit more, it gave me the momentum to carry on. I decided to lift my head free from the sink and let the weight of the water help, it did it was moving, I got my left thumb under near my cheek my eye lid has opened a fraction, I pushed and pulled, it was slow going it took a long time, but it was gathering momentum, until it dropped onto the floor, water must be flying in all directions, it was dark very dark, it is obvious there is no window, because if there was some sort of light. So now what?

It had took a long time, I was exhausted. I righted the chair and sat down to think, Sophie think, I must have nodded off, I don't know for how long but it refreshed me, I went to the sink and ran the tap and drank until my thirst was quenched. The chair, I could get further but the chair hinders me. I lifted it and with all my might I swung it into the wall nothing, only it was hurting my wrist I could feel more blood, so I decided to pack it with toilet roll to save it chaffing, that took a long, long time but I managed it with a few sheets at a time, wrapping it round and round, so the handcuff was not actually next to my skin, I picked the chair up again, did it time and time until I was out of breath, I righted it to sit on it, but it creaked something had cracked somewhere, I sat until I had got my breath back, then smashed it again and again, suddenly there was wood flying in all directions one hit me in the face, one on my right arm, that is more blood trickling down my arm, but now the chair was broken, there is a big piece of frame attached to the hand cuff.

I felt round the wall, it was a very small room, more like a little cloak room, there was no bath or shower, but I just could not reach the door, I knew where it was, because I could feel the door frame with my left hand, my right is stretched as far as it would go because I was still chained to the water pipe. I sat on the floor my legs were weak, I have no idea how long I have been here?

I have gone through feeling peckish, to being hungry, to being dying of hunger, to not feeling anything at all now only pain. I got back to the sink, drinking from the tap as I had been doing all the time.

How can I get this handcuff off the pipe? find a piece of wood from the chair and try to see if I can force the cuff open, I try, nothing, I keep trying it is hopeless, hang on how thick am I, pipes have joints, if there is enough movement won't that joint give, so I start pulling on the chain with both hands nothing, if I move further up the chain nearer the pipe, there is a lot of banging and clanging, obviously no one is here otherwise they would come and stop me. I am so hot I throw some more water over me to cool me, I wonder if it is day time? Is it a lovely summer day, we could have the paddling pool out for my babies, I start crying I have tried not to think of anything outside this room, but now I have thought about them it is all to much, the waterworks are in full flow I sit for a long, long time, I cannot hear anything.

After a long time, suddenly, I hear a noise a door downstairs, it is not the original door, someone is coming. I think of my life and all that's happened, now I have happiness, but now what? tears are in full flood.

I feel round on the floor and find a big piece of wood from the chair, with the one still attached to the hand cuff, I have wood in each hand, I hold my breath, I hold both hands above my head and wait, however, whoever it is in no hurry, perhaps they do not know I am here, shall I shout, stupid why haven't you shouted before someone might have heard me? If anyone had been around they would have heard the racket and come to stop me. Only now, I don't think I could utter a word even if it did bring me help.

He's coming upstairs, he is close by, a door opens near, then a knock on the door, another knock, I hear the handle move, "Nat" The bastard, the bloody rotten fucking bastard, the animal come on in now I am fucking mad, I am ready for you, it IS Mat, he doesn't know my name? How did he find me? The door handle moved again, the door opens a fraction, the light streams in, it hurts my eyes, now is not the time to be a baby! The door opens fully, Mat walks round the door, I slam the lumps of chair onto his head, both hands are raining blows on him as hard as I can, he is trying to grab hold of me, he is cursing and swearing at me, he gets hold of my top at the front I move back, it tears, he moves round, grabs my skirt that just tears and drops off, he eventually gets me in his grip.

"You bloody little slut I told you, you were mine, you let anybody fuck you, your a bloody whore, like my fucking mother, even got landed with kids, you really know how to rub it in you slag, I wouldn't put my prick anywhere near you now, you dirty cow, I told you, you were mine and no one else could have you, this is your last fucking breath, you bitch" his hands went round my throat, I am gasping for my breath, he is choking me, I can't do anything.

Then all hell breaks loose, there are running feet and shouting, someone punches a fist in his face twice, his hands drop from my neck, I wilt to the floor, I see his head is pouring blood down his face, his hand are bloody, it drips onto me. Then there is a scuffle, someone says "No, sir, leave him" they are grabbing him, I am dirty, I am covered in blood, no skirt and a torn top hanging in rags. My wrists and ankles are bleeding, I feel sore everywhere.

Then I am being lifted by big strong hands "Sophie we have got you, you are safe now," I know that voice it's Michael "He holds me to him," then the tears start, I can hear men and women all over the place Michael says "Darling you are safe, they have him cuffed to two policemen," he kisses me on the lips, not a peck, he really kisses me, a police woman covers me in a blanket,

"Anything else, sir," she asks.

"No thanks," Michael replies. Sir I think to myself?

They all stand aside as Michael literally runs downstairs with me to a waiting ambulance, he takes me in and tells them to go," the doors are shut, there is a nurse and a Doctor in with us, then the sirens are going and we set off at speed.

He is still holding me "Sophie we thought we had lost you," he leans down and kisses me full on the lips again, he has tears running down his face "Let me get out of your way," he sits down at the side but holds onto my hand.

The nurse did the usual Blood Pressure, Pulse, Heart, Temperature and the Doctor said "Where is the blood coming from?"

"I am not sure but I think most was from him. Please Michael where's Charles and my babies?" my voice is very croaky.

"They are fine now, we have all been worried sick, but try not to talk now, you are going to have to give us a full report on what happened."

"What day is it please," I asked.

The Doctor said "It is Wednesday."

"Wednesday it seemed a lot longer than that?"

"Sophie my darling, they took you a week yesterday, you have been missing a week and a day, if Matthew had not turned up when he did, you would still be there, because we did not know where you were.

We had the house under surveillance, we felt sure if you were there, he would have made an appearance, we were beginning to give up, but it paid off in the end. He appeared up the road and disappeared round the backs of the houses. He must have got over all the walls and fences to get in that way. Please do not worry you are safe now, try to stay calm. Charles knows now where you are and he will be at the hospital waiting for you, he is in a Police car so he will definitely be there," I smiled.

"Thank you Michael, your father would be so proud of you," he squeezed my hand.

We were soon pulling into the private hospital, I was pulled out on the stretcher and hurried in on a trolley. The Doctor gave his report, I was stripped off, well the bit of clothing that was left, I was dirty and examined head to toe, the lump on my head had gone down, but they could still see the bruise on my scalp, my wrists and ankles were cut, grazed and bleeding, there was the gash on my right arm, also trying to make my escape my hands were cut and had splinters stuck in them, I had no finger nails they were all broken and my face had a jagged slash and was still bruised from him hitting me, as was my body from travelling in the boot. I assured them I had not been raped, but they insist on checking me, then they put their heads together. The most recent bruises were very apparent on my neck when he decided I was going to die, another few minutes or even seconds and I would have been dead and that is when it hit me, I began to tremble then water works started "Can I please see my husband and my babies?" they all left me then Charles appeared.

"Darling I have been going out of my mind, you really are a sight to behold, Christ darling you look as if you been in the wars, how did you get all these cuts, gazes and bruises my darling?" he did not wait for an answer, his lips were on mine, the tears were streaming from us both, then a Doctor appeared.

"Can we just get Mrs Roper showered, then you can be with her, we need to bandage her wrists and ankles and give her a bed for a while, because the police need their questions answered."

"Please can Charles come with me?"

"Of course he can," the doctor smiled.

"Darling where are my babies?"

"They will not let them in while you are in this state, where is all the blood from, where are you hurt?"

"No, a lot is mainly Matthews, I will tell you, in fact I am sure they will let you stay with me while I answer their questions," I was taken in to a shower, I said "I can do it myself and shampooed my hair, I just stood under the torrents and let it flow, along with my tears," then they wrapped me in a big soft towel and put me on the bed.

I was in Charles arms we were kissing. I was given a large cup of strong, sweet tea, I have never tasted anything so delicious in my life.

Then a Sister came in all business like "Now Mrs Roper you have had your shower, we would like to put dressings on your wrists and ankles because they are very sore, we will probably put a large bandage on your arm, so it can be checked easily," so we sat and watched while they did that, then they left.

A doctor entered "All is well, I am going to say officially that you were not raped, your wife knew while she was awake no one touched her but, she was drugged and she had no idea how long she was drugged for. However, we found six needle marks, so possibly while you were out, they injected you, to keep you under. We had to make sure all was well. However, we discovered something that you possibly were not aware of, you are three almost four months pregnant and it looks like twins around the 8th December, just in time for Christmas," he waits not sure.

"Are you sure?" I ask he nods and we are in each others arms.

"Sophie, you have got your wish my darling, I am so proud of you, can she see our twin boys now, they have been wondering where mummy had gone?" and they come running in.

"Mummy, mummy," they shout very clearly, apparently Charles has sat teaching them for hours, he got there. The tears are streaming, they came bounding in, I bend to scoop them up and they are hugging me and wetting me with their kisses, I have never felt anything so wonderful in my life. Charles has his arms round us all and I am crying buckets as is Charles, he is kissing me, wherever he can. We stay like that for a long, long time, then the twins decide they want to explore, just as Stuart, Bel, John and Polly come in.

It is hugs, kisses and tears all round even John, then Michael comes in "I am sorry folks, but before our Sophie can go home we have to get a statement from her, we will be as quick as we can, you can stay Charles," They said they would take the twins home and would see us later so more kisses and cuddles.

Michael went to the door and two plain clothes policemen came in. Charles is sat one side of me and Michael the other they are both holding my hands. I start right from the beginning and relate the events, once or twice they stop and ask something, I answer and carry on, I tell it as it was, but I have no idea of how long I had been drugged for, because I know I woke up several times? so I cannot help there, but the Doctors have found six needle marks. When I finish they said they were happy with it and I would have to sign after I read the typed statement, Michael said he would deal with that.

"I have nothing to wear they took my dirty rags off me."

"I do not think either me or my brother would mind if you went home naked," they both laughed.

As if by magic a nurse came in and said "The Doctors said you can go now Mrs Roper, and congratulations, you can have this," passed me a bath robe and left.

"Why is she congratulating you?" Michael asked.

We looked at one another Charles said "They have just given Sophie a head to toe examination, and discovered she is four months pregnant with twins 8th December, I will be a daddy a real daddy!" he had the biggest grin on his face.

"Congratulations to you both," Michael said, and shook Charles hand, he came to me "I am not shaking my gorgeous sister-in-laws hand," and he bent forward, put his arms round me and kissed me full on the lips. "You are the luckiest bugger, having Sophie, she is one very special lady and I love her very much."

I turned my back and tried to put my arms in the sleeves, but the towel fell to the floor leaving me naked, although my back is to Michael, with Charles help I manage to get it on "That sight is my reward is it? a pity you were turned round, do you want to do a replay? but please turn this way?" Michael said laughing.

"You have your own wife, get her to give you a show, my Sophie does a fabulous strip tease frequently, I know now why father never looked at another women once he had Sophie in his bed, I can assure you he certainly was not exaggerating," he looked satisfied with that.

"I may have my own wife, but sorry when you compare any other women to Sophie, she is the tops every time, she is a wonderful young lady, so calming, she has helped Jackie enormously, I must say sex got better after Sophie spoke to her, I have no idea what you said darling, but it helped a lot?"

"You do not stand a chance, not while I am alive, I can tell you now, that is one thing about Sophie, she would never cheat on any man she was with, father knew I was in love with her, but he knew she would not cheat on him, even knowing how much I was in love her, yes we used to kiss usually in fathers presence, come on lets get home."

"Sophie if no one came to you after first getting you there what did you eat and drink"? Michael asked.

"Nothing to eat, just drank water, there was that one cup of tea which must have been drugged, I still think that must have been Matthew, but he did not speak, not like the first man," I said.

"It could have been Matthew, because we would not have seen him go round the back, if it was dark when he came in the house," Michael said "So you haven't eaten for over a week and you are expecting, Charles they ought to have given her something here."

"Well what about the other man then? the one who gave me the tea? Was he not seen leaving, because I know he did I heard him going down stairs and the door slamming?" I said.

"I will see what the reports say, please stop worrying my darling, you are safe now, we will be throwing the bloody book at him, I could strangle the bastard with my own hands, for putting you and our families through all that, I only managed two good blows at him, and was advised to stop" Michael was fuming.

"Never mind now let's get her home, I will look after her, John and Polly are staying until we get sorted," Charles said.

Chapter seventeen

We waited at the door while Michael brought the car round. As we got in he put his lights on and we took off fast, everything had to move for us, even at red traffic lights we sailed through. I was told it was 5pm so it was busy on the roads, but it did not stop Michael, it was brilliant, we were soon home.

"That was a brilliant ride Michael thank you," I stood on tip toe and kissed him, I have no idea where my shoes are?

The twins came running out I bent to pick them up and both Charles and Michael shouted no, they picked them up instead. Polly, Stuart and Bel looked puzzled, so when we got in, I sat on the sofa in the kitchen before anything else Charles made his announcement, he was so pleased with himself.

"Can I have a bucket of tea please?" I asked, Bel was just pouring it out, it was like nectar.

So everyone was filled in by some of the events, then they realised I had not eaten, so Stuart said "I think she ought to have something like soup first and build up from there, so a slow to start with, no alcohol until you are built up, because you have lost a lot of weight, so please take it easy for at least a week.

"Are you staying Polly and John?" they said they were. "Sophie I want you resting, let everyone else do everything, I shall be very cross with you if I find you have done anything and Mr Roper no sex for a few days, I know what you two are like, please look after her, she must have complete rest, otherwise I will be packing her off to hospital, and I do mean that sincerely, come along Bel leave them to get sorted out. I will call tomorrow," he came and kissed me on the lips as did Bel.

Michael asked if there was anything he could do, if not he would get off home to his wife and Eleanor his baby daughter, he came and kissed me again, Charles went to the door with him. The boys were sat each side of me snuggled up, I felt very tired. "Have they had their tea?" I asked.

Polly said "We fed them about 4.30pm and as soon as you have got this soup, John and I will take them to bed then daddy and mummy can go and see them before they go to sleep."

"Charles you have not eaten much again, what can I get you darling?" she asked "I found a meat and potato pie you had made in the freezer I got that out to defrost, I hope you do not mind Sophie?"

"Of course not."

"I will have some when I see Sophie eat," he said.

"I am going to sieve some soup and then you can drink it Sophie, it won't take long, it will go down better and there is still some remaining," and she brought me a big breakfast cup with the soup in and I sipped it.

"This is good I can feel it going down."

"I have heated enough up you can have another cup full."

John and Polly went to get the boys to bed and Charles watched me drink the second cup of soup, I had a job to keep my eyes open.

"Charles I am so tired, could I go to bed when I have kissed my babies?"

"Darling of course you can, I think we all need a good nights sleep, I have worn a rut in the carpet pacing up and down, I was despairing that I wasn't going to see you again," he was crying again, I drew him to me and kissed him.

"I am home now my darling and I am having your babies, two more all your own, you have your wish and knocked me up, in fact I was knocked up when you married me, there was me fretting that I would never be pregnant again. I never thought about my monthly's I must have missed. How have the boys been without me feeding them at night?" I asked.

"It didn't seem to bother them, I think because you were not around they accepted it, they still went to sleep as easily, so because you are pregnant, it could be good thing, you will need what you have in December when my sons are born."

"Here we go again, your father was certain I would give him boys, now you are starting the same thing, what about girls, I thought Daddies loved little girls?" I said looking at him.

"Tell you what you can have some girls after these are born, how's that?" he did his fathers one raised eye brow.

"Darling you look just like him when you do that, I have missed you so much, I thought I was going to die and never see you again, that is why I started trying to get free and ended up looking like this," I sobbed.

"You look absolutely beautiful in my eyes, I am just so happy you are back with us, I am so in love with you," he was crying.

"Not half as much as I am in love with you," I said.

"Come on lets see if your babies want a kiss and cuddle?" he said as he took hold of me and was holding me so close to him "I am never letting you out of my sight again, I am having you chained to me, Oh God Sophie, I am so sorry I did not think," he was heart broken, we sat on the stairs in one another arms and cried for quite a while. Then we heard little voices;

"Mummy, mummy and another voice said Dadda, dadda,"

"They got the hang of mummy, but by the time they had got that I think they gave up with Daddy," he smiled.

"It was a lovely surprise," I said and we carried on upstairs, went into the nursery the boys were jumping up and down on the bed "Be careful you will fall off," I grabbed Elliot as he was about to topple off, John and Polly made themselves scarce.

Charles was holding Felix "Give mummy a big kiss good night," he said, then both Felix and Elliot came to me and both put their little hands down my front and were pulling the robe open, before we could blink they were both kneeling with my breasts in their mouths.

"You know we should be happy, because I am back we should be celebrating, but I cannot even do that at the moment, because that is what we need, each other, locked together in love the best way we know how, but you have gone and got me knocked up so we are banned from sex now!" that made him laugh and me smile, "Darling if you were very gentle with me, would anyone know, if you just put your little man in, and we did not actually do any fucking, no one would know, I so want you Charles," I was kissing his face, we suddenly stopped Felix must have gone to sleep, he was slipping off my knees heading for the floor Charles just caught him, he did not wake up, I looked at Elliot and yes he was asleep.

"No stay there let me, I will leave the side down so you can kiss them," which I did. Charles pulled the side up and locked the catch. "Come along Mrs Roper, let me put you in bed I will not be long, but I must eat something and it is your meat and potato pie, I can never resist your cooking, my darling, when I come to bed we will try what you have suggested, like you say who will know?" he was whispering in my ear.

He turned the bed down and closed the curtains at both windows, I climbed into bed and slid down under the sheets, he leaned over and kissed me longingly, then his lips some how slipped onto my breasts.

"I shouldn't have done that I have made myself more wanting than ever serves me right, but there is no milk?" he laughed and kissed my forehead and went downstairs. I turned over on my side, something hurt so I rolled over on to my tummy and do not remember another thing.

When I awoke the sun is pouring in through the open windows but I am on my own, I look at the clock it is 1.30? I must have slept all that time, I need the loo and dash, I am just wandering out when Charles appears "She's awake," he calls down stairs "Hello my darling how do you feel you have had a lovely long sleep, come on back in bed."

"No I want to get up."

"Mrs Roper, please do as you are told, otherwise I will tell Stuart and he will pack you off to hospital, please for me," he held me close and kissed me, then the kiss went deeper "I so want you Mrs Roper, be a good girl, you went to sleep on purpose last night, I did not get my little man inside you and he is dying to feel you, so if you go back to bed, I can sneak in and pleasure myself with your wonderful sexy body. In fact I nearly helped myself while you slept!"

"My darling, you can help yourself any time, you can do anything you want with me, I will always enjoy you," I whispered. "And if you mean what you say about sneaking in, my lover," I slipped into bed "Can I see my babies please?"

"Yes, Polly is bringing you a cup of tea, then she is making you some porridge to get something into you. I think you had better have a nightie on, you do not want to be flaunting those beauties in front of John, otherwise there will be another one trying to get into your knickers," he laughed going into the walk-in and found a lace nightie.

"It would be easy, because I haven't got any on," I lifted one eye brow or I did a Michael as we now put it.

"You're playing with fire Mrs Roper, you are going to have to be spanked if you do not behave," he just looked at me, then Polly appeared with a tray, Charles pulled a table closer to the bed.

"I thought you might like more than one, morning my darling, you look a lot better than you did yesterday, Charles was telling us last night about what you went through, I cannot imagine how terrible it was for you?" she kissed me and left closing the door behind her.

"Charles what happened after I was taken, did you get any other messages? what was happening?" I asked.

"Darling it was hell, the boys were crying, I ran to see what had happened, they were pointing to the hedge, I shouted you but nothing, I ran into the house, with them under my arms and dialled 999, I gave our name and said someone taken my wife, the officer said is this the widow of, I did not let them any further I said yes, I then rang Michael at his office, within minutes three police cars arrived, they searched all the gardens in the road, asked at the few houses on the road, they found a hole had been cut through the hedge behind the shed, it was obvious that is where they came in and took you."

"Michael told the officer in charge about the note we had received, they immediately went to his address that the Probation Office gave them, but that was about 6pm, there was a car parked in the front of the property behind a tall hedge, it's plate was checked it was not Matthews, it came out of the property around midnight, but no other car had come in or out it took a while to set up surveillance, it was watched for twenty four hours, until you were released. They nearly gave up but Michael persuaded them to wait a bit longer, and it paid off that is when the alert went out that Matthew gone into the property from the rear."

"Before that, three days after you were took, I received a letter in the same hand, but with a piece of your hacked off hair in the envelope, it said that if I kept the police out of it, it will cost five million pounds, I would be told where to take it, if you get Mr Plod, you can kiss good bye to the trollop, she's my wife, I do not accept a divorce, she is mine to do what I want with. So the stupid sod had told the police who had you, but he did not show up at his house, we assumed he'd taken you elsewhere but they could not get a lead, but it's all turned out alright," I can't stop the tears.

"Can you let me in" It is Polly she is carrying another tray.

"That tea was like nectar again, thank you for bringing the pot I have had three cups," thank you for all you are doing Polly."

"I've been glad to be of help, you know the weddings next month."

"Crumbs I had forgotten," I said.

"All the more reason Mrs Roper we build you up," Charles said. John knocked and came in with the twins, he lifted them on the bed and they started jumping up and down. Charles said;

"No," very firmly "No you do not do that, you will hurt

Mummy and we have got to get her better," they stopped at the first no, I thought they would cry, they looked from daddy then to me, I smiled and held my arms out, "Gently boys mummy has been poorly," they put their little arms round my neck, then they dived their little hands down my nightie, trying to get hold of my breasts.

"No darlings it is not bedtime," they are nodding, I shake my head so they go back to loving me.

"Strikes me it is in the Roper blood," Polly said, Charles and John turned to look at her.

"What do you mean Polly?" Charles asked.

"Well you all seem obsessed with breasts," she burst out laughing.

"I agree Polly," I said.

"Right now Polly and I have something we want to tell you, we wanted to be sure before we said anything," John was saying.

Charles butted in, "Your pregnant Polly!"

"No," she almost screamed "I am not, my mother would have a heart attacked if I was pregnant before I got married, it's alright you lot you do not know my mother."

"If I can continue, the house next door is up for sale, we have been and looked round and we think we could get it into something we want, we seem to spend a lot of time here, we thought we would move next door, it was your money Sophie, thank you so much."

"I am so pleased that will be lovely one big happy family." Charles said "I could not have wished for anything better."

"I agree it will be lovely," I say.

"I think I should crack open a bottle of champagne in celebration," John says.

"No you can't, Sophie can't have any, wait until she can, then me and Sophie can get legless together," Polly laughed.

I was gradually getting down my porridge, "I am sorry I cannot eat any more, I think you thought you were feeding the five thousand."

"You have done very well, John and me thought after we feed them, we would take the boys to the park and feed the ducks, then they will probably nod off in the pushchair on the way back, giving you some peace, Charles looks all in," Polly said "I am getting very good at this nappy changing lark aren't I John?"

"Yes sooner you than me, I nearly heave with the smell, they look such lovely boys but Christ what they get rid of is disgusting," we all fell about laughing, so the boys joined in.

"Thank you darling you are so good, yes Charles can lie here with me, I am shattered, it is very tiring laying in bed sleeping, drinking and eating," they all left laughing, not Charles he was quite happy with the arrangement. I went to the loo, sat on my friend the bidet and then cleaned my teeth, took my nightie off and slid back into bed, Charles went to the loo and came out naked, "Now that has made me feel 150% better, that sight is worth a mint, you are a very sexy man, do you know that Mr Roper?" I am all but drooling, he slid in next to me and held me tight and kissed me "I missed you my darling, I missed your little man so much," he didn't speak his eyes spoke volumes, he knelt above me and gently he slid in "That is what I needed most of all, not all this food and drink, just you my dearest, darling husband," he began to move very gently "Oh yes," I said with a big sigh.

Unfortunately we were unable to continue for long, I was so wanting, we both soon climaxed together, he started to slide off me "No Charles."

"Shush," he said "Turn over you little witch," I did as I was told, I pushed my bottom towards him, he gently slid inside me again "Now this time we are going to be very, very good and not come too early," I laughed, I wondered what he was going to say, after that climax he told me "If you are a very good girl and have a sleep, we might find something to do again, to keep us both happy," he said kissing my ear.

"I do not think I will sleep," I said. He put his an arm round me holding my breast, the other one he slipped in between my legs, as he normally does. I do not remember anything else.

When I awoke I was wrapped in Charles arms I felt so safe, I thought he was still asleep but he wasn't he turned his head, "You have been a very, very good girl you have had a lovely sleep."

"Did you have a sleep?" I asked him.

"Yes, not quite as long as you, but I have only been awake about ten minutes, I was laying here with my arms round you, thanking someone above for bringing you back to me. I could not have lived without you, you are my world. I am in dire need of you, I have such of lot of catching up to do, I still want to make sure you are pregnant."

"Tut Charles, you are so demanding."

He turned me on my back and kissed me very deeply, how can anyone hold out when they are so in love "Take me to heaven and forget the Doctors orders, I will stay in bed as long has he insists I do, but I am not forgoing my favourite hobby with my gorgeous husband, not for any Doctor, it has got to be doing me more good than frustration. I have to keep my husband happy otherwise he will be looking elsewhere," I kissed him with all the feelings I could put into a kiss.

We had a very happy couple of hours, then we crept into the shower, I put my nightie back on Charles put some clean clothes on and lay on the top of the bed, I snuggled down and I could not believe it I had fallen to asleep again, but when I awoke there was no Charles!

Charles came in and sat on the bed and dragged the boys up, Polly and John pulled two chairs over and we sat and had a cup of tea and all the odds and ends they could find. "Mummy has to hurry up and get better we have run out of all the cakes and pies and biscuits haven't we boys?" he nodded his head so they did.

Most days Stuart popped in to see me, he was pleased and said I could start getting up tomorrow which was Monday, as long as did not do too much, he said he was surprised how soon I had reached this level, Charles and I knew why!

John and Polly decided they had better go home, there was so much for them to do for the wedding, I could not thank them enough for all they had done. She told me to try my 'Maid of Honour' dress on to see how it fits, what with being four months gone but having lost weight, it could go either way, it fit perfectly, because it was not a very tight fitted one and had a flared skirt so everything there was brilliant.

John and Charles had to go to get their 'Morning Suits' and things, so they decided to take the boys with them, so I was left in peace.
I was just relaxing on the patio in the sun, when the side gate catch rattled, "Anyone home?" it was Michael.

"Hang on," I went and unlocked it, he came in but locked it behind him "My why have we got this honour, on a Wednesday morning, all casually dressed, where's Mr Policeman then?" he laughed.

"Hello darling how are you doing?" he held me in his arms and kissed me on the lips "Where is everyone?"

"I am doing well, Charles and John have gone to be fitted for their morning suits and took the boys with them, to give me some peace, now that's gone and you arrive," I laughed.

"Sorry pet, I should have telephoned, I forgot about the wedding. I had a few days owing so I decided to take some, I just thought I would drop in and see how you are getting on, I must say you look mighty fine to me," he smiled. "I am glad we are on our own I wanted to ask something. You know the note that was sent to Charles after you were taken, do you mind talking about it, this is strictly between us two."

"If I can answer your questions I will," I smiled. What's coming I should have known he would want to know everything?

"You were married to Matthew I know that, but he went on to say you had seduced not one but two brothers, is that correct?"

"No I did not seduce anyone, I would not have known how."

"Sorry pet, I seem to have put that wrong, I do not want to upset you, that is the last thing I want to do, you are one very nice young lady.

"Until I was sixteen, I had two older brothers. Then my mother, decided to break the secret and told me I was found on the door step and was no relation whatsoever." I went on to tell him every step of my life.

"Sophie you are very honest and open, sorry please do not think I was prying, it was just I did not understand how you can marry two brothers and get away with it, until you have now explained, can I ask one more thing?" I nodded "Did my father know about your background?"

"Michael, your father knew everything about me, I had nothing to hide, I never had any friends at all girls or boys. Charles knows everything about me, I think you have to be honest, if you lie, some stage later you are found out, I cannot be like that," by now the water works are back, I thought I was doing well. He stood up and came and sat next to me.

"Sophie I am so sorry, I did not want to upset you, you are the last person I want to hurt, I am already ashamed of the way I treated you when you were introduced to the family, you are a truly wonderful girl, I admit I got you wrong, can you please forgive me? I do not want any animosity between us, I have grown very fond of you, I love you Sophie very much," he put his arms round me, held me close kissing my forehead,"Please forgive me darling, I will always be there for you, no matter what happens."

"I have nothing to forgive you for, I for gave you a long time ago. After that first meeting, I decided you weren't so bad after all."

"You have such a lovely calming way with you, you put people at ease." he looked at me, he passed me his handkerchief. "I am happy to be in your life and be your brother-in-law, there is nothing I would not do for you. If anyone ever hurts you, they had better watch out, that is why they got Matthew away from me, they knew how I felt, I only got two fists to land on him, but I would have gladly murdered him, especially when I saw you, I cried." he was very emotional. "Also you have made my marriage a lot more satisfactory in the bedroom department, I do not know what you said, but I have you to thank for it, if Jackie starts acting up I ask her what Sophie would do and it works like a charm, I am not unreasonable with my demands. I have had extramarital affairs, but I do not want to be my father, where I have to go elsewhere for it, sex is very important to the Roper men, that is why I know you are very unique, you tamed my father, he never looked at another woman after he got you in his bed and from what Charles says, you are one very special young lady," he kissed me full on the lips. "That is as far as my affection goes. You are unique, you dress very sexily, but you always look very innocent, untouched, we all love you, I think I can speak for all the Roper boys there is not one of us who would pass up a chance to sleep with you, but we will not, I think we are different to most families."

"Thank you Michael. You know your father was a very unique man, I thought I would be with him forever, with a big family, but fate is cruel. I knew Charles loved me, he told his father often enough, but he knew for one thing that Charles would never go any further than kissing me, but even if Charles did try to take me from his father, it would not have got him anywhere, your father knew me inside out and I would never cheat on the man I am with or married to. Then he left us those beautiful letters, I do not know how he managed to write them, he was a very special man, you all loved him and made him so happy. I cannot help it as soon as I think of those letters it just creases me up and I cannot stop the tears, I do not know where they all come from?" he just holds me and lets me cry, after a while I say. "I am so sorry I have not offered you a drink, do you want tea, coffee or something cool?"

"Do not apologise my love, I am so glad we have had this talk, I will have whatever you have," so I popped in and made some fresh coffee, I am fed up with this instant stuff "I am making coffee do you want milk or cream?"

"Fancy tempting me, it will have to be cream, thank you, can I have a walk round the garden it looks lovely, your ideas I believe?"

"Yes," I answered.

"I took the tray out and put it on the table," he was coming back, "You will have to come and give us some suggestions on ours."

"There is nothing wrong with yours, it is lovely, nice and easy to maintain," I said.

"No we are moving, that was something I had come to tell you and Charles, I will wait now until he comes back. I know Jackie loves you and she says she has never had such a good friend, however, I know you will not say anything to her about my affairs, they are in the past. I sometimes have to work hard to get what I want, but she is more receptive, thanks to you,"

"Charles will not be long the boys will be wanting their dinner," and as I said that we heard the car. I went and opened the gate, Michael came with me, Charles was just getting the out of the car.

"Hello my boys," I went to pick one up, Charles shouted.

So Michael picked him up and swung him round, so I think it's Elliot, was pulling on his jeans he wanted Uncle Michael to swing him, so he did, then they wanted more, so he did it again.

Charles said "They will have you at it for hours come on boys, have you been here long, it's unusual to see you on the spur of the moment."

"I know I should have telephoned," Michael said.

"Darling do you want a coffee I have only just made it?"

"Yes please," he replied, I put the two baby cups with milk in and Charles coffee on a little tray and took it outside.

"Michael has some news for us I am dying to know what?"

"We are moving, when we were are on a big job like Sophie's kidnap, we get draft men in from all over, I was talking to this officer about where you lived, he said his father lives out this way, but he lost his mother and the house is much too big, he is going to sell and find something nearer him the other side Derby, I asked where it was he told me, so we went and looked and we decided we wanted it, it wasn't even on the market, we offered a good price because we thought we would use that money you gave us Sophie."

"Yes but where is it, is it fairly close?" I asked.

"Well you could say that, it's that one next door," we sat gob smacked he was pointing the one next to us, the opposite side to John's. Although we were not too close because either side all three houses had very wide plots.

"Michael did you know John and Polly are moving the other side? that will be fabulous altogether," Charles said.

"That is wonderful Michael," I said leaning over and kissed him on the lips, he looked a bit surprised I just looked him in the eye and smiled.

"That evening I told Charles about Michaels conversation and his honesty and that he kissed me," I looked doubtful.

"My darling he can kiss you as often as he wants as far as I am concerned, because I know you love me and I am happy, and I like to think my brothers envy me, because I am the one fucking you. In fact one of these days I might just take you in front of my brothers (not the girls) so they can see what a fantastic, sexy, wanting fucking piece of art you are, I could arrange for them to come round and watch you in action," he was leering at me.

"I did not know you were up for exhibitionism? It's okay with me, but I draw the line in letting them join in!" I did keep my face straight.

"Be careful what you say, I may just do it, however I think you are going to have that beautiful arse spanked," he laughed.

"You wouldn't dare Charles Roper," I said.

One eye brow raised "Wouldn't I, I think you might like it, cannot say I have ever done it, but I have read about these things, and it could be arousing, mind I do not think you need anything to arouse you, you are always up for it! You are one easy little slut, do you know that Mrs Roper." he asked, eye brow up again.

"Well if I am, I am your easy little slut, so do you want to fuck me now, or ring your brothers first?"

He grabbed me and threw me on the bed, he had a very big erection, he was straggling me, but just above my breasts, he was almost near my lips, "Now Mrs Roper you are going to have to have that sexy mouth well and truly fucked, then I might just fuck your arse, how does that grab you?" he didn't wait for my answer, because I opened my mouth to let him in. "Ooh Sophie I will never tire of you, what that mouth does to my cock is out of this world," he was unable to utter another word. It was late but we did eventually go to sleep, both well and truly satisfied.

We all went up to Chester for the wedding, Michael and Jackie looked after the boys because Charles was the best man and I was Matron of Honour, it was a very big wedding and the reception was brilliant, I ended up dancing with all my brother-in-laws except the groom. While I was dancing with Junior, Michael I keep forgetting, he held me very, very close, kissed me round my ear and whispered, I love you so much my darling, then carried on dancing. We were all tipsy by the time we went to bed, we had the boys in with us, originally they would have been with Charles because I would have been with my lovely Michael. It is strange how things change in such a small space of time and from nowhere the tears came, I do miss you my darling, but Charles is helping, I thought to myself.

I was woken up by my Charles fucking me like he had been without sex for weeks, "Good morning my darling, what a wonderful way to be woken up, you know I might insist on you doing this every day," I am having difficulties speaking he is taking me up fast. Before I know it I am having a very loud climax, with Charles following close behind.

"My darling I will gladly wake you up every day, fucking you, I cannot get enough of you. Would you like me to make love to you now before the boys wake up?"

"You do not have to ask, when you already know the answer? I do like you helping yourself, does that make me kinky? but I want to tell you something first, I forgot last night because we could not keep our hands off one another. Whilst I was dancing with Michael he kissed me round my ears and told me that he 'Loved me so much' I have not encouraged him darling, please believe me," I am begging.

"My darling, first, I do believe you, second, I know he loves you, I have known a long time, even before he kissed you that first time before the wedding. I could not care less because it is you, and I know from the past you would not let anyone else anywhere near that cunt but me, if he wants to kiss you occasionally, I do not mind because it will keep reminding him what he cannot have. Unless you would rather he didn't then I will tell him, but I would rather you let him and that you respond and kiss him in your really sexy way.

Our new neighbours moved in each side, we all helped all we could, we made an entrance both sides so we could see each other easily, instead of walking via the road. Whatever we were doing we would all do it together, I gave birth to twin sons Charles junior and Michael, the boys were over awed with them, we could not get them to understand they were ours they would be living with us. We all spent Christmas at our house because we were more established than the others, it was lovely now the boys were bigger, it was lovely watching them open their presents.

We built a big two storey extension to the other side of the garage and extended the whole house across the back where the long patio was, then made another patio at the front of the extension and knocked the original outside walls out and made the lounge and kitchen bigger, the extra part at the back of the garage, off the kitchen we made into a large dinning room, the area was quiet big, we needed it now we all spent a lot of time at our house having big family meals. The ground floor extension to the other side of the garage, housed a big swimming pool for all of us, we incorporated a Gym with every conceivable piece of equipment for all of us adults not just the men, the children loved it as well. Also a big play room for all the children, when it rained they all had somewhere to play.

The upper floor extension enabled us to have a new master suite for us with en suite and walk-in wardrobe, also a double and single bedroom with en suite between the two, and we altered some of the original bedrooms and made more en suites. So although our family had grown we could still accommodate James and Simon and their wives, because we had the largest house.

We had some wonderful times altogether it was really special how we all got on together if ever there was a crisis, we all helped one another. The in-laws was what the men called us wives, all three of us were very good friends, we had a very close bond between us, we did everything together.

The boys all came into just over seven million pound each when all the grand parents died and the properties, land, antiques were sold, plus there was a lot of capital. So we decided to buy a huge villa in Italy, so we all went on holidays together, it was never the same if we did do something on our own something was missing, and all three families agreed we all felt the same.

Charles said one day when the adults were sitting relaxing, I think the only thing we ever do without one another is have sex, Michael and John agreed that it could be arranged to wife swap, it could bring a different meaning to our relationship. Charles said that was a stupid suggestion I am happy with my Sophie, and the only difference wife swapping would bring is divorce, we stay as we are, and you two to keep day dreaming about my Sophie, we all laughed including us girls.

Because the family was growing we employed a live-in Housekeeper, she always prepare breakfast and lunch, she also did the laundry. I usually cooked our evening meal, we always dressed for dinner. Part of her remit was she organised daily cleaners to come in.

John and Polly had twin boys in November 2001 and a daughter in August 2003 and another daughter in March 2006.

Michael and Jackie had twin boys in July 2003, Jackie said that is it, no more that is definitely it, three is enough. Michael confided in me that he still says what would Sophie do in a situation, he always got his way, that, he said was how he managed to get her to agree to another baby and ended up with twins boys!

Charles and I had the twin boys in Dec 2000, a daughter in March 2002, we had twin boys again April 2003 (We were all pregnant in 2003 we used to be swap stories), then May 2005 another daughter, I called her Celeste, we decided eight was enough, so I went on the injection. Charles really loved all his children, but I was right about daddies and their daughters there was something very, very special.

Soon after they moved next door Michael decided he did not need to work, as did John and Polly, we never got bored there was always something to do, especially until the children started going to school.

The in-laws decided between us, no boarding schools, they all went to private school and stayed at home where us Mums wanted our little ones, until they were older, then when they were old enough it would be up to them if they wanted to board out, but that would not be until they were eleven or twelve.

Charles and I are as happy now as we were at the beginning, we still spent a lot of time making love, our neighbours told us it was not healthy, although the brothers admitted they would like to be given the chance. I frequently think of my Michael and what he had missed, he would have been over the moon knowing three of his sons lived next to each other and that we had fifteen children between us.

We saw quite a lot of James and Simon but neither of them married the girls we had got to know, they were very successful in their business of Chartered Surveyors and Chartered Architects.

Neither married until they were thirty five and then when they got married they married twins from Derbyshire, so they settled just up the road in Edwalton of all places, they purchased a big plot of land and built two detached houses one each, so they were now close.

So you see eventually I did find Happiness and it has lasted longer than a few years, I knew Charles was the best of them all, fate had saved the very best until the very last, we knew we would grow old together, surrounded by goodness knows how many Grandchildren and Great Nephews and Nieces.

Word count 148,060

26179649R00188

Printed in Poland
by Amazon Fulfillment
Poland Sp. z o.o., Wrocław